A PIECE OF PEACE

A Place of Peace

Amy Clipston

ZONDERVAN®

ZONDERVAN

A Place of Peace

Copyright © 2011 by Amy Clipston

This title is also available as a Zondervan ebook. Visit www.zondervan.
com/ebooks.

This title is also available in a Zondervan audio edition. Visit www.
zondervan.fm.

Requests for information should be addressed to: Zondervan, Grand Rapids,
Michigan 49546

Library of Congress Cataloging-in-Publication Data

Clipston, Amy.
A place of peace / Amy Clipston.
p. cm.—(Kauffman Amish bakery series; bk. 3) ISBN 978-0-310-31995-5
(softcover)
1. Amish—Fiction. 2. Amish Country (Pa.)—Fiction. I. Title. PS3603.
L58P55 2011
813'.6—dc22   2010034654

Mass Market ISBN: 978-0-310-35416-1

Printed in the United States of America

18 16 17 18 19 / QG / 24 23 22 21 20 19 18 17 16 15 14 13 12 11 10 9 8 7 6 5 4 3 2 1

In loving memory of my father,
Ludwig "Bob" Goebelbecker

NOTE TO THE READER

While this novel is set against the real backdrop of Lancaster County, Pennsylvania, the characters are fictional. There is no intended resemblance between the characters in this book and any real members of the Amish and Mennonite communities. As with any work of fiction, I've taken license in some areas of research as a means of creating the necessary circumstances for my characters. My research was thorough; however, it would be impossible to be completely accurate in details and description, since each and every community differs. There-fore, any inaccuracies in the Amish and Mennonite lifestyles portrayed in this book are completely due to fictional license.

Glossary

ack: oh
aenti: aunt
appeditlich: delicious
Ausbund: Amish hymnal
bedauerlich: sad
boppli: baby
bopplin: babies
bruder: brother
bruderskinner: nieces/nephews
daed: dad
danki: thank you
dat: dad
Dietsch: Pennsylvania Dutch, the Amish language
    (a German dialect)
dochder: daughter
dochdern: daughters
Englisher: a non-Amish person
fraa: wife
freind: friend
freinden: friends
freindschaft: relative
froh: happy
gegisch: silly
Gern gschehne: You're welcome

grossdaddi: grandfather

grossdochdern: granddaughters

grandkinner: grandchildren

grossmammi: grandmother

gschtarewe: dead

Gude mariye: Good morning

gut: good

Gut nacht: Good night

Ich liebe dich: I love you

kapp: prayer covering or cap

kind: child

kinner: children

kumm: come

liewe: love, a term of endearment

maedel: young woman

mamm: mom

mei: my

mutter: mother

naerfich: nervous

narrisch: crazy

onkel: uncle

Ordnung: The oral tradition of practices required and
    forbidden in the Amish faith

schee: pretty

schweschder: sister

Was iss letz?: What's wrong?

Willkumm heemet: Welcome home

Wie geht's: How do you do? or Good day!

wunderbaar: wonderful

ya: yes

zwillingbopplin: twins

FAMILIES IN
A PLACE OF PEACE

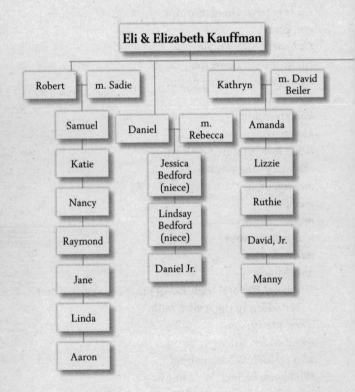

Eli & Elizabeth Kauffman

Robert — m. Sadie

Kathryn — m. David Beiler

Samuel

Daniel — m. Rebecca

Amanda

Katie

Jessica Bedford (niece)

Lizzie

Nancy

Lindsay Bedford (niece)

Ruthie

Raymond

Daniel Jr.

David, Jr.

Jane

Manny

Linda

Aaron

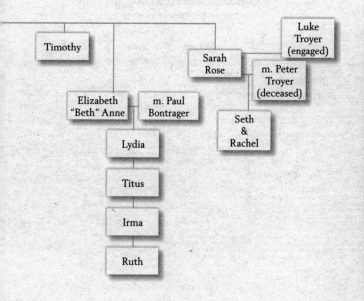

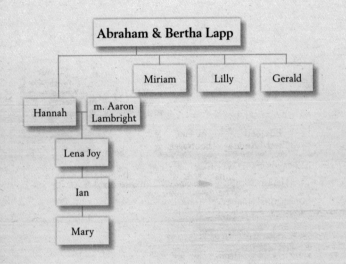

Abraham & Bertha Lapp

Miriam

Lilly

Gerald

Hannah — m. Aaron Lambright

Lena Joy

Ian

Mary

CHAPTER 1

Miriam Lapp leaned over the counter and smiled at the little redheaded girl, her favorite patient at the Center for Pediatrics. "Good morning, Brittany. How are you feeling today?"

The four-year-old scrunched up her nose, causing her freckles to wrinkle. "My ear hurts."

Miriam swallowed a chuckle at the girl's adorable expression. "I'm sorry. I'm certain Dr. Sabella can help you."

Brittany's face was grim. "Yeah, but I don't want a shot."

Miriam leaned down, angling her face closer to the girl's, and lowered her voice. "I have a hunch he won't give you a shot. I bet he'll just look in your ear and make sure it's not full of potatoes."

"Pee-tatoes!" Brittany squealed a giggle, covering her mouth with her hand.

Glancing at Brittany's mother, Miriam smiled. "It's so good to see you today. How's Mr. Baker?"

"He's doing well, thank you." The woman pulled out her wallet. "How are you?"

"Doing just fine, thank you." Miriam straightened her purple scrub top. "I'll take your co-pay, Mrs. Baker."

"Thank you." The woman handed Miriam her debit card.

Turning, Miriam swiped the card through the credit card machine and snatched a pen from the counter.

"Miriam!" Lauren, the office manager, rushed over from the inner office. "Miriam, there's a call for you on line two."

"I'll be just a minute," Miriam said, punching the keys on the credit machine. "I'm running through Mrs. Baker's co-pay." Lauren took the pen from Miriam's hand. "I got it." Frowning, she nodded toward the inner office. "Use my phone."

Arching an eyebrow in question, Miriam studied her co-worker's worried face. During the year Miriam had worked for Lauren, she'd never seen her look so concerned about a phone call. "Who is it?"

"Go on," Lauren said, nodding toward the office again. "I'll take over up here. You take your time."

"Who is it?" Miriam asked again. "Hannah," Lauren whispered.

"Hannah?" Miriam's mind raced, wracking her brain with thoughts of who it could be. She only knew one Hannah . . . "My *sister* Hannah?"

Lauren gave a quick nod. "Yes. Now go."

Miriam's stomach twisted. In the nearly four years since she'd left her family in Lancaster County, Pennsylvania, not one member of her family had ever called her. Only Hannah had written her, but called— never. Miriam had made it a point of giving Hannah her cell, home, and work numbers, and Hannah said she would only use them in case of an emergency.

Something is wrong.

Her thoughts moved to Hannah's eldest daughter, Lena Joy, who'd been born with a genetic disorder. Had something happened to her?

Her eyes widened with worry.

"Go!" Lauren nudged her toward the office. "Take all the time you need."

Taking a deep breath, Miriam rushed to the inner office, dropped into Lauren's chair, lifted the receiver to her ear, and punched the button for line two.

"Hello?" Miriam held her breath, waiting for her sister's familiar voice.

"Miriam," Hannah said. "How are you?"

The voice was sweet and familiar, bringing tears to Miriam's eyes as memories assaulted her mind. She'd treasured those nights long ago when they would lie awake late into the evening in the room they shared, whispering their future plans. Funny how it all came true for Hannah—she'd married the love of her life and had a family. Miriam, on the other hand, was the disappointment of the family. She'd left the community and never joined the Amish church or married.

Hannah was the only one who'd seemed to understand when Miriam made the choice that changed her life forever—when she left the love of her life, her family, and the only community she'd ever known. Hannah forgave her when the rest of the family did not.

Oh, how Miriam had missed her sister.

"I'm good. You?" Miriam stared absently at the date and time glowing on the phone while winding the cord around her finger.

"*Gut.*" Hannah's Pennsylvania *Dietsch* brought another flood of family memories crashing down on Miriam.

"It's so wonderful to hear your voice, Hannah," Miriam said. "How is your family? How are the children?"

"Oh, the *kinner* are *gut, danki,*" Hannah said. "They grow so fast."

"And Lena Joy? She's doing well?" Miriam asked and then held her breath in anticipation of the response.

"She has good and bad days, as to be expected. If only there were a cure . . ." Hannah paused for a moment as if collecting her thoughts or perhaps censoring her words. "Miriam, I'm afraid I have bad news." Her voice was cautious, causing Miriam's heart to thump in her chest.

"What is it?"

"*Mamm . . .*" She paused. "*Mamm iss gschtarewe.*"

"What?" Miriam gasped. "Mom died?" She groaned and covered her face with her hands. "No. No, no, no. Hannah, you don't mean that."

"*Ya,* I'm sorry to say I do." Her sister's voice trembled. "I can't believe it either."

"When?"

"Last night. In her sleep, from complications due to pneumonia. *Daed* found her this morning. He didn't know that she'd . . ." Her voice trailed off, the unspoken words hanging between them like a thick fog.

Miriam wiped the tears trickling down her hot cheeks. "How can she be gone? I was planning a trip home over the holidays to try to make everything right."

"I'm so sorry to call you at work and tell you this."

"No, no." Miriam plucked a tissue from the box on Lauren's tidy desk and dabbed her eyes and nose. "I'm glad you let me know. I'll go home and pack and then get on the road. I'll be there as soon as I can." She glanced at her watch and then mentally calculated the trip from her home in LaGrange, Indiana, to Gordonville, Pennsylvania. "I should be there before midnight."

"Oh, *gut*. I was hoping you'd come." "Of course I will. We're family."

"*Ya*. We are." Hannah's voice trembled. "Drive safely. *Ich liebe dich, Schweschder.*"

"I will." Miriam tried in vain to stop the tears flowing from her eyes. "I love you too, Sister."

After dropping the receiver into the cradle, Miriam cupped her hands to her face and sobbed while memories of her mother flooded her mind. The last time she'd seen her mother was the night she snuck out of the farmhouse and left the community to move to Indiana and live with her cousin Abby.

Lifting the receiver to her ear again, Miriam dialed Abby's office and groaned when voicemail picked up.

"You've reached the voicemail for Abigail Johnston, paralegal

with Wainwright, Morrison, and Rhodes," Abby's voice sang into the phone line. "I'm either on the phone or away from my desk. Please leave a detailed message, including your name, the time and date of your call, your phone number, and the nature of your call, and I will call you back as soon as I return. Thank you."

After the shrill beep ended, Miriam took a deep breath. "Abby, it's me." Before she could stop them, the tears started, and her voice was thick. "Call me. I just got the most horrible news. Hannah called me, and my *mamm* . . ." Her voice trailed off; she couldn't say the word. "I'm heading home to pack up and leave for Gordonville right away. Call me. Bye."

She slammed the phone down and stood. After explaining the situation to Lauren, she rushed to the apartment she'd shared with Abby since Abby's husband left her two years ago. Miriam was drowning in memories and packing when the door to her bedroom whooshed open, dragging across the worn tan carpet.

"What's going on?" a voice behind her asked.

Miriam turned to find her cousin standing in the doorway, clad in her best blue suit. Her light brown hair was cut in a short, stylish bob, perfect for a professional climbing the corporate ladder. She looked the part of an aspiring lawyer.

"Abby," Miriam said. "What are you doing here?"

"I left the office as soon as I got your voicemail." Her eyes were full of concern. "What did Hannah say?"

"*Mamm* passed away last night." Miriam's voice broke on the last word. Covering her mouth with her hands, she choked back a sob.

"Oh no." Abby encircled her in a hug. "I'm so sorry."

"I can't believe it," Miriam choked through her sobs. "I was going to surprise her with a visit over Christmas and try to work things out. I wanted to make things right. I wanted to see her and talk to her in person. But, now . . . Now she's—"

"Shhh." Abby patted her back. "It's going to be all right."

"But how?" Miriam swiped her tears away with the back of her hands.

A somber smile turned up her cousin's lips. "Remember what you told me when that snake of a husband of mine left me for his perky secretary?"

Miriam shook her head. "Not really."

"You reminded me of a very important verse from Isaiah—'those who hope in the Lord will renew their strength.'" Abby's eyes were serious. "We'll get through this. I promise."

Biting her bottom lip, Miriam nodded.

"I'll pack a few things, and we'll get on the road." Abby headed for the door.

"You're coming with me?"

Abby gave a little shrug. "Of course I am. Did you honestly think I'd let you face the family alone after nearly four years?"

Miriam let out a sigh. "I'd hoped not."

Abby gestured toward the suitcase. "Get packed, and we'll get on the road. With any luck, we'll be there before midnight. I imagine your dad and my parents won't welcome us with open arms. I guess we'll stay with Aunt Edna?"

Miriam nodded. "I was thinking that. As far as I know, she's still living alone in that little house on my *daed's* farm."

"I should have said *Aenti* Edna." Abby smiled. "Guess I better brush up on my Pennsylvania *Dietsch*, huh? Man, how long has it been since I've been back there?"

"Six years, right?" Miriam lowered herself onto her double bed next to her suitcase.

"Yeah, I guess so." Abby shook her head and stepped toward the door. "Well, we have a long ride ahead of us. We better get on the road."

Taking a deep breath, Miriam rose from the bed and fished a few blouses from her dresser. Closing her eyes, she whispered a prayer for strength and courage as she embarked on this painful trip to her past.

CHAPTER 2

The tires of Miriam's Honda Accord crunched down the winding rock path leading to the house where she'd grown up with her three siblings. Her heart pounded against her ribcage as the three-story whitewashed farmhouse with the sweeping wraparound porch came into view. Memories of late summer nights sitting on that porch swarmed her mind.

Sitting with her mother chatting about friends and relatives.

Lounging with her siblings, singing their favorite hymns.

Curling up on the porch swing, reading the Bible.

Miriam nosed the car up to the front porch and stared at the steps reflected in the beam of light. Memories mixed with regret and heartache crashed down on her. She knew that members of the community would have visited and offered condolences to her father and siblings all day today, staying from six in the morning until ten at night. She wished she'd been with them.

"I see a lamp burning in the kitchen. He must still be up." Abby's comment slammed Miriam back to the present.

Glancing toward the front windows, Miriam spotted the faint light creeping under the green shades. "It must be the first time in the last sixty years that he has stayed up past eight o'clock." She blinked back tears. "He must really miss her."

Abby touched Miriam's arm. "You want me to walk up to the door with you?"

"No, thanks." Miriam shook her head. "I need to do this alone."

Abby snorted. "I wouldn't be much help anyway. I'm the derelict who left the community, married a heathen, divorced the heathen, and am pursuing my completely un-Amish dream of becoming a lawyer."

Reaching over, Miriam squeezed Abby's hand. "I don't care what any of them says. I think you're wonderful."

Abby grinned. "You mean *wunderbaar*."

"*Ya.*" Miriam returned a smile as she wrenched the door open. "Say a prayer for me." Climbing from the car, she took a deep breath despite the humid July air closing in around her. Her heavy feet felt as if the weight of the world bogged them down as she climbed the steps of the old farmhouse.

Standing at the front door, she suddenly felt self-conscious of her attire. She glanced down at her pink T-shirt, blue jeans, and her painted pink toenails sticking out from her open-toed sandals. She then lifted her hand to her dark brown hair, cut to fall just past her shoulders and pulled up into a thick ponytail, affixed with a purple rubber band. Her attire broke every Amish rule—from her hair being cut to her hint of eye shadow and blush. Her father would surely comment on the disappointment and dishonor Miriam Lapp had brought to his family.

Despite her negative thoughts, Miriam squared her shoulders.

I have as much a right to be here as my siblings. She was my mother too.

She cleared her throat and tapped on the door. Her heart pounded in her chest as she held her breath. Beyond the door, she heard feet pound against the hardwood flooring. The bolt clicked, and the door opened with a protesting groan.

"Who's there?" a young man's voice called.

"It's Miriam." She hated how her voice trembled when she was nervous.

"Miriam?" The door swung open, revealing her brother, Gerald.

She blinked, stunned by how mature he was. He was now eighteen, five years her junior. Towering over her at close to six feet, he was handsome, resembling her father when he was younger. He wore traditional Amish clothes—a dark shirt, suspenders, and trousers, and his dark brown hair was cut in a bowl shape.

She wondered if Gerald had met someone special and was courting her, taking her to singings and bringing her home in his courting buggy. Would he marry a sweet Amish girl and have a family, following in the footsteps their parents always dreamt their four children would?

Gerald's eyes scanned her attire, and she folded her arms across her chest as if that gesture would hide her *English* clothes.

"What are you doing here?" he asked, his eyes accusing.

"Hannah called me." She cleared her throat. "I heard about . . ."

"Who's here at this hour?" Her father's voice bellowed from inside the house.

Gerald turned toward the voice. "It's Miriam. Hannah called her."

"I don't know anyone named Miriam." Her father's voice was cold, dead of emotion. "Tell her to leave."

Miriam's heart sank, and tears filled her eyes. She opened her mouth to speak, but Gerald slammed the door before the words escaped her lips. She stood staring at the door as the tears gushed from her eyes.

"Hey." Abby's voice was soft behind her.

Turning, Miriam found Abby standing at the bottom of the stairs. Miriam wiped her eyes and cleared her throat. "When did you get out of the car?" she asked.

"I saw Gerald's expression when he opened the door, and I thought you might need moral support. Don't let them get to you." She climbed the stairs and nodded toward the car. "Let's go to *Aenti's* house. When she called my cell phone from her phone shanty, she said we could arrive at any time. The door's unlocked for us."

Miriam followed her cousin toward the car.

They drove in silence to the cabin located at the back of her father's eighty acres. Her father and his brother had built the small home for Edna many years ago after their parents had died and another brother had moved into their parents' home with his family. Since Edna never married, she lived in the home alone, and her brothers provided for her living expenses. She baked Amish pastries and provided them to local bakeries for extra money.

Miriam parked alongside the cabin and stared at the small pond behind it, sparkling in the beams of the headlights. She remembered hot summer days when she and her siblings would splash in the pond after their chores were completed.

"She said she'd leave a lantern burning for us, and we should make ourselves at home," Abby said while gathering her purse.

Miriam nodded and cleared her throat, wishing the lump would subside.

"Hey, it'll be okay." Abby rubbed her arm. "The funeral will be in a couple days. You can visit with *Aenti* and Hannah and then head back home."

"Where's that?"

"Huh?" Abby's eyebrows knitted together with confusion. "Where's home exactly? It's certainly not here." Miriam gestured toward the large field separating the cabin from her father's house. "And it's not in Indiana."

"Why would you say that?"

"No one wants me here, so that doesn't make it home. And my life in Indiana consists of work and a small apartment."

"Gee, thanks a lot," Abby deadpanned, leaning back against the door.

Miriam sighed. "I didn't mean it that way. You know you're my best friend. I just meant I don't fit in anywhere. I'm not quite *English*, and I'm certainly not Amish."

"Why do you need to label yourself? You're Miriam Lapp." Abby touched Miriam's arm. "You're beautiful inside and out. You're sweet, kind, and loving. And if you hadn't chickened out and quit nursing school, you would've been the best pediatric nurse that LaGrange, Indiana, has ever seen."

Miriam's eyes narrowed to slits. "For the hundredth time, Abby, I didn't chicken out. I ran out of money. That's not the same as chickening out."

"You could've applied for more student aid. That's how I got my paralegal certificate and how I plan to get through law school." Abby pushed a lock of dark brown hair back from Miriam's face. "You sell yourself short. You're an amazing person. Don't let your family's judgment hold you back from achieving your dreams."

"But that's just it." Miriam unfastened her seatbelt and angled herself toward her cousin. "I don't know what I want or where I belong. I've been gone for nearly four years, but I still feel like I left something here. I still feel incomplete."

Abby frowned. "Because of *him*?"

Miriam shrugged. "Maybe."

"It is, isn't it? You haven't gotten over him."

Biting her bottom lip, Miriam glanced toward the pond. "He's probably married and has two children with another on the way by now," she whispered.

"If he is, then it was never meant to be."

Sniffing, Miriam shook her head. "But that's not just it. God is punishing me for what happened to Jeremy Henderson. It's my burden to be alone and suffer."

Abby scowled. "No, you're wrong. What happened

to Jeremy wasn't your fault, and it's time you realized that." Her expression softened. "God's in control, so have faith. That's what you told me when I was down in the dumps about Rich's escapades, and you helped me through. I thank God for you and your faith." She gave Miriam a quick hug. "You're my best friend too. We'll get through this. I promise." Abby pushed the door open. "Let's head to bed. It's nearly one. We're going to be exhausted tomorrow when *Aenti* gets us up at four-thirty."

Miriam groaned while retrieving her purse from the back-seat. "I hope she allows us some time to sleep."

"Don't bet on it." Abby sighed.

They lugged their bags up the front step of the cabin and stepped into the small living area. Scanning the room, Miriam found the sofa made up with sheets and pillows. The door to the guest room was open, revealing the single bed also ready for a visitor.

"Should we flip a coin to see who gets the guest room?" Miriam asked, letting her bag fall to the floor.

"Nah." Abby shook her head and yawned. "You take the guest room. I'll bunk on the sofa."

"How's that fair?"

"Just go." Abby nudged her. "I'll be fine."

"But—"

"You did the driving and look absolutely wiped out. I'll tell *Aenti* to let you sleep." She gestured toward the door. "Go on. Git!"

"Thanks. You're the best." Miriam gave Abby a hug and then dragged her bag to the guest room, which was devoid of decorations and held only a few pegs

on the wall, a small bureau, a sewing machine, and
the bed. After freshening up in the small bathroom in
the hall, she changed into her simple white nightgown
and crawled between the sheets of the bed. Snuggling
down, Miriam closed her eyes and silently said her
prayers.

As she drifted off to sleep, she was accosted by
thoughts of Timothy Kauffman—his sandy blond hair,
his powder blue eyes, his tantalizing smile that could
melt her within seconds of his lips curling . . .

She wondered if he'd ever married the girl her sister
Lilly had said he was courting behind Miriam's back.
Did he still live in that house he had built for himself
and Miriam on his father's property? Was he still as
handsome as she remembered?

Her thoughts faded as sleep overtook her exhausted
body.

* * *

Miriam awoke to the aroma of bacon, eggs, and freshly
made bread. She yawned, stretched, and hoisted herself from the bed and dressed in her jeans and a fresh
T-shirt.

After running a brush through her dark brown hair,
she stepped into the small living area and found Abby
and Edna chatting and drinking coffee. A spread big
enough for a small army covered the table, including
plates full of bread, bacon, eggs, oatmeal, and sausage.

"Miriam!" Edna attempted to stand. She looked older
than Miriam remembered. Her white hair was parted in

the middle and covered by a white prayer *kapp*, and she wore a traditional dark blue frock with a black cape and apron. Her skin was pale, but her deep brown eyes lit up with her warm smile.

"Please, don't get up." Miriam rushed to her side and hugged her. "It's so good to see you." Tears filled her eyes. How she'd missed her aunt.

"Have a seat, and let me have a good look at you." Edna patted the chair next to her, and Miriam lowered herself into it. "Ah, you're just as *schee* as your sisters. You look just like your *mamm*."

Miriam's eyes overflowed at the mention of her mother. "Thank you." She quickly corrected herself. "I mean, *danki*. It's been a long time since I used *Dietsch*."

"*Ya*. It's been too long, *mei liewe*." Edna patted Miriam's hands. "Please fill your plate and tell me about your life in Indiana. Do you have a special boy?"

Miriam glanced at her aunt's hands and nearly gasped at how curled her fingers were. Her arthritis had progressed. "Oh, *Aenti*." She touched Edna's frail hand. "How are you?"

Edna shrugged. "I get by. I'm just not as active as I used to be. I can only bake one thing a day to sell anymore. I used to have several dishes ready for Beth Anne when she came by, but now I struggle just to get one finished." She patted Miriam's hand again. "It's no bother. I want to hear about your life. I've heard about Abigail's already."

Abby rolled her eyes while chewing some bacon. "It didn't take long to tell her about my boring life."

Miriam smiled at her cousin and then glanced

back at her aunt. "Did you say Beth Anne? Beth Anne Bontrager?" *Timothy's sister!*

"*Ya*, that's right." Edna passed the plate of bread to Miriam. "You need to try some of my sweet bread. It's delicious. Beth Anne still comes by every day to pick up some desserts from me. They're shorthanded at the bakery these days."

"Why's that?" Miriam loaded up a plate with scrambled eggs and bacon.

"Sarah Rose had *zwillingbopplin* back at Christmas and isn't working right now. There's a rumor she's getting married soon too." Edna shook her head and smiled. "And Rebecca has a baby now too. Her little one was born a month or so after Sarah's *zwillingbopplin*, so I guess he's about six months old now."

Miriam gasped. "Sarah has twins and Rebecca had a baby?" "Oh *ya*. Rebecca was given custody of her nieces and then wound up pregnant after all those years of praying for a baby.

Sarah lost her husband, Peter, in a fire at the furniture store."

"Oh no!" Miriam said. "That's terrible."

"*Ya*," Edna said. "It was a tragedy, but she found love again when she met Peter's brother, Luke. The Lord works in mysterious ways."

"Ain't that the truth," Abby deadpanned while buttering another piece of bread.

"I keep forgetting how long you two have been gone. A lot has changed around here."

Edna's hand shook as she lifted her coffee cup to her lips, and Miriam squelched the instinct to reach out and help. She didn't want to insult the older woman, who had lived alone for a long time. She bit into the sweet bread and closed her eyes. It tasted like heaven. She longed to ask Edna how Timothy Kauffman was, but she didn't want to give the impression that she cared. After all, he'd broken her heart.

"What time will Beth Anne stop by?" Miriam asked.

"Rebecca's *English* niece brings her by around mid-morning

to pick up my desserts."

"We can help you make some pastries, right, Abby?" Miriam cut her eyes across the small table to her cousin, who responded with a horrified expression.

"You want me to try to bake?" Abby jammed her finger into her own collarbone. "Remember what happened when I attempted lasagna last month? Our neighbor wound up calling nine-one-one. The only good thing that came from it was I got a date with a handsome firefighter, but even he turned out to be a dud. Such is the story of my life, though."

"Perhaps you're looking in the wrong places, Abigail." Edna gave a knowing expression. "Are you going to go by and see your *mamm*?"

Abby shrugged, lifting her cup. "What's the point? They won't answer my letters or return the voice-mail messages I leave for them at the phone shanty. Apparently I don't exist."

"It's more difficult to ignore someone when they are standing on your front porch," Edna said.

"My brother had no problem with it last night," Miriam quipped.

"Give them time, Miriam. Wait until the funeral and then try again. Your *daed* has a hard exterior, but deep down, he has a heart of gold." Edna smiled and patted her hand. "So, tell me about Indiana. I know you work for a pediatrician. What else occupies your time?"

Miriam shrugged. "That's about it. Abby and I hold our own Bible studies, which is fun."

"No special someone in your life?" Edna raised her eyebrows, and Miriam stifled a laugh.

"No, sorry. We're both single," Miriam said between bites of egg.

"And we're happy that way. At least I am." Abby stood and carried the empty dishes to the sink.

"I find that difficult to believe," Edna said. "You were married once."

"I'm sorry, but it's true." Abby filled up the sink and added soap. "Just the other day Rich had the nerve to call me and ask if he could come back because his girlfriend left him. As if I'm supposed to drop everything and let him move in after the way he left me."

Miriam shook her head while snatching a piece of bacon from her plate. She loved Abby's confidence and wished some would rub off on her. Abby was more *English* than Miriam, and Miriam assumed working for a powerful law firm had given Abby all the courage and boldness she needed in the professional world.

To Miriam's surprise, Edna chuckled. "Abigail, you have your *mamm's* fire in you. You should go visit her. I would imagine she'd love to see you. You've grown into a beautiful young woman."

"*Danki, Aenti,*" Abby said while drying the dishes.

"I don't think my parents would see it that way. I disappointed them when I went against their wishes and left. They would probably throw me off their porch like Gerald did to Miriam last night."

"We'll see at the funeral." Edna's expression clouded. "Will you dress appropriately for the funeral?"

"I was already thinking about that," Miriam said. Abby nodded.

"That might help open the communication with your parents," Miriam said.

Abby sighed. "I'm certain you're right."

"How about we do some baking before Beth Anne comes?" Miriam carried her dishes to the sink. "I think I still remember how to make your famous shoofly pie."

"*Wunderbaar*." Edna nodded toward the counter. "Grab my cookbook, and let's get to work."

CHAPTER 3

Timothy Kauffman stood in the center of the work area of Kauffman & Yoder Amish Furniture and scanned the sea of carpenters for his father. The large, open warehouse was divided into nearly a dozen work areas separated by workbenches cluttered with an array of tools.

The sweet scent of wood and stain filled his nostrils. The men working around him were building beautifully designed dining room sets, bedroom suites, entertainment centers, hutches, end tables, desks, and coffee tables. Pieces crafted at the Kauffman & Yoder Amish Furniture were favorites among Lancaster County tourists and residents alike.

Timothy's father, Eli, had built the store with his best friend, Elmer Yoder, before Timothy was born. The business had been his father's dream come true, much like his mother's bakery, located a few miles away.

Hammers banged, saw blades whirled, and air compressors hummed. Since it was an Amish-owned business, the air compressors powering the tools ran off diesel generators.

Scanning the work area, Timothy spotted his brother

Daniel; his sister Sarah Rose's fiancé, Luke; and Elmer's grandson, Jake, all hard at work creating masterpieces for customers. Yet there was no sign of Eli.

Timothy sidled up to his older brother and spoke over the chorus of tools around them. "Have you seen *Dat*?"

Daniel shook his head and wiped his sweaty brow with a rag. "No, I haven't. Are those fans working? It's hotter than the mid-afternoon sun in here."

Timothy glanced toward the battery-powered fan sitting next to his brother's workbench. "*Ya*, it's working. I'll tell Elmer to order more fans. It's been a hot summer."

"I agree with that." Daniel blew out a sigh.

Timothy glanced around the shop again. "I guess I'll check up front for *Dat*."

"What did you need him for?"

"I wanted him to check this bureau. I'm having a difficult time with the shelves on the hutch. They just don't look right."

Leaning back against his workbench, Daniel took a gulp from a cup of water. "Want me to look at it?"

Timothy waved off the question. "You've got your hands full with that entertainment center. I don't want to burden you."

"Don't be *gegisch*. I have time." He smacked Timothy's shoulder. "Let me just finish this one piece, and then I'll come look at yours."

"*Danki*." Timothy pointed toward the doorway. "I'm going to check on *Dat* and then I'll be at my bench."

"*Dat's* probably up front since Jessica won't be in for

a little while. She's still driving Beth Anne around for errands."

"*Ya*, that's right. I forgot."

Daniel nodded. "See you in a bit."

Timothy maneuvered around the sea of work-benches and stepped through the doorway to the front of the store, which consisted of large glass windows and samples of furniture.

Elmer stood chatting with an *English* customer while Eli sat at the desk behind the front counter and spoke in Pennsylvania *Dietsch* into the receiver of the push-button phone. The small desk was covered in piles of furniture catalogs, phonebooks, and stacks of paper. Jessica Bedford, Rebecca's *English* niece, would be in soon to help run the front of the store. Jessica was visiting for the summer before starting her senior year of high school in Virginia.

Leaning on the counter, Timothy waited while his father finished his conversation.

"*Danki* for the call. Of course, the Lapps are in our prayers . . ." Eli met Timothy's curious expression and frowned. "*Ya*. I will, and we'll talk about Matthew too. It sounds *gut*. *Danki*, Manny. See you Thursday." *Dat* hung up the receiver and rubbed his temple. "Bad news is always tough to take."

Timothy raised an eyebrow. "*Was iss letz?*"

"Bertha Lapp passed away in her sleep Sunday night." Eli shook his head. "Apparently she succumbed to pneumonia. Her family thought she was on the mend, but the Lord saw fit to take her home. So tragic for her family. So sad."

Timothy swallowed and shook his head. "Bertha Lapp?"

Miriam's mamm.

Timothy closed his eyes for a moment, fighting in vain against the images of Miriam overtaking his mind.

Miriam smiling up at him while they sat on a quilt in the park. Miriam holding his hand. Miriam whispering she loved him. Miriam's lips brushing his lips . . .

He swallowed a groan. Why did these memories, ones he'd suppressed for so long, have to surface now? He'd worked so hard to put her behind him. His family had told him he needed to concentrate on making a new life.

So then why did thinking of her set his heart back four years?

"The funeral is Thursday." Eli tapped the counter. "We'll

close up and all go as a family."

Tongue-tied, Timothy simply nodded. His father wanted him to go into the Lapp home, and he would possibly face . . .

"Is Miriam in town?" The words escaped his lips before he could stop them. He groaned at his transparent emotions. A lecture from Eli would ensue for certain.

Eli shrugged as he stood. "I don't know. If so, then you will treat her with respect. I know she left you without an explanation, but the past is the past. Miriam made her choice when she left the community without joining the church. God tells us to forgive each other and love our neighbors, and that would apply to Miriam as well as to the rest of the community."

Timothy resisted the urge to roll his eyes. He was thirty and didn't need this lecture. "I know. I will be respectful."

"*Gut.*" Eli patted his arm. "We may have a new employee in the next couple of weeks."

"Oh?" Timothy's eyebrows careened toward his hairline in question.

"A young man named Matthew Glick who just moved here with his mother. Manny recommended him."

"When will he start here?"

"That I'll need to figure out. I'm going to see if I can talk with him later this week." Eli then gestured toward the shop. "We have more orders to fill, so we better get back to work."

"*Ya*, I wanted to talk to you about that bureau. I need your advice on the shelves. They aren't coming out the way I'd planned."

"Let's take a look." Eli led him back into the shop, where they finished building the bureau.

After Eli moved on to another project, Timothy began the tedious job of sanding, losing himself in memories of Miriam. No matter how hard he tried, thoughts of her flooded his memory and hijacked his thoughts.

"Timothy." A voice behind him caused him to jump with a start. Turning, he found Naomi King grinning while holding a picnic basket in one hand and a quilt in the other.

"Naomi." He set the sander on his workbench and wiped his hands on a red shop towel. "*Gude mariye. Wie geht's?*"

Her smile faded and her eyebrows knitted above her deep brown eyes, which shone with disappointment. "Actually, it's after twelve." She set the basket on the sawdust-covered wood floor. Her dark brown hair stuck out from under her white prayer *kapp*.

"Oh." He forced a smile. "So it's good afternoon."

She hugged the quilt to her purple caped dress. "We had a lunch date. Remember?"

"Right!" He tossed the rag onto the bench. "Let me get cleaned up."

He'd completely forgotten he'd had her reschedule her promise of a picnic for today. Naomi was always eager to bring him lunch. He knew she wanted more than friendship, but he hadn't yet convinced himself that marrying her was the right choice. He hoped he didn't set her up for heartache; however, she hadn't mentioned where their relationship was headed, which he took to mean that they were both comfortable with the friendship.

He overheard her mutter something in *Dietsch* about forgetful men as he moved past her toward the restroom. After dusting off his clothes and washing up, he met her by the back door. They stepped out into the warm July air and took their usual spot under the large oak tree beyond the parking lot.

While Timothy spread out the quilt, Naomi poured him a cup of water and then began fixing their chicken salad sandwiches. Sitting across from him on the blanket, she prattled on about gossip she'd heard while working at her mother's quilt stand at the farmer's market.

He stared at his sandwich and grunted at the appropriate times. Although he gave the appearance that he was interested in what Naomi was saying, he was immersed deeply in thoughts of Miriam.

His mind swirled with questions. He wondered if Miriam was in town for the funeral. Had she become a nurse? Did she have children? If so, then what would he say to her?

And most importantly—why should he care about her when she was the one who'd left him?

When the sound of Naomi's voice faded, he looked up, meeting her annoyed gaze.

"Did you hear a word I said, Timothy Kauffman?" she demanded, placing her half-eaten sandwich on a plate.

He gave his best mischievous grin and lifted his cup of tea. "Of course I did. You said I have the best smile in all of Lancaster County."

Her cheeks flushed a deep crimson, and an embarrassed giggle sang from her lips. "You do have the best smile in Lancaster County, but that's not what I was saying. I asked if you'd heard about Bertha Lapp's passing."

He nearly choked on his water. "*Ya*, I did. So *bedauerlich*."

"I spoke with Lilly this morning." Frowning, Naomi shook her head. "The family is devastated. They'd thought she was recovering from the pneumonia. It was completely unexpected."

He nodded at the mention of Miriam's younger sister. He wanted to ask if Naomi had heard anything about Miriam's coming to town, but he couldn't form the words.

"Will you go to the funeral with me?" she asked.

He nodded again, chewing his sandwich. "Of course."

"I feel so bad. I don't know what I'd do if I lost my *mamm*." She sniffed, and he hoped she wouldn't cry. He couldn't handle it when women cried. Too much raw emotion for him.

"Poor Lilly," she continued, her lip quivering. "And Hannah too. She has her hands full with Lena Joy's illness, along with her other *kinner*."

Timothy continued eating the rest of his sandwich. While Naomi chatted, a strange wave of guilt rushed through him. Although he and Naomi had been friends for a month now, he'd never officially asked to court her. He enjoyed their time together. She brought him lunch nearly every day, and she joined him for family suppers on weekends. She was sweet, but she was a friend. He didn't feel a romantic connection to her. Not like he'd had with . . .

He let the thought evaporate. No use in dwelling in the past. Four years had gone by, and he'd never heard from Miriam. It was over. If he could somehow convince his heart of that fact, he could move on with his life and settle down before he was too old.

"What's wrong, Timothy?" Naomi's sweet voice broke through his mental tirade.

"Nothing." He poured himself another cup of water and hoped she would drop the subject of his odd mood.

"Something's wrong. I can tell." Her eyes bored into his. "You're a million miles away. You normally at least respond to me when I speak." She pulled two slices of chocolate cake from her basket and set them on two napkins. "Today you haven't acknowledged one word I've said." Her expression became coy. "And you haven't even complimented my chicken salad."

He couldn't help but smile. "Your chicken salad is superb, Naomi. *Danki.*"

"*Gern gschehne.*" She handed him the cake. "Your dessert."

"*Danki.*" While they ate their cake, he asked her how her day was going at the farmer's market.

Once their lunch was finished, Timothy helped her pack up her basket and then walked her to the front of the shop, which was located across the street from the farmer's market in Bird-In-Hand.

"*Danki* for another *appeditlich* lunch," he said, handing her the quilt.

"*Gern gschehne*, Timothy. You know I love bringing you lunch." She batted her long lashes and gave him a coy smile.

He inwardly groaned. Did she expect a kiss? His *gut* had told him to cut off the friendship because she would wind up expecting more. He was going to have to tell her how he truly felt sooner or later, and from the expression on her face, it was going to have to be sooner.

But now was neither the time nor the place. He couldn't break her heart and then send her back to work.

Besides, wouldn't breaking her heart put me in the same category as Miriam after what she did to me?

The thought hit him like a ton of bricks. He was wrong to mislead Naomi. He was obligated to not hurt her.

"There you go again!" She gestured dramatically and

sighed. "You're off on another planet. I wish I could read your mind, Timothy."

"No, you don't," he muttered.

"What was that?" She tilted her head in question.

"Nothing." He touched her shoulder. "I best let you get back to work before your *mamm* prohibits you from having lunch with me."

"I doubt that will happen." Her flirtatious grin was back. "How about I bring you lunch again tomorrow?"

Oh, she was so eager. If she only knew the inner turmoil he was battling. He forced a smile. "That would be *wunderbaar*. Enjoy the rest of your day."

"You too." She turned and trotted toward the farmer's market.

Timothy watched her disappear across the parking lot and shook his head. Naomi deserved a suitor whose intentions were clear and whose emotions were focused on her. He said a silent prayer that he could be the person she deserved and that he would find the strength to get Miriam Lapp out of his mind and his heart.

. . .

Miriam set a German apple cake on the table next to the shoofly pie. "How are those oatmeal cookies coming along?" she asked Abby.

Her cousin grimaced. "I think I burned this batch too." She set the cookie sheet on the stove and huffed. "I'm not a good cook."

"*Ya*, you are." Edna rubbed Abby's back. "You are too harsh with yourself, just as you always were when you were a *maedel*." She moved the cookies around on the sheet with a spatula. "Some of these are good. Grab the plastic wrap, and we'll package up the good ones."

Miriam was wrapping up the German apple cake when she heard a car motor up the driveway. Her stomach flipped at the thought of seeing Beth Anne for the first time in nearly four years. She hoped Beth Anne would speak to her and not treat her like Gerald had.

A tap sounded on the door, and Miriam bit her bottom lip. "Answer that please, Miriam," Edna called. "We're almost done with these cookies."

Miriam hesitated and glanced at Abby, who nodded toward the door as if reading her worried thoughts.

"Go on," Abby said with a sweeping gesture. "She's only human like you."

Miriam pulled the door open and found Beth Anne standing on the porch alongside a young *English* woman with dark hair.

Beth Anne's eyes widened with shock. "Miriam." She touched her arm. "I'm so very sorry about your *mamm*. I've been asking the Lord to comfort your family."

Beth Anne's gesture brought tears to Miriam's eyes. "*Danki*," Miriam whispered.

"This is my niece, Jessica Bedford." Beth Anne nodded at her, and the girl smiled. "She's staying with Rebecca and Daniel for the summer."

"It's nice to meet you," Miriam said. Stepping back, she opened the door wide. "Please come in."

"*Wie geht's*," Beth Anne said, stepping into the kitchen. "I'm sorry I'm late, but Jessica and I brought food to Abraham and visited with the family. I'm so sorry to hear about—" She stopped when she turned to Abby. "Abigail Lapp!" Rushing over, Beth Anne took her hand. "Another surprise! How are you?"

Abby hugged Beth Anne. "It's good to see you too. I'm doing all right. How are you? Last I'd heard, you'd married Paul. How many *kinner* do you have?"

"Four, but we're hoping for more." Beth Anne grinned. "My little sister has twins now, and we're wondering if there may be more in the future. Robert has seven *kinner*, but we think he and Sadie may be finished."

Abby shook her head. "I can't imagine having one, let alone seven."

"We believe *kinner* are a gift from God." Beth Anne shrugged. "It's our way. I'm sure you remember."

"Oh, I do." Abby chuckled. "My older sister is working on number eight from what I've heard."

Miriam shifted her weight on her feet and then turned back to the cake to stop herself from asking how many children Timothy had.

A digital melody sang out from across the room and Abby jumped. "I'm sorry. That must be my boss. We're working on a big deposition." She hurried across the room and pulled her BlackBerry from her briefcase. "Yup, it's him. I'll take it in the guest room. Excuse me." Holding the electronic device to her ear, she disappeared into the guest room, gently closing the door behind her.

"How are you, Edna?" Beth Anne asked. "You look well."

"A little tired today but *froh* to have my *bruderskinner* with me." Edna placed a hand on Miriam's shoulder. "It's a sad occasion, but I'm so *froh* they came."

Beth Anne's eyes flickered back to Miriam, and Miriam felt her cheeks flame with embarrassment. Edna had always been good at putting her on the spot. She was reminded of the time when Edna had announced to the entire Lapp family that Miriam had received her first kiss after catching Miriam and Timothy smooching in the barn. Miriam's brother and male cousins had taunted her about it for weeks.

"How is Abraham?" Edna asked.

Frowning, Beth Anne shook her head. "He looked as if he was in shock. Lilly said he hasn't slept since he found out the news. The funeral is planned for Thursday."

Miriam's lip quivered. She would bury her mother on Thursday. She was ashamed she hadn't spoken to her in four years. How could she let that much time go by without visiting her parents? Miriam wiped an errant tear from her cheek. She wasn't much of a daughter. She'd deserved to have the door to her father's house slammed in her face.

Edna lowered herself into a kitchen chair. "I was thinking of walking up to the house later on to check on him, but my knees and hands are bothering me today. I think I may need to rest for a while. I believe an afternoon nap is in order."

"You should take a nap," Miriam said. "Abby and I will take care of everything."

"*Danki.*" Edna looked at Jessica. "How are you enjoying your summer?"

"It's been good." The girl smiled. "It's nice to be back here with my Aunt Rebecca and my sister."

"You're working in the furniture store too, *ya*?"

Jessica nodded. "I run the front."

"And her friend works there." Beth Anne grinned and elbowed Jessica in her ribs. "Jake."

Jessica's cheeks flushed pink. "We're just *friends*, Aunt Beth Anne."

Miriam's stomach tightened. She assumed Timothy still worked at his father's furniture shop. Would Jessica share that Miriam was in town? Miriam did a mental headshake. Why would Jessica share that information with Timothy? Jessica didn't know about their past.

However, Beth Anne could tell Jessica the story, and then Jessica could share the story . . .

Miriam swallowed a groan.

Edna nodded toward the refrigerator. "There are three more pies in there. I made them last night." She frowned. "I'm sorry I couldn't make more, but my fingers are very painful lately."

"Oh, I understand," Beth Anne said. "I hope you're feeling better soon."

"Abby and I helped her make some more desserts this morning," Miriam said. "We'll help again tomorrow." She fetched the pies from the refrigerator and then turned to Beth Anne and Jessica. "I'll help you carry everything outside."

"*Danki.*" Beth Anne took the pies from the table. Turning, she smiled at Edna. "*Danki.* I'll see you tomorrow."

Jessica grabbed the bags of cookies and said goodbye. Miriam took a deep breath while following Beth Anne outside, where they approached a dark blue SUV with Virginia license plates.

Smiling, Beth Anne took the desserts from Miriam's

hands and placed them on the back floor of the SUV. Miriam bit her lower lip, holding back the questions bursting forth in her mind. Was Timothy married? Was he a father?

Had he ever loved Miriam or was their whole relationship a mistake?

But if he did love her, had Miriam messed up by leaving? Still, she couldn't imagine doing otherwise, considering what Timothy had done and what had happened to Jeremy. Then there had been her dream of going to nursing school. She sighed. Leaving Lancaster County had once seemed so right. So why did it now seem so wrong?

Jessica said good-bye and climbed into the driver's seat.

"I'm very sorry about your *mamm*," Beth Anne said, closing the back door to the SUV. "She was a *wunderbar fraa*."

"*Danki*." Miriam cleared her throat and sniffed. "How are your parents doing?"

"*Gut*." Beth Anne opened the passenger door and leaned on it. "The bakery and the furniture store are doing *gut*. We've been so busy at the bakery that Edna has been a big help. Sarah Rose and Rebecca are taking some time off to be with their *kinner*."

"Edna told me. I'm so glad to hear Sarah Rose has found someone. I was sorry to hear about Peter and the fire."

"*Ya*." Beth Anne frowned. "It was tough on us all, but she and Luke seem very *froh*."

Miriam nodded. "I'm glad to hear it."

An uncomfortable silence fell between them, and Miriam wracked her mind for something to say. She longed to ask about Timothy, but it felt too risky. Beth Anne was being so nice. What if mentioning Timothy changed her attitude toward Miriam?

"How are you doing?" Beth Anne asked. "Are you still living in Indiana?"

"*Ya.*" Miriam leaned against the banister at the bottom of the stairs. "I've been working for a pediatrician for almost two years now. I love being with the children—I mean *kinner.*"

Beth Anne smiled. "I guess *Dietsch* feels foreign now, *ya*?"

"*Ya.*" Miriam smiled.

"You're a nurse, yes?"

Miriam shook her head. "I started nursing school, but my scholarship money ran out. I'm an office assistant."

"Oh. Do you like it?"

Miriam shrugged. "I do."

"Do you have a family?"

"No. Abby and I share an apartment. She was married, but her husband left her. We're helping each other out."

Beth Anne's expression was surprised. "You don't have a family?"

"No."

"Were you ever married?"

"No." Miriam tilted her head in question. "Why do you ask?"

Beth Anne smiled again. "I was just curious. I better get back. The tourist crowds have been rather large."

"I guess I'll see you tomorrow."

"*Ya.*" Beth Anne climbed into the car, and the engine revved. "*Danki* for the pastries."

"*Gern gschehne.*" Miriam waved as the SUV drove off.

She then breathed a deep sigh and lowered herself onto the stairs. Gazing at the back of the SUV disappearing down the driveway, she wondered how she would survive the funeral with the Kauffman family present. How was she going to keep her emotions intact—especially if Timothy was there?

Glancing across the field, she spotted Gerald trotting toward the row of barns behind her parents' house. A row of buggies parked near the barn represented the host of friends and neighbors who were visiting and offering condolences to the family. Miriam longed to be a part of the outpouring of support. Oh, how she missed her family. She wished she could get one more chance with them.

She needed to talk to someone who understood. She needed some of her family behind her.

She needed to go see Hannah.

CHAPTER 4

After nodding to her children, nieces, and nephews carousing in the playground behind the bakery under the supervision of her niece, Beth Anne balanced the pies and cookies on her arms and climbed the steps leading to the back door. The sweet aroma of freshly baked bread filled her senses while she placed the desserts on the counter.

She then crossed the floor and scrubbed her hands in the sink. The large open kitchen had plain white walls, and keeping with their tradition, there was no electricity. The lights were gas powered, as was the row of ovens.

Due to the humidity of the summer, they did the bulk of the baking in the early morning in order to keep the heat to a minimum. Five fans ran through the power inverters and gave a gentle breeze. Nevertheless, the kitchen was still very warm. The long counter included their tools, plain pans, and ordinary knives and cutlery.

Beth Anne made her way to the long counter to begin separating the desserts and getting them ready for sale.

"*Aenti* Beth Anne!" Lindsay, her teenaged niece, rushed over, plucking a pie from the stack and grabbing a knife. "Thank goodness you're back! The tourists haven't stopped since you left. I don't know how we're going to make it through the summer." She began slicing the pie and placing the pieces on small paper plates to sell individually. "Amanda and Ruthie are running the front, but I need to get back out there."

"*Gut*," Beth Anne said. She was glad two of her sister Kathryn's daughters, Amanda and Ruthie, had joined them at the bakery. Without the girls' help, they would've had to hire someone outside of the family.

"How did your visit go?" Elizabeth, her *mamm*, sidled up to Beth Anne and began helping prepare the pastries for the front counter.

"I guess it was *gut*." Beth Anne began separating the cookies. "Abraham was very quiet. Lilly said he's having a hard time, which is to be expected. They appreciated the food very much."

"*Dat* and I will go visit them tonight," Elizabeth said. "I really liked Bertha. The Lord decided it was her time, but we'll certainly miss our friend."

Beth Anne continued to separate the cookies, while her thoughts were back at Edna's home. She'd been surprised to see Miriam there with Abby. Beth Anne had often wondered what had become of Miriam and why she had truly left. Lilly's story about Miriam pursuing her dream of becoming a nurse didn't fit the Miriam Lapp that Beth Anne had known and called her dear friend.

Although Beth Anne was hurt and disappointed

Miriam had broken her brother's heart, she had also missed her friend.

Kathryn crossed the kitchen with a tray full of whoopie pies. "Glad you're back," she said to Beth Anne. "It's been crazy here today. We may need to hire some more bakers. How are the Lapps?"

"They're devastated." Beth Anne shook her head. "I think I'll cook some more for them tonight and stop over again in the morning."

"I'll make some chicken supreme tonight," Kathryn said. "We can visit together."

Beth Anne nodded. "Sounds good."

"I can help you wrap those, *Aenti* Kathryn, after I take these out front," Lindsay said over her shoulder as she carried the tray full of individually wrapped pieces of pie toward the front.

"*Danki*." Kathryn stood at the far end of the long counter and began wrapping the pies.

Beth Anne sidled up to her mother. "I visited with Edna for a few minutes when I picked up the desserts."

Elizabeth wiped her hands on a towel. "How was she?"

"I think her arthritis is getting the best of her." Beth Anne cut her eyes to her sister and found her engrossed in wrapping the whoopie pies. She knew Kathryn would be upset as soon as Miriam's name was spoken, since Kathryn was very emotional and defensive of their family—much more so than Beth Anne or Sarah Rose. "I was also surprised Edna had two house guests."

Elizabeth's eyebrows lifted, her curiosity piqued.

"Miriam and Abby." Beth Anne braced herself for her mother's reaction.

"What?" Kathryn was standing next to Beth Anne before she could blink. "Miriam had the arrogance to come back after the way she abandoned Timothy? And Abby came back too? I can't believe it!"

"Kathryn," Elizabeth began, "you must calm down. Remember what Jesus teaches us about forgiveness." She then turned to Beth Anne. "How are they doing?"

"Miriam seems . . . unhappy." Beth Anne leaned against the counter. "She said she was doing fine, but there was something in her eyes. She looked sad."

Kathryn jammed her hands on her hips. "She should be after what she did to Timothy."

"Why are you being so harsh toward Miriam?" Beth Anne asked. "You were the one who defended your sister-in-law Anna Mae when she came to visit after being shunned. You stood by her when her father didn't welcome her back for Christmas."

"This is different," Kathryn snapped. "Anna Mae was always honest with her intentions. Miriam lied and hurt Timothy badly."

Elizabeth shook her head. "You've always seen yourself as Timothy's other mother since he's your younger brother, but you have to take a step back. Anna Mae had her reasons for leaving, and Miriam surely had hers also. It's not your place to judge."

Kathryn scowled. "No, it's not my place to judge, but it's my place to defend my brother. She shattered his heart, and she's not to be trusted."

"Kathryn . . ." Elizabeth's eyes were serious. "'Do

not judge, and you will not be judged. Do not condemn, and you will not be condemned. Forgive, and you will be forgiven.'"

Nodding with defeat, Kathryn frowned.

"Does Miriam have a family?" Elizabeth asked.

Beth Anne shook her head. "She's not married and she didn't finish nursing school. I got the impression she was sorry she'd left."

Elizabeth nodded. "I'm surprised."

Kathryn headed back to the other end of the counter. "I can't believe you even talked to her. Timothy would not be *froh*."

"It's the Christian thing to do," Beth Anne said. "Besides, it's been nearly four years. It's time to heal."

Lindsay bounced through the door and made a beeline to Kathryn. "*Aenti* Kathryn, I finished putting the pie out on the counter. I'm ready to help you with the whoopie pies and continue my *Dietsch* lesson for today."

Soon Kathryn and Lindsay were engrossed in a discussion of Kathryn's favorite hymns that were sung in German. Relieved Kathryn was distracted, Beth Anne moved closer to Elizabeth.

"*Mamm*, this may sound crazy, but I think Miriam's return to Lancaster County might be the Lord's work," Beth Anne whispered. "Perhaps God is using this solemn circumstance to bring closure and healing to Timothy and even to Miriam. I know Timothy never got over Miriam's leaving. It's not my business, but I don't think he's going to commit to Naomi. I know they've only been seeing each other for about a month now, but I don't see love in his eyes like I did when he was with Miriam. The passion isn't there."

Elizabeth gave a wide smile. "You are a very smart *fraa*, Elizabeth Anne."

Beth Anne felt her cheeks heat. "If I agree with you, then I'm prideful, but I guess that means you think I'm right about Miriam and Timothy?"

Elizabeth chuckled and looped her arm around Beth Anne's shoulder. "I do think you're right. I've watched Timothy mope and mourn Miriam for too long. It's time he move on."

"I'll talk to him tonight and tell him he should see Miriam and talk it out with her. Maybe then he can find some happiness and settle down."

"You're a *gut* sister, Beth Anne." Elizabeth lifted a tray of cake and cookies. "I'm going to take this out front and check on the girls."

Beth Anne glanced over at Kathryn and Lindsay. When her sister's gaze met hers, Kathryn frowned. Beth Anne hoped she was right about Miriam. She hoped Timothy would speak to her and would finally find some peace.

. . .

Miriam stood on the wide, sweeping porch of her older sister's large farmhouse. Glancing down, she assessed her purple T-shirt, blue jeans, and sandals, wishing she'd worn something nicer. She touched her hair, which hung loosely past her shoulders. A frock and prayer *kapp* would've been more appropriate, but

Miriam had disposed of her Amish clothing soon after relocating to Indiana.

Miriam gave herself a mental shake. She was being too tough on herself by worrying about her attire. Hannah was the only member of her family who hadn't judged her before she left for Indiana. Taking a deep breath, Miriam stood straighter and licked her lips. She then knocked on the front door and held her breath.

Footsteps sounded and then the door creaked open, revealing the young and pretty face of an adolescent girl with dark hair, yellowish eyes, and matching yellowish skin.

"Lena Joy," Miriam whispered.

Remaining beyond the cracked door, the girl raised her eyebrows in question. "Don't I know you? Aren't you my *Aenti* Miriam?"

Miriam took a cautious step toward her. "That's right. I'm your *Aenti* Miriam. Your *mamm* is my sister."

"I haven't seen you in a long time. Let me get my *mamm*." Lena closed the door and yelled something.

Quick footsteps rushed toward the door, which swung open, revealing Hannah beaming with her arms opened wide. "Miriam! I was hoping you'd come."

Miriam launched herself into her older sister's embrace and held on for dear life as tears spilled from her eyes. "Hannah," she whispered into her sister's shoulder.

"It's so *gut* to see you," Hannah murmured, rubbing her back. "*Willkumm heemet!*"

"*Danki.* I just wish I could call it home." Pulling out of the embrace, Miriam swiped her eyes with the back of her hand.

"To me, this will always be your home. Please, come in." Hannah grasped Miriam's arm and led her into the spacious den where Lena Joy stood with two younger children, a boy and another girl. "*Kinner*, this is your *Aenti* Miriam. Miriam, I'd like you to meet Lena Joy, Ian, and Mary."

Miriam smiled. "It's so good to see you."

"You're not Amish," Mary said, pointing to Miriam's clothes. "How come you're *English*?"

"Mary!" Hannah shook her head. "I'm sorry about that. Mary is only five and doesn't know when to be quiet."

"It's okay." Miriam squatted down to the little girl's level. "When you were a baby, I left Gordonville and moved to Indiana. I live there now, and I'm not Amish anymore."

"How come?" Ian asked, stepping over to her.

"I guess I wasn't sure I wanted to be Amish. I wanted to try the *English* life for a while. I sort of lost track of time and just stayed *English*."

Lena Joy gave a cautious frown. "Did you come because *Grossmammi* died?"

Standing, Miriam faced her eldest niece. "*Ya*, that's true. Your *mamm* called me and told me the news, and I came as soon as I could."

Lena Joy folded her hands in front of her blue frock. "You used to come and play with me when I was little. We used to play dolls together, *ya*?"

"That's right. You remember." Miriam nodded, tears filling her eyes. "We used to sit on the porch for hours at a time." She pointed toward the door. "I cherish those memories with you."

Lena Joy pushed out her chin. "If they meant so much to you, then why did you leave us?"

"Lena Joy!" Hannah snapped. "You apologize at once for your tone. You know better than to speak to an adult that way. Your *daed* will hear about this. Go to your room—"

"No, no." Miriam touched her sister's arm. "It's a valid question. I'll answer it." She met her niece's gaze. "I've been wrong not to come here, and I regret it now. The truth is I was planning to come and visit later this year and I was going to talk to your *grossmammi* about why I'd left. But now it's too late, which only proves you shouldn't take your family for granted like I did. Don't ever let the years come between you and your parents, okay?"

Lena Joy's expression softened as she nodded. "I missed you," she whispered.

"I missed you too." Miriam wiped her eyes and touched Lena Joy's arm. Her niece gave her a sad smile.

"*Kinner*, those are enough questions for now." Hannah waved them off. "Please go finish your chores while your *aenti* and I talk in the kitchen."

The children filed through the kitchen and out the back door.

Hannah led Miriam over to the kitchen table and pointed to a chair. "Please have a seat, and I'll get us some water and cookies."

"*Danki*." Miriam lowered herself into a chair and glanced around the plain kitchen. "Your home is still lovely. I always dreamed of having a house like this."

Hannah chuckled while carrying a pitcher of water

and two glasses to the table. "I'm sure what you have in Indiana is much fancier than this old place."

"Not really. Abby and I share a tiny apartment, but it's enough for just the two of us."

Hannah placed a plate of butterscotch cookies on the table and sat in a seat across from Miriam. "For you."

"Oh, my favorites!" Miriam snatched two cookies from the plate. "You remembered." She bit into a cookie and moaned. "You still are the best cookie maker in the county."

Hannah snickered. "You're an easy audience." She lifted a cookie to her mouth. "I guess you're staying with *Aenti* Edna?"

Miriam nodded. "I went to *Daed's*, and Gerald threw me off the porch."

Hannah shook her head. "I don't understand why they are still angry with you. It's been four years. I bet *Aenti* is thrilled to have you and Abby."

"She is. Her arthritis looks like it has progressed. Abby and I helped her make some pastries, and Beth Anne picked them up today for the bakery. I plan to help her again tomorrow." Miriam chewed the cookie. "How's Lena Joy? She looks so . . ."

"Jaundiced." Hannah sighed. "I wish there was a cure for Crigler Najjar Syndrome, but our only hope is a liver transplant. The bilirubin keeps building up in her body, and she doesn't get as much time under her phototherapy lights as she did when she was younger. We could control the yellowish tinge in her skin better when she was younger and wouldn't fight spending eight hours at a time under the lights."

Miriam reached over and squeezed Hannah's hand. "I'm so sorry. I pray for Lena Joy every night."

"*Danki.*" Hannah squeezed her hand in response. "Lena Joy came to me one night a few months ago and told me she was ready to have her liver transplant. We'd known since she was born that she would need one. It was just a matter of time. Lena Joy said she's tired of sleeping uncovered under the lights, and she's tired of people staring at her."

Miriam wiped a tear from her eye. "She's so brave."

"*Ya.*" Hannah sniffed and cleared her throat. "She's growing into a young woman, and she's ready to live a normal life with her friends. She wants to go out and do social things without worrying about looking different. We took her to Pittsburgh to meet with the transplant doctors and to get her evaluated. She's on the list, and we hope she'll get a liver soon." Hannah pulled out a cell phone. "We have this with us at all times. We never know when we'll get the call that a liver is available for her."

Miriam's eyes widened. "The bishop allowed you a phone?"

"Of course. This is considered a medical emergency." Hannah frowned. "I want my child well. I pray for it all the time, but I feel so guilty praying for a liver, since it will take someone losing their life to give Lena Joy another chance at hers."

"Remember it's not our place to question God's will. It's God's choice when Lena Joy gets her liver."

"*Ya,* that's true." Hannah wiped a tear from her cheek. "What if I were tested to see if I could donate to her? Do people donate part of their livers?" Miriam asked.

Hannah squeezed Miriam's hand. "You're so generous. The doctor says the most successful transplants are from cadaveric livers, but *danki* for asking."

Miriam shrugged. "It's the right thing to do. I believe in organ donation."

"You're a *gut* person." Hannah's expression turned to concern. "How are you really?"

"I'm okay." Miriam shrugged and lifted her glass of water. "I'm not convinced." Hannah's eyes studied Miriam's. Even at thirty, Hannah still had the same perfect, clear creamy skin and dark brown hair that she'd had in her early twenties. "How was it when you saw Beth Anne today?"

Miriam paused and took a drink while she considered the question. "It was awkward, but Beth Anne was still the same sweet person she was back when I was here and a part of the community."

"Did she mention Timothy?"

Miriam shook her head. "I didn't ask, but I wanted to." She bit her lip, wanting to ask if he was married.

"Last I heard he was seeing a girl in his district."

Miriam bit into a cookie to keep from showing too much emotion even though the news cut her like a knife.

"I don't know if they're going to get married or not." Hannah broke a cookie in half. "Will you go see him while you're here?"

"No," Miriam said, a little too fast. "I–I wouldn't even know what to say," she stammered. "I have nothing to say. He was seeing someone behind my back. It's obvious he never cared for me as much as I cared for him. It was a long time ago. It's over. Besides, I made my choice when I left. I wanted to pursue my dream of becoming a pediatric nurse. I didn't just leave because of him. I left because I wanted to see what being *English* was like."

Hannah sipped her water. "It's a shame it didn't work out for you two. I really miss you, and now that *Mamm's* gone . . ." Her voice trailed off.

Miriam sniffed. "I miss you too."

"Then you should stay." Hannah tapped the table for emphasis. "You could stay with me or you could even stay with *Aenti* for a while. She'd love to have company. I could get you a job working for my mother-in-law's quilting business. I'm sure you remember how to—"

"No, no." Miriam shook her head. "I don't think that would work out."

"Why not?" Hannah's eyebrows knitted together with confusion.

"I don't fit in here anymore."

"Why would you think that? You're family."

"No, I'm not." Miriam grabbed another handful of cookies from the serving plate. "I'm not Amish, and I'm not *English*. I'm stuck somewhere in between. Besides, *Daed* made it perfectly clear I'm not welcome in his home."

Hannah glowered. "I'll have a talk with him after we get through the funeral. He has no right to treat you that way. You didn't join the church, so it's not like you're shunned. I'll get him to realize he's being an old fool, and he'll welcome you home." Her expression brightened. "Then you can join the church and meet a nice Amish man. Soon you'll be married and having *kinner* of your own."

Miriam sighed. Her sister made it sound so easy. "I'm not sure I want to stay."

"Why not? What do you have waiting for you back in Indiana?"

"A new identity. In Indiana, I'm not judged by my past and what happened to Jeremy Henderson." Her voice trembled.

Hannah shook her head. "Sister, I love you no matter what. I see the person you really are and how beautiful you are, inside and out. You're the only one who clings to that past."

Miriam felt a lump swell in her throat at her sister's loving words. "Thank you."

CHAPTER 5

Timothy dried his dinner plate and placed it in the cupboard. He then headed through the kitchen into his den, where he flopped into his favorite easy chair and lifted his Bible from the end table. This was his favorite part of the day—when he could let go of his burdens and enjoy some quiet time with God. He flipped open the cover and found his way to Romans.

He was just settling in to his devotions when he heard a knock on the front door. He popped up, crossed the small room, and wrenched the door open. He found his middle sister standing on the front porch holding a pie plate.

"Beth Anne?" He leaned on the door frame and eyed her mischievous smile with suspicion. "What are you doing here?"

She feigned insult with a dramatic frown. "Is that how you greet a person who brings you your favorite dessert?"

He raised his eyebrows. "You brought me crumbly peach pie?"

"*Ya.*" She stepped toward the door. "Are you going to

invite me in, or are we going to discuss crumbly peach pie on the porch all evening?"

"Of course." Stepping back, he opened the door wide and gestured for her to enter. "I'll make some coffee." He led her through the den to his small kitchen.

"*Danki.*" Beth Anne rifled through the cabinets and retrieved plates and utensils while Timothy grabbed the percolator to make coffee. He added water to it and set it on the stove, turning on the burner.

Beth Anne sat at the table and sliced the crumbly peach pie. "How was your day?"

"*Gut.* Yours?" He leaned against the counter while the coffee dripped, the rich aroma permeating the room.

She licked her fingers. "*Gut.* I went to visit the Lapps."

"How are they coping?"

She grimaced. "They're taking it hard. It wasn't expected. Bertha had been improving, but the pneumonia took a sudden turn for the worse."

He shook his head. "We're not to question God's will, but sometimes it isn't easy."

"*Ya*, that's so true." Beth Anne pursed her lips, and her expression clouded as if she were choosing her words carefully.

He eyed her again with suspicion. It wasn't like her to just drop by without a specific reason.

The coffee pot gurgled, announcing that it was finished brewing, and Timothy poured two cups. He then brought the cups, sugar, and creamer to the table and lowered himself into a chair across from Beth Anne.

"Why are you really here?" he asked.

She flinched at the direct question, and he stifled a laugh. He relished catching her off guard.

"Can't I visit my favorite brother?" Her phony innocent smile was back.

Shaking his head, he added cream and sugar to his coffee and then passed them to her. "You're incorrigible." He forked the crumbly peach pie into his mouth and groaned with delight. It was sweet, moist, and smooth.

Almost as good as the ones Miriam used to make for me.

He pushed the thought away.

"Wow," he muttered while taking another bite. "You almost have me convinced that you just were being nice by bringing me this crumbly peach pie. It's heavenly."

"Glad you like it." She sipped her coffee, set the mug down, and folded her hands on the table. "I stopped by to see Edna Lapp after I visited Abraham and his *kinner*."

Nodding, Timothy took another gulp of coffee before forking in more pie.

"Edna had a couple of visitors staying with her."

"Anyone I know?"

"Abby Lapp." She paused, her expression becoming serious. "And Miriam."

Timothy dropped his fork, which fell to the floor with a loud clatter. His eyes locked on his sister's, and he glowered. "I knew you had an ulterior motive by coming here. You came to tell me you saw Miriam. I'm *froh* you saw her, but I don't see how that has anything to do with me."

Beth Anne's eyes remained focused on his, challenging him. "I think it has everything to do with you."

"How could that be?" He leaned back in his chair, folding his arms across his chest. "She made her choice and left. End of story."

"No, it's not the end of the story." Beth Anne leaned forward, slicing her fork through the air like a sword and showering the table with crumbs. "If it were, then you'd be married by now."

His eyes widened with shock. "What did you say? You think my not being married is due to Miriam's leaving?" He laughed with bitterness. "Beth Anne, you don't know me at all."

"Don't I?" She dropped her fork on the table and folded her hands. "I know you haven't made a commitment to Naomi or any other woman because you're not over Miriam."

"Naomi and I are just friends, but that's none of your business. Besides, we've only just started to get to know each other. It takes longer than a month to decide if you want to marry someone. You and Paul dated for longer than a month."

Not backing down, her stare was steady. "It's time you moved on, Timothy. You're not getting any younger."

He jammed a finger in his chest. "It's my business if I choose to stay single. You need to be concerned about your marriage and your *kinner*. I can handle my own life, and it's none of your concern."

"*Ya*, it is my concern. You're my brother, and I care about you. I want to see you *froh*. You need a *fraa* and a family. It's part of who you are."

He glowered. "I choose to be alone. I appreciate your concern, but I'm happy."

"Are you?" Sitting up straight, she looked unconvinced. "Then why are you stringing poor Naomi King along?"

He shook his head. How dare she criticize his relationship! "Naomi and I are good friends. I'm not stringing her along as you say. I resent that accusation."

Beth Anne shook her head. "Naomi is in love with you. She's just waiting for you to propose to her."

"She is not. You don't know her." He knew Beth Anne was right, but he didn't want to hear it. *How is it that Beth Anne can read people just like Mamm does?*

"I can tell. It's obvious by the way she looks at you. You have her wrapped around your finger, but you refuse to acknowledge the love she wants to give you." Beth Anne shook her head and sighed. "I'm not here to accuse you or upset you. I want you to have closure with Miriam. That's why I think you need to talk to her and—"

"No." Timothy slammed his hand on the table, causing the plates and mugs to rattle. "I have nothing to say to Miriam. What we had is gone. It's the past. Talking to her will just rehash things I let go a long time ago."

"You didn't let it go. That's the problem." She ran her fingers over a napkin as if collecting her thoughts. "I truly believe God sent Miriam here to settle things between you two. I think it's God's will that you talk with her and work out all your hurt feelings. It's just what you need so you can move on and make a new life for yourself. I think it's the Holy Spirit working in your life, Timothy. I talked to *Mamm*, and she agrees with—"

"You discussed this with *Mamm*?" He ran his hands down his face, imagining his sisters analyzing his life while they baked sand tarts. There had to be chitchat more interesting than his sad, sorry life.

"Please, just listen, okay?" Reaching across the table, she touched his arm. "*Mamm* and I want what's best for you, and we think that working through your feelings for Miriam would be healthy for you. Besides, when I talked to Miriam, she seemed really sad. I think she's carrying around some regret and unresolved feelings for you too."

He raised his eyebrows in disbelief. "You actually feel sorry for her? Are you serious, Beth Anne? She left me. Don't you remember how it happened? We had plans." He gestured around the kitchen. "I built this house for us. We were supposed to live here together and raise a family, but she left me. She went to Indiana to move in with her boyfriend and become a nurse." His eyes narrowed to slits as anger boiled through his veins. "How could you feel sorry for her when she was the one who ruined it all?"

"I didn't say I felt sorry for her." Beth Anne held her hands up in defense. "I'm just saying I think she needs to talk to you too."

He couldn't stop the questions that bubbled up to his lips. "What did she say to you?"

"Not much. I do know she's not married, and she didn't finish nursing school because she ran out of money. She's sharing an apartment with Abby and working in a pediatrician's office."

"Did she ask about me?" He wished he could take the question back after he asked it. Baring his soul made him uncomfortable.

"No, but I think she wanted to."

"She wanted to, *ya?*" He snorted with sarcasm. "Just like she wanted to marry me and have a family. It's all false. She's a liar." Leaning over, he plucked the fork from the floor and then grabbed the empty plates from the table. "It's getting late. I'm sure Paul and the *kinner* are expecting you home. *Danki* for the *appeditlich* pie."

He carried the dishes and utensils to the sink, and she followed with the remaining pie and mugs.

"I didn't mean to upset you," she said while he washed the dishes and set them in the drain. "I just want you to be *froh*."

"I am happy. I have a job I love and my own little house. What more could I want?"

"Someone to love who loves you in return. It's what we all want." She touched his arm. "I think you'll find that once you let your feelings for Miriam go. Talk to her and let her explain why she left. Then you can concentrate on building a life with Naomi."

Timothy blew out a deep sigh. He knew his sister wasn't going to drop it until he agreed. "Fine. I will."

"*Danki*." She gave him a quick hug. "I best get home. Will I see you at the funeral Thursday?"

Facing her, he leaned against the counter and wiped his hands on a rag. "*Ya*. Naomi asked me to go with her."

"*Gut*." Beth Anne followed him to the door. "Maybe you and Miriam can chat there."

He pursed his lips. "I don't think her mother's funeral is an appropriate place to discuss our broken relationship."

Beth Anne nodded. "You're right. Perhaps you can go visit her at her *aenti's* and speak alone."

He frowned. "Don't push it. I said I would talk to her, but I'm not going to make any promises about when or where."

"Fair enough." Beth Anne smiled. "See you later."

"*Gut nacht.*" He watched her hurry down to her buggy, and then he closed the door.

Timothy returned to his easy chair but couldn't concentrate on his devotions. Instead, his mind was flooded with thoughts of Miriam and Beth Anne's insistence that he needed to speak with her in order to let go of the past. The idea seemed utterly preposterous, but then why did he find himself considering it?

After a quick shower, Timothy climbed into bed and stared at the ceiling. He knew Beth Anne was correct when she said he was stringing Naomi along, but he couldn't bring himself to make a commitment to her. Whenever he considered broaching the subject of their future, the words would remain lodged in his throat. Perhaps Beth Anne was on to something.

Groaning, Timothy rolled onto his side. He didn't want to go down this road with Miriam. Talking to her would bring back so much—good and bad. He couldn't help but remember what she looked like—her deep brown eyes, her long eyelashes, her silky dark hair, her creamy white skin, and the infectious lilt of her laugh . . .

Although she thought she was plain, ordinary, and too skinny, Miriam lit up a room when she entered. She'd captured Timothy's heart the first time she'd smiled at him. She'd known just what to say to him, and she'd understood and forgiven his unpredictable moods. Timothy was sure Miriam was his soul mate, the love of his life.

He'd never felt that with Naomi. She was a pretty and sweet young woman, but she wasn't Miriam. He'd never felt that connection with her.

Guilt rained down on him. How could he compare Naomi to someone who had broken his heart into a million pieces? He felt Naomi's eagerness to be loved; he knew Beth Anne was right about that. But how could he marry someone he didn't love with all his heart?

And how can I string her along?

Moving onto his stomach, Timothy groaned into the pillow. He needed to sort through all of these feelings. Maybe Beth Anne was correct when she said he needed to talk to Miriam.

However, he knew one thing for sure—a funeral was no place for that conversation. It would be disrespectful to Bertha's memory and to Abraham's family to speak to Miriam then.

How would he manage to keep his emotions in check when he saw Miriam for the first time since she'd left him nearly four years ago?

Closing his eyes, Timothy fell asleep imagining how Miriam looked today.

CHAPTER 6

Miriam wished she could evaporate into thin air or melt into the hardwood flooring beneath her feet—anything to help her escape the pained glances radiating around her.

Standing at the back of the large living room, she scanned the sea of faces before her—members of the community in which she'd been born. There were people present who'd been there when her parents were married and others who remembered when she took her first steps as a toddler. Yet she felt like a stranger, an alien visiting from another planet.

She was clad in a plain black dress and her hair was gelled and forced into a tight ponytail.

However, even though she was dressed so conservatively, the clothes felt strangely comfortable, which surprised her. She had to admit the paradox—she didn't belong in the community, yet the clothes comforted her soul. Perhaps they served as a connection to her mother, whom she missed beyond words.

Miriam had stood with Hannah during the morning of the visitation. Keeping with tradition, Bertha had been dressed in all white, including her white apron and cape that had been saved from her wedding. The color represented the final passage into a new and better life. Hundreds of members from the community had marched through Abraham's house to offer their sympathy. Unlike the *English* funerals she'd attended in Indiana, which featured hugs and long discussions of memories of the deceased, the Amish were quietly respectful, giving a handshake and offering few words to Miriam and her family.

The hour-and-a-half afternoon service had been beautiful. Miriam had sat with Hannah and found herself holding her sister's hand during some of the sermon. At first, the Pennsylvania *Dietsch* was foreign, but after only a few minutes, the language came back to Miriam, and she hung on every word, frequently wiping her eyes in response to the emotion overflowing from her soul. The sermon emphasized the importance of yielding to God's will and was followed by prayers and Scriptures.

The graveside service was more painful for Miriam. Her mother was transported in her coffin by a horse-drawn hearse, which was a large black buggy. Bishop Gideon Swartzendruber read a hymn by the graveside before she was laid to rest in a grave dug by hand in an Amish cemetery located within their district. Her grave marker was simple and identical to those around her, keeping with the belief that in death, as in life, the Amish are all equal. The service and burial were plain and devoid of flowers.

The finality of her mother's death was almost too much to bear, and Miriam's regret for not contacting her mother sooner was a raw wound in her heart. Abraham, her father, wouldn't meet her gaze during visitation, service, or burial, which pushed the knife further into her soul.

In keeping with tradition, they returned to a neighbor's house after the funeral to share a meal prepared by members of the community. While family members and friends milled around the house balancing plates of food and cups of water, Miriam attempted to sneak out the back door and retreat to her Aunt Edna's house across the street. Her efforts were foiled when Hannah caught her by the arm and insisted she stay for the family gathering.

Hannah soon became distracted by an old friend from a neighboring district, allowing Miriam to slip into the kitchen and grab a drink.

Miriam moved unnoticed past the women volunteers who were serving the meal and then found a place along the back wall where she stood sipping her ice water and watching the knot of mourners float about the room, chattering, most likely about her.

While a chorus of voices speaking *Dietsch* sang around her, Miriam rubbed her temple where a migraine was brewing.

"You must be starved," a voice beside her said. "You haven't eaten all day." Abby stood next to Miriam with a plate of food in one hand and a cup in the other. "Cookie?" Abby held out the plate. "It's not one of the ones I made, so it's safe for consumption."

"No. *Danki*." Miriam blew out a sigh. "I don't think I could eat anything if I tried."

"You're gonna pass out if you don't eat." Abby set the plate on a small table next to her and adjusted her black suit jacket. Miriam placed her empty cup on the table. She plucked a cookie from the plate and scanned the crowd while Abby babbled on about the latest community news.

"I was talking to Millie Yoder, and she told me—" Abby began.

Abby's words faded into the background when Miriam spotted a man moving through the crowd accompanied by a petite young woman. Although she couldn't see his face, his stature and swagger were all too familiar. When his face turned in Miriam's direction, she sucked in a breath and dropped the cookie onto the floor.

"What's wrong?" Abby asked, her voice urgent. "You okay?"

Miriam shook her head as her eyes took in Timothy Kauffman's countenance. He looked the same as he had when she'd last seen him. Standing at six-foot-two, he was muscular, complete with a wide chest and thick arms filling his dark blue shirt. His sandy blond hair was cut in a traditional Amish bowl cut, and his powder blue eyes sparkled in the light pouring in from the large windows around him.

And then the reality hit her—he was clean-shaven, which meant he wasn't married. Her stomach flip-flopped.

Hannah was right! Timothy's still single!

He leaned down to hear what the pretty young brunette was saying. When he smiled down at the girl, Miriam nearly swooned. Why did that man still have power over her emotions years after she'd left him?

"Miriam?" Abby moved closer. "Are you all right?"

"No." Miriam's voice trembled. "I'm not even close to being all right."

Abby followed her gaze. "Wow. That tall hunk must be Timothy Kauffman."

"*Ya*." Miriam nodded. "He's still perfect."

Her cousin snorted. "No man is perfect. Trust me, I know."

Timothy's gaze met Miriam's, and she held her breath. For a long moment, their stares held, and his smile faded. Her cheeks flamed as he studied her. She wanted to run, but an invisible force held her, cemented her in that spot until the young woman grabbed Timothy's arm and shook it. He glanced down at the woman, breaking the trance.

"I've got to go," Miriam muttered, bolting for the door.

"Miriam?" Abby called after her.

Miriam rushed through the back door and down the steps, running right into Zach Fisher, causing him to stumble backward.

"Whoa!" Zach exclaimed, righting himself. "I'm sorry. I didn't see—"

"Excuse me," Miriam mumbled, slipping past him and moving toward the path leading to the road.

"Miriam Lapp?" Zach ran after her.

Miriam groaned and kept walking. She was in no mood for another tedious and pointless conversation about where she'd been, how long she planned to stay in Pennsylvania, and how sorry he was about her mother.

"Wait up!" He trotted over and took her arm. "I haven't

seen you in four years, and you can't stop to say *Wie geht's?*"

"Miriam!" Abby loped toward her.

Miriam bit her lip to keep from screaming in frustration. *Would you just leave me alone?*

Forcing a smile, Miriam turned toward Zach. "Just give me one second, okay?" She then faced Abby and they moved out of earshot of Zach. "I'm fine. I just needed some air."

Abby's eyes were full of concern. "Are you sure you're okay? You look a little green. I think maybe you need to get something substantial to eat." She rubbed Miriam's arm. "I'm really worried about you. How about I take you back to *Aenti's* so you can put up your feet for a while? It's been a long and emotional day."

Miriam closed her eyes for a moment, willing her body to stop trembling. The image of Timothy's gorgeous eyes trained on hers was burned into her brain, causing her body to continue to shake. "I think I need to go to *Aenti's* and unwind in some peace and quiet. But you don't need to go with me. I know you want to try to talk to your sister and brother." Opening her eyes, Miriam found Abby still studying her.

"I really don't mind taking you," Abby said. Her expression became grim. "I need to tell you something. I checked my voicemail messages on my phone earlier. My boss really needs me back at the office right away. Would you be okay if I went back tomorrow?"

Miriam nodded. "I understand. I think I need to stay and spend some more time with Hannah and *Aenti*. I also want to try to work things out with my *daed*." She touched Abby's arm. "You go talk to your sister and brother. I'll head back to *Aenti's*. I saw Lilly and Gerald helping Edna home earlier. I want to be sure she's okay."

"All right," Abby said. "You take it easy. I'm going to go see if my sister will actually talk to me. I'll see you at *Aenti's* later. I'll book my flight so I can get back to my *wunderbaar* job." She nodded toward Zach. "That cute guy is waiting for you. Seems like you may have more here than just Hannah and *Aenti*. You definitely should stay a while."

"Please. He's just an old friend."

"And he's handsome." Abby elbowed Miriam in the arm. "Seems like you've got your pick between Timothy and Zach."

"Not quite. Timothy seems to have found someone already." She shook her head. "Go talk to your sister. I'm going to see what Zach wants and then head back to *Aenti's* for some sanity time."

Miriam walked back to Zach, finding the same attractive face and caring eyes she remembered. She was surprised to see he was clean-shaven too. Miriam had always assumed he'd married since a few young women in the district had hoped to court and marry him.

"I'm sorry, Zach," she said when she stepped over to him. "I didn't mean to take so long with Abby. It's just been a rough day. *Wie geht's?*"

"No, no, no." He gave her a sly grin. "That was forced. I want a real greeting from my old *freind*."

She couldn't stop the genuine smile forming on her

lips. Zach had been a friend to her when no one else had cared—after Jeremy Henderson had died. He was the only person who'd asked her what had happened and had listened without judgment to her explanation. He didn't blame her for the child's death as her family and many others in the district had.

"Zach, it's so good to see you," she began with overdone politeness. "*Wie geht's*, my dear, dear *freind*."

"Ah!" He laughed. "Now, that's a greeting. I'm doing *gut*." His eyes turned serious. "I'm so sorry about your *mamm*. She was a *wunderbaar* woman. How are you holding up?" His expression said he truly cared.

She cleared her throat, which was suddenly dry. "I've been better."

"Want to talk about it?" He touched her arm. "We can go somewhere private to chat. My front porch still has the best swing in all of Lancaster County."

"Not today, but maybe soon." She gave him a sad smile. "It was really good seeing you, but I have to go. I need some time alone."

"I'll let you off the hook for now, but I expect to hear from you within the week." He patted his pockets and frowned. "I don't have a card on me, but the number to my shop is still the same. I'd bet your *aenti* has the number."

Miriam touched his arm. "*Danki*. I'll call you."

"Promise?" His expression was hopeful.

"Promise." She turned and hurried toward the street and toward the path leading to Edna's house.

• • •

Timothy glanced across the room again, and she was gone.

Vanished into thin air.

Was she a figment of his imagination?

No, she wasn't a figment; she was in the flesh, real. Miriam had been standing on the other side of the room with her cousin Abby mere moments ago. However, he had looked over at Naomi and then back at Miriam, and she was gone.

He was certain he hadn't imagined her, though. He could still envision her in his mind's eye. She was as beautiful, if not more beautiful, than he'd remembered. Her skin was flawless, and her eyes, oh those deep, rich chocolate eyes, were wide with . . . innocence?

Could she still be innocent? Lilly had said Miriam left to be with a man she'd met through a personal ad. For all he knew, she'd lived with the man and then decided he wasn't for her. Bile rose in his throat at the thought of Miriam living intimately with another man.

He swallowed a groan. Why was he jealous when she was the one who had left *him*?

But his assumptions could've been wrong. Miriam's eyes were still the same. And those beautiful orbs gazed at him with an intensity he couldn't forget and that sometimes haunted his dreams.

Did that mean she still cared for him?

His heart thumped with that silly hope.

No, that wasn't possible. If she'd cared, then she would've stayed and married him. She wouldn't have broken all of those late-night promises they'd made while sitting on her father's porch.

"Timothy?" Naomi's voice broke through his mental tirade. "What's wrong? You've got that million-miles-away look on your face again."

"Sorry." He cleared his throat and cut his eyes toward the back door. "How about we go for a walk?"

He yearned to see Miriam again. He needed to know he hadn't imagined her standing there, staring at him, causing his pulse to leap and his throat to dry.

She shrugged. "Okay."

Weaving through the knot of mourners, Timothy led Naomi out the back door. While Naomi spoke to a friend, Timothy stopped dead in his tracks when he found Miriam standing in the grass talking to Zach Fisher. His stomach soured when Zach touched her arm. Miriam stepped closer to him, and they shared a quiet conversation. After more coy expressions, Miriam touched his arm and then started toward the road leading to Edna Lapp's house.

Had Miriam dumped her *English* boyfriend and returned to Lancaster County to begin a new relationship with Zach Fisher?

Seething with anger, Timothy shook his head.

What had Beth Anne been thinking when she said it was God's will for him and Miriam to talk? How could it be God's will for Miriam to break his heart all over again?

How could Timothy consider speaking to Miriam when the mere sight of her flirting made him physically ill?

Beside him, Naomi finished her conversation with one of her friends from the district. She turned back to him and tugged his arm. "Timothy?" she asked. "What's bothering you today? You've been acting strange ever since we got to the funeral."

Frowning, Timothy met her eyes. "I'm sorry."

She pursed her lips and folded her arms in front of her chest. "You keep saying that, but you keep getting this dazed look on your face. You can talk to me. You can trust me."

He sighed. *No, I can't tell you because the truth will hurt you too much.*

"How about we head home?" He touched her arm. "I'm really tired."

She lifted her chin in defiance. "You're avoiding the question, Timothy Kauffman."

He smiled. "You got me there, Naomi. I'm avoiding it because it's too boring. I was thinking about a job I've been struggling with at work. I'm trying to figure out how to fix this one bureau that has been giving me a fit since Monday. See?" He shrugged. "It's not that exciting. Let's head home. I'm tired of the crowd."

Her eyes said she wasn't convinced, but she didn't push the subject any further. "Let me say good-bye to Lilly first. I didn't get to talk to her earlier."

While Naomi stepped back into the house, Timothy cut his eyes toward the field once more. He spotted Miriam crossing the street and heading toward her aunt's house, and he glowered.

Would he ever figure out who Miriam Lapp truly was? And what did that intense expression she gave him mean?

Why did she still make his toes curl with just one gaze?

Shaking his head, he stepped into the house and tried in vain to put Miriam out of his mind.

. . .

Miriam slipped off her shoes and walked into the den, where Edna sat with her feet elevated on a hassock. "How are you?"

"Tired, Miriam." Edna frowned. "Arthritis is a nightmare."

Miriam stepped over to the kitchen area, fetched a glass of ice water, and brought it to Edna. "This should help you feel better."

"*Danki, kind.* You're so thoughtful." She took a long drink and then set the glass on the end table beside her. "The funeral was nice."

"*Ya.*" Miriam lowered herself onto the sofa. "I can't believe my *mamm* is gone. I wish I'd spoken with her one last time. I wish I'd had one more chance to tell her I loved her." She sniffed as the tears began to flow down her hot cheeks.

"Oh, *liewe.*" Edna reached out with a gnarled hand. "Come sit with me."

Swiping her hands down her cheeks, Miriam moved to the chair next to her. Miriam sobbed while Edna rubbed her arm.

"There, there," Edna cooed. "You mustn't punish yourself. Your *mamm* loved you and knew you loved her. Lift your burdens up to God. He will help heal your soul."

Miriam sniffed. "Abby said she's going to book a

flight home. I'm sorry to see her go, but she says she has to get back to work."

Edna shook her head. "That *maedel* works too much. I think she's forgotten what matters most in life."

Miriam studied her bitten fingernails. Who was she to judge Abby when her life was nearly parallel, except for the big-time corporate job?

"What about you?"

"What?" Miriam looked toward Edna.

"Are you leaving me too?"

Miriam shook her head. "I want to stay a while so I can spend time with you, Hannah, and Lena Joy. I'd also like to work things out with *Daed*. He ignored me at the funeral, and I need to get him to realize I'm not to blame for what happened at the Hendersons."

Edna patted Miriam's hands. "I think that's a good plan. You can wait a few days for things to settle down and then try to talk to him again."

"I'll call my boss in the morning and tell her I'm finally going to use that two weeks of vacation I have set aside." Miriam stood and headed for the kitchen.

"What are you doing?" Edna asked.

"Baking. Beth Anne will be here tomorrow to pick up more pastries for the bakery. We need to have them ready, don't we?"

Edna rose. "Let me help you."

"No, no." Miriam gestured for her to sit. "I've got it. Your cookbook is right here. I'll start with a chocolate cake. I'm going to take over your baking duties while I'm here. You look like you could use a good rest."

Edna smiled. "You're an angel, Miriam."

Miriam sighed.

If only Timothy agreed with you . . .

Pushing thoughts of Timothy out of her mind, Miriam set out to make the best chocolate cake that had ever been sold at the Kauffman Amish Bakery.

Funeral Pie

Pastry for 9-inch crust and strips for top
1 cup seeded raisins, washed
2 cups water
1 ¾ cups sugar
3 ¾ Tbsp flour
1 egg, beaten
1 tsp lemon juice
2 tsp grated lemon rind Pinch of salt

Soak raisins for 3 hours. Mix sugar, flour, and eggs. Add raisins and remaining ingredients. Cook in a double boiler over hot water for 15 minutes, stirring occasionally. When mixture is cool, empty into pie-dough lined pie plate. Cover pie with narrow strips of crisscrossed dough and bake at 350 degrees for 50 minutes or until brown.

CHAPTER 7

The following morning, Miriam awoke at the crack of dawn and drove Abby to the airport. With tears in their eyes, they hugged and promised to keep in touch over the next two weeks. Abby insisted Miriam call her every day with news of how things were progressing with Miriam's family.

Miriam stopped at the grocery store on her way back from the airport. When she arrived at the cabin, she finished baking while insisting Edna relax and supervise from the comfort of her favorite easy chair.

By the time Jessica's SUV hummed up to the house, Miriam had six dishes awaiting her and Beth Anne—peanut butter bars, pumpkin pie squares, angel cookies, strawberry pie, chocolate shoofly pie, and a chocolate cake.

Miriam met Beth Anne and Jessica at the door and gestured for them to come in. "*Gude mariye,*" Miriam said. "How are you today?"

"*Gut. Danki.* How are you?" Beth Anne asked. "I'm sorry I didn't get to talk to you yesterday."

"I'm doing okay," Miriam said with a nod. "*Danki* for asking."

"I'm sorry about your mom," Jessica said. "I've been thinking of you."

"Thank you," Miriam said.

Beth Anne examined the desserts displayed on the table. "My! You and Edna have been busy. It all looks *wunderbaar.*"

"Miriam gets the credit," Edna said from her chair. "She's been baking since last night and wouldn't let me lift a finger."

Beth Anne gave Miriam an impressed expression. "You're a *wunderbaar* baker."

Miriam shrugged, her cheeks burning with embarrassment. "It was nothing really. I thought I would help her out since I'm going to stay a couple of weeks or so."

Beth Anne's eyes widened with surprise. "You're staying a while?"

"*Ya.* I have some things I want to work out here. I also want to spend some time with my family. Since I have a couple of weeks of vacation at my work, I'd like to use them for something important, like getting to know my sister's *kinner* and taking care of *Aenti* for a while."

Edna beamed. "You were always such a *gut maedel,* Miriam."

"I'm sure your family will be *froh* to have you around again." Beth Anne lifted the pies. "*Danki* for these."

Jessica grabbed the cookies.

"Let me help you carry them out." Miriam retrieved the other desserts and followed them to the SUV.

"I appreciate all you're doing to help the bakery," Beth Anne said after loading up the desserts.

"I don't mind helping out my *aenti*," Miriam said. "She was always very supportive of me, even with what happened before I left."

Beth Anne seemed to study Miriam's expression, and Miriam immediately regretted her words.

"It's *gut* to have you back," Beth Anne finally said. "I think your being here will give everyone a chance to heal."

Miriam blanched, unsure of what to make of her comment.

"See you later," Jessica said, climbing into the vehicle.

"I'll see you tomorrow. Have a *gut* day." Beth Anne climbed into the SUV and waved as it headed down the driveway toward the main road.

Miriam stared after the SUV, wishing she understood what Beth Anne meant by everyone having "a chance to heal." Did she mean Timothy, or was she referring to the Henderson family?

Miriam contemplated Timothy, wondering if he had any healing to do. He sure seemed to be over her by the way he behaved with the young woman at the funeral. Yet, there was something unnerving in his stare when he gazed at her. Did he have some unsettled feelings about her?

Deep in thought, Miriam headed back into the cabin.

. . .

"Miriam made all of them," Beth Anne said, placing the desserts on the large counter in the center of the bakery's kitchen. "She said she's going to stay a couple of weeks to work things out with her family and to care for Edna."

"That's very generous of her," Elizabeth said, examining the chocolate cake. "It looks like she does good work."

"I'm surprised she remembers how to cook since she ran off to be a nurse," Kathryn quipped, unwrapping the strawberry pie.

"I think we should hire her," Beth Anne blurted out, eyeing her mother for a reaction.

"What?" Kathryn exclaimed. "You can't be serious, Beth Anne. Why would you hire someone who hurt our brother?"

Elizabeth's expression was curious. "Why do you think we should hire her?"

Beth Anne made a sweeping gesture over the desserts. "Look at her work. It's *wunderbaar*, and we're drowning here with the tourist boom this time of year. We could have Miriam back here, baking and restocking along with us. The girls are having a hard time keeping things straight up front. We could put Lindsay out with them all day. It makes sense."

Beth Anne ignored her sister's glare and continued studying Elizabeth's reflective expression. "Think about what I said the other day," Beth Anne said. "Perhaps bringing Miriam in here would force her and Timothy to actually talk. I'm certain he avoided her at the funeral, and I can't think of any other way to get them together. I feel like God is speaking to me about this and telling me to hire her. I know it sounds *narrisch*, but I feel like this is the right thing to do. It feels like God's will, and I need you to believe me."

"You're not crazy." Elizabeth patted Beth Anne's hand. "I happen to agree with you. We'll hire her, and let God do as He sees fit with Miriam and Timothy. We'll leave it in His hands."

"You're both *narrisch*!" Kathryn exclaimed. "I can't be a part of this. Timothy will explode when he hears about it. The last thing he needs is Miriam here in his face. She broke his heart, and you two seem to have forgotten that." She grabbed the plates of peanut butter bars and pumpkin pie squares and stomped toward the front counter.

Beth Anne raised an eyebrow. "She's upset."

"She'll have to let it go." Elizabeth shrugged. "It's my bakery. Therefore, I make the rules."

Beth Anne chuckled while cutting up the strawberry pie. "Monday morning you offer Miriam the job," Elizabeth said, mixing up cookie dough. "Tell her I'm anxious to see her again and have her working with us while she's here for two weeks."

. . .

Sunday afternoon, Miriam curled up on the sofa and read from the book of John in Edna's Bible.

The weekend had flown by quickly. She had a nice conversation with her boss on Friday afternoon. Lauren said she

understood why Miriam wanted to spend a couple of weeks in Lancaster County to bring some closure to the issues with her family. Miriam had promised to call Lauren next week and give her an update on how things were going.

Miriam had spent Saturday helping Edna clean before doing the grocery shopping. Then she'd baked all afternoon in preparation for Beth Anne's visit Monday morning. She hoped her sand tarts, chocolate peanut butter cookies, and peanut blossoms were good enough to give to Beth Anne. Since baking was considered work, it wasn't allowed on Sunday.

Although Sunday was an off-Sunday, meaning no formal community worship service, the day was still considered holy. Miriam and Edna had spent some time reading from the Bible and singing hymns together after breakfast.

After devotions, Edna had retreated to her room for a nap, and Miriam was concerned by how exhausted she'd appeared.

While reading the Bible, Miriam's thoughts kept wandering. She found herself analyzing Beth Anne's comment about everyone needing to heal. She couldn't stop herself from wondering if Beth Anne had been speaking of Timothy.

A knock on the door pulled Miriam from her thoughts. Placing the Bible on the end table beside her, she headed to the door and wrenched it open, squealing when her eyes fell on Hannah and her children.

"Hannah!" She embraced her sister. "It's so good to see you!"

"*Danki.*" Hannah returned the hug before directing her children into the cabin. "Say hello to your *aenti.*"

Miriam hugged each of the three children and then led them to the kitchen, where she pulled a container from the refrigerator. "You all can be my guinea pigs and try these sand tarts."

"Guinea pigs?" Ian asked. "What do you mean?"

Miriam chuckled to herself while setting the cookies on napkins. "It means you'll test the cookies for me."

"Oh," Mary said, grimacing. "So we'll tell you if they're bad."

"I hope they aren't bad." She patted Mary's head while handing her the napkin full of sand tarts. She then handed napkins to Lena Joy and Ian.

"How about you *kinner* take them out back and eat them, so *Aenti* and I can talk," Hannah said. "Play nicely outside."

They filed outside, and Miriam tapped one of the kitchen chairs. "Sit. I'll bring us some tea and cookies."

"*Danki*." Hannah lowered herself into the chair.

Miriam brought the tea and cookies to the table and sat across from her. "Abby went home Friday. She wanted me to tell you good-bye."

"That's a shame." Hannah frowned. "I'm sorry I didn't get to talk to her more. We spoke briefly at the funeral."

"She had some emergencies come up at work, and she had to leave right away. She's married to that job, you know?" Miriam sipped her tea and then smiled. "I have exciting news."

Hannah snatched a cookie from the plate. "What is it?"

"I'm staying for two weeks."

Hannah squeezed her hand. "I'm so pleased! What led you to the decision?"

"*Aenti* has been exhausted and in a great deal of pain from her arthritis. I want to help her out, and I want to spend more time with you and try to work out things with *Daed*, if that's possible."

Hannah nodded, chewing the cookie. "This is delicious, Miriam. You did a *wunderbaar* job."

"*Danki*. I'm baking them for Beth Anne. *Aenti* makes desserts for the bakery for extra money."

"I think Beth Anne will be pleased." Hannah sipped the tea. "As for *Daed*, he'll come around. I think you should visit later in the week. I'll go with you, if you'd like."

Miriam nodded, biting into a cookie. "I may take you up on that. He intimidates me."

Hannah waved off the comment. "Don't let him. He's really a big puppy under that hard exterior."

"I'm not so sure." Miriam shook her head. "I never did anything right in his eyes. I never did the laundry correctly, my grades were never good enough, and I messed up the Henderson job. I was the black sheep, so to speak. He was probably *froh* when I left."

"That's so far from the truth, Miriam." Hannah touched her hand. "He missed you after you left."

Miriam snorted. "Please, Hannah. There's no need to lie to make me feel better."

"I'm not lying!" Hannah tapped the table for emphasis. "You ask Lilly. He talked about you incessantly for a long time, saying how there was no need for you to leave. I think his ego was hurt, but he missed you."

"How's Lena Joy?" Miriam asked, needing to take the conversation away from her father.

Hannah sighed. "It's hard to say. She has good and bad days. Some days she's completely exhausted, but other days she's full of energy. We're praying that she'll get a liver soon."

"Do you know why she got sick?" Miriam asked, plucking another cookie from the plate. "What causes the disease?"

"The doctor says it's genetic." Hannah broke a cookie in half while she spoke. "He said that since we're carriers for the disease, there was a one-in-four chance our *kinner* could get it, and she was the only one who did. It's a miracle the other two didn't. It's all biology."

Miriam nodded, chewing another cookie. "These didn't turn out half bad."

"I told you they were delicious." A smile crept across Hannah's lips. "I saw you chatting with Zach Fisher at the gathering after the funeral. He's still a bachelor."

Miriam rolled her eyes. "Please don't try to play matchmaker with me. I'm not interested."

"Why not? He owns a successful saddle shop, and he's handsome and sweet. He'd be good for you."

Miriam shook her head. "We're friends, and that's all."

"Friendship is a great way to start courting." Hannah wagged a finger at her. "If you're friends first, then you really know each other."

"I'm sure that's true. I'm just not looking." Miriam made an attempt to change the subject. "The funeral was nice, wasn't it? It was good to see some old friends." She bit into a cookie.

"Did you see Timothy?"

Miriam nearly choked on the cookie. She sputtered and then took a long drink.

"I'll take that as a yes," Hannah muttered. "Did you speak to him?"

Miriam shook her head. "I only saw him across the room. We stared at each other and then I left as fast as I could, like the chicken I am."

"Why didn't you talk to him?"

"I have nothing to say to him."

Hannah's stare was accusing. "Then why did you almost choke when I asked about him?"

Miriam glared at her. "I have nothing to say to him, and that's that."

Hannah shrugged. "Suit yourself. Go on wondering why things turned out the way they did instead of asking him. He's not married, so something held him back from moving on."

"Maybe the *maedel* he was seeing behind my back left him too. It would serve him right for what he did to me. Nevertheless, that's really none of my concern. He made his decision by not marrying me. End of story."

Hannah nodded. "I guess you have a point."

Miriam stood. "Let's go see what the children are doing. I haven't had a chance to catch up with Lena Joy." Miriam followed Hannah out the back door to the small porch. She called the children over and they sat on the porch together.

Miriam listened while Ian and Mary shared school stories about their friends and teacher. When they ran out to the field to play with a ball, Miriam turned to Lena Joy and asked about her friends. They talked until it was close to suppertime and Hannah had to get home to cook for her family. Miriam walked Hannah and her children out to the buggy, and she hugged each of them before they climbed into it, promising to visit them soon.

As they drove off, Miriam smiled and sent up a silent prayer thanking God for Hannah and her nieces and nephew. She also said a prayer that she too would someday have a family.

CHAPTER 8

These are *wunderbaar*," Beth Anne said, studying the half-dozen desserts Miriam had waiting for her Monday morning. "They're so *gut* that I have a question for you."

"What?" Miriam asked, wiping her hands on a dish towel. "Would you consider coming to work for us at the bakery full-time?"

Miriam blanched. "Are you serious?"

"*Ya*." Beth Anne laughed. "Why would I ask if I weren't serious?"

"You should do it," Edna said from her favorite chair. "You shouldn't mope around here all day."

"I don't mope," Miriam said, defensive.

"*Ya*, you do mope," Edna countered. "You need to get out. You're young. Go work with Beth Anne and her family. It'll be *gut* for you."

Miriam bit her bottom lip, pondering the offer. Would going to work for Timothy's mother be a good idea? For some unexplainable reason, she couldn't say no.

Glancing down, she examined her faded jeans and her peach T-shirt, caked in flour. "I have to find some appropriate frocks, along with aprons and capes. I can't dress *English*."

"I have frocks that will fit you," Edna said. "You can let the hem down on a few of my dresses, and we'll make you a few spares too. We can work on that this afternoon, and you can start tomorrow."

Miriam glanced at Beth Anne, who smiled.

"It's settled," Beth Anne said. "You start tomorrow and work for the two weeks while you're here. It'll be *wunderbaar.*" She started toward the door with Jessica in tow, carrying desserts.

"Can you be there by five?" Beth Anne asked. "That's when we start baking."

"*Ya.*" Miriam inwardly groaned. She'd forgotten how early she used to get up when she lived in her father's home.

Miriam helped Beth Anne and Jessica to the SUV and then watched them drive off, stunned at the course of events. As of tomorrow, she'd be an employee of the Kauffman Amish Bakery, owned by the woman who'd once planned to be her mother-in-law.

A strange excitement coursed through Miriam's veins. She would be a member of the Kauffman's extended family. Why did this inspire her? Her future with Timothy had been shattered the day she'd left Lancaster County.

Could God be giving her a second chance with him?

Miriam shook her head at the naïve notion. There was no hope for a second chance with Timothy. He'd made his choice, and Miriam had made hers.

Yet something inside her awakened at the thought of being welcomed by his family.

Pushing that thought aside, Miriam hurried back into the house. She had a full day of sewing ahead of her.

• • •

Jessica dropped into the swing on her aunt Rebecca Kauffman's porch. Pulling her cell phone from her pocket, she checked the time and sighed.

"He'll be here," Lindsay, her younger sister, said, leaning on the doorway. "Jake has never let you down."

Jessica lifted her can of Diet Coke from the small table beside the swing. "You're right. He's kept all of his promises, and he's the only man who's ever done that for me, aside from Dad."

"That's true." Lindsay leaned on the porch railing. "Can you believe Mom and Dad have been gone over a year now?"

Jessica absently fingered her mother's wedding ring, hanging on a chain around her neck. "It's gone by so quickly, hasn't it? It seems like only yesterday we moved in here. So much has happened."

Lindsay gave a bleak smile. "I miss you."

Jessica crossed her legs. "I miss you too. It feels weird not having a little sister to argue with. Aunt Trish's house is too quiet." She studied her sister's plain purple dress, black apron, and prayer *kapp*. "Don't you get hot in all those clothes?"

Lindsay shrugged. "I'm used to it." She nodded toward Jessica's legs. "I think it would feel weird to wear jeans again. I'm used to dresses and aprons."

"Do you get headaches having your hair plastered to your head in a bun?"

Lindsay snickered. "No. Like I said, I'm used to it."

Jessica shook her head. "It's beyond me why you

would want to wear that stuff. Don't you want to be a normal fifteen-year-old and listen to alternative music and go to the movies and the mall? You know, Aunt Rebecca wouldn't love you any less if you weren't Amish. You don't need to feel pressured to fit in here."

"I don't feel pressured, Jessica. I only feel pressured by you because you keep telling me that I don't need to be Amish. I'm comfortable here. I feel like a Kauffman."

"I'm just saying—"

"Let's not fight tonight, okay?" Lindsay smiled. "Today's a special day. Today you turn seventeen. I'm still surprised you didn't want a party."

Jessica gave her a look of disbelief. Did her sister have a selective memory? "Are you serious? Don't you remember the fiasco it was last year? I ran away. Then I got hit by a car in Virginia and wound up in the hospital."

"I remember what happened, but things are better now with the family. They would've been happy to celebrate with you." She shrugged again. "That's okay. We can still celebrate without a party." Lindsay pulled an envelope from a pocket in her apron and handed it to Jessica. "Happy birthday, big sister."

Jessica's eyes widened. "Lindsay, you didn't need to—"

"Of course I did." Lindsay sank onto the swing next to her. She gestured toward the envelope. "Open it, silly, before he gets here."

Jessica tore open the purple envelope and found a purple and pink card covered in flowers with a sweet poem about the importance of sisters. Opening it, she gasped at the sight of a fifty-dollar gift card for Walmart. "Lindsay, you shouldn't have spent this much."

Lindsay looped her arm over Jessica's shoulder. "You deserve it. I know you wanted to get a few things before you head back to school, so I thought a gift card was the best gift. You can combine it with the gift card from *Aenti* Rebecca."

"Thank you." Jessica gave her a quick hug.

The rumble of an engine sounded on the dirt road leading to the farmhouse.

"Your date's here," Lindsay said, waggling her eyebrows. "Go have fun, but be home by midnight."

Jessica smacked her sister's shoulder. "I'm the older sister, not you." Standing, she put the card and gift card back into the envelope and handed it to Lindsay. "Would you put this in my room?"

"Of course. See you later."

"Thank you." Jessica gave her sister a quick hug and then rushed down the porch steps and climbed into the cab of Jake's dark blue Chevrolet pickup. Since Jake was Mennonite and not Amish, he was permitted to drive a vehicle and wear *English* clothing. "Hey," she said, fastening her seatbelt.

"Hey yourself." Leaning over, he pulled her into his arms. "I've been wanting to do this all day. Happy birthday."

"Thank you," she said, resting her cheek on his shoulder and breathing in the scent of his musky cologne. Closing her eyes, she wondered if she'd made the right choice when she'd left Jake to live with her parents' best friends in Virginia.

But she needed to finish high school and go to college—to make Mom and Dad proud.

"Hungry?" Jake pulled back and clicked his seatbelt.

"You betcha." Jessica rubbed her hands together. "I only had a yogurt for lunch, so I'm starved."

He raised an eyebrow. "Bird-in-Hand Restaurant?"

"Sounds great."

. . .

Jessica sat across from Jake in a booth and swirled her straw in her glass of Diet Coke while he pored over the menu as if he'd never seen it before.

Glancing up at her, he grinned, and her heart thumped in her chest. She'd imagined his face in her mind nearly a thousand times every day they were apart after she'd left Pennsylvania. His dark brown hair was cut short, accentuating his bright blue eyes.

"Do you know what you want?" he asked.

"The usual. Ham loaf." Lifting her glass, she took a sip. "I can't have that back at the beach, so I need to enjoy it here."

"That's true." His smile deepened. "Or you could stay here permanently."

She sighed. "Jake, we've been through this a million times. It's my senior year."

"Right." He gripped the menu. "And you can finish up here and go to college here."

"But my friends . . ."

He frowned. "If my memory serves me correctly, they weren't very good friends to you last summer."

The waitress appeared and took their order.

When the woman was gone, Jessica leaned forward onto the table. "I've made new friends," she said. "I know you want me to move here, but it's important to me to graduate with my class."

His eyes were hopeful. "And what happens after graduation?"

Jessica leaned back in the booth and bit her lip. "I'm going to college. I know that for sure, but I don't know where I'll end up."

He gestured widely with his arms. "Why not here with me?"

"It's a possibility, but I can't make any promises."

"Well, no matter where you wind up, I have a promise for you." He reached in his pocket and pulled out a small felt box. "Happy birthday."

He held the box out, and Jessica stared at it, her mouth gaping with surprise.

A jewelry box. What could be in it? A ring?

But Mennonites don't wear jewelry.

A key? But a key to what?

"Take it." He took her hand and placed the box in it, closing her fingers around it.

The warmth of his touch sent her pulse galloping. With her heart banging against her ribcage like a bass drum, she flipped open the top and found a simple gold cross shimmering up at her.

Tears filled her eyes as she looked up into his. "It's beautiful," she whispered.

"Look at the back." He pulled the necklace from the cardboard insert and held it up.

Jessica grasped the cool metal with her fingers and flipped over the cross. The tiny engraved letters spelled out, "To Jessica. Forever, Jake."

Her eyes filled with tears as they met his probing gaze. "It's gorgeous," she whispered.

Reaching across the table, Jake took her hand in his. "I know it's not customary for a Mennonite to buy or wear jewelry, but I wanted to do this for you. You always wear your mother's wedding ring on a chain on your neck. I wanted to give you something to remember me by while we're apart. A cross seemed appropriate, since Jesus brought us together."

He squeezed her hand. "I know you'll make whatever choice is best for you next year after you graduate, and I promise I won't pressure you to come here for college. But just the same, I don't want you to forget our friendship. The cross is a symbol of how much you mean to me."

"I could never forget you," Jessica said, her voice trembling with the admiration surging through her. She unlatched the catch on the chain and fastened the cross around her neck. Holding the cross to her chest, she cleared her throat. "I'll keep it here, next to my heart."

"Good." He smiled and then lifted his glass. "Happy birthday."

"Thank you." Jessica gripped the cross in her hand. No matter where she went to college, she knew she would keep the cross and Jake close to her heart forever.

. . .

Later that evening, Miriam nudged the porch swing and floated back and forth. She breathed in the sweet, humid air and yawned. She'd accomplished her mission to tailor three of Edna's old dresses for herself, along with the capes and aprons. She also started three new dresses but didn't finish them.

She ran her hands over the thighs of her old jeans and examined her peach T-shirt. As of tomorrow, she would be dressing Amish again. What a strange turn her life had taken in the past few days. She'd gone from pediatric assistant to Amish baker in less than a week. Yet, somehow, she was comfortable with the change. It felt right, despite the years she'd tried to convince herself that she belonged in Indiana working in a pediatrician's office.

Was God trying to tell her something about her life plan?

The clip-clop of a buggy caught her attention as it approached the cabin. Miriam stood and leaned on the porch railing, anxious to see who would arrive to visit Edna.

The horse and buggy came to a stop at the hitching post in front of the cabin, and Miriam smiled when Zach climbed from the buggy and tethered the horse.

"Zach Fisher," she said, pushing an errant lock of hair back that had fallen from her ponytail. "What on earth are you doing here?"

"*Wie geht's* to you, too," he said, climbing the stairs with a mischievous smile. "Since you've forgotten how to use the phone shanty, I thought I'd come visit you. I was in the neighborhood returning some books to the library. I had a pile of overdue books in the back of my workshop."

"You're still reading those Christian novels, huh?" Miriam laughed. "I meant to call you, but I've been so busy."

"Of course you have," he deadpanned. "That's what all the girls tell me when they're trying to avoid me."

"I doubt you've ever had that problem." She motioned toward the porch swing. "Please join me."

"I'd be honored." He followed her to the swing and sat next to her, gently rocking it back and forth in the warm breeze. "What has kept you so busy?"

"I sort of got a job."

"Here? You got a job here?" His smile was genuine and wide. "You're staying?"

"For a couple of weeks. I'm going to work at the Kauffman Bakery and use my vacation time from my job in Indiana." She grasped the cool chain that held up the swing. "I want to try to make things right with my *daed*, help out *aenti*, and spend time with Hannah and her children."

"Is Abraham still treating you badly?"

She cleared her throat, hoping to stop her threatening tears. Why did the thoughts of her father upset her so? "He wouldn't speak to me at the funeral. I'm not sure how to get through to him. Hannah says to wait a few days and go over there, but I'm not sure what I would even say to him."

"Listen to your heart. The Lord will guide you."

She nodded, afraid if she spoke, she would wind up crying in front of him.

"Maybe you'll work things out and decide to stay," he said. His hazel eyes were hopeful, and she wondered why.

"I don't know." Miriam glanced toward the large field separating the cabin from her father's house. "I'm not sure if I belong here."

"What's keeping you in Indiana?"

She shrugged. "I like my job. I love working with the *kinner*."

"You can find a job like that here."

Meeting his gaze, she found an intensity in his eyes that surprised her. She braced herself when he opened his mouth to speak.

"Miriam," he began, his expression serious, bordering on nervous. "I have something I've wanted to say for a very long time." He cleared his throat and looked down at his hands, then back up to her. "I care for you. I didn't get a chance to tell you before you started courting Timothy, but I've always cared for you."

She opened her mouth to speak.

He held up his hand to stop her from answering. "No, please. Let me finish. I had always hoped and prayed you'd come back. I'm sorry your return was under a very sad circumstance, but I have to admit, it's good to see you again. I hope you do decide to stay, and if you do, I would be honored if I could have a chance to court you."

"Zach," she said. "I'm not sure what to say."

"You don't need to say anything." He looked toward the field. "You don't need to make any decisions now. I just wanted to be honest with you for once. I've longed to tell you that for quite some time."

She studied his handsome face, wondering if he'd practiced his speech throughout the entire ride to the cabin. A calmness enveloped her. His friendship had always been a comfort to her, especially during the tough times.

Without thinking, she took his warm hand in hers, and he gave her a surprised smile.

"I value your friendship," she said. "You were the one person who listened to me when Jeremy Henderson died. You believed me when I told you it wasn't my fault."

"I know who you are as a person, and I've always believed in you." He squeezed her hand. "If you stay, and I hope you do stay, I want to be the first in line to court you."

Dropping his hand, she laughed. "I doubt there would ever be a line for me."

"Just you wait. There will be a line, and I'll be up front."

They sat in a comfortable silence for several minutes, staring out across the field. Miriam contemplated Zach's words, stunned by them. If only she cared for him the way he did for her. However, her feelings for him weren't romantic; they were loyal friendship and deep respect. She couldn't imagine courting him, and she wasn't sure if she wanted to stay in Lancaster County. She appreciated that he wasn't pressuring her for an answer. She valued his friendship and didn't want to lose it because she didn't want to court him.

When the sun began to set, Zach stood. "I guess I should let you get some rest. You can't show up to your first day of work yawning."

Miriam followed him down the stairs to his buggy.

"You still owe me supper," he said with a smile while yanking open the buggy door.

"I promised to call you, but I never promised supper."

"Since you haven't called, I now expect a call and supper," he said. "If I don't hear from you in a few days, I'll show up on your doorstep and demand my supper."

She chuckled. "I imagine you will."

He climbed into the buggy and leaned out the window. "Think about what I said."

She nodded. "I will. *Danki* for coming to visit."

"*Gern gschehne.*" Reaching out, he touched her nose. "*Gute nacht.*"

"*Gute nacht, mei freind.*" She smiled as he drove off toward the road.

CHAPTER 9

Miriam's Honda bounced along the road leading to the Kauffman Amish Bakery. The terrain was hilly, and the roads were winding and rural. Soon she spotted a farm with a cluster of large houses set back off the road and surrounded by four barns, along with a beautiful lush, green pasture.

The property was owned by Elizabeth and Eli Kauffman, Timothy's parents. Her stomach roiled when she spotted the home Timothy had built in anticipation of his marriage to her. Nearby was the home Sarah Rose had shared with her late husband, Peter. The bakery was the fourth house, the one closest to the road. Timothy and his five siblings grew up in the biggest house, where his parents still lived.

Miriam steered her gray Honda down the dirt road and nosed it into the large parking lot in front of the large, white clapboard farmhouse with a sweeping wraparound porch. A tall sign with "Kauffman Amish Bakery" in old-fashioned letters hung above the door.

Out behind the building was a fenced-in play area, and beyond that was an enclosed pasture. The three other large farmhouses and four barns were set back beyond the pasture. The dirt road leading to the other homes was roped off with a sign declaring "Private Property—No Trespassing." A large paved parking lot sat adjacent to the bakery.

After pulling her small sedan into a parking space, Miriam turned off the engine and gripped the steering wheel. Glancing down, she examined her black dress, symbolizing her mourning of her mother, and black apron. How ironic she was dressed Amish and driving a car. She'd considered asking to borrow a horse and buggy from her father, but she doubted she would get any help from him or her brother. Without any help, she had no choice but to rely on her own transportation. Besides, the drive would take much longer by buggy than by car.

For now, she would have to be a driving anomaly. Since most of the Amish paid full-time *English* drivers to take them to and from work, she would consider asking for a ride from Jessica or one of their other drivers once she got to know her better.

Taking a deep breath, Miriam climbed from the car, locked it, and slipped the keys into the inside pocket of her apron. She then crossed the parking lot and climbed the back steps of the bakery.

Memories of her visits to the bakery with Timothy assaulted her mind. He had often brought her here to enjoy a delicious dessert and visit with his sisters. She'd cherished those times, sitting at a little wrought iron table on the wraparound porch, enjoying whoopie pies and conversation with the man she'd thought was the love of her life.

Pushing those thoughts away, Miriam stepped through the back door of the bakery and inhaled the sweet smell of baking bread. Elizabeth, Beth Anne, Kathryn, and their nieces rushed around the kitchen preparing desserts for the day.

"*Gude mariye. Wie geht's?*" Beth Anne called while washing cookie sheets.

"*Gut.* How are you all doing?" Miriam rung her hands and cleared her throat, standing before Timothy's mother and sisters.

Kathryn frowned and looked down, mixing dough for her next creation.

"Miriam!" Elizabeth rushed over. "It's so *gut* to see you. How have you been?"

Miriam blinked, studying the older woman's genuine smile. She'd always considered Elizabeth an angel on earth, a loving, forgiving woman.

"I'm doing okay. How have you been?" Miriam stepped back and forced a nervous smile.

"*Gut. Danki.*" Elizabeth gestured around the kitchen. "You can see the bakery looks the same. I don't mean to sound prideful, but I have to admit business is booming. We're glad you can help us out." She turned to her granddaughters. "Lindsay, Amanda, Lizzie, and Ruthie, please come meet Miriam." The four girls crossed the room and smiled. "These are my *grossdochdern.* Lindsay is Rebecca and Daniel's niece who came to live with them from Virginia last year, and Amanda, Lizzie, and Ruthie are Kathryn's *dochdern.* I'm sure you remember them."

Miriam nodded and smiled. "*Ya,* I do. You've grown up."

Amanda tilted her head in question. "You know us?" She tapped her finger to her chin, concentrating. "You were courting *Onkel* Timothy, *ya*?"

Kathryn muttered something inaudible across the counter, and Beth Anne shot her older sister a warning look.

Kathryn blew out a frustrated sigh and then met Miriam's gaze. She pursed her lips. "It's *gut* to see you," she said without the hint of a smile. "Welcome to the bakery."

"*Danki*, Kathryn." Miriam smiled, and Kathryn looked away.

"As you know, we're open from eight until five," Elizabeth said. "The girls take turns taking care of the younger *kinner*. Right now Kathryn's daughter Lizzie is on duty. She'll switch off later with Ruthie."

Elizabeth put her hand on Miriam's shoulder and led her toward the row of ovens, refrigerators, and freezers. "Let me give you a tour of the kitchen." She pointed out the cooking supplies and ingredients and then discussed their schedule for the baking.

"You were always a *wunderbaar* baker." Elizabeth led her to the refrigerator. "I thought you'd like to start out with crumbly peach pie."

Miriam paused and met Elizabeth's eyes.

Timothy's favorite.

Pushing the memory away, Miriam cleared her throat. "I'd be happy to."

"*Gut*." Elizabeth opened the refrigerator. "You'll find everything you need in here and in the stand-alone freezers." She nodded toward a shelf full of binders, journals, and books. "We have several volumes of traditional recipes. Feel free to leaf through them or bake from memory. We trust your judgment. I know your *grossmammi* taught you well."

"*Danki*," Miriam whispered, winding her finger around the tie of her prayer *kapp*.

Elizabeth's gaze softened. "Please feel comfortable here, Miriam. We're *froh* to have you, despite what my stubborn Kathryn said. The past is the past, *ya*?"

"*Ya*," Miriam said. "*Danki*, Elizabeth."

Elizabeth patted her shoulder as she headed back to the center of the kitchen.

Miriam hummed her favorite hymns while she worked in the corner of the kitchen alone all morning long, baking four crumbly peach pies and then four dozen sugar cookies.

She was deep in thought, comparing her life in Indiana to her life in Pennsylvania, when a tap on her shoulder surprised her. She turned to find Beth Anne smiling at her.

"You've been working nonstop for hours," Beth Anne said. "Are you ready to take a lunch break?"

Miriam shrugged. "I'm ready anytime. There's no rush."

"I made some turkey sandwiches." Beth Anne nodded toward the other side of the kitchen, where the office and the playroom/nap room for the children were. "The sandwiches are in the office around the corner. You can sit at the little table by the desk and eat if you'd like. There's some ice water in the refrigerator."

"*Danki*." Miriam wiped her hands on a towel.

"I should be thanking you," Beth Anne said. "You're doing a fabulous job. We're so glad to have you."

"Kathryn isn't," Miriam said, staring at the pretty blonde across the kitchen talking to Lindsay. "She's done nothing but glare at me all day. I wonder if this was a mistake."

"No." Beth Anne shook her head with emphasis. "Kathryn means well. She's just defending Timothy because you broke his heart. But she'll come around and realize that the past is the past, and it was God's will that you and Timothy didn't marry."

Miriam's eyebrows careened upward while her mouth fell open. *I broke Timothy's heart? I think you have it backward.*

"I'll talk to Kathryn," Beth Anne said. "Don't worry about her. Her bark is worse than her bite." She waved toward the office. "Go on and enjoy your lunch. I'll finish these cookies."

Miriam contemplated Beth Anne's comment while eating her turkey sandwich and glancing through *The Budget*, the Amish newspaper. Beth Anne's remarks didn't make any sense. Why would she say Miriam broke Timothy's heart when it was Timothy who had cheated on her?

The questions were still twirling through her head when she cleaned the table and then headed back toward the kitchen. She stopped near the doorway when she heard a familiar masculine voice.

Her heart thumped in her chest when she entered the kitchen and found Timothy standing with Elizabeth, Beth Anne, and the young woman from the funeral.

With his back to Miriam, he forked a piece of one of her crumbly peach pies into his mouth. "*Wunderbaar!*" he exclaimed. "Beth Anne, you outdid yourself this time. This is the best crumbly peach pie I've had in a very long time." He chewed more. "I mean no offense, but this is better than the one you brought me the other night. I'm not sure what you did differently, but it's sweeter."

Miriam's eyes widened.

"I didn't make it." A sly smile grew on Beth Anne's lips as she met Miriam's horrified gaze. "I can't take credit for it, *Bruder.*"

"No?" He glanced at Elizabeth. "Then you must've made it. We all know you're the best baker."

Elizabeth snickered. "There's no need to flatter me, Timothy. You know I'll give you one dozen whoopie pies to take back to your *dat*. And besides, I didn't make the crumbly peach pies."

"Kathryn?" His voice nearly squeaked with disbelief. "She hates peaches. I can't see her making these."

"It wasn't Kathryn, nor was it your nieces. And you're not going to guess." Beth Anne's grin widened, and Miriam fought the urge to run and hide in the office.

Looking confused, Timothy set the plate on the counter. "You bought it at the supermarket?"

Miriam held her breath and then glanced at the door. If she ran now, she could make it to her car and speed from the parking lot before she had to face him.

"No." Beth Anne gestured toward Miriam, standing behind him. "She made them."

Timothy turned toward the direction of Beth Anne's

nod. He faced Miriam, and his eyes widened to the size of saucers.

Miriam's cheeks heated and her pulse raced. She wanted to run and avoid another gut-wrenching staring contest like they'd shared at the funeral.

"Miriam's working for us now," Elizabeth said. "We're shorthanded at the bakery, and as you can see with peach pies, she's a *wunderbaar* baker."

Timothy's stunned gaze never left Miriam. She tried to smile, but her lips formed a pained grimace instead.

"Miriam Lapp?" the young woman asked, stepping over to Miriam and sticking out her hand. "I'm Naomi King. I'm *gut* friends with your sister Lilly."

Miriam shook her hand. "Nice to meet you," she managed to whisper while feeling Timothy's eyes burrowing into her. She then glanced toward Elizabeth. "I best get back to work. I have to make more cookies."

With Timothy's gaze boring into her back, she crossed the kitchen.

. . .

Timothy watched Miriam cross the kitchen. Had he heard his mother correctly? Miriam was working in the bakery? She was employed by his mother?

He glanced at Elizabeth. "She's working here?"

"*Ya.*" Elizabeth beamed. "She's an excellent baker, and we need her help."

"Naomi," Kathryn called, stepping into the kitchen from the front. "*Wie geht's*? How's your *mamm*?"

Naomi stepped over to speak to Kathryn, and Beth Anne moved closer to Timothy.

"You should go talk to her," Beth Anne said. "She's very self-conscious about being here."

"As well she should be," he seethed, glaring at his sister. Anger coursed through him. "I know this was your idea, and I'm not happy about it."

"I agreed to it, too," Elizabeth cut in. "And Beth Anne is right—you should go speak to her. Start a conversation, so you two can work this out."

"There's nothing to work out." He cut his gaze across the kitchen to where Miriam was leaning on the counter reading a cookbook. She was so beautiful in her black frock.

But she broke my heart into a million pieces. She has no right to be in Mamm's bakery.

"Go speak to her," Elizabeth said. "Remember what Jesus teaches us about forgiveness."

Timothy frowned at Elizabeth. "I'll go speak to her." He then turned to Beth Anne. "This isn't over. We'll talk about this later."

"That's fine." She shrugged, her disregard of his feelings causing his anger to spark.

"Go, Timothy. Speak to her. Reach out to her. You'll be glad you did." Elizabeth gave him a gentle push in Miriam's direction.

His heart thumped in his chest as he strode over to Miriam. Standing on the opposite side of the long work counter, he watched her read the recipes. When she glanced up and met his gaze, her deep chocolate eyes widened, and she drew a sharp breath.

"Sorry," he muttered, running his fingers over the wood counter his father had built more than twenty years ago. "I didn't mean to startle you."

She bit her bottom lip and nodded, as if to say it was okay.

He cleared his throat, at a loss for words, and she watched him, hesitation clouding her eyes.

"I'm sorry about your *mamm*," he finally said. "She was a nice *fraa*."

"*Danki*," she whispered, her voice still the sweet lilt he remembered.

"You look well." He absently continued to trace his fingers over the counter.

She nodded. "You do too."

The silence hung in the area between them like a dense fog.

"Timothy," Naomi called while holding two large boxes, which he assumed were the whoopie pies his father had requested. "We better go. My *mamm* runs a tight ship. We've been gone close to an hour."

"*Ya*," he said to Naomi. He turned back to Miriam, who eyed him with an anxious expression. He wished he could read her mind. He needed to know why she'd left. What had he done to make her leave him? Was it simply her yearning to experience the *English* world and follow her dream of being a nurse? Was it to pursue another man? Or was it something else—something he'd done wrong?

"Good-bye," he told her.

She nodded without speaking.

He then crossed the kitchen to Naomi. After saying

good-bye to his sisters and mother, he led Naomi to the buggy.

He stared out the windshield and contemplated Miriam while steering down Gibbons Road toward Highway 340. Anger mixed with regret flowed through him. He was angry with Beth Anne and his mother, since he couldn't comprehend why they would consider hiring Miriam.

Unless it was part of Beth Anne's plan to honor God's will and help Timothy move on.

He groaned.

Elizabeth had won today, forcing him to talk to Miriam. However, she couldn't force him to "work things out" when there wasn't anything to work out. Miriam had left him—end of story.

"Timothy Kauffman, you're going to answer me if it's the last thing you do." Naomi's demand jerked him back to the present.

"I'm sorry," he muttered. "What were you saying?"

"I was asking you to come to supper tomorrow night, but now I'm reconsidering my invitation." She folded her arms across her chest in defiance. "You've got that same million-miles-away expression like you had at the funeral."

Guilt nipped at him. He needed to treat Naomi better, but Miriam was a distraction over which he had no control. Now that he was with Naomi, he needed to shut off any thoughts of Miriam and concentrate only on Naomi.

"I'm sorry," he said. "Please repeat what you were saying about supper tomorrow night. What time would you like me there?"

For the first time since he'd known Naomi, she was silent. And the silence was unnerving.

Something's wrong.

He glanced over and found her staring out the window. "Naomi?"

Still no answer.

He reached for her, brushing her shoulder, but she moved away from his touch.

"Naomi," he said. "I'm sorry if I've hurt you."

Finally, she faced him, tears streaming down her face.

"Naomi?" He steered to the side of the road and halted the horse. "What's wrong?"

"I figured it out." Her voice quavered. "You love her!"

"What?" He shook his head, confused. "I love who?"

"Her!" She pointed in the direction of the bakery. "Miriam! You love her!"

"What?" His eyebrows knitted together. "You're talking *narrisch*. I don't love her."

"Yes, you do!" She wiped her eyes with the backs of her hands. "Lilly told me who Miriam is. She broke up with you four years ago." More tears spilled from her eyes. "It all makes sense now!" She gestured wildly for emphasis. "That's why you stopped talking to me at the funeral and why you became quiet just now. Oh, I'm such a fool." Burying her face in her hands, Naomi sobbed.

Timothy leaned over and rubbed her back. "It's true that I did court her, but it's also true that she left. I don't love her, Naomi. I'm sorry I've been quiet. I just have a lot on my mind."

"*Ya*, you do—her!"

"No, that's not true, Naomi." He sighed, wishing he could take her pain away.

"Then why aren't you courting me?"

He blanched, surprised by the direct question.

"My *mamm* says you're leading me on and using me." She cleared her throat. "I told her you were just taking your time. But after seeing how you behave around Miriam, I'm starting to agree with *Mamm*." Her lip quivered and her eyes filled with more tears.

He swallowed a groan. Today was not the day for her to demand a declaration of his feelings for her. His heart was a mess after seeing Miriam. He had too much to comprehend. Figuring out his feelings for Naomi would only be the tip of the iceberg.

Taking a deep breath, he touched her face, wiping a tear from her cheek. Her expression softened at his touch.

"Naomi, I care deeply for you. You've been a dear and special *freind* to me." He forced a smile. "I intend to treat you right. I'm just not ready to make any promises right now."

"I won't wait forever, Timothy. I'm not getting any younger, and I want *kinner*."

He nodded. "That's fair. I just ask that you give me a little more time."

She turned toward the windshield. "We better get back. *Mamm* will send out a search party for me."

He flipped the reins and the horse came to life, clip-clop-ping down the road. Glancing over, he found Naomi still staring out the windshield. "Are you angry with me, Naomi?"

She shook her head.

"We're still *freinden*?"

"*Ya*," she said, flashing him a coy smile.

Turning back toward the road, he frowned. He was going to give Beth Anne and his mother a piece of his mind as soon as he left work tonight.

CHAPTER 10

Timothy stalked up the stairs leading to his parents' porch and marched into the kitchen, where he found his sisters and parents eating supper. Nieces and nephews raced around the kitchen, laughing and shrieking.

"Timothy!" his mother exclaimed. "I'm so glad you came in time for supper."

"I'm not hungry," he said, folding his arms in front of his chest. "I'd like to speak with you and Beth Anne—alone."

Beth Anne shot Elizabeth an apprehensive look.

"What's this about?" Sadie, his oldest brother's wife, asked, her eyes wide with excitement. Timothy was certain Sadie hoped the subject would be worthy of gossip at her next quilting circle.

"Timothy wanted to discuss how we'd like the porch fixed at the bakery," Elizabeth said, proving how fast she was on her toes.

Beth Anne's lips formed a smile that she quickly shielded with her hand.

"Let's go to the front porch," Elizabeth said, steering

Timothy through the den to the foyer. "That way we can talk without competing with the *kinner's* voices."

"I'm not going to miss this," Kathryn muttered, shuffling in line behind Beth Anne.

Once Elizabeth and his sisters were seated in the porch chairs, he leaned back on the railing and glared at them.

"What were you thinking, Beth Anne?" he demanded, gesturing with his arms. "You know I've been trying for four years to put her out of my mind, and yet you parade her in front of me at the bakery. It doesn't make sense. I spent all afternoon turning it over and over in my mind while I was working, and I can't get any logic out of it. You need to keep your nose in your own relationships and stay out of my life."

Beth Anne flinched and then glowered. "There's plenty of logic in it, Timothy. You just said you've been trying for four years to get her out of your mind. It's obvious you need help to do it, and speaking with her is the only solution."

Frustrated, he rubbed his temple and groaned. "You don't understand. Putting her in my face stirred it up all over again."

"See, I was right." Kathryn gave a smug smile and crossed her legs. "I told them not to, but those two"— she pointed between Elizabeth and Beth Anne—"never listen to me. They do their own thing, and look where it got them."

"Timothy, you need to let go of this anger and let God sort through it for you," Elizabeth said.

Lacing his fingers behind his head, Timothy swallowed

a sigh. His mother had the strongest faith he'd ever known, but sometimes he wanted her to just keep it to herself. He'd prayed many, many times, asking for the Lord to unburden his soul, and yet, Miriam continued to haunt his dreams—both during the day and at night. Praying just wasn't going to do it for him.

"You know what I always say, Timothy," Elizabeth continued.

"'Be joyful in hope, patient in affliction, faithful in prayer,'" he replied, letting his hands drop to his sides. "I know, *Mamm*, I know."

Elizabeth gave him a soft sigh of disappointment. "You say you know, and yet you still look at me as if I'm *narrisch*."

"I never said you were crazy." He glanced across the field to where his youngest nieces and nephews were chasing each other. A rumble of thunder in the distance snapped his gaze to the sky, where dark clouds crept across the horizon. "I just need to work through this in my own way," he said, turning back to her. "You can't force me."

Elizabeth nodded. "You're right. However, Miriam is a good baker, and we need her help. She's going to work there whether you and Kathryn like it or not."

Kathryn shook her head. "I won't like it."

Beth Anne rolled her eyes. "You're so immature. Sometimes I forget you're my older sister."

Timothy stood up straight and glanced down the driveway, where he spotted Sarah Rose, his younger sister, and her fiancé, Luke, walking slowly up the driveway holding her seven-month-old twins. Sarah

Rose stopped, turned to her fiancé, and gave him a loving smile.

Seeing that tender moment caused something deep in Timothy's soul to somersault.

Maybe they're right. Maybe I do need to talk to Miriam—face-to-face—and find out the truth.

"I need to go." He loped down the stairs and headed for his buggy.

"Where are you going?" Beth Anne called after him.

Ignoring the question, he increased his speed, not stopping to greet Sarah Rose and her family.

. . .

Miriam moved back and forth on the porch swing while clutching a cool glass of water and watching the ominous clouds creep across the sky. Thunder rumbled in the distance.

Taking a sip of water, she reflected on her first day of work. Overall, the day had gone well, and when Edna asked if she had liked it, Miriam had to admit that she had. She'd enjoyed making the traditional dishes. Some were her favorites, and some were new. Elizabeth, Beth Anne, and the children had made Miriam feel welcome with their smiles and their compliments on her baking.

Her only negative experience was connected with Kathryn and her disapproving looks. It was obvious Kathryn blamed her for the breakup with Timothy, and Miriam wished she could convince Kathryn that it wasn't that simple. While Miriam had wanted to experience the *English* world, she also left because Timothy had broken her heart. It seemed that Kathryn had the scenario backward if she blamed Miriam for hurting Timothy.

But that wasn't the end of Miriam's emotional day. There was also her pointless conversation with Timothy. Why had she turned to gelatin when he tried to speak with her? Her throat had gone dry as soon as she met his gaze, and her hands had shaken like leaves in a tornado. She wished she'd felt confident enough to ask him why he'd left her. She wished she'd shared what was on her mind and in her heart, but she'd stared at him blankly and spoken like a child.

The clip-clop of hooves drew Miriam's attention to the end of the dirt lane. A buggy she didn't recognize bounced toward the cabin.

Standing, Miriam set her glass on the small table next to the swing and then cracked open the front door. "*Aenti*," she called. "Are you expecting company?"

"No, dear," Edna replied from the bedroom. "I'm going to bathe and head to bed. If it's for me, tell them I'm sleeping."

Miriam smiled and shook her head. When Edna decided she was done for the evening, there were no discussions.

The horse and buggy steered up to the cabin, stopping near her Honda. Assuming the visitor was Zach, showing off one of his new buggy designs, Miriam stood at the railing while the driver wrenched the door open and unfolded his lean body from the seat. However, the man appeared to be too tall, and his hair was too blond to be Zach's.

When he turned and faced her, Miriam's mouth

gaped in response to finding Timothy's piercing blue eyes focused on her. He gave a slight smile and then tied the horse to the hitching post.

She absently smoothed her frock and then touched her *kapp*, making certain it was straight and her hair was neat. Shaking her head, she wondered why she was so worried about her appearance when her looks didn't seem to matter to him four years ago.

Timothy made his way to the bottom of the stairs, and she took a deep breath, hoping her voice wouldn't sound timid and her throat wouldn't dry as it had been when he came to the bakery earlier.

"*Wie geht's*," he said, leaning on the railing at the bottom of the steps. "May I visit with you?"

"*Ya*." She made a sweeping gesture toward the porch chairs. "Would you like a glass of water?"

"*Danki*. That sounds nice." He gave her his electric smile, the genuine one she remembered from long ago, and her knees wobbled in response.

"Make yourself comfortable. I'll be right back." Her heart thumping in her chest, Miriam rushed into the kitchen and filled a glass with ice and water.

When she returned to the porch, Timothy was seated in the chair next to the swing, turning his straw hat around in his hands like a Frisbee. When his eyes met hers, he popped the hat back onto his head.

She handed him the glass and lowered herself onto the swing, lifting her drink from the small table between them.

"I reckon we may get a storm," he said before sipping the water. "Those clouds look mighty threatening."

"*Ya*," she said, clutching her glass and running her fingers through the cool condensation.

His eyes met hers, and her cheeks flamed in response. When he smiled, she cut her gaze to the toes of her black sneakers. Why did the mere sight of his face turn her into a shy little girl?

"You still make the best crumbly peach pie in Lancaster County," he said.

"*Danki*," she whispered, still studying her shoes.

"How do you like working at the bakery?"

"It's fun." Staring out at the field, she took a sip of her drink, hoping it would wet her parched throat. Why did her throat have to betray her now when she needed confidence?

The rumbling thunder sounded closer and drizzles of rain sprinkled the path leading up to the porch.

"Are you moving back here?" he asked, breaking the silence. She looked at him, finding his eyes searching hers. "I'm not certain. Right now, I'm taking my vacation time from work, so I can spend time with Hannah and help Edna. Her arthritis has progressed, and she can't bake anymore. I'm working at the bakery to help her out. I plan to give her my paychecks."

"How long is your vacation?"

"Two weeks," she said.

They stared at each other in silence for a moment, and Miriam wished she could read his mind. Her thoughts flashed to him and Naomi together at the funeral and then at the bakery.

Thunder rolled louder, and the drizzle transformed to a light rain.

"Are you courting Naomi?" she asked before she could stop the words from leaving her lips.

"*Ya*," he answered quickly. "How about you? Are you courting?"

She shook her head. "I'm not seeing anyone. I've been alone for four years now."

He snorted. "Do you expect me to believe that?" His smile was wry.

"Excuse me?" She turned her body to face him.

"Please, Miriam." He glanced toward the field, and lightning flashed across the night sky while the rain beat a rhythm on the roof above them. "I'm not stupid."

"I never said you were." She placed her glass on the table. "Timothy, I'm sorry, but I'm not sure what you're implying."

"Lilly told me." When his eyes met hers again, they were full of anger and hurt.

"She told you what?" Miriam searched his expression, trying to read where his anger had originated.

"That you left to go live with your pen pal in Indiana." He shook his head in disgust.

"What?" Miriam stood up like a shot just as thunder crashed above them, shaking the porch beneath her feet. "What pen pal?"

"The man you met through a personal advertisement or something like that." He took a long gulp of water.

Miriam paced back and forth. "Lilly told you that? My sister?" She stopped, facing him. "It's not true, Timothy. It's not true at all. I left because you were seeing Annie Raber behind my back. I thought that since you didn't love me, I had no reason to stay here. That's why I went ahead with pursuing my dream of living among the *English* and going to school."

"Annie Raber?" His eyebrows knitted in confusion. "That *maedel* who worked with my *mamm* for a short time? I hardly even knew her, Miriam."

Tears of anger and disgust flooded her eyes. "I saw you with her one time. You—you—you were holding her hand as she walked down the porch stairs. I saw it with my own eyes, Timothy!" Trembling, she stammered over her words and wished she could speak with confidence. Oh, she hated when she got upset and stuttered!

"Holding her hand?" He got a faraway look in his eyes as if trying to remember something. "She slipped on the wet kitchen floor one time and twisted her ankle. Maybe that was why, but I never was courting her behind your back. I wasn't seeing anyone behind your back, Miriam. I would never do that. *Ever.*" He enunciated the word as more thunder crashed, louder this time.

"But that's not it." She swiped her tears as more flowed from her eyes, her body shaking so hard that she was sure he could see it. "I also heard that you told some others you couldn't marry a *maedel* who wasn't pretty enough. You said I had a body like a twelve-year-old boy because I'm so skinny."

The rain beat harder above them, and drops sprayed the back of Miriam's body.

"Who told you that?" He stood beside her.

"Lilly," she breathed the name, trying to control her tears.

"That's not true." He stomped his foot for emphasis. "I never, ever said that about you. None of it is true. I never saw Annie behind your back, and I never said you weren't pretty enough. I loved you. I loved you with everything I had and thought you were the most beautiful woman in the world."

Miriam bit her lip and stared into his eyes, finding truth in them.

Lightning flashed, lighting up the porch like the midday sun, and then thunder crashed, shaking the porch and causing Miriam to shriek with a start.

Timothy reached out and took her hands in his, and something sparked between them, sending liquid heat coursing through Miriam's veins.

She gasped, pulling her hands back.

She stared into his eyes, and the time they had spent together flashed before her like a movie. All of the love she'd felt for him in the past boiled up in her soul, and she wanted to reach out and hug him.

Instead, she stood still and held his gaze as his blue eyes studied hers.

"We were fed lies," he whispered, his look so intense that her breath paused.

Speechless, she nodded.

"Why didn't you tell me all this the day I came to see you at the Hendersons', the day that Jeremy—" He stopped short of the word *died*. "And then afterward, when I came to see you, you wouldn't speak to me. Why? Why did it go this far, Miriam? Why did you leave me without an explanation?"

"I—I was afraid," she whispered.

"Afraid?" He raised an eyebrow. "When did I ever give you a reason to fear me?"

She shook her head and stepped over to the railing to avoid his probing stare. She willed her body to stop trembling. "My family blamed me for Jeremy Henderson's death. My *daed* said I was an embarrassment to the Lapp family for neglecting him. He used every word except *murderer*." Her voice quavered. "He said I wasn't smart enough to leave the house. He wanted me to stay home and work the fields with my brother."

She glanced at Timothy and found his sympathetic eyes still on her. "When Lilly told me that you were cheating on me and didn't want to marry me, I thought it was my cue to leave. Everything was happening so fast. I thought you and my family had betrayed me. I had no one to turn to except Zach. He was the only one who believed me about Jeremy."

Timothy frowned at the mention of Zach's name.

Is that jealousy?

The thought evaporated when he stepped toward her. She held her breath as he reached out, but his hand dropped before he touched her.

"I believed you when you told me what happened with Jeremy, but you never gave me a chance to tell you," he said. "The day you came home from the police station after you were questioned was the last day I saw you, but I couldn't get you alone."

She nodded. "I remember. Jeremy died while you and I were arguing on the Hendersons' porch. My father said that was a sign from God that you and I weren't meant to be together. He said I wasn't responsible enough to be a mother at all."

Timothy shook his head, his eyes smoldering. "That isn't true."

Miriam sniffed and wiped her eyes. "*Ya*, it is. I'm destined to be alone, like my *aenti*."

"No," Timothy whispered. "Don't say that."

She studied his eyes, wishing she could turn back the clock to the day Jeremy died. If only she'd gotten to his crib before he'd stopped breathing. If only she'd told Timothy to come back and talk to her later. Maybe she could've saved Jeremy *and* her relationship with Timothy.

But she couldn't turn back time. God wanted this to happen. It was His plan that she was alone and Timothy was with Naomi King. That was why she'd dragged her feet when Timothy had proposed. That was why she shied away from joining the Amish church. None of it was meant to be.

Timothy's expression softened. "We've lost so much time," he whispered. "I don't know what to say."

Miriam wanted to let go of her apprehension and lose herself in those eyes. She wanted him to kiss her. She wanted to feel his powerful arms around her as he pulled her in for a hug.

She wanted to hear him say he still loved her.

But those things would never happen. That was all in the past.

Timothy had forgotten about Miriam. He was courting someone else.

She had a job to return to in Indiana. She couldn't let herself fall for him again.

It was too late for them. Their chance was gone.

God didn't give second chances.

The thunder rolled off in the distance, and the rain slowed. "There's nothing to say." She squared her shoulders. "It's over between us. It's time we moved on." She held out her hand, and he took it. "*Danki* for coming to see me." She shook his hand as if they were casual acquaintances. "It was *gut* to see you again."

He gave her a questioning expression, and Miriam wracked her brain for a reason for him to leave. She needed him to go—*now*—before she burst into tears and begged him to take her back. She had to make him leave before he realized how much she still loved him. Her dignity was all she had left, and she couldn't let him steal it from her.

"I best let you get on home. It's getting dark, and it's dangerous to go on the main roads in a buggy too late at night," she said, taking his arm and steering him toward the stairs. She ignored the feel of his taut muscles and the way his body heat radiated through his shirt to her hand.

He gave her a stiff nod. "*Ya*, that's a good point."

They descended the stairs and stood by his buggy in the light rain. His eyes met hers, and her pulse skittered.

"You best run in before you get soaked," he said, untying the horse. "*Gut nacht.*"

"*Gut nacht*," she said, hugging her arms to her chest.

He climbed into the buggy and clicked his tongue, bringing the horse to life. As he drove off, she felt as if her future had just slipped through her fingers—again.

Miriam glanced toward her childhood home and frowned. She'd lost everything because of one person—
Lilly!

With white-hot rage surging through her, Miriam marched across the field, stomped up the steps of the house, and pounded on the door until it creaked open, revealing Gerald.

His eyes met hers, and he glowered. "You're not welcome here." He began to close the door, and Miriam blocked it with her foot.

"No!" she yelled. "I'm not leaving here until I talk to Lilly."

Gerald shrugged. "Fine." He turned and hollered. "Lilly! You have a visitor on the porch." He then faced Miriam. "She'll be right down."

"*Danki.*" She paced until the door opened, and her sister, who was twelve months younger than she was, appeared with a book in her hand. Judging from the cover, it was one of Lilly's favorites, a Christian novel.

Lilly hugged the book to the front of her black frock and tilted her head with annoyance. "What do you want? Didn't *Daed* tell you you're not welcome here? That's how we all feel about you."

"I have a bone to pick with you, Lillian Lapp." Miriam came at her, wagging her finger.

Lilly stepped back and held up her hand. "Calm down, Miriam. I have no idea what you're talking about."

"It's about Timothy!" Miriam's body shook. "You lied to me! Why? Why did you do it? Why did you ruin my life?" Angry tears spilled from her eyes, and she wiped them away. "You encouraged me to leave. You pushed me to go to nursing school. Why? What did you want, Lilly? You had three men chomping at the bit to court you, and yet you had to break up Timothy and me."

Lilly's stare was cool. "I have no idea what you're talking about. You're *narrisch*." She nodded toward the stairs. "You should leave before I get *Daed* out here."

Miriam threw her hands up and blew out an angry sigh. "You're such a liar. I should've known!"

"I never lied to you. Timothy Kauffman is a snake in the grass. He was cheating on you. You even saw him with Annie Raber, so you know it's true. I was doing you a favor."

"No! It's not true," Miriam said.

"*Ya*, it was true. Now go back to the cabin where you belong. Better yet, go back to Indiana, to your *English* life."

Miriam turned her glare back to her sister. "He told me everything tonight, Lilly. I know you convinced him I was leaving him for someone else in Indiana. I don't understand you. You never cared for Timothy. Why would you do that?"

Lilly leaned in close. "Perhaps it wasn't Timothy I was after."

"What?" Miriam studied her sister's eyes. "What are you talking about? All I ever wanted was Timothy, but you had to ruin that for me. I had nothing else you would want, Lilly. It doesn't make sense."

The door opened, and Abraham stood in the doorway. "You're not welcome here, Miriam. You need to leave now."

Miriam stared up at him, her lip trembling. "Why, *Daed*? What have I done to offend you?"

"She's *narrisch*," Lilly said with a sly grin only Miriam could see. "She's here accusing me of breaking up her and Timothy, but we all know the truth."

"Get off my property," Abraham barked. "You broke your *mamm's* heart. I don't want to see you until you're baptized and made right with the church."

"But, *Daed*—" Miriam began.

"Go on! Get out of here." He stepped toward her and waved toward the steps. "Go on."

Miriam rushed down the stairs and trotted across the field. When she arrived back at the cabin, she climbed the stairs, rushed into her room, flopped on the bed, and cried herself to sleep, dreaming of Timothy and all they'd lost.

Dutch Almond Cookies

1 cup shortening
$1/2$ cup white sugar
1 cup brown sugar
$1/4$ tsp baking soda
2 eggs
$1/2$ tsp vanilla
3 cups flour
$1/2$ tsp cinnamon
$1/2$ tsp nutmeg
$1/4$ tsp salt
$3/4$ cup ground blanched almonds

Cream shortening with white and brown sugar. Add eggs and work in sifted dry ingredients. Add chopped almonds. Shape dough into long rolls. Roll in wax paper and cover with cling wrap to keep in moisture. Chill in refrigerator for 12 hours. Slice thin. Bake at 375 degrees for 20 minutes or until lightly browned.

CHAPTER 11

The following morning at the bakery, Miriam mixed up the dough for Jumbies cookies. Once she'd placed the sheets in the oven, she crossed the room and tapped Beth Anne on the shoulder.

"*Ya?*" Beth Anne asked, wiping her hands on a towel.

"May I speak with you alone in the office?" Miriam asked, keeping her voice low to ensure Kathryn wouldn't hear.

"Of course." Beth Anne followed her into the office, where Miriam gently shut the door behind them. "What's wrong?"

"I was awake most of last night."

Beth Anne sat on the edge of the desk. "Is something the matter?"

"*Ya.*" Miriam paced, wringing her hands together. "I heard something yesterday, and I need to know the truth."

Beth Anne folded her arms in front of her chest. "Go ahead and ask. I'll tell you whatever I know about the subject."

"Did Timothy ever cheat on me when we were

courting?" Miriam held her breath while awaiting the answer.

Beth Anne gave a bark of laughter. "No. He would never cheat on anyone, especially you. You were the love of his life."

Miriam blew out a sigh and flopped into the chair across from the desk. "I can't believe I fell for it." She shook her head. "I ruined everything."

"What are you talking about?" Beth Anne looked confused. "I heard *you* cheated on *him*."

Miriam threw her hands up. "That's just it—I never cheated, and Timothy told me last night that he never cheated."

Beth Anne's expression was pensive. "Someone interfered between you two and broke you up?"

Miriam nodded. "Exactly."

"It's not the end of the world, Miriam." Beth Anne smiled. "You're both still young. You can work things out."

Miriam shook her head. "I don't think that's possible. He's seeing someone else."

"With God, all things are possible." Beth Anne stood and patted Miriam on the shoulder. "Just take it slow and see what happens. We better get back out there. The lunch rush will be here before you know it."

Miriam followed Beth Anne out to the kitchen and spent the rest of the morning thinking of Timothy while she baked.

At lunchtime, Lindsay told Miriam she had a visitor out front. Stepping out into the front of the bakery, Miriam found Hannah waiting with a basket.

"I brought you lunch. Can we sit outside and talk?" Hannah asked.

"That would be *wunderbaar*." Miriam walked with her to the front porch, where they sat at a secluded table away from the items for sale. "Where are the *kinner*?"

"Home with Lena Joy." Hannah unpacked the makings for sandwiches and two bottles of water. "I thought we could have some adult conversation without little ears listening in."

"Sounds *wunderbaar* because I have a story for you."

While they made their sandwiches, Miriam told Hannah about her conversations with Timothy and Lilly. Hannah's eyes were wide with shock throughout the story. When Miriam finished, Hannah shook her head and glowered.

"I should've suspected Lilly." Hannah's words were laced with anger. "She's lied to me a few times over the years. She once told me she was going to a singing, and I heard that she'd skipped the gathering to be alone with a young man and a few friends. Another time, she said she couldn't babysit for me, and I found out later she'd spent the day entertaining friends. She's a sly one. I'm sorry I never picked up on the lies she'd told you."

Miriam shook her head and blew out a sigh. "It's all in the past. I simply need to find a way to accept it. But I just wish I knew why she did it. She said that she wasn't after Timothy, but she didn't say what or whom she was after."

"Hmm." Hannah rubbed her chin, deep in thought. "It doesn't make sense to me."

"I know. She always had young men wanting to court her, so she wasn't lonely."

"That's very true." Hannah reached over and squeezed Miriam's hand. "Now that you know the truth, what are you going to do about it?"

"Nothing, I guess. He's courting Naomi King. It's too late for us."

Hannah shook her head. "Don't say that. He loved you once."

"It was four years ago, Hannah. Our time is gone."

"He's not married yet."

"But he might as well be." Miriam bit into her turkey sandwich and glanced across the parking lot toward the sea of cars and tourists. "It's funny to think we could've been married and expecting our second *boppli* by now."

"Zach really likes you, Miriam." Hannah smiled. "If you truly believe it's over with Timothy and you want to make a new life here in Lancaster, you should consider Zach."

"He came to see me Sunday night, and he asked me to court him."

"No!" Hannah squealed. "He's a *wunderbaar* and sweet man. You'd be a fool to let him go."

Miriam sighed. "Maybe I should just go back to Indiana and get my nursing degree. Maybe I don't belong here at all."

"Oh, please!" Hannah waved off the comment. "You've taken to dressing Amish like a duck to water, and you love your job at the bakery. I can tell by the way you smiled when you saw me. You're a different person than you were when you wrote me letters and when you first arrived here. Stay here. Make a life."

"I don't know . . ."

"I'll help you work things out with *Daed*, and I'll even make sure we get Lilly to admit what she did. Don't give up on your family yet." Hannah gave her a sad smile. "I love you, Miriam. It would break my heart to see you leave again. My *kinner* love you too. I need you here with me. I need you with me when Lena Joy gets the call that there's a liver for her."

Miriam gave a melancholy smile. "Let me think about it, okay?"

"*Ya*," Hannah said. "You think about it, and I'll continue to nag you about it until you stay."

Miriam laughed. "I'm sure you will."

Once they finished lunch, Miriam walked Hannah back to her buggy and hugged her before she left.

Miriam spent the rest of the afternoon contemplating Hannah's pleas for her to stay and the possibility of starting a life with Zach Fisher.

. . .

Timothy lowered himself onto a stool and wiped his sweaty brow with a rag. He couldn't concentrate on the bureau in his work stall. Instead, his mind was back in Gordonville and on the porch with Miriam.

All day his thoughts had been with Miriam, remembering how beautiful she looked standing in the rain with her radiant eyes trained on him. He'd wanted to sweep her into his arms and kiss her until she was breathless.

Regret mixed with love had slammed through him when he found out the truth—she'd never cheated on him!

Oh, how he wished he could get back those years they'd lost. They could've been married and had children of their own by now. They could've been happy—living together in the house he'd built for her.

Timothy wanted to start fresh with Miriam. He wanted to pour his heart out to her and beg her to stay and marry him. But he didn't know how to begin. He'd tried to form the words last night, but she'd scooted him off Edna's property before he'd had a chance to sort through his raging emotions. She seemed determined to be rid of him, but he didn't know why.

He regretted telling her he was courting Naomi, but he'd lied in defense of his broken heart. He'd believed she was seeing someone else, and he didn't want her to know that he hadn't moved on with his life after she'd left. Now he wished he could take that lie back and pick up where they'd left off.

He needed to tell Miriam he loved her before she returned to Indiana. He needed her to know the truth.

But what if she rejected him when he told her that he still loved her?

It was a chance he was willing to take.

But what about sweet Naomi?

Timothy sighed as he snatched a cold cup of water off his workbench and gulped it down.

He hated the thought of hurting Naomi, but the truth was he didn't love her. Was it worse to court someone he didn't love than to tell her the truth and let her find her lifelong love?

Timothy set the cup down and glanced at the clock. Only two hours until closing time. Tonight he would go see Miriam and tell her how he felt. Then he would gently let Naomi down and encourage her to find a suitor who truly loved her. He had to be honest with both of them. He had to be true to his heart.

Was this God's will that Beth Anne had been talking about?

Standing, Timothy stepped over to the bureau. His pulse skittered at the thought of seeing Miriam again and telling her that he loved her. He prayed she loved him too.

. . .

Miriam stepped through the door of the cabin later that evening and found Edna sitting in her favorite easy chair, reading the Bible.

After placing her bag on the bench by the door, Miriam sat in the chair across from Edna and smiled. "*Wie geht's?*" she asked.

"*Gut.*" Edna set the Bible down. "How was your day?"

"*Gut.*" Miriam ran her finger over her apron, thoughts of her future and of her past sorrow spinning through her mind. "May I ask you a question?"

"Of course. What's on your mind?"

"*Aenti*, do you have any regrets?"

"Regrets?" Edna tilted her head in question. "What do you mean?"

"Do you wish you'd made different choices during your life?"

"I have one huge regret." A smile grew on Edna's lips. "His name was Herman."

Eyes wide with surprise, Miriam leaned forward and gasped. "*Aenti!* You had a boyfriend?"

Edna's smile sparkled. "We courted for a few months, and we had a wedding date set. But things changed."

"What happened?"

"My *daed* didn't approve. Herman was from another district, and he didn't have much. He was a farmer, and crops were bad that year. Not enough rain. He was poor, but I loved him so. I let my family talk me out of marrying him. He married another *maedel* the following fall."

"I'm so sorry." Miriam shook her head. "I had no idea."

"Of course you didn't. I kept that to myself. There was no reason to burden you with it." She smiled again. "He was such a sweet man. He was thoughtful and kind." She got a faraway look in her eyes. "But I made the mistake of letting other people run my life. I should've stood up for myself, but I didn't know how. I didn't have any strong women in the family to follow."

Leaning forward, Miriam squeezed her hand. "You're a very strong woman, *Aenti.* You made it on your own despite your decisions. I admire that."

"*Ya*, I did, but it wasn't really by choice. Once my

parents died, Abraham moved his family into the house, and I could tell your *mamm* wanted to run the house without my interference. I respected that since it was her family. Therefore, Abraham and my other brothers built me this place." She gestured around the cabin. "Last I heard, Herman had about thirty *grandkinner*. But I'm not alone. I have my *wunderbaar* nieces and nephews."

Miriam leaned back on the chair and frowned. "How do you know if you're making a bad choice?"

"Why don't you tell me what's truly on your mind, Miriam? It would be easier for me to give you advice if I knew what you're battling in your pretty head."

With tears in her eyes, Miriam told Edna everything she'd learned, from the lies that separated her and Timothy to Zach's offer of courtship.

When she finished her story, Edna squeezed Miriam's hand and gave her a knowing smile. "Don't make my mistake. You're standing at a crossroads between your lonely life in Indiana and your life here with your family. I chose to stay with my family, but I also chose to be lonely. By the time I realized I'd made the wrong choice, it was too late for me. I wish I could take that time back, but you have youth on your side. Come back home, join the church, and make a life for yourself."

Miriam wiped an errant tear and nodded. "*Danki.*"

"Now, Zach said you owe him a meal." Edna hoisted herself from the chair. "How about I make us a meat-loaf, and you get that young man over here for that promised meal?" She winked. "The best way to a man's heart is through his stomach. He fancies you, Miriam.

Don't let that one get away." She shuffled to the counter and pulled a small business card from a drawer and held it up. "Here's the number to his shop. Run down to the phone shanty in front of Abraham's house and give him a call. I'll start supper."

Crossing the room, Miriam gathered her aunt into a hug. "*Danki.*"

"*Gern gschehne.*" She patted Miriam's back. "Go call that boy before he changes his mind like my Herman did."

Grasping the business card, Miriam trotted across the field, hoping she was making the right choice.

CHAPTER 12

Timothy tethered his horse to the hitching post outside Edna Lapp's cabin. A cool, light mist of rain kissed his cheeks as he moved toward the cabin steps. He'd practiced his speech over and over in his mind during the drive from his house to hers.

Yet now, standing in front of the cabin and staring at the door separating him from his possible future, he'd forgotten every single word, except for his plea: "Miriam, please give me a second chance. I love you."

He climbed the stairs, stood before the door, and took a deep, cleansing breath.

I can do this. It's God will. Miriam and I belong together.

Lifting his hand to knock, he stopped and listened to voices filtering through the solid oak door. Although he couldn't make out the words, he was certain he could hear a masculine voice. He squelched the jealousy rising within him, reminding himself that Miriam had insisted she wasn't seeing another man. There had to be an explanation. Perhaps her family, including her brother or brother-in-law, had come by for supper.

Timothy rapped on the door, and laughter emanated from the other side.

A few moments later, the door creaked open, and Miriam's face appeared. When her gaze met his, her wide smile transformed to a look of shock. "Timothy?" she whispered. "What are you doing here?"

Hope evaporated from his soul. He'd expected a happier welcome from her. Mustering his last shred of courage, he opened his mouth to speak.

However, she turned to her guests and spoke first. "Please excuse me. I'll be right back." She then squeezed through the door and gingerly closed it behind her.

Timothy couldn't help wondering if she were hiding her guests from his sight. Or was she embarrassed Timothy was visiting?

"I'm sorry for interrupting your supper," Timothy began, studying her eyes.

She appeared anxious. He wished he could read her mind. What was she hiding? She'd seemed so transparent last night. Why was her demeanor different now?

"Oh, that's fine." Her smile was forced as she hugged her arms to her body and glanced out toward the field. "Is it raining again?"

"*Ya*," he said. "It's just a mist now, but I think another storm is coming."

She met his eyes again. "*Wie geht's*?"

"I was hoping we could talk." He gestured toward the swing. "Do you have a moment?"

"Oh." She frowned. "Well, I have company."

"I see." He blew out a sigh and wracked his brain, wondering if he should just cut to the chase and ask her to court him.

"What if we talked tomorrow?" Her forced smile

was back. "You could stop by the bakery—if that's okay with Naomi, of course."

"*Ya.* That's a good idea." He stepped toward the stairs.

The door opened, and Zach Fisher stepped out with a curious expression. "Is everything all right, Miriam?"

Timothy's stomach roiled.

So this was her mysterious guest.

Zach Fisher.

He inwardly groaned. He should've known better after Zach's actions with Miriam at the funeral. Zach had looked like a man on a mission to win a young woman's heart when he spoke to Miriam that day. From the looks of things now, Zach had won.

Zach met Timothy's eyes and smiled. "Timothy. *Wie geht's?*"

"*Gut.*" Timothy cut his gaze back to Miriam. "I'm sorry I bothered you. Enjoy your supper." As he started down the stairs, a hand on his arm stopped him.

"Wait." Miriam's eyes were urgent. "I didn't mean to run you off."

"It's fine. We'll talk later." Timothy frowned. "It was nothing at all. I didn't mean to waste your time. *Gut nacht.*"

"Timothy—" she began.

Ignoring her, he untied his horse and climbed into the buggy. As he drove past the cabin, he saw Zach place his hand on Miriam's shoulder. Bile rose in Timothy's throat at the sight and at the realization that he'd lost Miriam again—forever this time.

Unless, of course, he'd never had her at all.

Perhaps he'd been wrong last night. Maybe Lilly had

told the truth, and Miriam had left him for someone else. Now she had Zach.

The mist turned to large drops, and Timothy shook his head, red fury surging through him. He'd been played for a fool—again—and he was tired of it. He was also tired of missing Miriam, or pining for her, as Beth Anne had said.

Now was the time to make a change. He needed to take control of his life and his emotions.

He wanted a future. He longed for a family. He was sick of being the only Kauffman without children running around and tearing up his mother's house.

He'd been a fool to hold onto a memory that had been nothing but a lie.

Steering onto the main road, he headed back to Bird-In-Hand and Naomi. It was time he made things right and concentrated on a real future.

• • •

Miriam stared after Timothy's buggy. Guilt soaked through her like the rain splashing on the railing in front of her. She wanted to kick herself for not inviting Timothy to stay, but the situation was awkward with Zach in the house and Timothy standing on the porch.

Now Timothy was driving off through the storm, and she couldn't help thinking he was driving out of her life—forever. His eyes had been so urgent. She'd longed to hear what he had to say, but she was worried about Zach's feelings. He'd dropped all of his plans to join her for supper, and he'd seemed so excited about it when she'd called to invite him.

Now she'd missed her chance to talk to Timothy, and he'd seemed so intent on speaking to her. Whatever he had to say must've been important.

I've made a horrible mistake.

"What do you think that was about?" Zach asked, breaking through her thoughts. "He left in a bit of a huff, *ya*?"

"I'm not sure what he wanted." Miriam bit her bottom lip and tried to stop the regret rising in her soul.

Taking her hand, Zach gently turned her toward him. "I'm so glad you called me." His expression was intense, causing her heart to thump with anxiety. "I was beginning to think I'd scared you off the other night."

She forced a smile. "You didn't scare me. You're harmless, Zach."

He gave a bark of laughter. "I'm not so harmless." He lifted her chin with the tip of his finger. "I'd be honored if you'd court me, Miriam Lapp. What do you say?"

Alarm slammed through her. She was at another crossroads. Should she make a commitment to him? How did she know if this was how her life was supposed to go? But she couldn't risk losing Zach's friendship either.

"How about this," she said, the words escaping before she could stop them. "I care for you, Zach, but I want to take it slow. I've had my heart broken, and I don't want to experience that again."

He smiled. "We'll take it as slow as you'd like. I'll never hurt you, Miriam. You have my word."

Closing his eyes, he leaned down, and her hands trembled. He was going to kiss her, and she wasn't ready for it. It was too soon!

As if on cue, Edna's voice rang out. "Food's gettin' cold! Get back in here, you two!"

Stepping back from Zach, Miriam gave a nervous laugh. "We better go back in before she comes looking for us."

"*Ya.*" He took her hand and led her back into the kitchen.

"Who was at the door?" Edna asked as they sat down at the table.

"Oh, it was nothing important," Miriam muttered, more guilt poking at her as she spoke the words.

• • •

Raindrops splattered Timothy's hat and shirt as he approached Naomi's porch. Lifting his trembling hand to knock on the door, he stopped, closed his eyes, and breathed a deep sigh, willing the anger to leave his heart. Miriam wasn't meant for him, but Naomi was. Now was the time to come clean with Naomi and ask for her hand before she changed her mind and decided not to wait for him.

He tapped on the door and mustered all of his courage from the depths of his soul.

A few moments passed and then the door opened, revealing Naomi. She stared up at him, her eyes wide with wonder. "Timothy?" Her gaze raked over him. "You're soaked!" Taking his hand, she pulled him toward the foyer. "Come in and get dried off. We just started supper."

"No, I'm fine. Really." Grasping her hand in his, he gently stopped her from walking. "I was hoping we could talk. Alone."

Her smile transformed into a frown. "It sounds serious."

"It is."

"I guess I knew this was coming. I'll save you the trouble. It's over. You don't love me, and you want me to move on and find someone who does." Tears filled her eyes. "I understand. *Danki* for the time we spent together."

She attempted to yank her hand back, but he held onto it, pulling it to his chest.

"You got it all wrong, Naomi." He shook his head.

"I do?" Her eyes widened, and her expression softened.

"Absolutely. I didn't come here to break it off, but I understand if you want to end it with me." He braced himself, awaiting her rejection, the second of the night.

"No, no." She stepped toward him. "I don't want to end it."

"*Gut*." He paused, collecting his thoughts. "I'm here to apologize."

"Apologize?"

"I've thought about what you said in the buggy yesterday, and you're right." He took her other hand in his and squeezed them both. "I'm sorry for taking you for granted. You were right about Miriam—I did still care for her, but I've realized I was totally wrong."

She studied his eyes, her expression anxious.

"I spoke with Miriam, and I thought I still wanted to be with her. But what she and I had years ago is over. We both agreed the past is the past, and it's gone." He ran his thumbs over her palms. "She's seeing Zach Fisher now. At first I was angry when I found out, but now I see I'm not supposed to be with Miriam. I'm supposed to be with you. I'm sorry for not seeing that before."

Naomi gasped, and a single tear trickled down her face.

He swiped the tear away with the tip of his finger. "I've spent the past four years pining for Miriam, convinced God had wanted me to marry her. I blamed myself for our breakup, thinking I'd driven her away. Yet I see now I haven't been listening to God at all. You've been right before my eyes, and I didn't see it. I'm so sorry for not treating you right. You deserve someone so much better than me."

"Stop," she whispered, taking his hand in hers. "You're talking *narrisch*."

He chuckled. "Funny, I keep hearing that word."

Leaning down, he brushed his lips against hers, expecting to feel the electricity that had flashed through him when he touched Miriam's hand last night.

Instead, he found her lips warm and sweet, but no spark. No explosions. No heat. Perhaps that was how love was supposed to feel—warm, comfortable, complacent, and nothing more.

Meeting her gaze, he found her eyes wide and sparkling. "Would you allow me to court you, Naomi?"

"*Ya*," she breathed.

"Would it be too bold to ask you to marry me in the fall?"

"*Ya!*" She squealed, wrapping her arms around his neck. "I mean, no, it's not too bold. Of course, I will marry you. I love you, Timothy Kauffman."

He held her close. "I love you, too." As he spoke the words, they felt like a lie. He hoped he could say he loved her and mean it—soon.

CHAPTER 13

Saturday night, in keeping with Kauffman family tradition, Timothy, his brothers, brothers-in-law, and father leaned against the fence surrounding Eli's pasture and listened to a story his brother Daniel shared about one of the young workers at the furniture store. Timothy laughed at appropriate times, but his thoughts were tied up with his future.

Ever since he'd proposed to Naomi on Wednesday, she'd been different. She seemed to cling to him every time he saw her, and she was even bubblier, chatting endlessly about their wedding. She'd arranged for them to meet with the bishop next week in order to obtain his blessing and begin their plans.

Timothy longed to ask his brothers if they too had felt such a heavy load on their shoulders when they were planning their weddings, but it was an Amish tradition to keep upcoming weddings a secret, until they were "published," meaning announced at a worship service closer to the wedding.

He suspected deep in his heart that he wouldn't feel this aversion to her behavior if they were truly meant to be together. Yet, he couldn't face that fact. He didn't want to even consider breaking Naomi's heart—not after the way Miriam had broken his. He couldn't bear inflicting that pain on sweet Naomi, who longed to have a family with him. Miriam had told him that she was his past, and it was time he faced that reality.

He wished he could get Miriam out of his head and concentrate on his new life with Naomi, but Miriam's beautiful face still haunted his dreams at night and his thoughts during the day.

The screen door leading to the kitchen banged shut, drawing Timothy's eyes to the back porch across the dirt driveway.

Beth Anne stomped down the stairs as if on a mission. She stalked across the dirt lane and stood by the fence. After nodding at the group of men, she trained her eyes on Timothy. "May I speak with you in private?"

"*Ya.*" He followed her through the fence, and they strolled toward the large barn across the vast field. "*Wie geht's?*" he asked when they were out of earshot of the group of men behind them.

"Don't play coy with me," Beth Anne said.

He stopped and gave her a confused look. "What did I do?"

"I hear congratulations are in order," she said with a knowing smile.

"What's that supposed to mean?"

She folded her arms in front of her chest. "I hear you proposed to Naomi."

He groaned, covering his face with his hand. "She told you?"

"She told all of us while we were doing the dishes.

She said that she was so excited she couldn't wait until you were published." Beth Anne frowned. "You don't love her, Timothy. Why are you marrying her?"

He glared at her. "It's my decision who I marry. I don't need your permission."

"You don't love her." Beth Anne enunciated each word. "You're going to be miserable and make her miserable too."

"How do you know I don't love her?"

She wagged a finger at him like a schoolteacher. "I just tested you, and you failed. You groaned when you found out she told me. If you loved her, you'd be overjoyed right now."

He blanched as if she'd struck him.

She's right.

"The poor girl is nearly turning cartwheels in there. She's so young and desperate to be in love and have a family. I remember being that immature and lying in bed at night imagining what it would be like to be in love and getting married. She's a sweet girl, but she has a lot of growing up to do. I was really stunned when I heard the news." Beth Anne gestured toward the house. "I snuck out while she was surrounded by our sisters and *Mamm*. Everyone is thrilled. Naomi said she knows she should've waited to tell us when you're published, but she's so thrilled she can't keep it to herself. She told Lilly Lapp yesterday, and it was so easy to share that she wanted to tell the whole district."

He grimaced. "She told Lilly?"

Beth Anne raised an eyebrow. "Are you afraid Miriam might find out?"

He stared at her, speechless.

"Miriam will know soon. In fact, with the way Naomi is celebrating, I'd wager she knows already." Beth Anne clasped her hands to her hips. "Why didn't you just speak to Miriam instead of taking the coward's way out?"

"I did speak to her," he began through gritted teeth. "And?"

"She said I'm part of her past, and she's moving forward. She's courting Zach Fisher."

Beth Anne's expression was surprised. "Zach Fisher?"

"Ya. Zach Fisher. He was at her house for supper Wednesday when I went to see her."

"That doesn't make sense."

He raised his eyebrows. "Why wouldn't it make sense? Miriam has moved on, and so have I."

"But just the other day, Miriam asked me if you'd ever cheated on her, and I told her you hadn't. Then she explained about Lilly's lie."

"What?" He shook his head, shocked. "When did she ask you that?"

"Wednesday. I told her God could give you both a second chance, and I said to have faith. But she said you were courting Naomi. I thought you and Naomi were only friends, but I felt it wasn't my place to tell her your business."

Again, he groaned. "How did things get so confused?"

"I don't know." Beth Anne bit her lip. "I guess I should've told her that you and Naomi were only friends. And I should've told you that she was asking about you. However, I felt it was better to leave things in God's hands."

"But why was she asking about me if she was courting Zach?"

Beth Anne threw her hands up with frustration. "I have no idea. She never mentioned Zach to me."

He folded his arms in front of his chest. "It doesn't matter. She's made her choice. She has Zach, and I have Naomi."

Beth Anne scowled. "It's all my fault. I should've stayed out of it and maybe now you and Miriam would be together."

"It's not meant to be." His expression softened. "I know you mean well, but God doesn't see us together."

"But you love each other. You are supposed to be together."

"You think she loves me?" He studied her eyes. *Could Beth Anne be right? Does Miriam love me?*

"Timothy!" a voice yelled behind them. "Get over here!"

Turning, he found Elizabeth, surrounded by his sisters, waving to him.

"I bet they pulled out the ice cream," Beth Anne muttered as they started toward the crowd.

"We need to celebrate with some ice cream," Elizabeth called, beaming. "My last *kind* is finally getting married."

"Told ya," Beth Anne whispered, smacking his shoulder.

The men and children joined the group of women, and Timothy wished he could crawl under a rock. He forced a smile as his gaze met Naomi's wide grin.

"It's about time," Daniel called, his arms wrapped around his wife.

"We were beginning to worry about you," Robert chimed in, and the crowd laughed in response.

Timothy and Beth Anne stepped through the fence and were swallowed up into the crowd. He approached Naomi, and the knot of relatives began to clap.

"I just couldn't keep it to myself," Naomi gushed, taking his hand in hers.

He gazed down at his bride and pushed a flyaway lock of hair back from her face. How could he hurt this woman, whose eyes shone with love only for him? He was meant to be with her and to forget Miriam.

"I'm so *froh*," Naomi said.

"Me too," he replied, praying that statement would come true.

. . .

Lindsay sank onto the swing and smiled at the scene unfolding in the pasture. "They sure are happy about Naomi's announcement."

"They get riled up about weddings, don't they?" Jessica chomped her gum and fingered her necklace.

"I think *Englishers* are the same." Lindsay leaned back and pushed the swing. "Everyone gets excited about weddings. *Aenti* Rebecca once made a comment that Elizabeth worried Timothy would never settle down."

Jessica frowned. "You always talk about '*Englishers*,'" she began, using her fingers as quotations as she said the word, "as if you're Amish. Linds, you're not Amish. You're a poser." With hypercritical eyes, she gestured toward Lindsay. "You're trying too hard to fit in. You need to just be Lindsay Bedford and not try so hard to be Lindsay Bedford, Amish girl."

My own sister doesn't get me. Or maybe she's just not listening!

Lindsay gritted her teeth to stop the angry words from escaping her lips. Taking a deep breath, she silently counted to ten.

"What?" Jessica asked, still chomping her gum. "You look like you have something to say."

"I don't want to fight with you, Jessica," Lindsay said, enunciating the words. "You're going back to Virginia soon, and the last thing I want to do is let you leave on bad terms."

Her older sister shrugged. "I'm not mad at you. I'm just stating the obvious."

"That's just it." Lindsay angled her body toward her sister. "You keep saying that I'm posing as an Amish person, but this is who I want to be. You need to respect that this is my choice." She pointed toward Jessica. "You do what's right for you." She then pointed to her chest. "And I'll do what's right for me. I don't plan to join the church until I'm certain that this is the life I want to lead. But right now, it feels right, and you need to accept that or we're going to have problems between us."

Jessica's expression softened. "You're right." Reaching over, she squeezed Lindsay's hand. "I'm sorry for not respecting your decision."

Lindsay smiled. "I forgive you. Just don't do it again."

"Deal." Jessica looked toward the dirt road leading up to the house. "Jake decided to show up after all."

Lindsay glanced toward the headlights as the pickup truck rumbled toward the house. The truck stopped in front of the barn and Jake climbed from the driver's seat. The passenger door opened, revealing a tall, slender Amish man.

"I guess Jake has Matthew with him tonight," Jessica said.

"Who?" Lindsay asked.

"He just moved here and started working at the furniture store."

With Jake talking and Matthew frowning, they strolled toward the porch. Lindsay's gaze was glued to Matthew, taking in his tall, lean physique. As he approached the porch, she was struck by brown curls escaping from beneath his straw hat. His eyes met hers and then darted toward the fence, where the cluster of Kauffman family members congregated.

"Hey there," Jessica said, standing. "What are you guys up to this evening?"

"Not a whole lot." Jake climbed the porch steps and leaned back against the railing. "We thought we'd come over and see what was going on at the Kauffman homestead."

Matthew's stare moved from the Kauffman clan to the toes of his boots. Lindsay longed to know why the man was so quiet. He looked to be approximately seventeen, and his clean-shaven face told her that he was single. She wished she could see his eyes.

"How's it going, Matt?" Jessica asked. "Long time no see, huh?"

Matt looked up, his expression somber.

"I don't think you've met my little sister. Matt, this is Lindsay." Jessica gestured between them. "Linds, this is Matt Glick."

"It's nice to meet you," Lindsay said, hoping his eyes would meet hers.

Matthew's eyes met hers, and her pulse leapt. His eyes were a light shade of brown that was nearly golden. "You too," he said, looking back toward the pasture.

Lindsay opened her mouth to speak but was overshadowed by Eli's voice booming from the pasture.

"Matthew!" he called. "It's so good to see you. Come visit with us, son!"

Matthew gave Lindsay another quick nod and then loped toward the fence. His slim body moved with a grace mirroring a gazelle.

"He doesn't talk much at all, does he?" Jessica asked, as if reading Lindsay's thoughts.

"No, he doesn't." Jake glanced across the pasture toward Matthew. "He's a bit shy."

Lindsay watched Matthew as he approached Eli. While the older man spoke, Matthew folded his arms.

Biting her lip, Lindsay watched Matthew lean on the fence. He turned and met her eyes and then quickly looked away. Lindsay hoped to learn more about Matthew Glick.

. . .

Miriam sat on the porch swing that evening and stared across the field at her father's house. She longed to be welcomed back into that home and to feel the love of a family she missed so much.

Hannah and Edna had told her to give Abraham time, but she wanted to work things out soon. If she were going to consider courting and marrying Zach, then she wanted her family's blessing. She wanted her future children to know their family.

She crossed the field and climbed the porch steps. She knocked on the door and waited a few moments. When no one answered, she turned the cool knob and entered the house.

Stepping into the foyer, she felt as if she'd traveled back in time. The house looked exactly as it had before she'd left. The foyer opened into a large living room with the same plain furniture and white walls. Memories made within that room consumed her—family devotionals, birthdays, Christmases, weddings, church services. She imagined her mother sitting in her favorite chair while quilting or giving much-needed advice.

Miriam closed her eyes, fighting the threatening tears. Oh, how she missed her family. How could she have left them? She walked through the living room to the large kitchen, but she didn't see anyone. She padded through the laundry room to the mudroom and back porch. Still no one.

"Hello?" Miriam called, heading for the stairs. Not receiving an answer, she climbed the steep stairs.

"Hello?" she called down the silent hallway. She moved past her brother's room and Hannah's former room and then stopped in the doorway of the room she'd shared with Lilly since their birth.

Late-night talks with her younger sister, sharing hopes and dreams, twirled through her mind. Miriam tilted her head, reflecting how things hadn't worked out the way they'd hoped. Neither of them was married. Neither had a family.

She crossed the room and stood by her sister's battery-operated treadle sewing machine. A pile of unfinished quilts sat folded neatly beside it. Lifting the pile, she unfolded a purple and blue quilt created in the Lone Star pattern. She ran her fingers over the stitching, marveling at the intricate design.

Lilly was a talented quilter, and she'd learned all she knew from their mother. The two had sat together for hours quilting and talking. Miriam had spent her time in the kitchen with their grandmother learning all she could about Amish cooking, but she'd never learned to quilt very well. She could make a fairly decent quilt, but it would never have been as beautiful as Lilly's.

Flipping through the pile of quilts, she found another in the Log Cabin pattern and a second Lone Star. She touched each one, imagining the hours her younger sister had spent on them. Like their mother once had, Lilly created them for *English* customers who had ordered them from Naomi King's booth at the farmer's market. Miriam was certain her parents were proud of Lilly for following in Bertha's footsteps.

Unlike Miriam.

Sighing, Miriam refolded the quilts and set them down where they'd been, next to the sewing machine. Turning, she found a stack of books on the floor. She reached down and moved the books, glancing through the covers. Each title and cover seemed to be a Christian novel. Miriam recalled how Lilly would keep the lamp burning well past their bedtime in order to continue reading, despite Miriam's requests to turn the light off and go to sleep. There were a few times when Lilly had almost gotten caught by their parents, but she'd managed to snuff the flame, hide the book, and snuggle under the quilt before the door had creaked open. While Miriam enjoyed reading, she wasn't a voracious reader like her younger sister, but she knew that Zach enjoyed reading for pleasure. Miriam absently wondered if Lilly and Zach enjoyed the same authors.

Miriam's gaze moved across the hallway to her parents' room, and tears filled her eyes again. She couldn't imagine how lonely the room must feel for her father.

Pushing the door back, Miriam stepped into the room as a loud crash sounded, causing her to jump. Glancing beyond the door, she found a stack of papers she'd knocked off the bureau. She knelt on the floor and retrieved the stack, setting it as neatly as possible in its place.

She scanned the floor for missed papers and spotted a shoe-box under the bed. Miriam dropped to her knees and yanked the box from under the bed. She opened the lid and gasped at a stack of envelopes addressed to her.

Miriam pulled out an envelope and unfolded the plain stationery inside. Her eyes filled with tears as she read a beautiful letter addressed to her and written in her mother's handwriting.

Liewe Miriam,

It's been six months since you left us, and I don't understand why you won't respond to my letters. I miss you every day. While I see your smile reflected in your sisters' faces, it's not the same without you. Timothy Kauffman stopped by the other day asking if we'd heard from you. I had to tell him the truth, which was no.

You'll be happy to hear Colleen and Trevor Henderson are doing a little better. I saw Colleen at the market the other day, and she asked about you. She had tears in her eyes, and I believe she wants to talk to you and make peace. I'm certain she has forgiveness in her heart for you and wants to share it with you.

You must put your guilt to rest and let yourself heal, Miriam. You weren't responsible for Jeremy's death. Unfortunately, some *bopplin* don't make it past the first year of life. I learned many years ago that there's something called Sudden Infant Death Syndrome. A doctor explained it to me and he called it SIDS for short. He said that it happens, and sometimes it can't be prevented. You must trust me that I know more about this than you could imagine. I wanted to explain this to you, but I never got a chance to speak with you alone before you left.

Please read this letter carefully and understand what I'm trying to say to you. Miriam, you need to accept that this wasn't your fault. Don't listen to what everyone said about you. Their hurtful words were said out of grief and sadness, and you need to forgive them as Jesus forgives us.

I hope you're doing well and are finding happiness in Indiana. Please tell Abigail her mother misses her. Remember, you'll always be welcome home.

All my love,

Mamm

Miriam sobbed as she read the letter a second time. Pulling out a few more envelopes, she found similar notes. She counted all of the envelopes in the box and found twenty. Each one was stamped but never mailed. She wiped her eyes, wondering why.

"What are you doing here?" a voice barked behind her.

Startled, Miriam gasped, turning to find her father standing over her.

"Give me those! They're private." He reached down and ripped the letters and box from her hands before she could react. "Now, get out!" He pointed toward the door.

Miriam scrambled to get up, fury and hurt rushing through her. "Why didn't *Mamm* mail those?"

He stuffed the letters back into the box and placed them on the bureau. "They're none of your concern."

"They're addressed to me, *Daed*." She jammed a finger in her chest. "Remember me—Miriam? Your middle *dochder*?"

He stood silent, his eyes stone cold.

She shook her head, ignoring the angry tears streaming down her hot face. "Why are you treating me this way?"

Scowling, he didn't answer.

"*Mamm* forgave me. See the letters?" She pointed to the box. "Have you read them?"

"Your *mamm* had a soft heart. I remember transgressions."

"What transgressions do you think I've made?" Her voice trembled with her heartbreak.

"You were seeing many men behind Timothy Kauffman's back. You were irresponsible and allowed Jeremy Henderson to perish while you stood on the porch kissing and doing other inappropriate things with Timothy Kauffman."

She shook her head and stepped toward him. "None of that is true. I wasn't seeing anyone but Timothy, and we weren't kissing when Jeremy died. Did Lilly tell you those lies? Lilly has been telling a lot of tales lately."

"I know it's the truth." He nodded toward the door. "Go now. Go back to Indiana and leave us be. You're not welcome here."

"But I—"

"Go!" His voice boomed off the white bedroom walls.

Swallowing a sob, Miriam rushed down the stairs and out the front door, nearly knocking over Lilly and Gerald. Miriam pushed past them and started down the path to the cabin.

"Miriam!" Lilly called after her. "Wait up!" Miriam increased her speed, loping down the path. "Miriam!" Lilly called.

A strong hand reached out and yanked Miriam back. "Just wait a minute."

Miriam faced her younger sister and wiped her cheeks.

"I wanted to tell you something. I figured it would be best if you heard it from family."

"What?" Miriam asked, her voice thin.

"I talked to Naomi King yesterday." A smirk spread across Lilly's lips. "She's marrying Timothy Kauffman in the fall."

Miriam's eyes narrowed to slits. "What makes you think I'd believe anything you tell me?"

Lilly's smirk was replaced with a frown. "Suit yourself, but it's true. She said Timothy came to see her Wednesday night and admitted he'd taken her for granted. For four years he'd been pining for you. He'd talked to you and you said he's your past but Zach is your future. Apparently, Zach was at Edna's for supper Wednesday night."

Miriam cupped her hand to her mouth.

Lilly's eyes narrowed to slits. "So it's true?"

Miriam glowered. "What do you care? Do you enjoy shoving the knife deeper into my back?"

Her sister's face fell to a frown. "Are you courting Zach Fisher?" she asked through gritted teeth.

Miriam shook her head. "I can't believe we share the same parents. You're the most hateful person I've ever met!"

She then rushed back to the cabin, flung open the door, and slammed it shut. She leaned back against it and sobbed. Staring up at the ceiling, she prayed for comfort and peace. She needed a sign.

"What should I do next?" she whispered.

Go back to Indiana.

The answer came from somewhere inside her, and a calm filled her, choking back the panic.

She had nothing left in Lancaster County, except for

Edna, Hannah, and Zach. But the hurt buried deep in her soul swelled.

She'd lost everything once again—Timothy and her family. She'd lost her family years ago, but she now had fresh pain with the knowledge that her mother had tried to reach out to her. Bertha had loved her despite all that happened, but Abraham wouldn't give her the benefit of the doubt.

And Timothy. She'd almost gotten him back—even as a friend—but now he was planning to marry someone else. Was that what he'd come to tell her? Did he want her to know he was going to marry Naomi before the news hit the grapevine?

A fresh stream of tears trickled down her cheeks. She owed all of this hurt to her sister, her flesh-and-blood sister, who'd set out to ruin her life and won. How could Hannah be so loving and supportive while Lilly was only focused on hurting Miriam?

Miriam knew what she had to do. She tiptoed to Edna's bedroom and found her sleeping. She backed out of her bedroom and closed the door.

Stepping into her room, Miriam changed into jeans and a T-shirt and then packed the rest of her things. After writing a letter, she left it on top of her frock on the kitchen counter before packing the car. She drove down the lane and stopped at the phone shanty. Pulling out her address book, she located the numbers for the bakery and Zach.

She dialed the bakery first. Elizabeth Kauffman's voice sang through the phone, explaining their location and hours of operation. After the introductory message ended, Miriam cleared her throat.

"Beth Anne, this is Miriam Lapp," she began, hoping to sound confident. "I wanted to tell you I'm heading back to Indiana because of an . . . unexpected emergency situation at my other job." She bit her lip, wracking her brain for another excuse. "*Danki* for your friendship." Her voice quavered with the regret and hurt swelling in her heart. "I'll miss you." She hung up the phone and swiped the tears from her cheeks.

Clearing her throat again, she dialed Zach's shop. His sweet voice brought a fresh batch of tears to her eyes. When the beep sounded, she had to fight to find her voice. "Zach, it's me, Miriam. I'm sorry, but I have to leave. Some things happened with my family and . . ." She took a deep breath, but the tears flowed despite her efforts. "I'm sorry. I have to go." She hung up the phone and dissolved in sobs, leaning against the shanty wall.

After a few moments, she collected herself and trudged to her car.

On her way out of town, Miriam slowed down and then parked at the side of the road in front of a large farmhouse, lit up like downtown Lancaster at night with outside lights shining from the four corners.

She wished she could go back in time and relive that awful day. If she had the chance, she never would've put Jeremy down for a nap. Instead, she would've held him, rocked him, and made sure he continued to breathe. She never would've answered the door when Timothy stopped by to talk. Their conversation had gone terribly wrong when they'd argued about their future.

If she'd held Jeremy and not spoken to Timothy, then maybe Jeremy would be alive today and turning five next spring. And maybe she would've worked things out with Timothy . . .

She wondered how the Hendersons were doing. Had they rebuilt their lives? Had they welcomed a new baby into their family? She cupped her hands over the keys and considered walking up to the house and asking the family how they were coping since losing their precious child, the child they'd left in Miriam's tender care that fateful day. Miriam turned off the ignition, yanked out the keys, and stared at the house.

Instead, she closed her eyes and rested her head on the steering wheel. She was too afraid of the answer. She couldn't face the guilt that would haunt her if Colleen told her that her marriage had fallen apart because of Miriam's negligence. The letter from Miriam's mother had said that Colleen and Trevor were doing well. Miriam hoped that she'd been right.

Shoving the key back into the ignition, Miriam started the car and sped down the highway, away from the only place she'd ever called home.

CHAPTER 14

Hannah hurried across the field behind Abraham's house Sunday evening. She'd been concerned when Edna and Miriam hadn't attended church service. After Lilly explained that Edna wasn't feeling well, Hannah's concern grew to worry. To make matters worse, Lilly didn't know where Miriam was.

While her children and husband visited with family at her father's house, Hannah headed to Edna's cabin to find out what was wrong. She tapped on the cabin door, and Edna called for her to come in.

"How are you?" Hannah asked when she found Edna lounging in her favorite easy chair.

"Heartbroken." Frowning, Edna held up a piece of paper.

Hannah knitted her eyebrows with confusion and flopped onto the sofa next to Edna's chair. "I don't understand."

"This will explain everything." Edna handed the letter to Hannah.

Hannah opened the paper and recognized Miriam's handwriting on sight. She cupped her hand to her mouth as she read it.

Dear *Aenti* Edna,

I've enjoyed our time together these past couple of weeks, but I must go back to Indiana now. Unfortunately, I'm not as brave as you thought I was.

Today was the worst day I've experienced in a long time, and it's made me realize I was fooling myself when I thought I could move back here and become a part of the community again by starting a new life.

Tonight I went to see *Daed* to try to make things right. I found the house empty and while walking by his room, I discovered a box of letters *Mamm* had written to me but never mailed. The letters were loving and forgiving, telling me how much she'd wanted me to come home. When I asked *Daed* about the letters, he said they were not my concern. He was angry and cold, and he said I had dishonored the family by seeing men behind Timothy Kauffman's back and by letting Jeremy Henderson die. When I tried to explain the lies he'd heard about me weren't true, he threw me out of the house. On my way back to the cabin, Lilly stopped me and shared the news that Timothy is going to marry Naomi King in the fall.

My heart is now in shambles, and I'm not strong enough to carry the pain in silence any longer. I can't stay in a community where I am considered dead to my family. Also, I can't stand by and watch the love of my life marry someone else. I'd thought I could fool myself into believing I would be happy with another man. However, I've lost Timothy all over again, and I can't bear it.

What hurts the most is that my own sister, Lilly, is the one responsible for the lies that have ruined my life. Lilly is the reason why I will never marry the one man I will always love, Timothy Kauffman, and she's the reason why I've lost most of the members of my family—everyone except for you and Hannah.

Please tell Hannah I'm sorry for not saying goodbye in person. I'll be in touch with her soon. I'm going to leave a message for Beth Anne explaining I had to return to work in Indiana. There's no need for me to explain it any further to her. I'm certain she thinks it's best if I let her brother move on with his life. In all honesty, I can't blame him for marrying Naomi since I was the one who left four years ago and didn't even try to work things out. I guess in some ways, I've gotten what I deserved.

Thank you again for everything. Don't worry about baking for extra money. I'm going to send you money every month to help cover your expenses.

All my love,
Miriam

Hannah wiped an errant tear and then met Edna's gaze. "When did you find this?"

"This morning." She nodded toward the kitchen counter. "She must've packed up and left during the night. I never heard a peep, but I've always been a heavy sleeper."

Hannah sniffed and folded the letter up. "I don't understand how things have gone this far. Why would Lilly possibly want to ruin Miriam's life?"

Edna's frown deepened. "The only reason I can imagine is jealousy. I reckon Miriam got something Lilly wanted, but I just can't figure out what it was."

"It ends now. I'm going to set things straight." Hannah stood and held up the letter. "May I keep this?"

"*Ya.*" Edna shook her head, her eyes shining with fresh tears. "If I read it again, I'll only cry."

"I'm going to go have a talk with *Daed* and Lilly. Do you need anything?"

Edna sighed. "I just need you to make things right in this family. It's gone on too long."

"I'll do my best." Hannah hugged Edna and then headed back to her father's house, where she found Lilly and Abraham visiting with other family members in the kitchen.

She asked them to follow her into the laundry room, and she closed the door behind them. "I've stayed silent long enough." She looked back and forth between her father and Lilly.

"What's this about, Hannah?" Abraham asked, scowling.

"It's about Miriam." Hannah eyed Lilly, and she could've sworn panic flashed in her younger sister's eyes. "She's gone. She went back to Indiana."

"*Gut,*" Abraham said, heading toward the door. "That's where she belongs. Now I'm going to finish my pie."

"I'm not finished," Hannah snapped.

Abraham faced her, his eyes narrowed to slits. "You don't talk to me like that, Hannah."

"I'm not a child anymore," Hannah challenged. "You can extend me the courtesy of hearing me out."

He folded his arms across his chest. "Make it quick."

She glanced at Lilly. "Your youngest daughter here is the one who spread the lies that caused all of this trouble for Miriam." Hannah trained her eyes on Abraham, ignoring the daggers his glance shot her way. "You may believe Miriam was having affairs behind Timothy's back, but it simply isn't true. Also, I don't believe she was responsible for Jeremy Henderson's death. There's a syndrome called Sudden Infant Death. It's also known as crib death, and it's completely inexplicable and tragic. No one could've saved Jeremy. You've misjudged Miriam, and it's time you forgave her. She's your *dochder. Mamm* is gone, and we all miss her. Her death taught us that life is precious, and we need to love each other while we have the chance."

Abraham's expression hardened. "Are you done?"

"No." Hannah shook her head. "I'm not done until I hear you will forgive Miriam and tell her she's your *dochder*, and you love her." She looked at Lilly, who was studying the toes of her shoes. "And you, Lillian, what do you have to say for yourself?"

"You're out of line, Hannah." Abraham wagged a finger at her. "Do you need help remembering your place?"

Hannah folded her arms in defiance. "I think you need to remember yours."

Abraham's eyes widened with shock. "Do you speak to your husband this way?"

"Only when he needs to be taken down a peg or two. You're wrong to judge Miriam. Remember the Word, *Daed*." She held her head high and quoted one of her favorite Scriptures. "'There is no difference, for all have sinned and fall short of the glory of God, and are justified freely by his grace through the redemption that came by Christ Jesus.'"

Abraham's eyes softened for a split second, and then his brow furrowed with resentment. "I don't have to stand here and take this from my own *dochder*."

"Fine. I'll collect my family, and we'll leave." Hannah started for the door, but then turned back to face them one more time. "You both should be ashamed of yourselves," she said, looking between them. "Miriam left this community heartbroken and went back to Indiana, where she has nothing except for a job. She was ready to start a new life here, but you both ruined that. I don't know how you sleep at night knowing you've mortally wounded your own family member. *Mamm* would be gravely disappointed in both of you."

She then marched from the laundry room in search of her family.

. . .

Monday morning, Timothy was sanding a cradle when a hand tapped his shoulder. He wiped his brow and turned to find Daniel. "You have a visitor out front," Daniel said, jerking his thumb toward the showroom.

Glancing at the clock, Timothy found it was only ten. Since Naomi usually came for lunch around noon, he was certain it couldn't be her.

After wiping his hands on a rag and dusting off his clothes, Timothy headed out front and was surprised to find Hannah standing by the sample furniture pieces. He silently marveled at the Lapp family resemblance. While Hannah was approximately two inches taller than Miriam, she had the same dark hair, clear creamy complexion, and brown eyes.

Hannah met his gaze. "Timothy. *Wie geht's?*"

"*Gut.* How are you?" he asked.

She shook her head. "I'm trying to right a wrong that's been done to my sister."

His eyebrows knitted in confusion. "I'm sorry, but I don't understand."

"Will you come outside with me?" She gestured toward the door.

"Of course." He followed her out to the parking lot, where they walked over to a sedan.

"Miriam went back to Indiana Saturday night," Hannah said.

Timothy's stomach plummeted. "Oh?" he asked.

"She left my *aenti* a note explaining why, and I'd like you to read it." Hannah held out a piece of paper.

He shook his head. "I don't think that's any of my business."

"Actually, it is." She waved the paper in front of him. "Please take it. I don't want to argue with you. I've had enough arguing

to last me a year, thanks to my *daed.*"

He gave her a confused look and took the paper. He skimmed the letter, and when he finished, his stomach was tied up in knots.

One paragraph kept replaying in his mind:

"I can't stand by and watch the love of my life marry someone else. I'd thought I could fool myself into believing I would be happy with another man. However, I've lost Timothy all over again, and I can't bear it . . ."

He cleared his throat and folded up the letter before meeting Hannah's probing stare. He couldn't let her know the letter was tearing his soul apart.

Marrying Naomi was the right thing to do. Miriam made her choice by returning to Indiana. Breaking his promise to Naomi would cause her the same pain he was experiencing now, and he refused to hurt Naomi that way.

"I'm sorry Miriam feels this way." He held the letter out to Hannah. "It's a shame she had to leave under these circumstances. Nevertheless, I'm sure it's for the best."

Hannah's eyes rounded with surprise as she took the letter from him. "You can't really mean that."

Timothy shrugged and feigned indifference. "What do you want me to say? Miriam made her choice. She left here four years ago to experience the *English* world. I guess she decided that she belonged there and not here. She returned to Indiana, and I'm marrying Naomi. I was hoping Miriam and I could be friends, but I guess that won't happen."

"Did you read the letter, Timothy?" Hannah's voice shook with anger. "Miriam loves you. She called you the love of her life. Do you have any tenderness at all?"

Although her comments stabbed Timothy in the heart, he remained calm. "Miriam left me years ago. I carried a torch for her for a long time, but I realized I had to move on. Unfortunately, it's too late for her and me. I'm marrying Naomi."

"Do you love her?"

"Who?" he asked, caught off guard.

"*Naomi*," Hannah enunciated the word.

Timothy paused. "*Ya.*"

Hannah gave him a knowing smile. "You're a coward, Timothy Kauffman."

His eyebrows shot up with shock. "Excuse me?"

"Good day," she said, opening the back door of her driver's sedan.

"Wait a minute," he said. "Why did you call me a coward?"

"Think about it," she said. "You'll figure it out." She climbed into the backseat and slammed the door.

He stared after the car as it drove away. Hannah's accusation echoed in his mind along with the words in the letter while he ambled across the parking lot.

Stepping into the showroom, he found Luke on the phone.

When Timothy walked by, Luke grabbed his arm. "Phone is for you."

"Now what?" Timothy muttered, taking the receiver. "Hello," he said.

"Timothy," Beth Anne said. "I got a message this morning that might interest you."

"Let me guess, it has to do with Miriam and the fact that she went back to Indiana," he said, dropping into the chair behind the counter.

"You knew already?" she asked.

"*Ya*. Hannah just paid me a visit."

"Really? What did she say?"

"Not much," he fibbed. "She told me Miriam went back home and was heartbroken when she found out I'm marrying Naomi." *And she wanted me to know I'm a coward.*

"I guess that means Lilly told her."

"*Ya*, that's what it means." He sighed and glanced across the showroom.

"So, what are you going to do?"

"I'm going to keep my promise to Naomi," he said.

"And be miserable," Beth Anne added.

He frowned. "I'd love to listen to you lecture me about my mistakes, but I have work to do."

"Fine, fine," Beth Anne sang. "You get back to work. But I want to tell you one more thing. Miriam sounded heartbroken when she left the message. I truly believe she loves you."

He covered his face with his free hand and swallowed a groan. *I'm the love of her life.*

"For what it's worth," she continued, "I think you're making a mistake with Naomi."

"You've made that perfectly clear," he said. "Now may I go? This cradle isn't going to build itself and the *English* customer wants it by next Monday."

"Have a good day."

He snorted with sarcasm. "I'll certainly try." Timothy hung up the phone and stared down at the desk.

Miriam's sweet words in her letter to Edna echoed through his mind. She'd called him the love of her life. She'd declared she couldn't stand by and watch him marry someone else.

Miriam said she'd always love Timothy.

And now Miriam was gone, and he had promised to marry a young woman whom he'd only considered a dear friend. He knew in his heart he didn't love Naomi.

But he couldn't break his promise to Naomi. She was an innocent bystander to this great big mess—a mess Lilly Lapp had orchestrated four years ago.

Groaning, he covered his face with his hands. "How did things get so out of control?" he muttered.

Dropping his hands, he sat up straighter. Although it was a mess, he was going to prove he was a man of his word. He would marry Naomi and build a life with her. While he knew he'd always love Miriam Lapp, God's plan was for him to marry Naomi. He closed his eyes and prayed for guidance.

He then stood and headed back to the shop. As he stepped through the door, a question rang out through his mind.

If marrying Naomi is God's plan, then why does it feel so wrong?

Jumbies

1/2 cup shortening

1 1/2 cups brown sugar

3 eggs

3 cups flour

1/2 tsp salt

1 tsp baking soda

2 Tbsp hot water

1 cup chopped nuts

1 cup chopped dates

1 1/4 tsp vanilla

Cream shortening, sugar, eggs, and vanilla. Dissolve baking soda in hot water and add with dry ingredients. Add dates and nuts. Bake for 15 minutes at 350 degrees.

CHAPTER 15

Miriam leaned over the counter and handed the small slip of paper to the young mother. "Here's your receipt, Mrs. Spencer," she said, forcing a smile. "Dr. Sabella will be with you shortly."

"Thank you." Mrs. Spencer took her six-year-old son by the hand and led him to a bench in the waiting room.

Once the patient was gone, Miriam slid the glass window shut and buried her face in her hands, blowing out a deep sigh. Since she'd been back in Indiana, the days had dragged on like molasses in February. She'd spent her days at the office watching the clock, and her evenings sleeping—sometimes twelve to fifteen hours.

Abby had invited her to go out several times, but Miriam had no desire or energy to go. Hannah had left Miriam several phone messages—at home, at work, and on her cell phone—but Miriam couldn't bring herself to call her back, knowing it would be too painful. Miriam had left her heart in Pennsylvania.

"Miriam," a voice behind her said. "May I speak with you—in private?"

Miriam glanced up at her boss eyeing her with a sympathetic expression.

"Of course," Miriam said, following Lauren to the inner office.

Once in the office, Lauren sat behind her long oak desk, and Miriam plopped into the chair across from her. While she expected to be reprimanded for her lack of emotion on the job, Miriam didn't seem to care. Her passion for the job had evaporated.

"I'm worried about you," Lauren began, steepling her fingers on the desk. "You're different. Ever since you returned to work last week, you seem . . . depressed. What happened to you in Pennsylvania?"

Miriam gave a sarcastic snort. "Where should I begin?"

"How about at the beginning?" Lauren leaned forward, her eyes full of concern.

Miriam glanced toward the window. She didn't want to relive the heartbreak of her trip back to Lancaster County. It was painful enough as a distant memory, and rehashing it would only make it worse.

She met her boss's gaze and found the sympathy still apparent in her eyes. "Things didn't go the way I'd planned. I thought by going back home, my family would finally forgive me. However, they still blame me for things I didn't do, and I found out the man I've always loved is marrying someone else in the fall."

Lauren shook her head, frowning. "I'm so sorry."

Miriam folded her hands in her lap. "I know I'm acting depressed, but I promise I'll get over it. I'll try harder to put all of my family drama out of my head. You don't need to reprimand me. I'll do better."

Her boss raised an eyebrow. "You thought I was calling you in here to reprimand you?"

Miriam nodded. "I deserve it."

"Honey, I was going to see if you were all right. Considering the circumstances, I think you should take some time off."

"No!" The word came out more forcefully than Miriam had intended, and Lauren's eyes rounded with surprise. "I'm sorry, but I'll go nuts if I'm stuck at home. Please let me work."

Lauren shook her head. "I think you need some time to yourself. You should take a few weeks off and read a book or take up a hobby. Have you ever tried painting? Watercolors help me relax when life brings me down."

"No." Miriam shook her head. "I need to work. Being here is how I relax. If I'm at home, I'll go crazy thinking about everything that happened back in Pennsylvania."

"Honey, those demons are going to get you one way or the other. It's healthier for you to face them now rather than later." Lauren flipped through her Rolodex and pulled out a card. After writing something on a hot pink Post-It, she handed it to Miriam. "This is the name of a therapist I saw after my divorce. She helped me sort through my feelings, and after about six months, I was good as new. That's when I met Mike, the love of my life. We've been happily married for ten years now."

Gripping the Post-It note, Miriam grimaced. The love of my life is marrying someone else. "I don't think therapy will cure me."

"That's what a lot of people say, but you should give it a try." Lauren stood. "I don't want to see you for at least two weeks."

"But I only have one week of vacation left," Miriam pleaded while Lauren led her to the door. "I really need to work. I can't go without a paycheck since I'm going to start helping out my elderly aunt. I have to have that paycheck."

"I've already taken care of that. Dr. Sabella approved the extra time for you."

"But I don't think—"

"Go on," Lauren said, waving her off. "Get out of here."

Miriam schlepped to her desk with a frustrated frown on her face. After packing up her things, she said good-bye to her coworkers and headed out to the parking lot.

She climbed into her car, rested her head on the steering wheel, and wept.

. . .

Abby studied Miriam across the supper table later that evening. "Let me get this straight. Lauren gave you two weeks off, paid, and you're upset about it? Do you know how rare it is to find a boss like her?"

Miriam spooned more meatloaf onto her plate. "Yes, I do, but you don't understand my side of it. I want to work so I can get my mind off everything."

"In order to avoid your feelings for Timothy."

"It's not just that." Miriam lifted her glass of Diet Coke. "I'm also upset about the horrible things *Daed* said about me."

"You mean your dad." Abby forked more meatloaf

into her mouth. "You don't have to talk Dietsch to me. You're not there anymore."

"But maybe I want to be," Miriam muttered, studying her dinner plate.

"What did you say?"

Miriam sighed. "I miss it, Abby." She met her cousin's astonished expression. "You got me to admit it. I'm miserable here. I can't stand my job anymore. I sit there all day and wonder how Hannah, Lena Joy, and *Aenti* are doing. I worry about Lena Joy and how her illness is progressing. I contemplate all of the things I should've said to Timothy that night he came over to see me and how stupid I was to let him go. I wonder if I could've prevented him from proposing to Naomi if I had asked Zach to give me a few minutes alone to talk to Timothy and find out what he wanted to say to me."

Abby shrugged and sipped her drink. "So, go back."

Miriam raised an eyebrow. "You make it sound so easy."

"Why should it be difficult? You just said you're miserable here. There's nothing keeping you here except for your fear of facing your father." Abby leaned toward her. "You've done nothing wrong, Miriam. The worst thing you did was leave in the middle of the night without explaining your reasons to Timothy."

Miriam ate more meatloaf while Abby's words soaked through her. She wondered if she should try going back to Pennsylvania since returning to Indiana wasn't working out. She couldn't spend the rest of her life miserable.

The phone rang, and Abby rose. "I know you won't answer it," she muttered, crossing the kitchen. She snatched the cordless off the counter and held it to her ear. "Hello? . . . Oh hey. How are you? . . . Oh no. You're kidding. I'm so sorry . . ." Abby faced Miriam. "Yeah, she's right here . . ." She put her hand over the receiver. "It's Hannah."

"Tell her I'm not here," Miriam said.

"She's pretty upset." Abby held out the phone. "It's an emergency."

"Oh no. Is it Lena?" Miriam jumped up and grabbed the phone. "Hannah? Is Lena okay?"

"*Ya*," Hannah said, her voice quavering. "It's *Daed*. He's in the hospital. He's had a stroke. Can you come back? Please, Miriam?"

Miriam sank into the chair, her mind racing with thoughts. She wanted to come back, but why would her father want her? "I don't know . . ."

"He's asking for you, Miriam."

"He's asking for me?" She met Abby's questioning gaze. "Why would he ask for me?"

"I think he wants to apologize," Hannah said. "Please, Miriam. I promise I'll let you go back to Indiana after he sees you. You have my word that I won't pressure you to stay. I just worry we're going to lose him. I feel he should go with dignity, *ya*?"

Miriam stared down at her dinner plate. While her head told her to stay in Indiana and let her family handle her father, her heart told her to go. It was the Christian thing to do. "I'll pack some things and head out as soon as I can."

"*Danki*, Miriam. Drive safely. I love you."

Miriam wiped an errant tear. "Love you, too. Are you at Lancaster General?"

"*Ya*. I'll meet you here," Hannah said.

Miriam turned off the phone and placed it on the table. "I guess that was decided for me."

"Your dad had a stroke and is asking for you?" Abby asked. Miriam stood and gathered up her dirty dishes. "That's right. I guess on his death bed he's realizing his wrongs and asking for absolution."

"It's better late than never, huh?"

"I guess so." Miriam began to scrape off the plates for the dishwasher.

"Leave the dishes. You have a long ride ahead of you." Miriam hugged Abby. "Thank you for everything."

"Don't you mean *danki*?" Abby asked with a laugh. "Call me when you get there. I'll be here worrying about you driving so late."

· · ·

Miriam nosed her Honda into a parking space and glanced at the clock on the dashboard. "Four in the morning," she mumbled.

After gathering up her purse, she made the trek into the main lobby at Lancaster General. She found her way to the ICU waiting area, where Hannah sat slumped in her seat, asleep with her head resting on Gerald's shoulder.

"Miriam," Gerald said. "You made it."

Hannah yawned and opened her eyes. "Miriam!"

She rose and pulled Miriam into a tight hug. "*Danki* for coming."

Miriam held onto her sister. "You're welcome."

"The nurses know what's going on, so they're going to let you go back to see him," Hannah said. Looping an arm around Miriam's shoulder, she led her toward the rooms.

"Wait," Gerald said, rushing over to them.

Miriam gave him a confused look.

"I wanted to say I'm sorry for treating you badly. I see how quickly we can lose our family and how precious they are. Hannah's been trying to tell us that, but it took *Daed* getting sick for us to realize it." He opened his arms to Miriam. "Would you please forgive me?"

"*Ya*," Miriam whispered, giving him a hug. "It's good to have a brother again."

"I'm glad to have my sister too," he said.

"Okay you two," Hannah said, taking Miriam's arm. "It's four in the morning. We can save this happy reunion for later, *ya*?"

"*Ya*," Gerald agreed. "I'll wait here while you two go see *Daed*."

Miriam followed Hannah back to a small room, where Abraham lay hooked up to a host of machines. He looked so pale, and the machines surrounding him clicked and hummed as if they were working hard to keep him alive.

She said a silent prayer he'd somehow make it through. Despite the hurt he'd caused her, Miriam couldn't bear the idea of losing him after losing her mother and Timothy.

"*Daed*," Hannah said, touching his arm. "*Daed*, Miriam is here. I told her you wanted to see her, and she drove all the way from Indiana."

Abraham's eyes blinked, and he stared at Hannah as if trying to focus on her words. His eyes then cut to Miriam's, and he held his hand out, beckoning her.

Miriam felt a lump swell in her throat as she moved over to him. All of the hurt and anger she'd felt for him dissipated as she stared at the sick, broken man before her on the bed.

He touched her hand and opened his mouth to speak. "M-m-m-ir-ium." His voice was hoarse and his words were garbled. "I'm s-s-s-sorry." He paused as if searching for the words to say. "You're . . . *doch-der. Ich lieb* . . . I . . . I wuv . . . y-y-you."

"It's okay, *Daed*," she said, patting his hand. "Just get well, okay? Don't worry about me."

"No," he said. "I . . . wrong. Hannah . . . right." He paused and reached out, as if trying to grab the words out of the air before him. "I . . . wr-r-rong."

"Please, *Daed*," Miriam said, wiping a tear. "You just get better. I forgive you. You concentrate on getting better."

"You . . . stay," her father said. "P-p-promise. Be in f-f-fam-ily."

Miriam glanced at Hannah, who nodded, encouraging her to make the promise. "I will," Miriam whispered to him. "I'll stay."

"Fat's *gut*," he said, closing his eyes. "Fat's *gut. Vanki*." He then closed his eyes and drifted off to sleep.

Hannah gestured toward the door, and Miriam

followed her out to the hallway. "*Danki*, Miriam. He was so insistent on seeing you that we worried he wasn't going to pull through."

Miriam wiped her eyes. "I think it was good for me too. I'm glad he finally believed me." She and Hannah met Gerald in the waiting area.

"What happened?" he asked.

"*Daed* apologized and begged me to stay here and be part of the family." Miriam's eyes welled with tears, and before she could stop herself, she was sobbing.

"It's okay." Gerald pulled her to him. "You go ahead and cry it out."

When she got control of her emotions, she stepped back and wiped her eyes. "Oh, I've waited so long to hear him say those words that it doesn't seem real."

Hannah rubbed Miriam's arm. "I'm so *froh*. We're finally a family again."

"Will you drive us home now?" Gerald asked. "We can come back to see him later."

"*Ya*." As Miriam walked out to the parking lot between her siblings, she said a silent prayer, thanking God for giving her back her family.

CHAPTER 16

When Miriam awoke in the guest room of Edna's cabin, she heard voices chattering in Pennsylvania *Dietsch* out in the kitchen. She dressed in her jeans and a T-shirt and then stepped through the door, finding Hannah, Edna, and Lilly eating and talking at the table.

"*Gude mariye*, sleepyhead," Edna said with a chuckle. "Join us. We have a lot of food."

"*Danki*," Miriam said, schlepping to the table with a yawn. She nodded a greeting to her sisters and then sat next to Hannah and admired the bountiful spread, including rolls, scrambled eggs, bacon, sausage, and ham. Mirroring most mornings at the cabin, there was enough food to feed the entire Lapp family.

"I was telling Lilly and *Aenti* that *Daed* apologized and made you promise you'll stay here and be a part of the family again," Hannah said, beaming while buttering a roll. "Even Gerald apologized last night. It was a *froh* occasion."

Miriam filled a plate with food. She felt eyes studying her and glancing up, she caught Lilly's gaze. Lilly blushed and cut her eyes to her plate full of bacon.

"Does this mean you're moving back for good?" Edna asked, her tone hopeful.

While her father's words were sweet, Miriam still couldn't see herself building a life in Lancaster. "Well, I, uh . . ." Miriam stammered.

"We'd love to have you here permanently," Hannah chimed in.

"*Ya*, we would," Lilly said, her voice soft.

Miriam studied her younger sister. "What did you say?"

Lilly met her gaze. "We would all like to see you back so we could be a family again."

"Even you?" Miriam asked.

Lilly nodded. "*Ya*. I'm sorry for everything I did to you. I'm sorry I tore you and Timothy apart. It was my fault. All of it."

Miriam's eyes widened. "Why this sudden change of heart with you and *Daed*?"

"It's Hannah. She made us realize how wrong we were." Lilly gestured at their older sister.

Miriam glanced at Hannah, who shrugged as if it were no big deal. Hannah was always humble.

"I mean it, Miriam," Lilly said. "I'm truly sorry. I don't think there's anything I can do to fix things, but I want to start over with you. You and Hannah are my only sisters. You mean so much to me."

Miriam set her fork down and let Lilly's words sink in. Was she dreaming? Was her family finally accepting her back?

Was this a sign from God that she should return to Lancaster?

But I still can't have Timothy. He's marrying someone else.

"What if I talked to Timothy and confessed what I did? Would that help?" Lilly asked.

Miriam shook her head. "No. He made his choice when he proposed to Naomi."

"Can you forgive me?" Lilly asked. "I'm truly sorry, Miriam. I was wrong, so wrong."

"Why did you do it?" Miriam asked. She braced herself for the answer.

Tears filled Lilly's eyes. "I was so selfish and so immature."

"Please, Lilly, just tell me," Miriam said.

Lilly wiped a tear from her eye. "Because you had your choice of men. You had two after you, and I had no one. *Ya*, I had suitors, but I had no one I loved in return. You did, and I was jealous and mean and horrible."

"What?" Miriam's eyebrows knitted together. "What are you talking about? I had Timothy, and he was all I wanted. What do you mean I had two?"

Lilly sniffed and swiped the trail of tears from her cheeks. "Think about it, Miriam. Who has been seeking your hand in marriage since you were seventeen? Who is the one man who has always wanted you and has never looked at me for a second?"

Befuddled, Miriam gave her a palms up. "Lilly, you're speaking in riddles, and I'm too exhausted to understand you. I drove nine hours to get here, and then I slept maybe three hours. What are you saying?"

"Oh, Lilly." Hannah sighed with empathy. "It's Zach, isn't it?"

"*Ya!*" Lilly swallowed a sob. "I've loved Zach since I was fifteen, and he has never, ever noticed me. I tried time and time again to get his attention at worship services, and he would merely say, 'Oh, hi, Lilly,' and then walk past me. He has no interest in me, and yet he's always wanted you, even when you were courting Timothy Kauffman. I was jealous, and I'm sorry, Miriam. I'm so sorry." Lilly buried her face in her hands and sobbed while Edna rubbed her back.

"There, there, *kind*," Edna cooed. "It's okay now."

Miriam looked at Hannah, who gave her a surprised expression in return. Shaking her head, Miriam groaned.

All of this was for Zach.

Never in a million years had Miriam dreamt that Lilly wanted Zach.

"Lilly," Miriam began, "if I had known, I would've helped you with Zach years ago. All you had to do was tell me."

"I'm sorry, Miriam. I'm so sorry," Lilly whispered. "Can you ever forgive me? Please, Miriam? I promise I will never, ever hurt you again. I promise with all my heart."

Miriam sighed. "Of course, I forgive you, Lilly. You're my sister."

"*Danki*," Lilly said, wiping her eyes again. "Will you move back?"

Miriam forked some egg into her mouth while she considered the question. "I don't know. It's a huge decision." Pouring a cup of coffee from the pot in the center of the table, she yawned. "I'm still not awake, so I can't make a decision like that right now."

"Will you take us to see *Daed* today?" Hannah asked before sipping her cup of coffee.

"Of course. I want to see him too," Miriam said.

"Give him my love, will you?" Edna asked. "My hands and knees are painful today."

"*Ya*, we will," Miriam said.

"When are you due back to work?" Edna asked.

"My boss instructed me to take two weeks off, so I have plenty of time here." Miriam sipped the hot coffee. "I'd like to spend more time with everyone."

"*Gut*." Hannah squeezed her hand. "The *kinner* will be so excited to see you. Lena Joy told me she wanted to have another good long talk with you soon. She loves spending time with you."

While her sisters updated her on the latest community news, Miriam savored her breakfast and contemplated their requests for her to stay. She couldn't help wondering what had inspired Lilly to apologize and confess why she fabricated the lies. Was it Hannah's influence or was it something more powerful and divine?

Was God telling Miriam she belonged here and not in Indiana?

• • •

When Miriam and her sisters arrived at the hospital, they found that their father had been moved out of ICU and into a regular room. He was resting in a reclined position.

His face brightened when Miriam and her sisters

entered the room. With his eyes focused on Miriam, he extended his hand and beckoned her to the bed. "Mir-um," he slurred her name in a hoarse whisper. "I . . . afraid I . . . dweamt y-y-y-our visit."

"*Ya*, I was here. I came as soon as Hannah called me." She took his hand and blinked back tears.

Her father looked so exhausted and so old. The stroke had taken a toll on his body. She'd never remembered him looking so pale and frail. All her life, she envisioned her father as a strong-willed, healthy man. But now he looked like a sad, ill, old man.

"Y-you acc%ept my 'pology?" he whispered, stumbling over the words.

"*Ya*," she said. "You just rest. I'll be here a while."

"Will you s-s-stay?" he asked, his tired eyes hopeful. "I . . . n-need . . ." He paused, his expression straining for the words. "Your *mamm* gone now . . . I need fa-fa-mil-y."

Miriam bit her bottom lip and contemplated his words. How ironic that her family had gone from ignoring her to begging her to stay in less than a month. "Let me think about it, okay? I'm not sure where I belong right now."

"You belong here," Hannah said, placing a hand on Miriam's shoulder. "You belong where everyone loves you, and we love you."

But Timothy loves someone else. How can I bear that?

Miriam ignored her threatening tears. "*Danki*," she whispered.

Lilly and Hannah sat in chairs across from her father's bed, and Miriam sat next to the bed, holding her father's hand until he let go.

While Hannah shared a story of Ian and Mary pushing each other down into the mud, Miriam mulled over the idea of moving back. She wished she had the right answer. Did she belong in Pennsylvania or in Indiana?

She was considering the question when the sound of snoring brought her back to the present. She glanced over at Abraham and found him fast asleep. His face was relaxed and content, and she couldn't help but smile.

Footsteps drew Miriam's attention to the doorway, where a man in a white coat stood with a clipboard. He motioned for Miriam and her sisters to follow him to the hallway.

"I'm Dr. Fulton," he said. "I've been following your father's case."

Hannah introduced herself, Lilly, and Miriam to the doctor.

"How's he doing?" she asked.

The doctor hugged the clipboard to his chest. "It was a fairly serious stroke, but I think he's going to do well. I plan to move him to a rehabilitation facility later this week, where he'll learn to walk again. Unfortunately, he has some paralysis in his right arm and leg."

Tears filled Lilly's eyes. "He's paralyzed?"

"Yes, but he'll learn to function after he spends some time in rehab. The therapists there will teach him how to dress and feed himself. He'll do just fine." The doctor examined the chart. "Does Mr. Lapp live alone?" he asked.

"No, I live with him, along with my brother," Lilly said, wiping her eyes.

"Good. I don't think it would be a good idea for him to be alone," the doctor said.

"Does he have to go to rehab? Can't we have someone come to the house?" Hannah asked.

"It would be best if he stayed in the facility in order for him to have around-the-clock care from health professionals. He'll be there for about a month." Dr. Fulton glanced between Miriam and her sisters. "Do you have any more questions?"

Miriam and her sisters shook their heads.

"Your dad will be just fine. It will take him a little while to get back on his feet. Just have patience with him." Dr. Fulton then stepped into the hospital room to see Abraham.

"Should we go down to the cafeteria and get something to drink?" Miriam offered. "Maybe it will do us some good to walk a little bit."

"That's a *gut* idea." Hannah looped her arm around Lilly, who was still sniffing back tears.

They walked in silence to the cafeteria, where Miriam bought each of them a soda. They sat at a corner table and drank in silence.

"I can't believe he's paralyzed," Hannah finally said. "I thought he was strong as an ox."

Miriam nodded. "I did too. It's amazing how life can change in the blink of an eye."

"*Ya*," Lilly said. "*Mamm's* gone, *Daed* had a stroke, and the summer isn't over yet."

"But we still have each other. We have our family." Hannah squeezed their hands. "Family is what matters most."

Lilly looked at Miriam. "I'm so glad to have my sisters and brother."

Miriam smiled, wondering what Hannah could've said to Abraham and Lilly to get them to change their minds about her.

"Gerald said he would visit this afternoon," Lilly continued. "We can head back home soon."

"How long do you think *Daed* will be in rehab?"

Miriam sipped her drink. "Didn't the doctor say a month?"

"*Ya*," Hannah said. "I believe that was it."

"We can take turns going to visit him." Lilly ran her fingers over the condensation on the cup. "I'll care for him when he comes home. I'm making quilts for Naomi's *mamm's* business, so that's no problem."

Miriam's stomach dropped at the mention of Naomi's name. Soon Naomi King would be Naomi Kauffman, and that thought made Miriam ill.

"You don't need to shoulder all of the work when he's home," Hannah said. "We can take turns with him. I'm sure other friends and relatives will visit with him and check on him too."

"We'll figure it out," Miriam said. "I'll help out as much as I can."

"So, have you thought about coming back here for good?" Lilly asked.

"Lilly, she hasn't had much time to consider it," Hannah chided. "It's not the kind of decision you make in a few hours."

"I'm still thinking," Miriam said.

"You should make a list of pros and cons," Lilly said

while fiddling with the straw in her Styrofoam cup. "That's what I do when I have a really serious decision to make."

Miriam nodded. "That's a really smart idea."

Lilly shrugged. "Sometimes I have good ideas."

"We better get back to check on him," Miriam said, standing. "He may wake up and think we abandoned him."

As they headed back to her father's room, Miriam couldn't help but think how wonderful it felt to be a part of the Lapp family once again.

. . .

Later that evening, Miriam sat at the kitchen table and wrote on a notepad by the light of the lantern. At the top of the page, she scrawled "Reasons to stay in Gordonville." In one column, she wrote "Pros" and in the other "Cons."

Gnawing on the end of her pen, she considered the pros and then began to make a list:

Be with family
Help Aenti with chores and expenses
Help Daed with recovery
Help Hannah with kinner
Get to know my nieces and nephew

She rubbed her neck with her hand for a moment and then crafted her con list:

> *Watch Timothy marry someone else*
> *Miss Abby*
> *Give up job in Indiana*
> *Miss friends in Indiana*

"What have you got there, Miriam?" Edna asked, causing Miriam to jump with a start.

"*Aenti*," Miriam said. "I didn't hear you come in."

"Sorry. I guess I snuck out of the bathroom." Edna leaned over Miriam's shoulder and read the list. "Hmm. Looks to me like the pros outweigh the cons."

"You think so?" Miriam asked.

Edna lowered herself into the chair next to her. "*Ya*, I do. I think in your heart your family matters most. From what you've told me, moving to Indiana was the hardest thing you had to do because you had to say good-bye to your family. Now your *daed* and your hurtful younger sister have realized the error of their ways, and they want you back in their lives. That's what you've always wanted. Honestly, I don't see what's holding you back from letting them welcome you into their lives again."

Miriam bit her lower lip and stared at the list.

"It's Timothy Kauffman, isn't it?" Edna's smile was sympathetic. "You love him, and seeing him marry someone else will truly be painful for you."

"*Ya*." Miriam sniffed.

"He's not married yet, Miriam."

"*Aenti*, you know as well as I do that a proposal is as strong a promise as the wedding vows in our community."

"They haven't taken their vows yet. If you tell him how you feel . . ."

"I can't do that." Miriam shook her head. "I can't do that to Naomi. She's good friends with Lilly. Besides, Timothy made his choice."

Edna shrugged. "Suit yourself."

Miriam glanced down at the list. "I just don't know what the right choice is. How will I know if I'm making the right decision?"

"Pray about it," Edna said. "He'll tell you."

"Right." She stared down at the list again. It seemed as if the answer was right there before her, but she couldn't see it.

Edna stood. "*Gut nacht.* I'll see you in the morning." She then began to shuffle toward the bedroom.

Watching her aunt walk slowly and with so much effort suddenly made the answer crystal clear: Miriam was needed right here.

"*Aenti,*" she said.

"*Ya?*" Edna faced her.

"I'm going to stay." She sat up straighter, confident in her decision. "I'm going to meet with the bishop tomorrow and see about being baptized into the faith."

"Oh, Miriam!" Edna sidled up to her and hugged her. "Did you know that the baptism is going to be held at your father's house? Abraham is hosting the baptism service that Sunday in October."

Miriam gasped. "It's a sign from God."

"*Ya.*" Edna cupped her hand to Miriam's cheek. "I believe it is."

"I know I've missed most of the pre-baptism classes

this summer, but maybe the bishop will make a special exception for me since we've lost our *mamm* and *daed* is ill. I can explain that I want to do it as soon as possible so that my *daed* knows I did it while he's still here with us."

"I'm so, so thankful to hear this," Edna said.

"Me too." Miriam smiled. She knew in her heart that this was the right choice.

CHAPTER 17

M iriam sucked in a deep breath and parked her car by the barn behind Bishop Gideon Swartzendruber's farm the following morning. She'd practiced her speech several times during the ride over, but the words had somehow evaporated from her head as soon as she halted her car. This would be a difficult conversation at best. In Miriam's church district, baptisms were performed once every other year before the fall communion service in order to allow the newly baptized to commune with the rest of the church members. Communion was held twice per year—in October and April—as a special daylong service.

Most Amish youth were baptized between the ages of sixteen and twenty-one; however, sometimes community members chose to experience the *English* world before joining, as Miriam had. Instruction sessions were held during the first thirty minutes of church services over the summer months, during which the class members met with the ministers while the rest of the church members sang hymns. The ministers and bishop reviewed the eighteen articles of the Dordrecht

Confession of Faith and emphasized aspects of the *Ordnung*. Four years ago, Miriam had completed the classes and then changed her mind a few days before the baptism. She'd left without consequence since she was never baptized.

The classes were required with rare exception, and Miriam knew she'd missed a good part of them. Therefore, she had to convince the bishop to allow her to make up what she'd missed so that her father could see her baptized as soon as possible.

Miriam's heart thumped in her chest as she yanked the keys from the ignition and climbed from the small sedan. Dressed in the plain black frock, black cape, and apron, she hoped she looked presentable for her impromptu meeting with the bishop. She touched her prayer *kapp* to make certain it was straight.

Rallying her courage, she approached the back door of the house, hoping the bishop was home. Since he ran a dairy farm and also grew crops, she assumed he had plenty to keep him busy at the house.

She knocked on the back door and then waited. A few minutes later, the door creaked open, revealing the bishop, his brow knitted together in confusion.

"Miriam Lapp?" he asked.

"*Gude mariye*," she said, plastering a smile on her nervous lips. "I was hoping to speak with you a few moments."

"*Ya*." He stepped out onto the porch. "I heard your *daed* has taken ill."

"He had a stroke." Miriam absently fingered her apron. "He's in Lancaster General now but is going to be moved to a rehabilitation facility in a few days. One of his arms and a leg are paralyzed."

The bishop folded his arms across his broad chest. "I'm sorry to hear it. I'll go visit him later. Some of the women in the district are putting together meals for your family and will deliver them today. Let us know how else we can help."

"*Danki*." Miriam cleared her throat. "I wanted to speak with you about another matter."

He gestured toward chairs on the porch. "Please, have a seat. Would you like a drink?"

"No, *danki*." Miriam lowered herself into a rocker. "I won't keep you long."

"*Wie geht's?*" he asked, fingering his gray beard.

"I would like to join the church," she said, her body trembling with anxiety and excitement. "I'm ready to be baptized."

His expression was stern. "You know this is a huge commitment, Miriam. You have to renounce all of your worldly possessions." He pointed in the direction of the Honda. "Foremost your car."

She nodded. "I plan to take the car back to Indiana and give it to my *English* friend. I'm ready to live by the *Ordnung* and give my life to Christ."

He rubbed his beard while studying her. "Are you certain?"

"Absolutely. I need to make a trip to Indiana to take care of some things and then I'll be ready to start instruction. I would like to be baptized this year. I know it's going to be held at my *daed*'s house, and it would mean a lot to him to be there. I know this is short notice since the classes are already in session this summer, but I wanted to ask you—no, beg you—for an exception for the sake of my father and his declining health."

The bishop shook his head. "I'm sorry, but I'll have to say no. You've missed too many instructional classes to be baptized this year. You'll have to go to another district next year or wait two years for our next district class."

"Please hear me out." Miriam took a deep breath, collecting her thoughts. "You may think that I ran off four years ago to sample the *English* life without any thought about how my leaving affected my family. However, that's not true."

Gideon held his hand up to stop her from speaking. "I'm in no place to judge you or anyone else. We leave the judgment to God."

"No, wait." She clasped her hands together as tears filled her eyes. "I want to explain. I left not only because I thought I belonged in the *English* world, but also because someone whom I loved had betrayed me. However, I've learned some hard lessons, including that I belong here with my family and the person I love didn't betray me. Losing my mother and almost losing my father taught me even more. Now I know with all my heart that I want to be Amish and I want to be here with my family." With her voice caught, she paused to wipe her eyes.

Clearing her throat, she continued. "My father's health is fragile. His heart is broken after losing my mother and he looks as if he's aged a decade in only a few days because of his stroke. He's finally let me back into his life after four years, and I want to show him

I'm still the girl he remembers. I want to be baptized with the current class. I take my vows seriously, and I'm begging you to let me into that class. Please let me share this moment with my father while he's still alive. I'll make up the classes whenever it's most convenient for you. I'll work hard and show you that I'm dedicated."

Compassion glimmered in the bishop's eyes. "You're absolutely certain about this, Miriam?"

She nodded. "There's no doubt in my mind."

The bishop paused for a moment. "You make that trip to Indiana and then come see me when you get back and we'll begin your instruction," he finally said.

"*Danki.*" Miriam stood and shook his hand. "I'll come see you next week. Have a *gut* day." She started toward the car, her heart pounding with excitement.

"Miriam," he called after her.

She turned, meeting his stern gaze.

"This is a very serious decision," he said. "It's not one to be taken lightly. Once you've joined, you're in for life."

"I know in my heart that it's the right time for me to make the commitment to Christ and my community."

"*Gut.*" His expression softened. "We'll go visit your *daed* later this afternoon."

"*Danki.*" Miriam climbed into her car. As she turned the ignition, bringing her Honda to life, she considered what it would feel like to give up her car, her driver's license, her job at the pediatrician's office, her laptop, her email address, her jeans, and her makeup. Although the sacrifices were great, the reward was so much greater. She would finally be a true part of the

Amish community, the community of her birth and her parents' birth.

Yes, she was ready to give it all up. She was ready to live as a true member of the Lapp family. The thought filled her with a warmth she hadn't experienced in a long time.

Nevertheless, there was one disappointment nagging at her.

If only I could have Timothy by my side.

The thought echoed in her mind as she drove to the Kauffman Amish Bakery. She parked in the lot out front and then headed in the front door, past the loud *English* tourists blocking the small aisles and filling their baskets with pastries and trinkets, including key chains, figurines, dolls, postcards, magnets, and T-shirts.

"Miriam!" Lindsay squealed and rushed around the counter, engulfing Miriam in a tight hug. "It's so good to see you!"

"*Danki.*" Miriam held her tight. "How are you?"

"We've been so busy. Please tell me you're coming back." She pulled away from the hug and examined Miriam's expression. "Please?"

"I need to discuss that with your *Aenti* Beth Anne."

"She's in the back." Lindsay jammed her thumb toward the kitchen. "You know the way."

"*Danki.*" Miriam patted Lindsay's shoulder while stepping past her.

Her smile deepened when she stepped back into the kitchen. While she enjoyed working for the pediatrician in Indiana, she loved the bakery. The sweet smell of icing and apple pie assaulted her senses, causing her stomach to growl.

Miriam's former coworkers were busy at work in the kitchen. Elizabeth was wrapping a pie while Beth Anne pulled a sheet of cookies from an oven. Kathryn was icing a chocolate cake.

Beth Anne spun to face the door, and her eyes widened when they met Miriam's. "Miriam!" Beth Anne rushed over and hugged her. "How are you?"

"*Gut.*" Miriam nodded a greeting to Elizabeth and Kathryn, who both looked surprised to see her. "Could I possibly talk to you in private?"

"Of course." Beth Anne led her to the office, shutting the door behind them. "Have a seat." She gestured toward the chair across from the desk. "*Wie geht's?*"

Miriam lowered herself into the chair. "I'm coming back to stay—permanently."

"Ack, that's *wunderbaar!*" Beth Anne clapped her hands together. "Will you come back to work at the bakery?"

"I'd like to—if you'll hire me again."

"Of course!" Beth Anne patted Miriam's shoulder and then sat in the chair across from her. "May I ask why you decided to come back?"

"My *daed* had a stroke."

"Oh no! I'm so sorry to hear that."

"*Danki.* He has some paralysis, but overall he's okay. He's at Lancaster General and will be moved to a rehabilitation center in a few days to learn to do basic daily tasks, like dressing himself." Miriam cleared her throat, hoping to hold back her emotions. "He asked me to come back. I left because my family had been treating me like a stranger. Only Hannah and *Aenti* Edna have been treating me like family—up until I came back to see my *daed*. Now *Daed*, Lilly, and Gerald have apologized and asked me to be a part of the family again."

"Oh my goodness." Beth Anne's eyes filled with tears. "I don't know what to say. That's a beautiful story. I'm so happy for you." She squeezed Miriam's hands. "I'm glad you're coming back."

Miriam bit her lip, internally debating if she should tell Beth Anne about Lilly's confession.

"What else is on your mind?" Beth Anne's expression was full of concern.

"There's something else Lilly told me, and I want to share it with you. But I don't want to make you uncomfortable."

"Please tell me." Beth Anne's lips curved into a sweet smile. "We're friends. You can be honest with me."

"I wanted to share something Lilly told me just to clear the air between us."

Beth Anne tilted her head in question. "What is it?"

"Lilly fabricated the stories about Timothy cheating on me and vice versa. She was jealous of me, and she wanted to tear Timothy and me apart." Miriam's voice quavered. "I wanted you to know I never did anything to hurt Timothy. I left the community after Jeremy Henderson died because I felt I had nowhere else to go."

Frowning, Beth Anne shook her head. "I'm so sorry your sister caused the breakup."

"*Ya.*" Miriam swiped away an errant tear. "I've

forgiven her, but I have disappointment and regret in my heart." She forced a sad smile. "But I know Timothy and Naomi are going to be married in the fall, and I wish him all of the happiness in the world." *Although I wish I could share that happiness with him.*

"Miriam." Beth Anne took her hand again. "You're a strong woman."

"I can't change the past." Miriam sat up straight. "God is in control, and I need to follow His lead. I'm going to be baptized in October."

Beth Anne's wide smile returned to her lips. "That's *wunderbaar!*"

"*Danki.* I'd love for you to be there."

"I'd love to come and share the special day with you. You just let me know." Beth Anne gestured toward the door. "When would you like to start back here? We need you as soon as you're available."

"I'm going to go back to Indiana tomorrow to tie up some loose ends. I need to get rid of my car, give notice to my employer, and pack up some things. I also need to explain to my cousin Abby exactly what my plans are. I'd like to start when I get back."

Beth Anne nodded. "That sounds perfect."

"My sisters and I will be caring for my *daed,* so I may need a day or two off during the week."

"Family always comes first." Beth Anne smiled. "I'm so *froh* you're coming back. You sounded so sad when you left me the message the day you left. I was worried about you."

"I was very upset. My *daed* had thrown me out of his house, and then Lilly had told me—" Miriam stopped mid-sentence. She was afraid to reveal too much of her feelings about Timothy to Beth Anne. Since Beth Anne was his sister, Miriam didn't want to make her feel uneasy or caught in the middle between them. "Lilly confessed she had lied to Timothy. It was too much for me to handle."

Beth Anne shook her head. "I can't imagine how that betrayal felt."

"I did some soul searching and decided I couldn't stay in a community where my family treated me like a stranger. That's why I left."

"It makes sense. Family members are our most important allies."

Miriam smiled. "It feels *gut* to be back. And I'm so thankful you'll extend the job to me again. *Danki*, Beth Anne. You're a *wunderbaar* friend."

"You're always welcome, Miriam." Beth Anne squeezed her hand again. "Don't forget that."

They chatted for a few moments about how busy the bakery had been and then Beth Anne led Miriam back to the kitchen. "Miriam is coming back to work with us," Beth Anne announced. "She's going to be baptized and join the church too."

"*Wunderbaar*!" Elizabeth rushed over and hugged Miriam. "I'm so *froh* to hear the news."

"That's *gut*," Kathryn said with a smile. "I'm glad to hear it."

Miriam wondered if Hannah had something to do with Kathryn's change of heart or if it was because Timothy had finally moved on with his life and was going to marry someone else.

"*Danki*," Miriam said. "I'll be starting in about a week. I need to travel back to Indiana to take care of a few things. Once I get back, I'll be here for good."

"I'm so *froh* for you," Elizabeth said, squeezing Miriam's hand. "You're welcome here anytime."

"I'll call you when I get back," Miriam said.

"Perfect. Have a safe trip." Beth Anne hugged her again. Heading to her car, Miriam whispered a prayer of thanks to God for her *wunderbaar* friends in Lancaster County.

. . .

Timothy was reading his Bible when a knock sounded at the front door later that evening. He crossed the room, opened the door, and found Beth Anne smiling on the porch with a pie in her hand.

He raised an eyebrow with suspicion. "I've fallen for this before, Beth Anne. You can't possibly think I will again, do you?"

"It's apple pie." She moved the pie back and forth in front of him. "Yum. Smell it? It's *appeditlich*."

He grinned and shook his head. "Incorrigible," he muttered, motioning for her to enter his home. He led her into the kitchen, where he grabbed plates and utensils. "What are we going to discuss this time? Or should I say, what will you lecture me about?"

"What if this is a friendly visit?" she asked, grabbing a knife from a drawer.

"What if I'm a monkey's uncle?"

She laughed while cutting the pie.

"Coffee?" he offered.

"No, thanks. But make it if you'd like some."

He lowered himself into the chair across from her and breathed in the warm, sweet aroma of the pie. "You and *Mamm* are the best bakers I know."

"Miriam is better than me by far." She served him a piece and then licked her fingers.

His stomach twisted.

So, this is about Miriam—again.

He swallowed a groan. He'd been trying in vain to forget Miriam, but her beautiful face filled his mind every time he laid his head on the pillow at night. She'd managed to capture his heart once again.

He forked some pie into his mouth and moaned with pleasure. "You've outdone yourself. It melts in my mouth."

She smirked. "*Danki.*"

"Are you here to discuss her again?" he asked.

"Who?"

He narrowed his eyes with annoyance. "Miriam."

"*Ya.*" She took a bite of the pie. "*Ack*, it is *gut.*"

After another bite, he stared at his sister. "Will you get to the point, please? I haven't got all night. I have to be to work early tomorrow to finish up a big project."

"She came to see me today," Beth Anne said.

His heart thumped in his chest. "Miriam? She's back?"

"Her *daed* had a stroke." She eyed him with suspicion. "Naomi didn't tell you? She's close to Lilly."

"She'd told me about the stroke, but I didn't know Miriam came back."

"Her *daed* finally forgave her for leaving, and Lilly

and Gerald apologized for how they'd treated her. They want her to come back and be a member of the family again."

"And . . . ?" He held his breath for the answer.

"She's coming back to stay and joining the church."

Timothy studied his sister while the words filtered through his mind.

Miriam is back.

She's joining the church.

She's back for good.

The words registered, and his eyes widened.

"There's more." Beth Anne leaned forward, her expression serious. "Lilly confessed she was responsible for your breakup."

He scowled in defense. "What does that mean?"

"She confessed that she made up the lies about Miriam cheating on you and you cheating on her because she was jealous. She fabricated those lies to ruin Miriam's life."

He studied his pie while he considered his sister's words. Unable to speak, he raked his fingers through his hair.

It was true—his plans for a life with Miriam were derailed due to a lie told by Lilly Lapp.

Yet it simply didn't make sense. What would motivate Lilly Lapp to do that? What could she have been jealous about?

However, the truth also didn't change anything. He would stick to his current life plan with Naomi. It was the right and decent thing to do. Timothy Kauffman was a man of his word.

"It doesn't matter," he finally said, meeting Beth Anne's intent gaze. "I've made a promise to Naomi that I intend to keep. It's only right."

Beth Anne paused for a moment. "I just wanted you to know she's going to be back for good, and she'll be working in the bakery."

"What do you mean she'll be back? I thought you said she was already back."

"She's going to Indiana to gather up her things and tie up some loose ends. Once she arrives back in town, she'll work for me in the bakery and help her sisters care for her *daed*. She'll be baptized in October."

He tried in vain to ignore the anxiety roaring through his veins at the thought of seeing Miriam in the bakery. How would he endure daily encounters with her when her brown eyes sent heat coursing through him, head to toe?

"I wish her well," he mumbled, forking more pie.

"Do you?" Beth Anne's stare was penetrating.

"*Ya*, I do." He made idle chitchat about work and how busy the shop was until Beth Anne stood and cleared the dishes. "*Danki* for the pie."

"*Gern gschehne.*"

He followed her to the door. "I'll most likely see you tomorrow."

"*Gut.*" She gave him a coy smile. "I just wanted you to know about Miriam. You know, you're not married yet."

"A promise is a promise."

"Right." She headed down the porch stairs. "*Gut nacht.*"

He echoed the parting words and then slumped against the door frame.

He shook his head with disbelief. Miriam's own sister had ruined their plans to be a family. How could she do it? Jealousy was a sin! It didn't make sense—Lilly had never shown interest in Timothy. Why had she been jealous?

And now Miriam was going to return and finally join the church. He'd never expected that news. How was he going to suppress his feelings for Miriam when she was going to be a member of the bakery staff?

Nevertheless, he needed to be strong—for sweet, innocent Naomi. He could never hurt Naomi the way Miriam had hurt him when she had left without an explanation.

The past was still the past.

Apple Butter Pie

Pastry for 9-inch crust and $1/2$-inch strips for top
$1/2$ cup apple butter
2 eggs, beaten
$1/2$ cup sugar
1 $3/4$ Tbsp cornstarch
1 $1/2$ tsp cinnamon
2 cups milk

Combine apple butter, eggs, sugar, cornstarch, and cinnamon and mix well. Add the milk gradually and blend. Pour into unbaked pie shell. Top with crisscrossed strips of crust. Bake at 350 degrees for 30 minutes.

CHAPTER 18

The following morning, Miriam steered her Honda down the paved driveway toward the Henderson farm, where she had worked for the *English* family as a nanny before she left the community and moved to Indiana. She'd convinced herself the only way to move forward was to face her past. With her heart beating an erratic cadence in her chest, she threw her Honda into Park in front of the barn and climbed from the car. While she was walking toward the back porch, the screen door opened and slammed against the wooden door frame.

Colleen Henderson stepped out onto the porch with a dishtowel in her hand. She looked just as Miriam remembered. Her hair was still shoulder length and a deep auburn. The only difference was a few lines around her eyes, revealing she was on the cusp of forty.

She studied Miriam. Recognition flooded her expression, and a tentative smile curved her lips. "Miriam?" she asked. "Miriam Lapp?"

Miriam cleared her throat and stood at the bottom of the porch steps, uncertain if she should climb them. "I was hoping to speak with you for a moment."

"My! You're all grown up." She waved the dishrag, beckoning Miriam. "Please, come in. Would you like a glass of cold lemonade?"

"*Danki*." Miriam climbed the steps and entered the spacious kitchen.

"How is your family?" she asked, pouring the lemonade into two large glasses from a clear pitcher with a drawing of a lemon on the side.

"*Mamm* passed away about a month ago, and *Daed* is in the hospital. He had a stroke and is partially paralyzed."

Colleen clapped a hand to her mouth. "I'm so sorry. I hadn't heard." She motioned toward the table. "Please sit."

Miriam sank into a chair, and Colleen passed her a glass of lemonade.

"I'm so sorry for all of the tragedy in your family." Leaning across the table, she squeezed Miriam's hand. "I'm sorry for your loss. Your mother was a wonderful lady. She always had a smile, and she never met a stranger."

"*Danki*." Miriam sipped the lemonade, avoiding the tears threatening her eyes.

"How is your father? Was it a massive stroke?"

Miriam cleared her throat, hoping to stop the lump from stealing her voice. "He's partially paralyzed— his arm and leg. But he's going to be transferred to a rehabilitation facility where he'll learn to care for himself—like how to dress and feed himself. My sisters and I will take turns caring for him when he comes home."

Colleen nodded. "I'd heard you left the community after—we lost Jeremy."

Miriam scanned the large, open kitchen as the events that transpired that day, the day that changed her life forever, returned to her. She'd been making chocolate chip cookies as a treat for Colleen and Trevor. Nearly four years later, Miriam could still smell the warm, sweet, freshly baked fragrance.

She'd been leaning over the oven to retrieve the cookie sheet when a soft knock sounded at the front door. After grabbing the cookie sheet and placing it on the rack to cool, she hurried to the front door, where she found Timothy frowning on the front porch. A shiver gripped Miriam's spine at the memory of that fateful conversation, the words of which ripped Miriam and Timothy apart for good.

Earlier in the day, Lilly had told Miriam that Timothy was cheating on her. Therefore, when Timothy arrived to tell Miriam he couldn't go with her to meet the bishop and discuss their wedding plans, Miriam had assumed Timothy was meeting his other girlfriend.

Miriam was cold to Timothy, saying she didn't believe he had to help his father with an important project at home. They'd argued, and he'd left in a huff.

If only Miriam had known then that Lilly had started those rumors about Timothy's cheating, then maybe, just maybe, Miriam and Timothy could've saved their relationship.

After Timothy had left, Miriam had rushed back into the house and burst into tears in the kitchen. Standing by the counter, she studied the monitor, noticing that Jeremy hadn't awakened for his four o'clock feeding. She rushed upstairs to his room and found he was eerily silent and still.

When she touched his body, it was cool, and he wasn't breathing. She had tried in vain to wake him, calling his name and gently shaking him. When he remained unresponsive, she had panicked, and with tears streaming down her cheeks, she called nine-one-one, praying and begging God to let little Jeremy be okay.

Please, God. Please let him be okay. Please protect him, God.

She called Colleen and, with a trembling voice and tears splattering her cheeks, told her to come home.

The emergency medical technicians had arrived at the same time as Colleen and Trevor, but it was too late. Jeremy was already gone.

Miriam could still see the hurt and blame in Colleen's eyes when she demanded to know why Miriam hadn't checked on her baby sooner.

"Miriam?" Colleen asked, breaking through Miriam's memories. "Are you okay?"

Miriam wiped a stream of tears from her hot cheek. "*Ya.*" Her voice quavered. "Just memories."

Colleen's genuine smile sent relief flooding through Miriam's heart. "Oh, Miriam, please don't blame yourself for what happened."

"I've worried about you and Trevor constantly the past four years," Miriam whispered, her voice thick while she studied the wood grain on the kitchen table. "I prayed for you both every day. I'm so sorry I wasn't in his room when he stopped breathing. I've replayed that day a thousand times in my mind, thinking of what I should've done differently. I should've sat outside his room and listened to him sleeping. I never should've answered the door when Timothy stopped by. I never should've stood out there and argued with—"

"Shhh." Colleen touched Miriam's hand. "Look at me."

Miriam met her gaze.

"Was that why you left? Because of what happened to Jeremy?"

Miriam nodded, swiping away another tear. "That was a good part of why I left."

Colleen shook her head, her eyes filling with tears. "I'm so sorry for that. It wasn't your fault."

Miriam raised an eyebrow. "What do you mean?"

"I was wrong, dead wrong, to blame you. Can you forgive me?"

"Forgive you?" Miriam let the words soak in. "Who am I to forgive you when I was negligent and allowed your child to pass away?"

Colleen wiped away her own tears. "See, that's where you're wrong. You were our scapegoat for our sadness and guilt, and really no one was to blame. What happened to Jeremy was no one's fault. He died of Sudden Infant Death Syndrome." She sniffed and cleared her throat. "There was nothing anyone could've done."

Miriam sucked in a breath. "So, you don't blame me?"

Colleen shook her head. "No. We were wrong to blame you. I wished I could've contacted you and told you, but I didn't know where you were. I always wished I could've apologized."

Miriam felt an invisible weight lift from her heart. The Hendersons forgave her.

A baby's cry rang through the kitchen. Confusion ringing through her, Miriam looked at Colleen.

Colleen smiled and gestured toward a baby monitor on the counter. "That's Deanna."

"Deanna?" Miriam shook her head. "I don't understand."

Colleen stood and pointed toward the stairs. "Come with me. She'd love to meet you."

Miriam followed Colleen upstairs, where they entered the bedroom across from Jeremy's former room. The room was decorated in pink with white lacy curtains. A white crib sat in the center of the room, and a little blonde girl stood in the crib, holding onto the sides and jumping up and down while giggling.

"She's beautiful," Miriam whispered, tears filling her eyes.

"Thank you." Colleen beamed. "Deanna, this is my friend Miriam. Miriam, this is Deanna Nicole Henderson. She's almost fifteen months." She glanced at Miriam. "Would you like to hold her?"

Miriam hesitated and then smiled. "Yes, I would." She lifted the little girl into her arms. "It's nice to meet you, Deanna." She inhaled the baby's fresh scent of lotion and soap.

Colleen directed Miriam to the changing table and changed Deanna's diaper. Miriam then followed Colleen downstairs and strapped Deanna into the highchair while Colleen poured juice into a Sippy cup.

Miriam sat in a chair next to the baby and stared at

her, marveling how much life had changed since she'd left the community. Jeremy was gone, but a beautiful, healthy little girl had joined the Henderson family.

"Are you visiting for a while?" Colleen asked, handing the Sippy cup to Deanna, who squealed and put it in her mouth.

"Actually, I'm moving back. I'm heading to Indiana to take care of a few things, and then I'm coming back to stay and join the church."

"That's wonderful." Colleen sat in a chair across from her and then asked how Miriam's siblings were doing, and Miriam filled her in on each of her siblings' lives.

While she spoke, Miriam touched Deanna's warm, chubby hand, and her thoughts wandered back to memories of Jeremy. Deanna had the same gray blue eyes and chubby cheeks as her brother. She hoped Colleen and Trevor were blessed with as many healthy children as their hearts desired.

After a while, Miriam glanced at the clock and found it was close to ten. "I better get going. I have a long ride ahead of me." She touched Deanna's arm before she rose and took the empty glasses to the counter. "*Danki* for inviting me in and visiting with me. It's so *gut* to talk to you." She glanced at the little girl. "It was so nice to see you, Deanna. You're a sweet girl."

Colleen opened her arms, inviting Miriam for a hug. "Come here."

Miriam walked into the hug and sighed. "*Danki*."

"No, thank you," Colleen said, patting Miriam's back. "I hope you'll visit again soon. I'd love for you to get to know Deanna."

"I'd like that."

Colleen walked Miriam to her car and they chatted about the weather for a few minutes before Miriam climbed in and backed out of the driveway. She tooted the horn when she merged onto the main road.

Motoring down the highway, Miriam smiled and whispered thanks to God for lifting the burden from her heart. Then she thanked Him for giving Colleen and Trevor a beautiful daughter to help heal their hearts after the tragedy of losing their sweet Jeremy.

. . .

Miriam unlocked the door to the apartment she shared with Abby at seven-thirty that evening. Stepping into the small foyer, she dropped her duffle bag with a loud thump.

"Hello?" she called. "Abby?"

"Hey!" Abby came through the kitchen and hugged Miriam. "How's your dad?"

Miriam nodded. "He's doing okay. He's going to be moved to a rehab center so he can learn how to do some things on his own, like feed himself."

"Good." Abby rubbed Miriam's arm. "I've been worried about you and your family."

"Thanks."

"Now what are you doing back here so soon?" Abby asked, looking curious. "I thought you were staying two weeks?"

"I have some news." Miriam glanced toward the kitchen. "But I'd love something to eat first."

"I've got some leftover pizza I can throw in the microwave for you." Abby lifted Miriam's bag and carried it to her bedroom, where she dropped it in the doorway.

"*Danki*, Abby," Miriam said, fiddling with her purse strap on her way to the kitchen. "I was going to call but then I thought I could just show up and surprise you."

"Oh really?" Abby gave her a suspicious look while slapping a piece of pizza onto the paper plate and placing it in the microwave. After slamming the door, she punched a few buttons, and the microwave hummed in response. "You seem anxious. This must be a great story."

The microwave beeped, and Abby tossed the plate onto the small table.

Miriam lowered herself into a chair in front of the pizza. "How have things been?"

"You're changing the subject." Abby sat across from her, eyeing her. "What's going on? It's not like you to just get in the car and drive to Indiana. You're up to something."

Miriam took a bite of the pizza, fanning the air when it burned the roof of her mouth. Popping up, she rushed across the kitchen and fetched a cold can of Diet Coke from the refrigerator. She gulped down nearly half the can, wishing the burning sensation would subside.

Abby shook her head as Miriam sat across from her. "You always do that. You need to learn to let pizza cool down."

Miriam sipped more soda. "I know."

"Now spill it. What's up?"

"I'm moving back to Gordonville, and I'm joining the church." She waited for the explosion from her cousin.

"You're *what*?" Abby's eyes widened. "Are you crazy?"

"Maybe so, but I feel in my heart it's the right thing to do."

"Why this sudden decision?"

"My family has forgiven me." Miriam sat up straighter, despite her cousin's wary gaze. "My *daed* asked me to stay. He apologized for how he's treated me. Lilly apologized and admitted that she'd lied to split Timothy and me up."

Abby frowned. "And you forgave her? She completely ruined your life, and you're going to just forgive her and move back to Gordonville like you're one big, happy family?"

"You remember what the Bible says in Luke 6:37, 'Do not judge, and you will not be judged. Do not condemn, and you will not be condemned. Forgive, and you will be forgiven.'"

"You've got to be kidding me," Abby deadpanned. "Your own sister sabotages your life, and you're going to sit here quoting Bible verses about forgiveness? What she did is worse than taking the last whoopie pie and then lying and saying the dog ate it."

Miriam took a deep breath, collecting her thoughts. She knew Abby would be against the idea. "You're right. What Lilly did was worse than wrong—it was horrible. However, she's my sister, and I want my family back."

Abby's expression remained unconvinced. "You know you can't change your mind after you're baptized.

If you leave the community, you'll be shunned, and then your family won't have much to do with you."

"I know that, but I don't plan to leave. I feel I belong there." Miriam took another bite of pizza and tried to ignore the sting as the pizza hit the roof of her mouth. "Colleen Henderson forgave me too."

Abby's eyebrows shot up in question. "You went to see Colleen Henderson?"

Nodding, Miriam smiled. "I stopped by her house on my way here. She has a beautiful baby girl, Deanna, who's about fifteen months old now. God has blessed her with happiness after taking Jeremy."

Abby shook her head. "Wow. That's a miracle."

Miriam took another drink.

"I guess everything is working out for you," Abby said. "Your family has forgiven you and you've made amends with the Hendersons. So you came back to say good-bye to boring ol' me, huh?"

Miriam met Abby's sad eyes. Guilt coursed through her. "I promise I'll visit."

Abby rolled her eyes. "Yeah, right. Like I haven't heard that a hundred times from my sisters who have never come once to see me."

"I'm not one of your sisters." Miriam touched Abby's hand. "You know I love you. I promise I'll come visit and you can come see me too. Hannah, *Aenti*, and I would love for you to come. You know that's true, Abby."

Abby's expression became serious. "I don't want you to get hurt again by Lilly or by Timothy. He's engaged to marry Naomi. You know that's a promise that isn't often broken in the Amish community, Miriam. Don't set yourself up for heartache."

Miriam nodded with emphasis. "I know that. I'm going back to be with my family." She sighed, thinking of Timothy and his electric smile. "It won't be easy, but I'll get used to seeing Timothy with Naomi."

Abby sighed. "Just be sure this is what you want."

Miriam smiled. "I will. Thank you for worrying about me. Now, how have things been here?"

They moved on to a discussion about mutual friends in Indiana.

When Miriam began to yawn, Abby nodded toward her bedroom. "I think it's time for you to hit the hay. You've got a lot of packing to do tomorrow."

Miriam swallowed another yawn. "You're right." She squeezed Abby's hand. "Thank you for taking me under your wing when I left Gordonville and came here. You've been like a sister to me."

Abby chuckled. "You don't have to thank me. That's what cousins are for."

"I won't forget it. You're a blessing in my life." Miriam stood. "*Danki.*"

"Yeah, yeah." Abby rose from her chair. "You can just say thank you. No need to get all Amish on me."

Chuckling, Miriam hugged her. "I hope you'll come visit me too."

"We'll see." Abby patted her back. "Just make sure you're making this decision for you, not because your family is pressuring you."

"I know in my heart that this is the path God has chosen for me. It feels right." Miriam tossed the empty plate in the trash can. "I'm going to go see Lauren tomorrow to tell her I'm not coming back to work. She once asked about buying my car for her daughter, so I'm going to see if she still wants it."

"You're going to sell your car?" Abby leaned on the counter. "How are you going to get back to Pennsylvania?"

"The train." Miriam laughed. "There are other modes of transportation besides cars."

"You love that car." Abby shook her head, her eyes full of awe. "You're serious about this."

"*Ya.* I am. Good night." Miriam headed toward her bedroom. After changing into her nightclothes, she scanned the room and wondered how she would manage to sort through all of the things she'd collected since moving to Indiana. She knew her Amish relatives were on the right track by not hoarding too many material things. She then crawled into bed and fell asleep, dreaming of what life would be like when she moved back to Lancaster County—for good this time.

. . .

"You're leaving permanently?" The following morning Lauren sat at her desk across from Miriam, her eyes wide with shock. "I only wanted you to take a couple of weeks off, not start a new life back in Pennsylvania."

Miriam bit her lip, hoping her boss would understand. "I know, but my relatives want to start over. We're going to work things out and be a family again. That's what I've always wanted."

Lauren's lips formed a sad smile. "I can understand that, but I'm sure going to miss you."

"Thank you." Miriam leaned on the desk. "Remember when you told me that if I ever decided to sell my car you would buy it for Kaitlyn?"

"You want to sell it?" Lauren raised her eyebrows. "You sure?"

"Absolutely. I can't have a car or a license when I join the church. I have to give up all worldly possessions. I'm ready to sell it to you today."

"Oh." Lauren nodded. "I'd love to have it. Kaitlyn has been really good about keeping her grades up, and she's been saving for a car. She may even have enough for half of the sale price already in her savings account. Let me talk to my husband, and I'll get you a cashier's check. How about I call you tomorrow?"

"That would be great." Miriam sighed. "I'm really going to miss you."

"If you ever change your mind for whatever reason, you always have a job here waiting for you."

"Thank you." Miriam leaned across the desk and hugged her. "I appreciate all you've done for me."

Lauren glanced at the clock. "How about I take you to lunch since you didn't give me time to plan a going-away party for you? It's almost eleven, so we can make it an early lunch—unless you have plans."

"No, I don't." Miriam shook her head. "I just have to stop by the bank and close out my accounts. I can do that on the way home."

"Great." Lauren stood. "Let me just tell the girls up front."

While Lauren disappeared out of the office, Miriam glanced around, remembering her first visit to the large room when she interviewed for the job. She'd felt so out of her element and lost. Yet, Lauren had given her a chance and taught her everything she now knew about running the front of a doctor's office. Miriam had loved the job and cherished her friendship with the patients and other members of the staff. It would be bittersweet to say good-bye to the friends who'd become her surrogate family.

"Okay, let's go," Lauren said, crossing to the desk and snatching her purse from the bottom drawer. "The girls said you'd better stop by and see them before you leave."

"I will," Miriam said, following Lauren into the hall.

Stepping into the front office, tears filled Miriam's eyes. She hugged each of her former coworkers and thanked them for their friendship.

She followed Lauren out to her car and silently thanked God for the wonderful friends she'd made in Indiana.

CHAPTER 19

Timothy steered the horse toward Naomi's house. He stared out the windshield of the buggy, trying in vain to concentrate on his passenger in the seat beside him.

"Supper was *appeditlich*," Naomi said, her voice cheery. "*Danki* for inviting me."

"Of course," Timothy said, glancing at her smile. "I'm glad you could join me and my family. My *mamm* always enjoys having you."

While Naomi yammered on about stories his sisters had been swapping, Timothy's thoughts wandered back to Miriam for what seemed like the hundredth time this evening. He couldn't stop wondering why she'd decided to move back to Gordonville and join the church. Was her family the real reason? Or did she think somehow they could get back together?

He pushed that thought aside since it was a moot point. He'd made a promise to Naomi, and he intended to keep it. As Miriam had said, Timothy was her past, and their relationship was in the past.

If she was his past, then why couldn't he get Miriam out of his head?

"Timothy?" Naomi asked. "Are you still with me? You're distracted again."

"I'm here," he said, hoping his thoughts weren't transparent. "It's been a long day for me."

"*Ya*, it has." She sighed. "It was nice getting to spend more time with you. Before you know it, we'll be spending a lot more time together." She squeezed his arm. "I can't wait."

He forced a smile. "It's coming up fast."

He wished he could be more excited about their wedding. It bothered him that he wasn't more enthralled about bringing Naomi home the night of their wedding. When he'd talked to Daniel, his older brother shared that he had often looked forward to his first days in his home with his new bride. Why didn't Timothy possess those feelings for Naomi?

Was he making a mistake marrying a young woman with whom he wasn't completely in love?

Timothy turned his thoughts toward maneuvering the buggy up the long rock lane to Naomi's parents' home.

"Lunch tomorrow?" Naomi asked. A smile grew on her face. "I'll bring you something special."

"That would be nice." He took her hand in his. "*Danki* again for having supper with my family and me."

"They'll be my family soon." Her expression turned expectant, and she sucked in a breath.

He knew she wanted a kiss, and he wished he were more excited about fulfilling the request. Leaning down to her, he cupped her face in his hands.

I wish you were Miriam.

The thought caught him off guard. He stared at Naomi's face.

Her eyes widened with worry. "What's wrong?"

"Nothing." He pushed a lock of hair that had escaped her *kapp* back from her face. "I was just thinking about how beautiful you are." He was ashamed of how easy his lips blurted out the fib.

Lying is a sin.

Her cheeks blushed crimson. "*Danki*," she whispered, shifting closer to him.

Leaning down, he brushed his lips across hers.

"I love you." Her words came in a tentative whisper.

"*Ich liebe dich*," he echoed, wishing with all his heart that the words were true.

Her expression brightened. "Lunch tomorrow?"

"I look forward to it." He began to open his door.

"No, no." She placed her hand on his. "I can find my way to the porch alone. You get on home. It's getting late and you must rise early. *Gut nacht*."

"*Gut nacht*." He watched her head up the steps of the porch and wave before disappearing into the house.

While he drove home, his thoughts were stuck on Miriam. He wondered about her visit to Indiana and when she would return. He thought about her baptism. Would she meet a thoughtful and understanding Amish man after she was a member of the church? Would she marry this unnamed man and have a large family?

The thought caused his stomach to tighten. Why should he care about Miriam's future?

Because it was Lilly who ruined their future

together, not Miriam. Their future was stolen—no, commandeered—by lies.

But then again, his lies to Naomi were no better.

He quickly dismissed that thought. To him, faithfulness to a promise was more important than truthfulness.

Another question struck him: Was God giving them a second chance by inspiring Miriam to come back to the community and join the church?

The question hovered in Timothy's mind as his mother's kitchen came into view. The lantern glowed in her window, signaling she was still awake and probably cleaning up from supper. He steered his horse toward the house, then dismounted and tethered the horse to the hitching post out front.

He climbed up to the back porch and stepped into the kitchen, finding his parents chatting at the table.

"Timothy," Eli said. "What brings you back here?"

"Just took Naomi home." Timothy tossed his straw hat onto the peg by the door. "I saw your light on and thought I'd stop in. Everyone left?"

"*Ya.*" Elizabeth patted the chair next to her. "Sit. You look like the weight of the world is on your shoulders. What's troubling you?"

Timothy lowered himself into the chair. "I'm wondering if I made the right decision with Naomi."

"What do you mean?" Elizabeth's eyes were full of concern. "Marriage?"

In an effort to avoid their shocked stares, Timothy traced a pattern in the top of the table Eli had built as a wedding gift for Elizabeth. "How do you know if it's right?"

Eli chuckled. "Cold feet, eh?"

Frowning, Timothy met his gaze. "It feels like more than that. I don't think I'd feel cold feet in my heart."

Elizabeth squeezed his shoulder. "Naomi is a *wunderbaar maedel*. She'll make a *wunderbaar fraa* for you."

"I don't doubt that. She's a *wunderbaar* friend. I trust her completely, but I doubt how I feel." He pointed to his chest. "How do I know if she's right for me?"

Elizabeth smiled. "Don't put so much pressure on yourself. Marriage is a big adjustment. Your doubts will disappear when the wedding is over, and you're settled in your home together." Timothy grimaced. His mother was making it sound so simplistic, but his doubts ran deep into his soul.

Eli's smile faded. "What's really bothering you?"

"I feel like I should be more excited about the wedding and about having her with me at home. I even talked to Daniel about it, and he said he was ecstatic before marrying Rebecca." He slumped back in the chair and crossed his arms in front of his chest. "I'm really beginning to think I made a mistake. Everyone was pressuring me to get married. Beth Anne gave me a lecture about stringing Naomi along. I felt like I had to do it or let Naomi go. Now that it's done, I keep thinking I moved too fast."

Elizabeth's expression was pensive. "Is this about Miriam?"

Caught red-handed.

Timothy couldn't respond.

"You've moved on with your life, and you're marrying Naomi, who loves you with all her heart. I can see the love shining in her eyes when she's with you. Let your doubts about her disappear and concentrate on your future with your bride-to-be." Elizabeth rose and crossed the kitchen. "Would you like a drink?"

"*Ya. Danki.*" Timothy sat up straighter. "If I've truly moved on, then how come I can't get Miriam out of my head?"

"It's only natural." Elizabeth poured a glass of ice water and brought it to the table. "You finally reconnected with her after all those years. You'll get over her. Before you know it, you won't think twice when you see her at the bakery. She'll just be another baker."

I doubt that.

"It feels wrong to be thinking of Miriam when I should be thinking of my future with Naomi. How do I turn off those thoughts?" Timothy sipped his water and then glanced at his father, hoping for his usual words of wisdom.

"You love Miriam?" Eli asked.

Timothy opened his mouth, but no words escaped.

Elizabeth gave Timothy's hand a reassuring pat. "Your love for Naomi will grow and mature with time. You're friends now, but the best marriages grow from friendship." She smiled at Eli. "Our love started out as a friendship."

Timothy watched the smiles passing between his parents and wondered if he'd ever have that with Naomi.

"Naomi deserves someone who knows for certain that he really loves her." The words surprised Timothy when they left his lips.

"You're worried about being a *gut* husband, and you will be," Elizabeth insisted. "You're *gut*, honest, and loyal, just like your *dat*. Believe in yourself, Timothy. I believe in you."

"It's not that." Timothy stared at the water swirling in his glass.

"Miriam and you weren't a good combination. It was rocky from the start."

His gaze snapped to hers. "Why do you say that?"

"It's just a feeling I had." Elizabeth shrugged. "Miriam always seemed to want other things. She didn't want to live out on this farm. She always talked about being a nurse, and then she left you heartbroken."

Resentment bubbled up inside him. "We were young. Besides, it was Lilly who broke us up. She told me Miriam was cheating on me, and she told Miriam I was cheating on her. If we were broken up by a lie, then who is to say that we weren't meant to be together?"

"Beth Anne and I only meant for you to work through your feelings for Miriam when we encouraged you to talk to her." His mother's expression softened, and she touched Timothy's arm. "You belong with Naomi, and you've made a promise to her. Let Miriam's memory go."

"I can't control the thoughts in my head," he said. He sipped his drink and glanced at the clock on the wall. It was nearly eight-thirty. "I reckon I should head home. It's getting late." Gulping down the rest of the drink, he stood and placed the empty glass in the sink. "*Danki* for the drink. I'll see you tomorrow. *Gut nacht*."

"*Gut nacht*," Elizabeth called.

Timothy stepped out onto the porch and inhaled the sweet night air. He glanced toward his house and tried to imagine sitting out on his own porch late at night with Naomi by his side, humming to herself.

The image felt forced, not genuine.

A door slammed, and Eli sidled up to him, lantern in hand. "Let's take the horse to the barn."

Timothy and Eli walked in silence to the barn. After putting up the horse and buggy, they stood in the doorway, gazing at the house.

"Your *mamm* means well," Eli said, breaking the heavy silence. "She thinks she knows what's best for our *kinner*. She only wants you to be *froh*."

Timothy leaned against the door frame. "I know."

"But you need to do what feels right to you." His father's expression was solemn. "Only you know what's in your heart."

Timothy studied Eli's tired eyes. "Did you know it was right when you married *Mamm*?"

A grin spread on Eli's face. "I was sure as the sunrise. Your *mamm* was my best friend. I'd known her since we were *kinner*, and our friendship grew to so much more."

"So you had no doubts at all?"

Eli shrugged. "I was *naerfich*, but I had no doubts. I knew I wanted to build a life with her."

Timothy stared down the lane to his dark house. "I need a sign. I need to know I'm doing the right thing."

Eli patted his shoulder. "You'll know. God will tell you. Just listen with your heart."

Timothy blew out a frustrated sigh. "*Gut nacht.*"

"See you tomorrow," Eli said, locking the barn. "*Gut nacht.*"

Timothy stalked down the lane toward his house with Eli's words echoing in his mind. He hoped he'd be listening when God revealed the answer to him.

CHAPTER 20

M iriam knelt on the floor of her bedroom in the apartment and closed up another box. She snatched a black marker and scrawled "DONATE" across the lid and then pushed the box against the wall, lining it up next to six other boxes ready for the local charities. She glanced around the small room and found most of it bare.

Almost done.

"Wow," Abby said, leaning on the door frame. "Looks like it did when you moved in." She nudged one of the boxes with the toe of her loafer. "Boy, you've got an awful lot to donate. Are you taking anything to Pennsylvania?"

"Not much." Miriam sat on the floor and crossed her legs. "Those boxes have my clothes, shoes, CDs, and DVDs. You know, stuff I can't wear or listen to." She nodded toward the closet. "My nicer clothes are in there. I thought you might like to look through them."

Abby crossed to the closet and examined the contents. Fishing out a red dress, she held it in front of herself and turned toward the full-length mirror. "This is nice." She faced Miriam and frowned. "You sure you want to do this?"

"*Ya*, I am. I've done a lot of soul-searching, and that's where I belong." Miriam pulled a shoebox out from under her bed and gasped. "Oh my gosh. I'd forgotten about this."

"What is it?" Abby asked, leafing through the clothes in the closet.

"These are some mementos I'd brought from Gordonville." She pulled out a couple of letters from Hannah and a rock Gerald had brought back from the creek. She moved around a few more letters and came to an envelope that caused her heart to thump in her chest.

Lifting it, she held her breath. "Miriam" was written in perfect script across the front. She opened it, and dried petals from a daisy, her favorite flower, fell like crumbs onto her lap as she opened the letter, which read:

My dearest Miriam,

I hope this letter finds you well. It's been four days since I've seen you, and it feels as if my heart will break. I hope you can meet me Saturday after your chores are done. When I think of you, my heart races in my chest as if I've chased my brothers across the backfield. I can't wait until the fall. After we're married, we can spend all of the time in the world together, and we won't have to worry about getting you home in time to avoid the wrath of your father.

Don't forget I love you more than all of the stalks of corn in Old Man Yoder's field.

Yours forever,
Timothy

Miriam wiped a tear and read it again.

"What do you have there?" Abby stepped over to her with a black skirt and purple blouse slung over her arm.

"A letter." Miriam folded it and stuffed it along with the dried petals into the envelope, hoping to avoid another lecture. "Nothing important."

"Apparently it *is* important." Abby tossed the clothes onto the bed and reached for the envelope. "Give it here."

Miriam stuffed it back into the box. "It's personal." She placed the shoebox into the bottom of an empty large packing box.

"From Timothy, huh?" Abby shook her head and stepped back to the closet. "You need to let that one go."

If only I could . . .

Miriam placed a few books into the packing box.

"What time does your train leave tomorrow?" Abby asked.

"Ten," Miriam said, filling the box with more books and letters.

"I guess Lauren got your car today?"

"*Ya.* She brought the check by this evening. Her daughter is thrilled." Miriam opened the bottom drawer in her bureau and sifted through photo albums and books.

"I'm really going to miss you," Abby said.

Miriam met her sad gaze. "We'll keep in touch. I promise."

Abby held up an armful of clothes. "I'll take these if you don't want them."

Miriam nodded. "Enjoy them."

While Abby moved the clothes into her closet,

Miriam finished packing up the last of the items in her room. Glancing at the clock, she found it was close to one in the morning. She said good night to Abby, took a quick shower, and then fell into bed, dreaming of what her life would be like back home in Gordonville.

• • •

"I guess this is it, Cousin," Abby said, pulling Miriam into a hug while they stood in the train station the following morning. "You're going to abandon me."

Miriam sniffed back tears. "Not abandoning. Just starting a new life. We'll have to visit each other and write letters."

"Yeah." Abby swiped her hand across her wet cheeks. "You better go or you'll miss your train."

Miriam squeezed Abby's arm and then hoisted her purse onto her shoulder. "You behave."

"Where's the fun in that?" Abby chuckled and sniffed back more tears. "You take care of yourself. And if you change your mind, you're always welcome back at my apartment."

"Thanks, but I'm sure I won't change my mind." Miriam gave her one last hug. "Thanks for being my best friend."

"No," Abby whispered in her ear. "Thank you."

Stepping away, Miriam gave a wave and then rushed to the gate for her train. Once she was settled in her seat, Miriam sat back and closed her eyes. She hoped she was making the right choice, and she asked God to guide her in her new life.

. . .

Miriam stepped into the chaotic concourse of the Lancaster station, wheeling her suitcase behind her. She'd shipped her boxes and brought only her essentials with her on the train. She glanced across at the overhead signs, searching for the taxi area. Weaving through the knot of passengers, she moved toward the exit and stopped dead in her tracks when she spotted Hannah and Lilly waving and grinning while running toward her.

"We found you!" Hannah wrapped her arms around Miriam's neck. "We were worried we missed you and you already got a taxi home."

"What are you doing here?" Miriam asked, hugging her back.

"We wanted to surprise you." Lilly hugged her when Hannah stepped back. "We didn't want you to ride home alone. Everyone's at the house waiting for you. We're so excited you're here."

"Lilly!" Hannah scolded. "That was supposed to be a surprise."

"Sorry." Lilly shrugged. "I couldn't wait to tell her."

"Tell me what?" Miriam looked between her sisters while Hannah glared and Lilly grinned.

"You'll see." Lilly took the handle of the suitcase and dragged it toward the door. "Our driver is waiting. Let's get you home."

Miriam smiled to herself while following them to the car. She already felt like a part of the family, and it warmed her soul.

Lilly loaded the suitcase, and Miriam greeted the *English* driver.

"How's *Daed*?" Miriam asked as they climbed into the van.

"Doing *gut*," Hannah said, slipping on her safety belt. "It looks like he may come home in a few weeks. The rehabilitation is going much better than the doctors had predicted. He's already feeding himself."

"*Wunderbaar!*" Miriam snapped her safety belt. "I can't wait to see him."

"He's asked about you," Lilly chimed in. "He'll be *froh* to see you. We told him you were coming back."

"What have I missed since I left?" Miriam asked, sinking back into the seat and yawning.

Hannah gave all the family news and then Lilly chimed in with community tidbits, rambling on about families in the surrounding area.

When they pulled up to their father's house, Miriam was surprised to find the first floor ablaze with lights. "Who's home?" Miriam asked, climbing from the van.

"You'll see." Lilly's grin was wide while she pulled the suitcase from the trunk.

Hannah paid the driver. "I figured you knew since Little Sister can't keep her mouth shut."

"I can't help being excited." Lilly started toward the house with the suitcase wheels crunching over the rocks behind her. "It's great to have the whole family back together."

Miriam trailed Lilly toward the porch. She climbed the stairs and entered the kitchen, where she found Edna, Gerald, Hannah's husband, Aaron, their children, and a few neighbors waiting. Sweet aromas of desserts emanated from the sea of plates cluttering the counter.

"*Willkumm heemet!*" they all yelled.

"*Danki*," Miriam said, tears spilling from her eyes. "It's so *gut* to be home."

. . .

Miriam walked next to Lilly down the hallway in the rehabilitation center the following afternoon. Her heart thumped in her chest when they reached Abraham's door.

"What if he's not happy to see me?" she whispered to Lilly. "What if he changed his mind about my moving back here?"

Lilly rolled her eyes and waved off the comment. "He's asked about you every time I came to visit the few days while you were gone. He's *froh* you're moving back. Trust me."

Lilly stepped into the room and greeted Abraham while Miriam stayed in the doorway. Lilly stepped over to the recliner where he sat and kissed his cheek.

His gaze met Miriam's, and his brown eyes brightened. "Ma-ma-miriam!" He gestured for her to come in. "*K-k-k-kumm!*"

Miriam smiled and crossed the room, silently analyzing her father. His pale skin and tired eyes caused him to resemble a man of seventy-five, rather than his real age of fifty-eight years old. His genuine smile touched her heart.

"How are you?" she asked, taking his cold hand in hers. "You look *gut*."

"Wa-want . . . t-t-to go . . . h-h-home." He glanced at Lilly as if awaiting permission. "Food ish ba-ba-ba," he said. His speech was slow and words were still garbled. He paused often as if trying to think of the word he wanted to say.

Miriam suppressed a bark of laughter. Although it was heartbreaking to hear his speech, his dislike of the food made her smile and gave her hope that he would recover quickly.

Lilly sank onto his bed, which creaked in response. "I told you, *Daed*, you'll come home in a few weeks. The time will pass quickly since you'll be busy with your therapy. The doctors say you're doing *gut*, but you have to finish your treatment."

"I'll have a chocolate cake waiting for you when you get home," Miriam promised. "I remember *Grossmammi's* recipe, your favorite."

"Sa-sa-sit." Abraham gestured toward the chair beside him. He then reached out as if trying to form the words he longed to say to her.

Miriam lowered herself into the chair and patted his hand. "Don't get yourself all worked up. I'll do the talking."

He nodded.

"I bet *Daed* wants to know what you've been doing," Lilly said.

"I went back to Indiana last week," Miriam said. "I took care of my affairs in Indiana and even sold my car."

He patted her hand and gave a proud smile.

Miriam took a deep breath. "I'm meeting with the

bishop starting next week. I'm going to be baptized and join the church."

Her father gasped and his eyes filled with tears. "*Mamm* w-w-would be f-f-*froh*," he whispered slowly, working hard to speak each word.

Miriam bit her lip, hoping she wouldn't cry. "*Danki.*" Anxious to keep the conversation going with her father, she then gave the details of her visit with Abby as well as her trip to her old job. She told him about packing up her belongings and taking the train home, adding how excited she was to meet her sisters in the station.

"Ab-by back too?" he asked, his expression hopeful.

"Unfortunately, no." Miriam shook her head. "I don't think that will happen anytime soon. She seems to like her life in Indiana."

"Ab-by de-de-vorce, *ya*?" Abraham asked.

Miriam nodded. "Her husband left her for his secretary."

"I know we're not supposed to judge others, but Abby doesn't deserve that," Lilly said, folding her arms in front of her chest. "No one does."

"I agree." Miriam nodded. "She deserves much better."

"What's keeping her in Indiana?" Lilly asked.

Miriam shrugged. "I'm not exactly sure. Maybe someday she'll have a change of heart."

"Mr. Lapp," a nurse asked from the doorway. "Are you ready for your physical therapy?"

Lilly stood and kissed Abraham's cheek. "We'll let you do your therapy. We'll come and see you tomorrow."

"Bye, *Daed*." Miriam kissed his cheek.

"*D-d-d-danki.*" He squeezed her hands.

Miriam nodded to the nurse on her way out into the hallway. She and Lilly walked in silence out to the parking lot, where they climbed into the van owned by their *English* driver, Kimberly Johnson. Kimberly was an *Englisher* who worked full-time as a driver for the Amish. During the ride home, Lilly explained their father's prognosis to Kimberly, sharing how much better he'd looked that day than he had earlier in the week.

When they arrived home, Miriam and Lilly walked side-by-side back to the cabin.

Miriam glanced up at the cloudless sky and breathed in the sweet smell of the fresh-cut hay. The warm sun kissed her cheeks, and she smiled. "The Lord has blessed us with a *schee* day," she said, smoothing her apron. "It's so *gut* to be home."

"*Daed* is thrilled you're back home," Lilly said. "I am too. I missed you." She climbed the porch steps, sank onto the swing, and patted the seat next to her. "Sit."

Miriam sat next to her. "I missed you too, *Schweschder.*"

"I'm sorry I was so horrible to you." Lilly frowned. "You didn't deserve it. You were always so *gut* and true. I wouldn't blame you if you hated me."

"I could never hate you, Lilly." Miriam touched her hand. "Why didn't you ever tell me you liked Zach?"

Lilly stared across the field. "It was pride. I was so jealous of you, and I know that's a sin. I just couldn't help it."

"Why?" Miriam shook her head with disbelief. "Why would you be jealous of me?"

"Because you had two men after you, and I had none." Lilly slumped in the seat. "Men never noticed me."

"That's simply not true." Miriam faced her sister. "Lilly, you're beautiful, and you're smart. You're also talented. You've made the most beautiful quilts I've ever seen. You sell yourself short. Besides that, you had men after you. I can think of three who wanted to take you home from singings, but you wouldn't give them the time of day."

"I didn't want any of them. I only wanted one man, and I still only want one."

"So go after him, Lilly. You're beautiful, and he'll notice you. Just try."

Lilly shook her head. "I've tried with Zach. I spoke to him at singings years ago, and he would just smile and walk away. I tried at church services too, but it's like I'm invisible. He's the only man I've ever been interested in, but he looks right through me. It's a lost cause. I was jealous, and that's why I did what I did. I'm so sorry, Miriam. I truly am. I wish I could take it all back and fix it for you and Timothy. You deserve to be happy."

"You should've told me, Lilly, and maybe I could've helped you with Zach." Miriam contemplated the thought for a brief moment. While she had considered pursuing Zach herself, she knew that she didn't love him. He was a dear friend, but not the man she longed to have as a life mate. However, she wanted to see her sister happy. Maybe, just maybe, both Zach and Lilly could be life mates, and it would bring Miriam joy to see her sister and her dear friend happy together.

Miriam sat up straight and grinned. "I still can help

you. I could set you and Zach up. Maybe you can come to supper one night, and I'll invite Zach too."

Lilly shook her head. "Don't be silly. I'm a grown woman. I should take care of these things myself."

"It's no bother at all. I love to cook. I can invite him over one night, and you can come too." Miriam patted Lilly's hand. "You name the night."

Lilly shook her head. "You don't need to go to such trouble."

Miriam snapped her fingers as a thought hit her. "Lilly, you and Zach would be perfect together!"

Looking intrigued, her sister raised an eyebrow. "What do you mean?"

Miriam grabbed Lilly's hand and shook it with excitement. "You both love novels!"

"He likes to read?" Lilly's eyes rounded. "I didn't know that."

"Why didn't I think of this before? You'll have so much to talk about." Miriam squeezed Lilly's hand. "Yes, you must let me cook dinner for you both."

Lilly hesitated and then shook her head. "It's not necessary." She stood. "I better get back home. I have two quilts I need to finish for Naomi. I'll see you later on." She gave Miriam a quick hug. "Have a good afternoon and kiss *Aenti* for me."

"See you later." Miriam watched her sister lope across the field and smiled. Despite her sister's hesitation, she was going to see to it that Lilly got her chance with Zach.

No one should be alone.

CHAPTER 21

Timothy climbed the stairs to the bakery and nodded at *English* customers who greeted him. Stepping through the doorway, the sweet smell of pastries filled his nostrils, causing his stomach to growl. He weaved through the sea of tourists to the counter and smiled at his niece.

Lizzie mirrored his smile. "Hi, *Onkel* Timothy."

He leaned on the counter. "*Gude mariye. Wie geht's?*"

"It's been crazy busy all day." She shook her head. "Ruthie and I are having a hard time keeping the counter stocked. It's like the tourists came out of the woodwork or somethin'. It's a good thing Miriam came back to help us."

His pulse leapt at the sound of her name. Without realizing it, Lizzie had answered the question that had been burning in his soul and caused him to make a mid-morning run to the bakery for "snacks for the workers." Timothy had a feeling his father knew the truth from the way he'd grinned and told Timothy to go get the pastries.

He'd trekked the mile to the bakery on foot since their *English* driver had taken Luke on a supply run.

Somehow the walk in the boiling heat hadn't bothered Timothy one bit, since he was hoping to see Miriam.

Let Miriam go! It's time to move on.

Timothy ignored the thoughts and glanced past the counter toward the kitchen. "Is your *grossmammi* back there?"

"*Ya.*" Lizzie nodded toward the doorway leading to the kitchen. "She's baking."

While a tourist stepped forward to ask Lizzie a question, Timothy slipped behind the counter and into the kitchen, where his sisters rushed around working on various baked goods, and his mother barked orders for more sand tart cookies.

His heart thumped against his ribcage when he spotted Miriam alone in the corner standing over a crumbly peach pie. Crossing the kitchen, his stomach growled with anticipation of the delicious pie.

Engrossed in her work, Miriam kept her eyes on her creation while standing at the island counter in the center of the work area. Her tongue stuck out from between her teeth, evidence she was concentrating.

She was the picture of beauty with long wisps of dark hair that had fallen from her *kapp* framing her perfect pixie face. Her lips were a shade of deep rose, and her high cheekbones were pink from the heat of the kitchen. She'd never looked more radiant, and he wished he could freeze the moment in time.

A smile turned up the corners of his mouth. "You were kind to make that pie for me."

Her eyes met his, and she sucked in a breath, cupping a hand to her chest. "Timothy!" She grabbed a rag and wiped her hands. "How long have you been standing there?"

"Long enough." Grinning, he leaned on the counter. "I'm sorry for startling you. I should've announced myself, but you were so deep in thought I couldn't help but watch you."

Her cheeks blushed a deeper red.

She's so schee.

"Is that pie for me? You know it's my favorite." He breathed in the scent of the sweet peaches. "It smells *appeditlich.*"

Her smile was coy. "All customers are welcome to purchase the entire pie if they choose to do so. I would imagine you'd get a Kauffman family discount."

To his surprise, she was playing along with his flirtatious banter—just like she used to do when they were a couple. His pulse skittered. He resisted the urge to swipe a crumb from her cheek. Touching would be too personal, too dangerous for his heart.

"I was sorry to hear your *daed* has fallen ill. How is he?" he asked, steering the conversation to a safer subject.

"*Gut.*" She leaned back on the supply counter behind her. "His rehabilitation is going well. He's learned how to feed himself, and he's working with a speech therapist. It's a miracle after the stroke he suffered. He's coming home in a couple of weeks."

"I'm glad to hear it." He absently ran his finger along the smooth counter as confidence surged through him. He longed to tell her how he felt about her. "I was glad to hear you came back and are going to be baptized.

Beth Anne told me you'd worked things out with your family. That's *wunderbaar*."

"*Danki*. It's good to be back." She fingered the ties on her *kapp*, a nervous habit he remembered her doing often.

An uncomfortable silence fell between them, and the air surrounding them felt electrified. He glanced down at the pie to avoid losing himself in her deep brown eyes.

She snatched a knife off the counter, sliced the pie, and placed a piece on a plate. She held the pie and a fork out to him, and her smile was genuine and sweet, turning his insides to butter.

"Here," she said. "Take a bite before you melt the pie with your stare."

"No, I couldn't." He shook his head. "That's for the customers."

She continued to hold the piece out for him. "Please. Just eat it. You'll insult me if you don't."

"I certainly don't want to insult you." Accepting the pie from her, he took a bite, and it melted in his mouth. "Miriam, you still make the best crumbly peach pie in Lancaster County. No one could ever hold a candle to you."

Her smile faded, and he instantly regretted the double meaning of the comment.

But it's true. No one could ever hold a candle to you.

Her smile reappeared, but it was forced, resembling a grimace. "Congratulations on your upcoming wedding to Naomi. Lilly told me the *wunderbaar* news."

He tried to smile, but his lips remained flat. "*Danki*."

"I wish you all of the happiness in the world." She fingered the ties in her *kapp*. "You deserve it."

He studied her eyes, wishing he could read her thoughts. Was she truly happy for him, or did she feel the same regret that was coursing through him?

"Timothy!" Elizabeth's voice sounded behind him, but he kept his gaze locked on Miriam's, awaiting a sign of her true feelings.

Elizabeth sidled up to him. "Did *Dat* send you over for whoopie pies again today? I'm going to have to start charging that man. He's hurting my profits."

Her eyes still unreadable, Miriam nodded toward Elizabeth. "I believe she's speaking to you, Timothy."

Timothy cut his gaze to Elizabeth. "I'm sorry. What did you say?"

Her frown was impatient. "I asked if your *dat* sent you for whoopie pies."

"Oh. *Ya*. He did." Timothy prayed he didn't look as frazzled as he felt. "Two dozen would be *wunderbaar*."

"Two dozen this time? Is he *narrisch*?" Elizabeth threw her hands up. "I don't know if I have that many made. He may have to settle for one dozen." She started across the kitchen. "He has to stop these mid-morning orders. It's not good for business."

She stopped and spun, facing Miriam. "Miriam, I forgot to tell you Zach called. It must've been an hour ago, but we've been so busy it slipped my mind. He wanted me to tell you to call him. I apologize for not telling you earlier, but it's been crazy."

Timothy's stomach knotted. Facing her, he found Miriam's cheeks blazing a deeper red.

She's seeing Zach Fisher.

Does she love him?

He wondered if she would be announcing her engagement soon. Was Zach the reason behind her joining the church? Would she follow through with their nuptials, unlike she had with Timothy?

"Timothy!" Elizabeth called. "Come help me package up these whoopie pies for *Dat*. We have work to do around here."

Miriam's expression softened. "You'd better go. She's a bit stressed today."

"I can hear it in her voice." He gave her a tentative smile. "It was *gut* seeing you, Miriam."

"Would you like to take some crumbly peach pie with you?" she asked, cutting her eyes to the pie. "I can make another one."

He shook his head. "I'd better not push it with *Mamm*. It's not wise to cross her when she's stressed out."

She chuckled, and her radiant smile was back. "You're right."

"Have a *gut* day," he said, fighting the urge to reach over and touch her.

"*Ya*," she whispered. "You too."

I hope to see you again soon.

He swallowed the thought and crossed the kitchen to join Elizabeth, who was loading whoopie pies into a large cardboard box.

"You tell *Dat* he has to stop these surprise orders," she mumbled. "I need some warning. If he called ahead then it wouldn't be a problem."

"*Ya*," Timothy said, adding pies to the box. "I'll remind

him." After the whoopie pies were loaded up, he hoisted the box from the counter. "*Danki, Mamm.*" He gave her a kiss on the cheek. "We'll enjoy them."

"*Ya, ya.*" She waved him off. "Tell your *dat* I'll give him a piece of my mind later."

He said good-bye to his sisters and then glanced across the room and found Miriam studying him, her eyes focused and intense. He'd give anything to be able to read the thoughts in that pretty head of hers.

Stepping out into the store area, he wondered what Naomi would think if she knew he'd made up an excuse to visit Miriam.

It would break her heart.

. . .

Miriam blew out the breath she'd been holding for what felt like several minutes. She stared at the doorway, wishing Timothy would realize he'd forgotten something, maybe the crumbly peach pie, and come back to get it.

He'd looked so handsome in that dark blue shirt. His blue eyes had sent her insides into a wild spin. And that smile, oh, that smile . . .

She closed her eyes and groaned. It was a sin to covet another woman's husband.

But he's not married yet!

Miriam suppressed her scheming inner voice and turned her attention to slicing the pie on the counter. She then grabbed the plastic wrap and began wrapping each piece.

While she worked, Timothy's smooth, warm voice echoed through her mind. His genuine interest in her and her family, along with his flirtatious jokes, had caught her off guard.

Was he toying with her emotions?

She'd never known Timothy to play games. Yet, she wondered why he would show her so much attention when he was marrying another woman.

Miriam's stomach lurched at the thought of Timothy and Naomi. Although Miriam held no claim to Timothy, she couldn't digest the thought of Timothy and Naomi living in the house he'd built for her.

But she'd left him. How could she expect him to wait for her?

However, on an inexplicable level, Timothy had seemed to be testing her today. Was he trying to tell her something? What had he meant when he said, "No one can hold a candle to you?" Was he referring to more than just her cooking?

The comment had struck so deep in her soul that she'd deliberately mentioned his wedding to remind him he'd chosen someone else to be his bride. Paying Miriam such a high compliment felt like a cruel joke.

He must've only meant my baking.

"Miriam?" Beth Anne asked, approaching the counter. "Would you mind making another chocolate cake? Lizzie says we're out again."

"Of course," Miriam said with a smile.

Beth Anne glanced down at the pie. "That looks *wunderbaar*. Did my brother steal a piece?"

Miriam loaded the individually wrapped pieces onto

a tray. "*Ya*, he did. I tried to get him to take the whole pie, but he said your *mamm* would scold him."

Beth Anne lifted the tray. "I'll take this out front."

"*Danki*." Miriam pulled out a cake pan and a mixing bowl from the cabinet behind her. Turning, she found Beth Anne still watching her. "*Ya*? May I help you?"

"Timothy seemed *froh* to see you," Beth Anne said.

Miriam shrugged, wishing her cheeks wouldn't flare at the sound of his name. "We're friends, and nothing more. He's marrying Naomi, and I'm happy for them." She hoped she sounded casual.

"*Ya*. Friends." Beth Anne sounded unconvinced, but she smiled. "You best get to baking that cake. The customers are fond of your recipe."

Miriam heaved a deep sigh while Beth Anne walked away. She hoped she could get used to seeing Timothy without wearing her heartstrings on her sleeve.

Miriam felt a hand touch her arm, and she turned to find Kathryn giving her an unreadable expression. She hoped Kathryn wasn't going to chime in on Beth Anne's observations. While Kathryn hadn't greeted Miriam with a warm hug, she also hadn't been rude since Miriam came back. She seemed almost happy to have Miriam there.

"I owe you an apology," Kathryn said slowly. "Beth Anne explained to me that you didn't walk out on my brother. She told me that your breakup with Timothy was due to lies, not your intention to hurt him."

Miriam nodded. "That's true. My sister Lilly told lies to Timothy and me out of jealousy."

Kathryn held out her hand and Miriam shook it.

"I'm sorry for being so nasty to you. I thought I was protecting my brother, but I was wrong."

Miriam smiled. "*Danki.*"

"I'm glad you're here," Kathryn said with a genuine smile. "You're a *wunderbaar* addition to our bakery."

As Kathryn crossed to the other side of the kitchen, Miriam leaned back on the counter and shook her head. What a confusing day it had turned out to be.

Crumbly Peach Pie

9-inch pie shell, unbaked
1 cup sugar
1/4 cup flour
1 tsp cinnamon
1/8 tsp nutmeg
1 stick butter
8 large peach halves
1/4 cup water

Mix together the sugar, flour, cinnamon, and nutmeg, then mix in butter until crumbly. Sprinkle half of the mixture in the bottom of the pie shell. Arrange peach halves cut side down over crumbs. Cover with remaining crumbs. Add the water and bake for 10 minutes at 450 degrees, then for 30 minutes at 350 degrees.

CHAPTER 22

"D o you need anything?" Miriam asked, standing in the living room of Abraham's house three weeks later.

Abraham shifted in the chair and cleared his throat. "Wa-water."

"I'll be right back. You get comfortable." Miriam crossed to the kitchen, where Lilly stood at the counter flipping through a recipe book. "I can't believe *Daed's* been home a week already. The days are flying by." Miriam plucked a glass from the cabinet, added a few ice cubes, and then filled it with ice water from the refrigerator.

"*Ya.* Before you know it, your baptism day will be here. It's difficult to believe September is upon us," Lilly said. "It's not that long now. How are your classes going?"

"*Gut,*" Miriam said with a nod. "I've been meeting with the bishop Wednesday evenings along with going to the classes on our church Sundays. I'm really enjoying it."

"That's *gut.*" Lilly smiled. "Hannah told me you've been spending a lot of time with Lena Joy."

"That's true. I visit her twice a week in the evening.

We're working on a few sewing projects together."
Miriam sighed. "She's such a sweet girl. I hope she has
her liver transplant soon."

"*Ya*, I know. I pray for that every day." Lilly tapped
the cookbook. "What if I made *Mamm's* meatloaf tonight? Sound good?"

"I think *Daed* would love it." Miriam headed for the
doorway. "I'm taking *Daed* a glass of water. I'll be right
back to help you with the ingredients."

She ambled back to Abraham and handed him the
glass. He took a few sips. "*D-danki.*"

"*Gern gschehne.* May I get you anything else? Maybe
a snack? Or the newspaper?"

He shook his head while placing the glass onto the
end table beside him. Leaning back, he closed his eyes.
"No. I rest."

She wagged a finger at him, even though his eyes
were closed. "Remember you must do your exercises
later to keep up your strength."

"*Ya, ya.*" He waved her off without opening his eyes.

Miriam shook her head. He was stubborn, but that
kept him strong.

Moving back toward the kitchen, Miriam heard an
unfamiliar feminine voice that didn't resemble either of
her sisters'. She stood in the doorway, and her eyes widened when she spotted Naomi standing at the counter
and speaking with Lilly. A basket of rolls, bagels, and
sticky buns sat on the table.

Mustering up all of her inner strength, Miriam
moved into the kitchen and plastered a smile on her
face. "Naomi," she said. "What a pleasant surprise."

"Miriam!" Naomi rushed over and shook her hand. "*Wie geht's?*"

Miriam stifled a groan. She couldn't fathom a close friendship with Naomi. "*Gut,*" Miriam said. "What brings you here?"

"I thought I'd stop by and see how you all were faring." Naomi's smile was genuine and bright. "Lilly told me that your *daed* came home last week, and I wanted to make a visit and bring some goodies for you." She nodded toward the basket. "I hope you're hungry."

Miriam's appetite had evaporated the moment she'd laid eyes on Timothy's fiancée, but she wasn't about to admit that. After all, jealousy was a sin.

"They look *appeditlich. Danki*, Naomi." Miriam glanced toward her sister, who gave a sad smile. Did Lilly sense Miriam's jumbled emotions? Miriam hoped her uneasiness wasn't so transparent.

"Have a seat," Lilly said. "I'll bring a few glasses and ice water."

"*Wunderbaar!*" Naomi clapped her hands. "We can visit for a while."

"*Ya. Wunderbaar,*" Miriam muttered. "I'll grab plates."

They sat at the table and filled their plates with the contents of Naomi's basket while Naomi chattered on about work.

"Your quilts are the most popular," she told Lilly. "The Lone Star pattern is the fastest seller we have."

"*Danki.*" Lilly buttered a roll. "I'll start another one in a few days. I've been concentrating on *Daed*, so I've fallen behind on my work."

"Oh, don't be *gegisch.*" Naomi waved off the thought.

"We understand. You take your time. Family first, of course." She turned to Miriam. "I was so *froh* to hear you're back to stay."

"*Danki*." Miriam picked a sticky bun from her plate. "It's *gut* to be home."

"I heard you're going to be baptized! That's so exciting." Naomi buttered a bagel. "I'm *froh* for you."

Miriam nodded, wondering why Naomi was so interested in her life. Was she trying to be a friend or did she have an ulterior motive? Naomi seemed genuine, but looks could be deceiving.

"It's hard to believe the summer is over," Naomi continued, her smile growing. "My wedding is coming soon."

Miriam sucked in a breath. When Lilly and Naomi snapped their eyes to hers, Miriam quickly lifted her glass and took a drink, hoping to hide her reaction.

Naomi glanced down at her bagel, and Lilly's gaze softened to empathy.

"I can't believe I'll be married in just about two months. I can't wait to live as husband and wife." Naomi lifted her bagel. "I feared I'd never get married. I'm very blessed."

Miriam studied her roll, trying to ignore the sick feeling roaring through her stomach. She wished she could excuse herself, but she couldn't dream up a feasible explanation. If only her father were awake and calling for her . . .

She glanced at Lilly, hoping her sister would think of a way to steer the conversation away from Naomi's impending nuptials.

"How's your *mamm* doing?" Lilly asked. Miriam breathed a sigh of relief. *Danki, Lilly!*

"She's doing well." Naomi's eyes sparkled. "She started on my wedding dress last week. I picked royal blue. I'm so excited." She paused to take a sip of water. "I told Timothy I want at least six *kinner*, maybe more. I asked him how many he wanted, but he said he didn't know. I guess men don't think about those things. He'll probably be *froh* with as many as God gives us. It's God's decision, *ya*? His plan."

Miriam coughed, feeling the room closing in on her. The thought of Timothy and Naomi becoming parents was too much. She had to leave before Naomi made her physically ill.

"Miriam?" Lilly asked, her voice a little too loud and deliberate. "Have you had a chance to check the voice-mail today? I was expecting a call from Hannah."

Miriam met her sister's gaze and raised her eyebrows in surprise. Was Lilly creating a reason for Miriam to leave this torturous conversation? Could her sister read her thoughts and emotions?

"Have you been to the phone shanty?" Lilly's expression was serious, as if it had a hidden meaning.

"No, I haven't."

"Would you please go check it now? I want to be sure Hannah is okay." Lilly winked so that only Miriam could see. "She mentioned Lena Joy wasn't feeling well last evening."

"Oh, right." Miriam stood up like a shot. "I best go make sure she's okay."

"*Danki*," Lilly said.

Miriam started for the door.

"And Miriam," Lilly added. "Take your time and be sure to call Hannah back. I must know how our niece is."

Facing her sister, Miriam swallowed a grin. "I'll do that."

Thank God for sisters!

Miriam rushed to the phone shanty, not knowing if she should laugh or cry. While she was thankful for Lilly for giving her an excuse to leave, she also wanted to ask Naomi if she had any idea how hurtful her words were. Yet, Naomi most likely had no idea how Miriam felt about Timothy. It would be difficult to believe Miriam still loved him after she'd left him four years ago.

The thought caused Miriam to stop dead in her tracks.

Did she still love him?

She groaned as she stepped into the phone shanty. She knew loving Timothy Kauffman was a lost cause. He was marrying Naomi, and Miriam needed to accept it.

However, her heart refused to let him go. He'd left an imprint on her soul. He'd stolen her heart.

Shoving those thoughts aside, she dialed the voicemail and punched in the password. The first message was from Hannah confirming supper for tomorrow night. The second was from Lilly's friend Mary Anne Hostetler checking to see how Abraham was. And the last was from Zach, asking Miriam to please call him back as soon as possible.

Remembering Lilly's order to take her time, Miriam dialed Zach's shop and hoped he would answer in order to avoid another round of phone tag.

"Fisher's Saddle Shop," Zach said. "How may I help you?"

"*Ya*, I'd like to order two dozen saddles, and I need them by Tuesday," Miriam joked with a grin.

"Why, Miriam Lapp," Zach began. "I'd thought for certain you'd moved back to Indiana."

"You can't mean that." Miriam lowered herself onto the small bench seat. "You think I'd move away without telling you?"

"You never returned my calls. I left a message for you at the bakery and in the phone shanty."

Miriam slapped a hand to her forehead. "I'm so sorry, Zach. I meant to call you. It's just been *narrisch*. *Daed* came home, and my sisters and I have been taking turns caring for him. I really meant to call you."

"How's your *daed*?"

"Doing *gut*. *Danki*," she said.

"You owe me supper," he said.

"*Ya*, I do. How about tomorrow night? You can come to the cabin, and I'll make your favorite."

"No. I'll come get you and make you supper."

"Oh." She blinked, surprised. "What time?"

"I'll pick you up around five."

"Sounds *wunderbaar*."

"*Gut*. Don't disappear again."

She chuckled. "I won't."

"See you then. Good-bye."

"Good-bye." Miriam replaced the receiver in the cradle and smiled. Zach was a good friend, and he would be perfect for Lilly.

She stood and glanced toward the house, her thoughts

moving to her younger sister. Lilly deserved a good man like Zach Fisher. Tomorrow night she would tell him how Lilly felt about him and try to get him to consider courting her. She knew it would be awkward since Zach had asked her to court him, but in her heart, she believed Lilly and Zach belonged together. She couldn't shake the feeling that they would click and become fast friends. They both loved to read, and Miriam was certain they would spend hours discussing books. Miriam had never considered herself a matchmaker, but this seemed so right. If Miriam couldn't have her true love, perhaps she could help Lilly and Zach find each other.

Miriam left a message on Hannah's voicemail saying she hoped everyone was doing well and she would come to visit in a couple of days. She then took her time walking back toward the house, hoping Naomi would take the hint and leave.

Climbing the porch stairs, Miriam took a deep, cleansing breath and then entered through the kitchen doorway. She forced a smile and nodded to her sister and Naomi.

"Did Hannah call?" Lilly asked.

"*Ya*, she left a message confirming supper plans for tomorrow night. She said Lena Joy is doing fine. Mary Anne also left a message asking how *Daed* is doing." Miriam stood by the counter. "I called Hannah back and left her a message telling her we were thinking of her."

"Oh, *gut*." Lilly smiled.

"It was no trouble." Miriam picked up the cookbook. "You two continue your conversation, and I'll start the meatloaf for supper."

"*Danki*." Lilly gave Miriam an exasperated look behind Naomi's back.

While Naomi prattled on about her family, the quilt business, and her upcoming nuptials, Miriam tried in vain to tune out her voice and throw together a meatloaf.

Miriam was thankful when her father awoke and called her in to sit with him. She sank into a chair beside him, and he handed her a piece of paper.

"Read," he whispered. "N-nurse w-wrote for me."

Miriam glanced at the note that the visiting nurse must have transcribed for her father. Her eyes welled with tears as the words echoed through her mind:

Miriam,

I'm sorry that I was so harsh to you after Jeremy's death. The truth is that your *mamm* and I lost a *boppli* before Hannah was born. The *boppli* died of SIDS, like Jeremy did, and I always blamed myself. I'm sorry. I love you.

Daed

As the words filtered through her mind, she recalled the letter she'd found from her mother. While discussing SIDS, her mother had written: "*You must trust me that I know more about this than you could imagine.*" Now it all seemed to make sense.

Glancing up at her father, she found tears in his eyes. "You lost a baby to SIDS?"

He nodded, a tear streaking his cheek.

"Is that why you were so upset with me?" she asked,

her voice trembling. "What happened to Jeremy opened up old wounds?"

He nodded again. "I-I-I'm so sor-ry."

She sniffed, hoping to curb her threatening tears. "Now so much makes sense, *Daed*."

"You . . . f-f-for-give m-m-me?" he asked, his voice soft and unsure.

"Of course I do. *Danki* for telling me." Leaning over she hugged him. "Would you like to read the Bible together now?"

He nodded.

She read the Bible to him and enjoyed the comfort of the Lord's Word.

An hour later, Lilly appeared in the doorway. "How are you, *Daed*?"

Instead of speaking, he nodded.

"Do you need anything?" Lilly asked. Shaking his head, he closed his eyes.

Lilly turned to Miriam. "Would you please help me in the kitchen?"

"Of course." Miriam placed the Bible on the end table, grabbed the note from him, and followed Lilly to the kitchen.

"She's gone." Lilly leaned against the counter. "I'm so sorry, Miriam," she touched Miriam's arm. "I thought Naomi would never leave. She's a sweet person, but she has no concept of appropriate topics."

Miriam stuck the letter into her pocket and pre-heated the stove. "It was nothing. She probably didn't even realize that Timothy and I were once a couple."

"No, she knew. You'd think she'd be a little more respectful of your feelings."

Miriam busied herself by placing the basket of rolls on the counter. "But Timothy and I are ancient history. She would have no reason to think I still have feelings for him." She glanced around for something to clean up, but Lilly had already straightened the kitchen.

"Miriam. Stop." Lilly placed a hand on her shoulder. "It's okay to be upset. Naomi was thoughtless. I wish I'd known she was coming to visit, so I could've stopped her. I could've come up with some excuse to put her off."

"It's not your fault." Miriam smiled. "Naomi had no idea."

Frowning, Lilly sighed. "That's where you're wrong. It *is* my fault. The whole reason why you left and didn't marry Timothy is because of me and my big, fat mouth."

"What's done is done." Miriam shrugged. "I can't change what happened. It's in God's hands. Timothy will marry whom-ever he's meant to marry. And maybe someday I'll marry someone too."

"I wish I could fix it."

"It's not yours to fix. It's up to God and His plan." Miriam pulled the letter from her pocket and handed it to Lilly. "Look at what *Daed* had a nurse write."

Lilly gasped as she read the note. "*Mamm* and *Daed* lost a baby before Hannah was born?"

Miriam nodded. "*Ya.* Now it makes sense why he was so angry with me when Jeremy died. He asked me for his forgiveness." Her eyes filled with tears. "I feel so much better knowing that *Daed* still loves me."

"Of course he does." Lilly hugged her. "I'm so glad you're back, and I'm so glad that it all worked out."

"Me too." Miriam stepped over to the refrigerator. "I'm in the mood for some freshly squeezed lemonade. How does that sound?" She was happy that she and her father had worked things out, but her heart still ached for Timothy. Pushing Timothy from her mind, Miriam took the near-empty pitcher from the refrigerator.

CHAPTER 23

Timothy climbed the steps to his porch Saturday night. Glancing up, he silently admired the clear September night. The stars twinkled in the bright light of the moon.

It had been a typical Saturday evening—delicious supper at his parents' house with the whole family, abundant desserts, and lots of chatter and sharing.

Naomi had joined Timothy again this Saturday and had taken to the Kauffman family like one of the fold. While Timothy had talked with the men, Naomi had joined the women as if she were already a Kauffman. Seeing her with his mother and sisters should've made Timothy smile and should've made him love her even more. Yet, an inkling of regret had nipped at him. He repeatedly found himself imagining Miriam standing with his sisters and mother.

Why am I torturing myself?

Sighing, Timothy shook his head. He was wrong to think of Miriam when Naomi loved him so. He could see the love shining in her eyes whenever she looked at him. It wasn't right of him to think of another woman. He should've been thinking of Naomi and only her.

The clip-clop of hooves drew his attention to the lane. Turning, he found a horse and buggy maneuvering past the house and steering toward his.

His eyebrows raised in question. He wasn't expecting company. In fact, it wasn't common for visitors to arrive unannounced so late at night.

Timothy leaned on the porch railing and pushed his straw hat up further on his head while he focused on the buggy that stopped in front of his house. A man hopped from the driver's seat and tethered the horse to the hitching post. The man met his gaze, and Timothy was surprised to see a member of the Lapp family.

"Why, Gerald Lapp," he said, stomping down the porch steps. "*Wie geht's*? What brings you out this way so late in the evening?" He smacked him on the shoulder.

"It's *gut* to see you, too." Gerald shook his hand and then gestured toward the passenger side of the buggy. "It was her idea to come out here. She asked me to drive."

Timothy faced the woman climbing from the buggy, and his heart thumped in his chest when he was certain she was Miriam.

With a closer look at her face, he found Lilly giving him a cautious smile while stepping toward him. Although she resembled Miriam, Lilly's beauty was less pronounced. Her cheekbones were not as high as Miriam's, and her eyes weren't as deep brown.

"Timothy," Lilly said. "I apologize for visiting so late, but I must speak with you."

"Oh." His smile faded in response to her serious tone. "Would you like to come in and have something to drink?"

She shook her head. "No, I don't want to impose. I just need a few moments to speak with you."

"Lilly, you're not imposing." Timothy nodded toward the porch. "Please at least sit on the porch, and I'll bring out some drinks."

While his guests sat on the porch, Timothy rushed into the house and brought out a tray, including three glasses, a pitcher of water, and a bowl of chocolate chip cookies Naomi had left for him. He placed the tray on a small table and sat next to Lilly. As he poured the water for them, Timothy spotted Lilly wringing her hands while staring across at the darkened fields. She was anxious, and he dreaded whatever it was that she had come to say.

Gerald took the glass of water and a handful of cookies and then sat in a chair kitty-corner to Timothy.

"How's your *dat*?" Timothy asked, handing Lilly a glass of water.

"*Gut.*" She nodded, her expression softening. "He's been home a week now, and he's progressing well. He's a lot slower than he used to be, but he's getting around by himself." She glanced at Gerald and smiled. "He thinks we made a run to the market for milk and bread. I bet he's wondering why we've been gone so long."

"*Ya.*" Gerald sipped his drink. "But Hannah's with him, so he's fine."

"How are your parents?" Lilly asked.

"*Gut.*" Timothy lifted his glass. "We had our weekly Kauffman family supper tonight, and everyone was there. Everyone is healthy."

"That's good to hear." Lilly placed her glass on the

small table and cleared her throat. "I came here because I have something to say. I thought about writing you a letter, but I decided you deserve to hear this face-to-face." She blew out a ragged breath.

"Take your time," Timothy said.

"I owe you an apology," she began. Her bottom lip quivered. "What I did to you is absolutely unforgivable, but I want you to know I'm sincerely sorry. I wish I could take it all back and fix it, but I know I can't." She sniffed and wiped her nose.

"Slow down." Timothy leaned over to touch her arm but stopped, knowing it was inappropriate to touch a woman he barely knew. "Just start at the beginning."

"I'm the reason why my sister left you and moved to Indiana. It's all my fault." Tears spilled from her brown eyes. "I told a terrible lie. Actually, I told more than one lie. It was sinful and selfish and unforgivable. I'm truly sorry, Timothy. I'm so, so sorry." She cupped her hand to her mouth and sobbed.

He glanced at Gerald, hoping for some guidance on how to handle Lilly's tears. Gerald shrugged and continued eating cookies.

You're a big help.

Unsure of what to do, Timothy handed her a napkin. "Lilly, we've all made mistakes. We're all imperfect in God's eyes."

Shaking her head, she wiped her eyes and nose with the napkin. "No, what I did was worse than anything you can imagine. I was jealous of Miriam, so I lied. I wanted to break you and her up, and it worked. I'm so, so sorry, Timothy."

Timothy took a long gulp of water in an attempt to calm his frayed nerves. "Why would you want to break us up?"

"I was jealous." Her voice trembled and more tears spilled from her eyes. "I had no one, and Miriam had two men who were interested in her."

"Two?" Timothy asked. "Who was the other man?"

"Zach Fisher." Lilly sniffed again and sipped her water.

Jealousy surged through him, but he pushed it back, focusing on Lilly's explanation. "I still don't understand why that would make you want to break us up."

"I was young and hateful." She shook her head. "I'm not proud of my actions. I was miserable and wanted Miriam to be unhappy too. I was determined to make things horrible for her. I told everyone you were cheating on her and she was cheating on you. After the tragedy of Jeremy Henderson's death, things got worse for her, and she left." She sipped her drink and then studied the glass. "I thought I would feel some happiness when she left because that meant that I had won. But I felt worse. The whole thing backfired. In the end, I'd lost my sister, and I was still alone."

Timothy bit his upper lip and stared down at his lap. Anger and regret coursed through him. He knew that as a Christian he needed to tell her she was forgiven, but he couldn't form the words.

"I wanted to come here to apologize, but I also wanted to tell you Miriam still loves you." Lilly's voice was soft and full of uncertainty.

Timothy's widened eyes cut to hers.

"It may seem like I'm betraying Naomi's friend-ship, but I don't mean to." She held her hand out as if to caution him. "Naomi is a very dear friend of mine, and I care for her deeply. However, my allegiance is to Miriam first. I haven't been a very good sister to her, but I've changed. I want my sister to be *froh*, and I know she won't be until she has you back."

Timothy shook his head.

This can't be happening. I'm engaged to Naomi.

"Lilly, I appreciate your honesty," he said, his voice hesitant. "However, what happened between Miriam and me was four years ago, and there's no use in reliv-ing the past. What's done is done."

Lilly shook her head, her eyes sparkling with fresh tears. "No, that's not true. You're not married to Naomi yet. There's still time for you—"

"No," he said, the word coming out a little too force-fully. "I made a promise that I intend to keep. I refuse to hurt Naomi. I can't make her suffer like I did when Miriam left."

"But Miriam left because of me." She jammed a finger in her chest. "*She* didn't hurt you. *I* hurt you, Timothy. I hurt you both, and I'm so, so sorry." She swallowed a sob as more tears rushed down her pink cheeks.

Timothy handed her another napkin and then shifted in his seat. Watching her cry was almost too much for him.

She sniffed, wiped her eyes and nose, and cleared her throat. "Timothy, please listen to me. I know you made a promise to Naomi, and that's very honorable and right and true. But please consider what I said about Miriam. Her heart belongs to you. You both are meant to be. Just give her a chance. She didn't leave you willingly. She thought she had no way out of her problems here, but the truth is that I caused those problems. It's all my fault you aren't married and living here together."

Speechless, Timothy stared at her.

"Just think about what I said." Lilly stood and smoothed her apron. "*Danki* for the water and cookies." She looked at her brother. "Are you ready?"

Gerald crossed the porch and placed his empty glass on the tray. "It was *gut* seeing you. We'll have to get together sometime."

"*Ya.*" Timothy shook his hand. "That would be *gut.*" He followed them down the steps to the buggy.

Lilly shook Timothy's hand. "*Danki* for the talk. Please think about what I said."

Timothy waved as they drove off.

Once they were out of sight, he sank onto the porch steps, tossed his hat down, and raked his fingers through his hair.

Never in a million years had he expected Lilly to show up on his doorstep begging for forgiveness for wrecking his relationship with Miriam. To make matters even more confusing, Lilly insisted Miriam's heart still belonged to him.

Turning his face up to the sky, he groaned. What was God trying to tell him? Timothy had thought marrying Naomi was what God had planned for him, but now Lilly had thrown a wrench into the plan. Was God trying to tell him to give Miriam another chance?

But how could breaking a promise and also breaking Naomi's heart be in God's plan?

Timothy swiped his hand over his face, grabbed his hat, and stood. He climbed the porch steps, took the tray of glasses to the kitchen, grabbed the lantern from the railing, and headed to the barn. The only way he'd know if being with Miriam was the answer was by talking to Miriam in person. Only she could tell him if she wanted to be with him.

After hitching up the horse, he steered toward the main road. In less than an hour, he'd be at Miriam's cabin, and then he could get answers straight from Miriam.

· · ·

Timothy gingerly knocked on the door to Miriam's cabin and then held his breath. It was late, but he hoped she was still awake and willing to speak with him.

A few moments later, the door opened, revealing Edna clad in a housecoat. She eyed him with suspicion. "Timothy Kauffman?" she asked. "Do you know what time it is?"

"*Ya.*" He held his hat in front of him and absently turned it. "I apologize. I was hoping I could speak with Miriam about an important matter. I knew I would be up all night if I didn't get to talk to her right away."

Edna shook her head and frowned. "I'm sorry, but she's not home yet."

"May I ask where she is?"

"She had supper with Zach Fisher. They've been gone several hours now."

Zach Fisher. There's that name again.

Timothy gritted his teeth.

"Timothy," Edna began, "I don't mean to pry, but I think it's time for you to move on. You're marrying Naomi, and Miriam is seeing Zach. It may be best for you two to just be friends and remember your past as a fond memory of your youth."

He nodded. "Perhaps you're right."

"Son, I know I am. I have a lot of regrets in my life, which is why I never married. The biggest mistake I made was letting a man I loved go. But in this situation, I think it's the best solution. You have Naomi now, so you must cherish her. Don't let her go."

Is this the sign the Lord was trying to send me?

He cleared his throat. "*Danki.* Please don't mention to Miriam that I was here."

"I won't," she said with a smile. "Drive home safely."

"*Gut nacht.*"

"*Gut nacht.*" She closed the door.

Timothy climbed into the buggy and let his head thump back on the seat, his emotions whirling inside him. His heart was numb. While he knew he loved Miriam, the roads seemed to be pointing to Naomi.

Nevertheless, what Edna said made sense. He'd made a promise to Naomi, and Miriam was seeing Zach Fisher. Even though the idea of being with Miriam felt right, it wasn't logical or practical.

He belonged with Naomi, and it was time he faced it.

. . .

Staring out of Zach's windshield, Miriam spotted a buggy passing them in the dark. "I wonder who that is," she muttered. "It looks like they're coming from my *daed's* house."

"Maybe it's Hannah heading back home?" Zach asked.

"*Ya.* Maybe." Miriam studied the mysterious rig as it passed. "Doesn't look like Hannah's. Besides, I can't imagine her driving home so late at night with the *kinner.* She doesn't like to drive in the dark."

"Maybe it was someone coming to visit your *daed,*" he said, steering onto the lane leading to Abraham's house. "Everyone has been concerned about him. I would imagine Hannah had a house full of visitors tonight while she cared for him."

Miriam nodded and glanced at Abraham's house as they bounced by in the buggy. Lanterns glowed from the kitchen. She hoped her father was in bed resting and not still awake.

"*Danki* for joining me for supper tonight," Zach said with a sideways glance. "I had a *wunderbaar* time."

"*Ya*, me too. *Danki* for inviting me." She gazed at the cabin, surprised to find lanterns still aglow. Edna must've decided to wait up for her.

Zach brought the horse to rest at the porch step and then climbed out and tethered the horse to the hitching post.

Climbing the porch, Miriam sat in the swing and patted the seat next to her, inviting him to join her.

He sank into the seat and turned and faced her, his

expression serious. "I'm glad you're back to stay. I was sad when you left. I'm thrilled you're going to be baptized." He leaned over and touched her hand.

Miriam smiled. She knew where this conversation would go next. He was going to suggest they court. Now was the time to mention Lilly, but she had to do it the right way so as not to insult him or hurt his feelings.

"Would you consider courting me?" he asked, his eyes hopeful.

"Zach," she began, choosing her words with care. "You know I care for you as a friend."

He frowned and pulled his hand back.

"Wait," she said, touching his hand. "Just hear me out. You may like what I have to say."

"I doubt that," he muttered, pushing his hat back on his head.

"Zach, you've been a *gut*, true friend to me for many years, and I appreciate that. However, I still see you as a friend and care for you deeply." She took his hand in hers. "But I'm not the *maedel* for you."

Sighing, he shook his head. "I think you are the *maedel* for me. I love you, Miriam. Can't you see that? I've always loved you."

Guilt shot through her.

Why did he have to love her? She wished she loved him in return, but she only loved one man, a man who was marrying someone else.

But Lilly loves Zach! He won't be alone like me.

She cleared her throat and tried to ignore the hurt in his eyes. "I know someone who has loved you from afar for many years now, and she would be honored to court you."

He raised an eyebrow. "What are you saying?"

"You've never noticed her." She gave him a coy smile. "You've never paid her any mind at all."

He grimaced and stood. "Please don't play games with me, Miriam. I'm not in any mood to joke. I just opened my heart to you, and you stomped on it. I understand that you don't want to court me, so let's leave it at that."

"Wait." She popped up and grabbed his arm. "I'm not toying with you. There's someone else who loves you. She's always loved you. In fact, she was so jealous of your friendship with me that she broke up Timothy and me."

Zach's eyebrows knitted together. "What are you saying, Miriam? Who would do something like that?"

"Lilly." Miriam hoped he would believe her.

His eyes widened, and his expression softened. "Lilly? Your sister?"

"*Ya.*" Miriam smiled. "She told me she's always loved you, but you've never given her much more than a nod at services or at singings when you were younger. She said she was jealous of our friendship."

"But why would she go so far as to ruin your engagement to Timothy because of her feelings for me?" He pointed to his chest. "That doesn't make sense."

"I know." Miriam folded her arms. "And she's very sorry and has learned from her mistakes. She and I have worked things out and renewed our friendship. I forgave her, which is the Christian thing to do." She paused, gathering her thoughts. "Did you hear what

I said? Lilly loves you, and only you. You should be courting her, not me. I can't be more than your friend, but you should think about Lilly."

He gave her a suspicious look. "Did she put you up to this?"

"No, no!" She shook her head. "She has no idea I'm telling you her feelings, and she would probably be upset if she found out I told you. She thinks you don't like her, and she didn't want me to interfere in her life."

He lifted his hat and gazed toward Abraham's house. "I had no idea. I never realized she was trying to get my attention."

"Probably because you were so focused on me."

Meeting her gaze, he smiled. "*Ya*, probably. You've always had me captivated."

"Zach, you belong with someone like Lilly."

He shook his head. "I don't know. I don't see how I can just change my heart so quickly."

Miriam nodded. "I know you care for me, but I can't give you the commitment you long to have. Lilly can. You should give her a chance."

He looked skeptical.

"You two have more in common than you think." Miriam grinned. "You'd be surprised."

"What do you mean?" He raised an eyebrow with curiosity.

"You both are crazy about books."

His eyebrows shot to his hairline. "Really?"

"*Ya!*" Miriam nodded. "She had so many in our room when we were growing up that my dad once joked that she could open a used bookstore."

He grinned. "You know, that's always been my dream. I've considered turning part of my shop into a little bookstore."

"Lilly would love that," Miriam said. "I would imagine she has enough books stuffed in her bureau to start a little book corner in your shop, with the bishop's permission of course."

"That sounds doable." He rubbed his chin and stared off toward the dark field. "Lilly Lapp has always loved me. I never knew it. I'm stunned."

"Give her a chance, Zach. You have my blessing."

He nodded. "I'll talk to her."

"*Danki*." She smiled. "I'd be *froh* to see you with my sister. You'd be a *gut* husband to her." Stepping back, she smiled. "*Danki* for supper. *Gut nacht*."

"*Gut nacht*." He descended the stairs and climbed into the buggy.

Miriam stood at the railing and watched the buggy disappear into the darkness. Stepping into the cabin, she found a lonely lantern burning in the kitchen. She glanced toward Edna's room and assumed Edna had gone to bed earlier. Miriam hoped Edna was feeling well. She snuffed out the lantern, retreated to her room, and changed into her nightgown.

Crawling into bed, she said her prayers, adding an extra special one for Zach and Lilly. As she fell asleep, she imagined celebrating Lilly and Zach's wedding with the community.

CHAPTER 24

Two weeks later, Miriam's hands trembled as she sat on a bench near the front of the room during a regular Sunday service held in her father's house. The walls in the downstairs were moved to make room for rows of benches. More than a hundred members of her church district were there for the service. Today was the day she would be baptized and would truly be Amish. Her heart thumped in her chest and her eyes filled with tears. Oh, how she wished her mother were here to celebrate this life-changing moment with her!

Earlier that morning, Miriam and her baptism classmates had met with the ministers one last time while the congregation began singing hymns. After their meeting, they filed into the church service together, first the young men and then the young women, and took their seats on the benches reserved for them at the front of the congregation near the ministers.

Miriam and her classmates bowed their heads and covered their faces with their hands as a symbol of their willingness to submit to God and the church.

She did her best to concentrate through the two sermons based on the book of Acts; however, her mind buzzed with thoughts of how much her life would change once she was a member of the church. She would follow in the traditions of her ancestors. She would participate in the fall Communion service coming next month. It felt so right, and her heart soared. This was her home. This was where she belonged, not in Indiana.

Once the sermons ended, the deacon left the room to retrieve the pail of water and a cup.

"Go down on your knees before the Most High and Almighty God and His church if you still think this is the right thing to do to obtain your salvation," Bishop Gideon Swartzendruber instructed Miriam and the rest of the candidates.

The bishop stood by Miriam first. Her body trembled. The moment had come.

"Can you renounce the devil, the world, and your own flesh and blood?" the bishop asked.

"*Ya*," she said, her voice a quavering whisper.

"Can you commit yourself to Christ and His church and to abide by it and therein to live and to die?"

"*Ya*," she whispered.

"And in all the order of the church, according to the Word of the Lord, to be obedient and submissive to it and to help therein?"

"*Ya*," she said.

Miriam closed her eyes and tried to calm her heartbeat as the bishop moved to the next candidate. Once he was finished asking the questions to each one, he asked the congregation to stand. He read a prayer from the traditional Swiss Anabaptist prayer book before the congregation sat again.

The bishop, his wife, the deacon, and his wife stood before Miriam. The deacon's wife removed Miriam's prayer covering. Miriam's body shook anew as the deacon poured water into the bishop's cupped hands before it dripped onto Miriam's head. The water was cool and refreshing; she truly felt reborn!

Bishop Gideon Swartzendruber then extended his hand to Miriam and she rose. She closed her eyes while he recited a prayer.

"May the Lord God complete the good work which He has begun in you and strengthen and comfort you to a blessed end through Jesus Christ," he said. "Amen."

The bishop's wife kissed Miriam as a symbol of the "holy kiss" before Miriam placed her prayer *kapp* back on her head.

Miriam closed her eyes and prayed while the baptism was completed for the rest of the candidates. When the process was complete, the bishop reminded the congregation to be obedient.

. . .

Once the service was over, Miriam greeted her friends and family members and accepted their handshakes and words of encouragement. She was now a member of the church. Her eyes filled with tears as she thought of her mother and how pleased she would've been.

"I'm so *froh* for you," Hannah engulfed Miriam in a warm hug. "*Mamm* would've loved to have been here."

"I was just thinking that," Miriam whispered into

her sister's ear while still holding onto her. "But it's better late than never, *ya*?"

"*Ya*." Hannah kissed her cheek and then stepped back from the hug. "You look beautiful."

"*Danki*." Miriam touched her new black dress. "*Aenti* helped me make the dress. We've been working every night for a week. I needed a few dresses of my own now that I'm back."

Lena Joy sidled up to her mother. "Hi, *Aenti* Miriam. You look pretty."

"Thank you." Miriam touched her arm. "How are you feeling?"

Lena shrugged. "*Gut. Danki*. I'm looking forward to finishing up that dress we started last week. I can't wait until you come over on Tuesday."

"Me too." Miriam touched her cheek. "I love spending time with you."

"I do too." Lena Joy glanced up at Hannah. "They need your help in the kitchen. *Aenti* Lilly asked me to come and get you. They need you to help serve the food."

"Oh. I better go then." Hannah smiled at Miriam. "Go talk to the other guests. I'm sure they want to congratulate you."

Miriam shook her head. "No, I'll help serve the food too." She followed her sister and niece into the kitchen, where they served the lunchtime meal to the men first. Miriam and her sisters had spent days preparing to host the service in the house. They planted flowers, cleaned the house, and cooked. Miriam and her sisters wanted to make their mother proud by having her home perfect for the special occasion.

After the men were finished eating, they went outside to socialize and the women and children ate. Miriam sat with her sisters, and they talked and laughed while eating. After they finished, Lilly excused herself and went to check on Abraham, who had retreated upstairs for a nap.

Beth Anne approached Miriam and shook her hand. "I'm so glad you invited me to come and witness your baptism. I'm so very *froh* for you. Welcome to the church."

"*Danki.*" Miriam smiled. "I'm glad you came."

"It was a beautiful service." Beth Anne sat next to Miriam on the bench. "I enjoy coming to services at other districts."

"I do too," Hannah said while picking up a cookie and handing it to Mary. "It's fun to hear another bishop speak."

"*Ya,*" Beth Anne said, nodding. "Are you coming to work tomorrow, Miriam?"

Miriam nodded. "*Ya,* I'll be there. Hannah is going to watch out for *Daed* tomorrow."

"*Gut.*" Beth Anne smiled at Hannah. "Your sister is a *wunderbaar* baker."

"*Ya.*" Hannah agreed. "She learned from *Grossmammi* Lapp."

Beth Anne and Hannah discussed their favorite recipes, while Miriam scanned the crowd of friends and family members. During the service and the meal, her mind kept wandering to thoughts of Timothy. She'd secretly hoped Beth Anne extended an invitation to him. Miriam also hoped Lilly had invited Naomi to come, and Naomi had invited him.

However, Miriam hadn't spotted Naomi or Timothy, and she was disappointed. Today was the most important day of her life. Miriam had pledged her life to God, and she wished she could share her excitement with Timothy.

But Timothy is marrying someone else.

Shooing away the thought, Miriam glanced toward the stairs, where Lilly stood with a wide grin. Tilting her head, Miriam spotted what was causing her sister's mirth—Zach standing across from her while talking and smiling.

Warmth flowed through Miriam. Although she might never have her true love, she was witnessing love in the making.

God is good.

Miriam turned back to Beth Anne, deep in a discussion about apple pie recipes with Hannah, who nodded in agreement about the best-flavored apples to use in the pies. They discussed recipes for a while longer until Beth Anne stood.

"I better get back home," Beth Anne said. "*Danki* for inviting me. My *mamm* wanted to come, but she was hosting a social in her home today."

"I understand." Miriam gave her a quick hug. "I'll see you tomorrow."

Beth Anne headed through the crowd toward the back door, and Hannah stood. "I better go check on my *kinner*. Then I'll get started cleaning up the tables."

"I'll get started out here." Miriam collected the dirty paper cups and plates from the surrounding tables and then started toward the kitchen. She was approaching the doorway when a hand tapped her shoulder.

"Miriam," Lilly said, her voice brewing with excitement. "You'll never guess who just talked to me."

"Who?" Miriam set the dirty cups and plates back onto the table and faced her sister, who was grinning ear-to-ear.

"Zach!" Lilly's cheeks flushed. "He came over to me and told me I looked nice. He told me all about his business and how much it's been booming. He told me he loves reading, and we spent about fifteen minutes discussing our favorite authors. He told me he always wanted to open a little bookstore, and I told him that was my dream too!" Her grin was electric. "He asked me to have supper with him tomorrow night. Can you believe it?" She bit her bottom lip. "He's so handsome, Miriam. I can't believe he finally noticed me."

"That's *wunderbaar*." Miriam hugged her younger sister. "I'm so excited for you. I wish you all the happiness in the world, *Schweschder*."

Lilly pursed her lips and eyed Miriam with suspicion. "Wait just a minute. You don't seem all that surprised." She wagged a finger at her. "Did you have something to do with this, Miriam Lapp?"

Miriam shrugged and picked up the dirty cups and dishes again. "I would imagine Zach Fisher finally got his head screwed on right and realized what an amazing person you are."

"Miriam . . ." Lilly grabbed her arm. "I have a feeling you're playing matchmaker."

Miriam gave her a knowing smile. "I may have suggested he talk to you, but he asked you to supper on his own accord. He is his own man with his own mind. His interest in you is genuine."

Lilly clasped her hands together and made a soft shrieking noise in her throat. "I feel like I've waited a lifetime for this."

"It's worth the wait." Miriam carried the dirty plates and cups into the kitchen and dropped them into the large trash bag by the door.

A group of women cleaned up the kitchen while talking about friends and family members. Miriam grabbed a wet rag and traipsed out into the living room to begin wiping down the tables. She glanced across the room and found Lilly and Zach talking in the corner. She smiled and continued her task.

"Miriam," Zach called. "Come here and tell your sister how well I cook. She doesn't believe me."

Chuckling, Miriam joined the couple.

. . .

Timothy followed Naomi up the porch steps to the front door of Abraham Lapp's house. While he was happy Miriam had joined the church today, he wasn't convinced it was appropriate for him to be here sharing this personal time with her. Considering how he still cared for her, he was worried his presence might make her uncomfortable—especially in front of her boyfriend.

Dread filled him at the thought of having to witness Miriam and Zach together. He wondered if Zach knew how blessed he was to have Miriam.

Timothy stepped into the living room behind Naomi.

He nodded greetings to familiar faces as they made their way through the knot of people toward a small group back toward the door leading to the kitchen.

His abdomen tightened when his eyes focused on Lilly, Zach, and Miriam. The three were laughing and talking, and his stomach roiled when Miriam reached out and patted Zach's bicep.

Couldn't she save the touching for a private location?

"Hi," Naomi rushed over and hugged Lilly. She then turned to Miriam. "Welcome to the church. I'm sorry we couldn't be here to see your baptism. We had some obligations to fulfill in our district."

"*Danki* for coming." Miriam met Timothy's gaze, and her expression became . . . anxious? "*Gut* to see you, Timothy."

"I was *froh* to hear the news," Timothy said, shifting his weight on his feet. "Beth Anne mentioned today was the day, and then Naomi invited me to come. I'm glad to be here."

Miriam nodded, her gorgeous brown eyes sparkling. She looked radiant, as usual.

"*Gut* to see you, Timothy." Zach held his hand out.

"You too." Timothy hesitated and then shook the man's hand.

Jealousy is a sin.

And why should Timothy be jealous? He was marrying Naomi, a woman who loved him. Devotion shone in her eyes and on her face. Timothy was a fool to pine for Miriam.

His sister Sarah Rose's words from the past echoed in his mind—*You can't help whom you love.*

Ya, he loved Miriam, but she was with Zach while he was with Naomi.

"Would you like something to drink?" Lilly offered. "Maybe a snack? We have plenty of desserts left. I think we went a bit overboard with the food."

Timothy shrugged. "Sure. *Danki.*"

"I'll walk with you," Naomi said.

Lilly and Naomi chattered away while they headed to the kitchen.

Timothy cleared his throat and faced Miriam and Zach.

This couldn't get any more awkward . . .

Looking between the two of them, Timothy wondered why he had come. "How's your *daed*?" he asked, folding his arms across his chest.

"*Gut.*" She gestured toward the stairs. "He's taking a nap. Today was a lot of excitement for him. Lilly checked on him earlier, and he was doing just fine."

"That's *wunderbaar.*" He scanned the room and found a few familiar faces. He wondered if Beth Anne was still there since she'd mentioned she was going to come. "Did my sister come by? She told me she was going to visit."

"*Ya.* She left already." Miriam smiled, and his heart thumped. "I was really *froh* to see her. She's a *gut* friend."

He nodded and looked at Zach. "How's business?"

"I don't mean to brag, but it's booming," he said with a grin. "I got an order for fifty saddles from a couple of *English* horse farmers the other day. I was really thankful. For a while, things had slowed down, but I may need to hire a helper now. How's the furniture shop?"

"The same," Timothy said. "We've been so busy my *dat* hired another carpenter. We can't seem to get caught up. The orders just keep coming."

"That's *gut*." Zach nodded toward a long table in the corner. "Why don't you two have a seat? I'll go give Lilly and Naomi a hand."

Miriam shot Zach a shocked expression, and he shrugged in response before heading toward the kitchen.

She then met Timothy's gaze. "Shall we have a seat?"

He followed her to the table and sank onto the bench across from her. He studied her eyes, wishing he knew what she was feeling toward him. She seemed very uneasy. He hoped his presence didn't make her that way. He remembered the days when they could say anything to each other. He missed those times so much that his heart ached.

"Naomi came to visit a couple of weeks ago," she said, lacing her fingers together. "She brought us a basket of breads. It was very nice."

"*Ya*, she told me." He rubbed his chin and then rested his arms on the table. "I was glad to hear she came out to see you." He knew lying was a sin, but he couldn't admit the truth to Miriam. He'd not been happy when he heard she'd come to the house and Miriam was there. He hoped she hadn't spoken about the wedding the whole time.

"She mentioned how excited she is about your upcoming wedding," Miriam said, a frown stealing her soft expression.

Timothy swallowed a groan. Naomi had done exactly what he'd feared.

"I'm *froh* for you," she said, but her eyes betrayed her words.

"*Danki*," he said, his voice sounding soft despite the neighboring conversations whirling around them.

Their eyes locked, and he could've sworn he saw tears in those deep pools of chocolate beneath her long, gorgeous lashes. But why would she cry over him? Their love was in the past.

Right?

She studied him, her gaze unmoving and her expression intense. His breath was ragged as memories of their time together assaulted his mind. He longed to reach for her, take her in his arms, and tell her he still loved her.

But he'd made a promise to Naomi, and Miriam was courting Zach.

Their time was gone. It was lost in the past.

However, he had a hunch that similar thoughts were floating through Miriam's mind. Her expression seemed to mirror the regret seeping into his soul.

"I hope you still like chocolate chip cookies," Naomi said, snapping him back to the present. "There's a mountain of them in the kitchen." She placed a plate of cookies in front of him. "I got you some ice water too."

"*Danki*," he said, grabbing a cookie from the plate. "They smell *appeditlich*."

Zach sat next to Miriam with Lilly at his other side. "These cookies are *wunderbaar*. Did you make them, Miriam?"

"I think so. We had a lot of people bring food, so there's no way to be sure." Miriam sipped her water.

Naomi slipped onto the seat next to Timothy and touched his arm before grabbing a couple of cookies.

Timothy tried to keep his eyes off Miriam while everyone chatted around him. Yet his eyes were drawn to her as if her face held an invisible magnetic force only he sensed. A few times, she met his gaze and blessed him with a shy smile before her cheeks blushed a bright pink. He tried in vain to look at Naomi instead, but his orbs defied him, opting for Miriam.

More than once, Lilly caught his eye and gave him a knowing smile. Had she noticed his staring at Miriam? If so, then she seemed to approve of it. However, Zach was sitting between her and Miriam as if to stake his claim. How could Timothy consider pursuing Miriam, when she had chosen Zach? He wondered where Lilly found her logic.

He felt a surge of relief when Naomi announced it was late and she had to get home. Watching Miriam was sweet torture, and he needed to get away from her beautiful face before his longing for her became transparent.

Naomi and Lilly headed out the front door and stayed engrossed in a conversation about quilting and the most popular patterns.

Timothy followed with Zach at his side, making conversation about their respective businesses and how to keep up with rising supply costs. Miriam trailed behind them, her eyes averted from his.

When they reached the barn, Zach accompanied Timothy inside and helped him hitch the horse to the buggy. He walked with Timothy out to the awaiting group of women.

"Keep in touch," Naomi said, hugging Lilly. "I'm so glad we came and got to see you." She then looked at Miriam. "We're *froh* you're here to stay. It's so *gut* to have you in the church."

"*Danki*," Miriam said.

"I guess we'll see you all Thursday at Sarah and Luke's wedding, *ya*?" Naomi asked.

"*Ya*, I guess so," Miriam said. She nodded at Timothy. "Take care."

"You too," he said.

They stared in silence for another moment, and then she turned and hurried back into the house.

He shook Zach's hand and climbed into the buggy. Naomi hopped in next to him and waved to Lilly.

When Lilly met his gaze, she winked. Timothy shook his head, wishing he knew what her secret code meant.

He steered toward the main road, hoping to put Miriam out of his mind.

Naomi reached over and squeezed his arm. "*Danki* for taking me. It was so *wunderbaar* to see Lilly. Miriam looked *gut*, didn't she? I think it's great that she's staying, don't you?"

"*Ya*, it's great." He kept his eyes on the road ahead.

"You okay, Timothy?" she asked. "You're quiet again."

He cut his eyes to her and forced a smile. "I'm fine. I'm glad you were with me today."

She studied him with suspicion for a moment and then changed the subject, discussing the quilt stand for the rest of the ride home.

Timothy settled in his seat and focused on her stories, pushing Miriam as far from his mind as possible.

CHAPTER 25

Thursday morning, Miriam sniffed and wiped her eyes as Sarah Rose and Luke recited their vows standing before nearly two hundred members of the community. Weddings always made her cry, whether they were Amish or the *English* weddings she'd attended during her days spent in Indiana. Amish ceremonies were very different from the *English* weddings. Held on Tuesdays and Thursdays in the fall, Amish weddings didn't include flowers, tuxedoes, or gowns.

The wedding ceremony was similar to a typical church service, and the benches were set up in the same manner, with the men and women seated separately. It began with the couple meeting with the minister while the congregation sang hymns from the *Ausbund*.

When the hymns were complete, Sarah Rose and Luke returned to the congregation and sat with their attendants, Rebecca, Daniel, Beth Anne, and Paul. Sarah Rose, with her attendants by her side, sat facing Luke, Paul, and Daniel. Sarah Rose, Rebecca, and Beth Anne wore matching navy blue dresses that they had made themselves, while the men wore their traditional Sunday black and white clothing.

After another hymn, the minister delivered a thirty-minute sermon based on Old Testament stories of marriages. The congregation kneeled for silent prayer and then rose for the minister's reading of Matthew 19 verses one through twelve.

Next Bishop Abner Chupp stood and preached the main sermon, continuing with the book of Genesis, including the story of Abraham and the other patriarchs included in the book. Miriam sat in the congregation with the other young women.

During the sermon, Hannah leaned over to Miriam. "It's such a blessing Sarah Rose found Luke after losing her Peter so tragically," she whispered.

Miriam forced a smile. "*Ya*, God is good," she whispered. She looked back toward the soon-to-be newlyweds. Sarah Rose, Timothy's younger sister, was radiant in her blue linen dress with her white *kapp*. She beamed at her groom, Luke, whose eyes shone with love for her.

That should've been Timothy and me.

The thought caught Miriam off guard. Before she could stop herself, her eyes moved to the sea of men at the other side of the room and honed in on Timothy. Her heart slammed against her ribcage when she found him studying her, his blue eyes serious. Was he also thinking of the plans they'd made and then lost?

No, he's thinking of his wedding to Naomi.

Miriam bit back a groan at the thought. How would she stomach sitting through Timothy and Naomi's wedding next month? The mere thought made bile rise in her throat. Perhaps she would feign the flu in order to miss the occasion.

She struggled in vain to remove her eyes from Timothy's stare. She felt a hand on her shoulder, and relief flooded her.

"Are you all right?" Hannah whispered.

"*Ya*," Miriam said in response, shifting her eyes back to the bride and groom, who looked to be listening intently to the bishop's lecture on Paul's instructions for marriage included in 1 Corinthians and Ephesians. Although she knew she should be listening, Miriam's mind still wandered to Timothy and all that could've been.

The bishop continued his sermon, instructing Sarah Rose and Luke on how to run a godly household, and then he moved on to a forty-five-minute sermon on the story of Sara and Tobias from the intertestamental book of Tobit.

When the sermon was over, the bishop looked between Sarah Rose and Luke. "Now here are two in one faith," he said. "Sarah Rose Troyer and Luke Hezekiah Troyer." The bishop then asked the congregation if they knew any scriptural reason for the couple to not be married. Hearing no response, he continued, "If it is your desire to be married you may in the name of the Lord come forth."

Luke took Sarah Rose's hand in his and they stood before the bishop to take their vows.

While the couple responded to the bishop's questions, Miriam glanced over at Timothy. She sucked in a breath when she found his eyes focused intently on her. She held his gaze with her heart pounding in her chest while the bishop read "A Prayer for Those About to Be Married" from an Amish prayer book called the *Christenpflict*.

Timothy turned back toward Bishop Abner Chupp when he resumed his sermon.

When the sermon was over, the congregation knelt while the bishop again read from the *Christenpflict*. After the bishop recited the Lord's Prayer, the congregation stood, and the three-hour service ended with the singing of another hymn.

Once the ceremony was over, some of the men began rearranging furniture while others joined the women to serve the wedding dinner, which included chicken with stuffing, mashed potatoes with gravy, pepper cabbage, and cooked cream of celery. The bountiful desserts that followed were cookies, pie, fruit, and Jell-O salad. They served them in shifts. The newly married couple received the food first, followed by their wedding party. Miriam stayed in the kitchen and helped prepare the food, hoping to avoid talking to Timothy and seeing him with Naomi.

Carrying a pitcher of iced water, Miriam set out into the large dining area. With the living room and moveable bedroom walls removed, the downstairs of Sarah Rose and Luke's home was spacious. Benches converted to tables lined the open area, and the men ate and gabbed, their conversations a loud drone among the crowd.

Miriam made her way across the room, filling empty glasses while smiling and exchanging pleasantries. As she turned and headed toward a neighboring table, she heard loud squealing coming toward her. She took a step toward the table just as Ian and Mary ran past her, knocking her off balance and sending her crashing into the table. The pitcher slipped from her hands and landed in the lap of a man seated at the end of the bench while Miriam came to rest on the floor next to him.

The man hopped up from the bench and crouched next to her. "Are you all right?"

Her cheeks ablaze with embarrassment, Miriam turned toward him, pain radiating from her knees to her shins.

When she found herself looking into Timothy's eyes, she gasped. She examined his soaked shirt and trousers, and she thought her face might combust.

"I'm so sorry, Timothy," she said. "Hannah's *kinner* ran by, and they tripped me."

His grin was wide. "It's all right. I won't need a shower tonight." He held out his hand. "Let me help you up."

A crowd gathered around them, including Lilly and Timothy's curious sisters.

"Are you okay?" Hannah asked.

"What happened?" Lilly asked.

"Why are you all wet?" Beth Anne asked Timothy.

"Everything is fine," Timothy said, gesturing for them to leave the scene. "You can get back to whatever you were doing." He then turned back to Miriam. "Let me help you up before we draw a bigger crowd."

She grasped his hand, and heat raced up her arm. After retrieving the pitcher from the floor, he pulled her up to her feet, and she grimaced as the pain worsened on her shins and knees.

"Are you hurt?" His blue eyes simmered with concern.

"I'm fine." She nodded toward his shirt that was dripping water. "Let's get you cleaned up in the kitchen."

Taking her arm, he steered her toward the kitchen. She cringed when the pain stung her legs.

"You really hurt yourself," he said.

She waved off his empathy, despite the pain. "I'm just a klutz."

"You might want to go into the bathroom and see if you need a bandage." He led her into the kitchen and placed the pitcher on the counter.

"I'll be fine." She hobbled across the room and grabbed two towels.

When she turned, she found a group of women gathered around Timothy, providing him with towels. She placed her towels on the counter, feeling like a fool for rushing.

His gaze met hers, and he gave her a worried expression. "Go check out your legs," he said over the chatter around him. "The bathroom is on the other side of the kitchen."

"I'm really sorry about this," she said, crossing her arms in front of her chest.

"Don't be silly. I can run home and grab something else to wear." His eyes locked on hers, and the intensity caused her pulse to leap. "I'm more worried about your legs. Please go take care of them. I'm sure Luke has bandages since he's known for hitting his fingers with a hammer."

Unable to speak, Miriam limped across the kitchen to the bathroom, closing the door behind her. She pulled up her dress and gasped at the sight of long, bloody scrapes and bruises turning purple on her legs.

"What an oaf," she mumbled.

Opening the medicine chest, she grabbed bandages and salve. She winced as she applied the salve, all the while concentrating on the intensity in Timothy's eyes. Why was he so concerned about her legs? And what was he thinking while he was staring at me during the service? She wished she could've read his thoughts.

If only he weren't getting married . . .

She pushed the thought away and covered her legs with the bandages.

. . .

Timothy pulled on a dry shirt and pair of trousers. Taking the stairs two at a time, he hurried down to the kitchen. While he filled a glass with water from the tap, he glanced around the room, and his thoughts wandered back to when he'd built the house—for Miriam. They'd spent hours discussing the house—how many rooms it would have, how to set up the kitchen, and how many children they'd wanted to fill the bedrooms upstairs.

Shaking his head, he lifted the glass to his lips. When Miriam had left, she'd taken his heart with her, and he'd considered moving in with his parents and selling the house to one of his newly married friends. However, his pride had won out and he remained in the house—alone.

He glanced out the window toward Sarah Rose and Luke's house, and he envisioned the expression on

Miriam's face after she'd fallen. While his first reaction was to laugh at the utter hilarity of the situation, his smile disappeared when he'd found she'd been hurt. He'd resisted the urge to pick Miriam up and carry her to the bathroom to help with her injury.

He dropped into a kitchen chair and rubbed his temple. He wished he could stop the memories of Miriam and feelings for her from assaulting his mind and wreaking havoc on his life. He planned to marry Naomi in only a month. He wished he could convince his heart that this was the best decision for his future.

However, he doubted his decision more than ever when he watched Miriam's expression during the wedding service earlier today. She seemed to be lost in her thoughts, just as he was. Did she harbor the same regrets as he did?

But it was her choice to leave.

Timothy placed the glass on the counter and ambled to the kitchen. As he stepped into the living room, the front door swung open with a squeak, revealing a grinning Naomi.

"I heard you had a run-in with a pitcher of water," she said with a laugh. "Are you all dried up now?"

He put his arm around her shoulders, escorting her to the door. "*Ya*, I'm all dried up. That's for certain."

· · ·

Lindsay sank into a seat across from her sister. "The wedding was beautiful. I even understood some of the *Dietsch*."

Jessica snorted and gave Jake a sideways glance. "That makes one of us."

Jake raised an eyebrow in response. "You don't understand any of the *Dietsch*?"

"*Ya* and *gude mariye* are about the extent of my *Dietsch*," Jessica said with a shrug. She lifted a glass of water to her lips.

Jake looped his arm around her shoulder. "I guess that means you need to spend more time here so you can learn more *Dietsch* words."

"We've been through this how many times?" She rolled her eyes. "Consider yourself lucky that Trisha let me take time off from school to come here for the wedding. She wasn't too keen on the idea at first, but my Aunt Rebecca had a long talk with her in order to convince her."

"I know, I know." Jake grinned. "I was just kidding. I'm very happy you got to come up for a few days."

Lindsay glanced across the room and wondered if she'd ever find anyone who cared for her as much Jake cared for Jessica. The love was apparent in his eyes, and she questioned when her sister would realize how special he was.

Her gaze locked on Matthew Glick, crossing the room with Elmer Yoder. Elmer spotted Lindsay and stopped in his tracks. He said something to Matthew and pointed toward her. Her cheeks heated as Matthew negotiated through the crowd to the table. He was handsome, clad in a dark blue shirt with dark trousers and suspenders. A few deep brown curls escaped from under his straw hat.

She touched her prayer *kapp*, hoping her hair was still secure beneath it. Then she wondered why she was so worried about her appearance since she'd never even spoken to the guy except for their brief first meeting at Elizabeth's during the summer.

Jake turned and waved. "Hey, Matt. How are you doing?"

Matthew shrugged. "All right." He glanced at Jessica. "You're back, huh? I thought you went to Virginia to return to school."

"I'm just in town for the wedding," Jessica said.

Matthew nodded.

Jake gestured toward the open seat next to Lindsay. "Pull up a seat."

Matthew dropped onto the bench next to Lindsay and gave a slight nod of greeting.

Lindsay couldn't keep from staring at his gorgeous golden eyes. She felt as if she'd been hypnotized. When he gave her a questioning expression, she cut her gaze to the surface of the bench that served as their tabletop, wishing her cheeks would cool.

"Where have you been?" Jake asked, lifting his cup of water. "I saw you just before the service started and then didn't see you again. It was as if you'd disappeared into thin air."

"I was trying to escape, but Elmer caught me."

"Escape?" The question left Lindsay's lips before she could stop it. "What do you mean?"

Matthew's eyes were curious. "Why should I hang around here? I really don't know anyone."

"You know me," Jake said.

"Don't you want to get to know people in the community since you're new here?" Lindsay studied his eyes, captivated by their unusual golden hue.

"Why are you so concerned about my social life?" Matthew's voice was warm and smooth, reminding her of whipped butter.

Lindsay tried to appear nonchalant, even though the attention he gave her was causing her insides to scream with excitement. "I know what it's like to be new, that's all."

"Maybe I prefer to remain anonymous." His eyes challenged her as he glowered.

Speechless, Lindsay turned to her sister, whose eyebrows were raised in question.

While Jake and Matthew discussed their current carpentry projects at the shop, Jessica gestured toward the kitchen.

"How about we go get the guys refills?" Jessica asked, enunciating the words a little bit too much.

"Okay." Lindsay followed Jessica to the kitchen, where they stood by the counter, away from the women who were cleaning up after the meal. "Why did you call me in here?" she asked.

A knowing grin grew on her sister's lips. She pointed at Lindsay. "You like him."

"What are you talking about?" Lindsay asked, jamming her hands on her hips.

"Matthew." Jessica pointed toward the doorway leading to the living room, and Lindsay grabbed her hand.

"Stop it," she ordered through gritted teeth. "You're calling attention to us."

"You *do* like him." Jessica's smile was conniving. "This could be good."

"What are you saying? I hardly know the guy, and he doesn't seem to like anyone. He said himself that he wants to be anonymous."

"But that's just a defense mechanism. Jake told me Matthew is shy. You and I both know how hard it is coming to a new place." She smiled. "So that means that you and Matthew have tons in common. You can help him meet people and feel like he fits in with the youth here."

Lindsay shook her head in protest, even though the words made perfect sense. "I don't know, Jessica. He doesn't seem interested in making friends."

"You never know what could happen." Jessica filled four cups with ice water from a pitcher. "Just be yourself, Linds. Everyone loves you."

Lindsay sighed as they headed back to the table. "I'm going to miss you. I wish you could stay longer than the weekend." She sighed. "It's going to be too dull without you."

Jessica smirked. "Not if you get to know Matthew."

"Quit it."

Jessica laughed. "Come on, Little Sister, let's get these drinks to our thirsty guys." They reached the table and distributed the water.

Lindsay's cheeks burned with embarrassment as she sat next to Matthew. When his eyes met hers, he gave her a slight smile, and her pulse skittered. She wondered if she could possibly break through his icy exterior and become his friend.

Only time would tell . . .

. . .

Saturday night Jessica grasped Jake's hand while climbing the steps to Rebecca's porch. The crisp breeze whispering through her hair signaled that autumn had descended upon Lancaster County.

"I had a great time this weekend," she said when they reached the porch.

He frowned. "You're leaving me tomorrow."

She touched his shoulder. "I know, but you'll see me again soon."

"How soon?" His eyes challenged her.

"The first vacation I get."

"Which is when?" His expression softened. "I want an exact date."

"I do too, but I don't know the exact date. Let's figure on Thanksgiving."

Crossing his arms in front of his wide chest, he shook his head. "That's not soon enough."

She gave him a coy smile. "You're going to just have to make do without me for a little while longer. You made it through almost two months without me when I went back to Virginia at the end of August, didn't you? You'll have to be a big boy."

"And how will you do without me?" Putting his hands on her waist, he pulled her to him.

"I'll be just fine."

"Right." He ran his finger down her cheekbone, sending shivers up her spine. "You'll forget all about me and have fun with those high school boys."

"Right," she deadpanned, rolling her eyes. "As if they could compete with you."

He grinned. "Good answer." Leaning down, he brushed his lips against hers, melting her insides. "Don't forget me," he whispered. He nodded toward the cross hanging from her neck. "The cross will remind you how much I care about you."

"Don't you forget me either." She cupped his cheek in her hand. "If you do, I'll beat you up."

He snickered. "Jessica, I could never forget you." His expression became serious. "I meant what I said about college. You should apply to all of the nearby schools so we can actually be together."

She shook her head. "Let's not argue on our last night together."

He sighed with frustration. "I don't even see why this is an issue. You tell me you care about me, but you won't tell me you want to stay here. It doesn't make sense."

"I'm just not ready to make this decision right now. It's going to be difficult enough to figure it out without my parents' help. I can't make a snap decision that's going to affect the rest of my life. Don't you understand that?"

"But what about us?" His eyes pleaded with her.

Her expression softened. "There will always be an us. You have to be patient with me."

"I have the patience of Job."

"Good, because you're going to need it." She glanced up at the sky. "Look at all of those stars. How about we sit on the swing and enjoy them for a little bit?"

He gave her a surprised expression. "Isn't it past your curfew?"

Grabbing his hand, she pulled him toward the swing. "It's my last night here. What's Daniel going to do—ground me?"

Jake chuckled. "You've got a good point."

Lowering herself onto the swing next to Jake, she laced her fingers in his and leaned against his shoulder. She closed her eyes and smiled.

"I wish this moment could last forever," she said, breathing in his musky scent.

The gentle whisper of his lips on the top of her head warmed her heart. She silently prayed Thanksgiving would come quickly.

Almond Macaroons

1 cup almond paste
3/4 cup sugar
3 egg whites
Pinch salt

Rub paste until smooth; gradually work in sugar until well mixed. Add a pinch of salt and beat in one egg white at a time, mixing thoroughly. Let stand for 20 minutes. Drop by teaspoonful on lightly buttered baking sheet. Bake at 300 degrees for 30 minutes until surface is dry. Keep in cool place overnight.

CHAPTER 26

Miriam placed an apple pie on the counter and wrapped it in plastic wrap. Once it was ready for the counter out front, she wiped her hands on a rag. "Order up!" she called to Beth Anne. "What do you need next?"

"*Danki.*" Beth Anne retrieved the pie from the counter and started toward the front. "How about a shoofly pie?" she called over her shoulder. "Lizzie said we're out."

"I'm on it." Miriam fished the recipe out of the binder on the shelf and then started pulling the ingredients from the cabinets.

"What a busy week," Elizabeth said, sidling up to her. "I can't believe it's Thursday."

"Feels like it was just Monday, *ya*?" Miriam began adding the ingredients to a large mixing bowl.

"Miriam!" Beth Anne called from the front. "Telephone for you."

Miriam hurried out front. "Who is it?" she asked, taking the phone from Beth Anne.

"Hannah." Beth Anne gave a serious expression. "You might want to talk in there." She nodded toward the back office. "Go pick up in the office, and I'll hang up out here."

Her heart racing with worry, Miriam rushed to the office and picked up the phone. "Hello?"

"Miriam!" Hannah's voice was urgent. "We're on our way to Pittsburgh."

"What?" Miriam gasped, sinking into the desk chair. "Oh no. Is Lena Joy okay? What happened?"

"She's fine. They got her a liver!" Hannah's voice quaked with emotion. "The doctor said it's a perfect match. We're so blessed, Miriam. We got the call and then got a ride right away."

"Oh my goodness." Tears filled Miriam's eyes. "It's a miracle. Do you need me to stay with the *kinner*? Where are they?"

"Lilly has the *kinner*. She's keeping them at *Daed's* house."

Hannah paused. "Is there any chance you can come to the hospital? I spoke with Aaron's parents for a while earlier, and they aren't well enough to make the trip to the hospital with us. His *daed* is still recovering from his bout with pneumonia last month. Would you please come and stay with us, Miriam? I need you. Lena Joy needs you too. She specifically asked for you."

"*Ya*, of course." Miriam wiped the tears from her cheeks. "I'll see if I can get a ride right away. How close are you to Pittsburgh?"

"We have another two hours. I'm sorry I didn't call you right away, but we were making calls to Aaron's family. It all happened too fast. I was hanging out laundry when the cell phone rang. I didn't even hear it. Lena Joy heard it, thankfully. We had to pack everything up and get on the road right away. We're blessed that Aaron was close to home. I've been making calls since we got in the van. The bishop allowed us to have another cell phone on hand, so we left it with Lilly. That way we can keep in touch and let her know what's going on," Hannah continued. "Aaron's parents have one too since his *daed* is still having health problems. I'm sorry they can't be at the hospital, but we can keep them updated with the surgery."

"I can't believe it's finally happening, Hannah. Lena Joy is going to get her liver!"

"*Ya.* I know." Hannah sniffed. "I need you with me, Miriam. You'll be my rock."

"Of course I will, Hannah. I want to be there for you and Aaron." Miriam cleared her throat and stood. "I'll talk to Beth Anne and get a ride out there. I'll be there as soon as I can."

"*Danki, Schweschder,*" Hannah whispered. "I'll see you soon. It's a four-hour drive. Just ask the nurses at the front desk to direct you to our waiting room when you get there."

"Okay," Miriam said. "I'll be there soon. I love you."

"Love you too," Hannah said before hanging up.

Miriam hurried out to the kitchen and approached Beth Anne, who was standing with Elizabeth. "Hannah got the call." She grabbed Beth Anne's arm. "There's a liver for Lena Joy. They think it's a perfect match. She asked me to come to the hospital in Pittsburgh. Aaron's parents can't come because their health is bad, so I need to go and sit with her and Aaron. They need me."

"Oh, you must go!" Beth Anne said. "I'll get Nina Janitz to take you right away." She started for the office. "I'll call her now."

"Oh, Miriam!" Elizabeth hugged her. "We'll be praying for her. You must let us know how she is doing."

Kathryn walked over. "What's going on?"

"There's a liver for my niece." Miriam swallowed a sob. "She's going to get her health back."

"Oh! Praise God!" Kathryn hugged her. "We'll be praying, Miriam. What a miracle."

Lizzie and Ruthie joined them and also hugged Miriam.

Beth Anne returned from the office. "Nina should be here in five minutes."

Miriam glanced across the kitchen. "Would you finish that shoofly pie for me, Kathryn?"

Kathryn laughed. "Please don't worry about the baking, Miriam. You just go take care of your sister and her family."

"*Danki*." Miriam hugged Kathryn again. "*Danki* for everything."

. . .

Timothy sat across from Naomi at the break room table. "You've outdone yourself," he said with a smile. "Chicken salad and chow-chow?"

"I hope you're hungry because there's chocolate cake for dessert." She pulled out a large container. "It's nice outside, no?"

He nodded. "It is. Not too brisk and not a cloud in the sky. The perfect October day."

She poured him a cup of water from a thermos and handed it to him. "I thought we could make a toast."

"Oh?" He held his cup up. "What are we toasting?"

She poured herself a cup and held it up. "Our wedding is three weeks from today."

"It is?" He shook his head. "Time is passing quickly."

She grinned. "It is. I can't wait. So, let's toast."

"Timothy!" Daniel's voice boomed from the doorway behind them. "Telephone call!"

He put his cup down and stood. "Excuse me."

Naomi shrugged. "Take your time."

Timothy faced his waiting brother. "Who is it? I'm at lunch."

"*Ya*, I know, but it's Beth Anne. She said it's urgent." Daniel led him to the office. "Take it in here so you have some privacy."

"*Danki*." Timothy sat at his father's desk and lifted the receiver to his ear. "Hello?"

"Timothy?" Beth Anne asked.

"*Ya*, it's me. *Wie geht's*?" He absently twisted the telephone cord around his finger.

"It's uncanny how much you sound just like *Dat* and Daniel," she said. "I had to talk to you. It's about Miriam."

"What is it?" he asked. "Is Miriam all right?"

"*Ya*, she's fine. It's her niece," Beth Anne said. "They found a liver for her, a perfect match. Miriam's on her way to the hospital to be with Hannah and Aaron during the surgery. I had a feeling I should call and tell you. I thought you would want to know."

"I'm glad you called," he said. "I can pray for her and her niece."

"Timothy, I know you care for her. I think you should go and be there for her."

"I can't go and be with her," he said.

"Why?"

"Because I shouldn't. She wouldn't want me there."

"*Ya*, she would. She's going to be there for Hannah and Aaron, since his parents can't go. You should be there for her. You could be her strength through this."

"Beth Anne, you know I'm with Naomi."

"But you love Miriam. I can see it in your eyes every time someone says her name. You love Miriam, and you should be with her."

He closed his eyes and pinched the bridge of his nose where a migraine brewed.

Beth Anne is wrong.

"I know you mean well, and you think you know what's best for me, but Miriam is with Zach Fisher," he said. "She made her choice."

"I don't think so," Beth Anne said. "I have a feeling she's not with Zach. She never talks about him. I truly believe they are just friends. She only has eyes for you."

Timothy sighed. "Beth Anne, I don't think I should go to the hospital. I think if Miriam wanted me there, she would call me."

"Would she really, Timothy? Or would she hope you would get the news and surprise her?"

He leaned back in the desk chair, and it squeaked under his weight. "I don't know, Beth Anne."

"Well, think about it. But remember it's a four-hour drive. You should get on the road soon."

"*Danki* for calling, Beth Anne."

"Call me later," she said. "I want to know how the surgery goes. We're all praying for Lena Joy."

Timothy set the phone back in its cradle and then rested his face in his hands. While he was glad Beth Anne had called him, he didn't know what to do. If he went to the hospital to be with Miriam, he would hurt Naomi for certain. It wouldn't be appropriate to ask Naomi to go with him either. However, to the very depth of his soul, he knew he wanted to be with Miriam. He wanted to be with her, to hold her hand, to comfort her.

What should I do?

He sighed and sent up a silent prayer asking for guidance.

The sound of a sniff behind him startled him back to the present. Turning, he found Naomi standing in the doorway with tears rolling down her pink cheeks.

"Naomi?" He popped up and crossed the room, reaching for her.

"Don't." She stepped back, holding her hands out to stop him. "Don't touch me, Timothy."

He tilted his head. "What's wrong?"

She shook her head. "You don't need to pretend anymore. I already know the truth."

Taking her hand, he pulled her into the office and closed the door behind her for privacy and to drown out the sounds of the tools whirling and the hammers banging in the shop. "What do you mean?" he asked. "You know what truth?"

"I'm not blind, Timothy." She swiped away her tears with the back of her hands and sniffed. "I can see what's going on here. You don't love me. You've never loved me. You love Miriam Lapp."

"Naomi, I don't—"

"Yes, you do," she said. "She's the reason why you're so quiet and completely shut me out after you see her. You did it after Bertha Lapp's funeral. And you were quiet after we went to Abraham's house and again after Sarah Rose's wedding. You see Miriam, and the rest of the world fades away."

She closed her eyes for a few moments as if collecting her thoughts. "I heard the conversation. Miriam is heading to the hospital to be with Hannah during the liver transplant?"

"How did you—?"

She gave a knowing smile. "You forget I'm best friends with Lilly Lapp. Lilly called me at the farmer's market as soon as she got the news. She's staying with their *daed* and Lena Joy's younger siblings while Hannah and Aaron take Lena Joy to Pittsburgh. I guess Hannah called Miriam and asked her to go too. And now you've heard the news from Beth Anne, and you want to go be with Miriam."

Naomi sighed as more tears spilled from her sad eyes. "It makes perfect sense. Of course you want to go comfort the woman you truly love with all your heart."

He shook his head. "I don't know what to say."

"You don't need to say anything." Reaching out, she cupped a hand to his cheek. "I love you, Timothy Kauffman, but I can't make you love me."

"Miriam is my past." He placed his hand over hers. "You're my future."

"No." Her voice trembled as more tears fell. "She's your past and your future. I can't marry a man who will always long for someone else. I want to marry a man who loves me and only me."

Clearing her throat, she wiped her eyes with her free hand. "When I really think about how I feel for you, I wonder if it's true love or if it's just infatuation. I'm in love with the idea of being in love. I've been searching for a husband without really slowing down long enough to find the person who is the right fit for me. I've been immature and too focused on getting married." She pulled her hand back from his gentle grip. "I release you, Timothy. Go to her. Be with her. Be with the *maedel* you love."

"But Naomi, I made a promise to you."

She shook her head and wiped more tears. "I can tell your heart belongs to Miriam Lapp, not to me. I'm sure the promise was made with *gut* intentions, but you can't force true love, Timothy. I don't think our marriage is part of God's plan for me. I think I'm meant to wait for someone else."

"Miriam loves Zach Fisher," he said. "I don't think she loves me."

Naomi shook her head. "No, I think you're wrong there. I think she's only friends with Zach. Lilly hasn't said anything to me about Miriam and Zach courting." She nodded toward the door. "Go to the hospital. Be with Miriam and ask her about Zach. You and Miriam belong together. Go and give her a chance. I'll be okay. I've bounced back before."

He hesitated, debating it in his mind and feeling as if he'd let her down. However, in his *gut*, he knew she was right, and she was a wonderful person.

Timothy kissed her cheek. "You have a loving heart. I know someday you'll find the right man who will love you the way you deserve to be loved."

She sniffed and her lips formed a sad smile. "Funny. I think I've heard that before."

"I hope we can be friends," he said.

She nodded. "I suppose so. Miriam's sister is my best friend, so I'm sure we'll see each other often."

He gave her a quick hug. "We better finish our lunch."

"Forget lunch. Go get a ride to the hospital. Miriam needs you." She squeezed his arm. "Go."

He rushed from the office to the front of the store, where he found Eli speaking with Elmer. "*Dat*," he said. "I need to get a ride to Pittsburgh. Miriam's niece is having her liver transplant."

"Oh." Eli gave him a strange expression. "Did Miriam call you?"

"No." Timothy shook his head. "Beth Anne did, but I know Miriam needs me. I can feel it in my heart."

"Then go, Son." He picked up the phone. "I'll call Roger right now and tell him to come pick you up. We'll figure out another ride home."

"*Danki*." Timothy wrung his hands. He had to get to Pittsburgh to be with Miriam. She needed him.

And he needed her.

CHAPTER 27

At approximately four in the afternoon, Miriam rushed into the waiting room where Aaron sat, holding Hannah close.

When Hannah's eyes met Miriam's, Hannah stood and enveloped her into a tight hug. "I'm so glad you're here," she whispered in Miriam's ears. "*Danki* for coming. I need you, *Schweschder.*"

"I wouldn't miss this for the world." Miriam held her close. "How is she?"

Hannah took Miriam's hand and led her to the sofa next to Aaron. "We were with her until a few minutes ago." She sniffed and wiped her eyes. "She was very excited and said she wasn't afraid at all. She's such a brave girl."

Miriam tried in vain to stop the tears pooling in her eyes. "*Ya*, she's very brave and very special. How long will the operation take?"

"It depends," Aaron said. "It could be eight hours, but a nurse will keep us posted on how it's going. It's going to be a long night."

Miriam squeezed his hand. "I'll do what I can to help you both through this. I promise."

"*Danki*. We're glad you're here." He gave her a forced smile. "The liver is a perfect match."

"Praise God!" Miriam held onto his hand. "A perfect match."

"There's a *gut* chance it will last a very long time," he said,

his eyes filling with tears. "The doctor said it should last at least ten years if all goes well with the surgery."

Hannah sniffed. "I just hate that someone had to die to give my *dochder* life."

"*Ya*, but it's God's will, Hannah. It's not our fault." He put his free hand on her shoulder and then pulled her closer to him. "We must trust God's will."

"Aaron's right," Miriam said. "We must trust God and have faith. As Elizabeth Kauffman often says, 'Now faith is being sure of what we hope for and certain of what we do not see.'"

Hannah wiped her eyes. "I know. It's just difficult sometimes. I've been praying for the family who lost their loved one today. That person is giving Lena Joy life. He or she has made the ultimate sacrifice as an organ donor."

"*Ya*." Aaron pulled Hannah to his chest. "Praise God for that person."

Miriam held Aaron's hand and also took Hannah's in hers. "Let's say a prayer for Lena Joy and for the donor." She closed her eyes, and they prayed silently together.

When she opened her eyes, she squeezed their hands. "Have you eaten?"

They shook their heads.

"Not since early this morning," Aaron said.

"Let me go get you both something. I have money." She stood. "I'll go ask the woman at the desk where the cafeteria is, and I'll bring you back something."

"No," Hannah said. "Let's all go together." She glanced at Aaron, who nodded.

Miriam asked the volunteer at the waiting room desk for directions to the cafeteria and then they headed down the hall-way toward the elevator.

. . .

Miriam carried a tray filled with three different sandwiches, three varieties of chips, three soft drinks, and three pieces of chocolate cake to a booth in the corner where Aaron and Hannah sat huddled together. Aaron's arm was draped over Hannah's shoulder while he spoke softly to her. Miriam ignored the glances from curious *Englishers* while she crossed the cafeteria.

Plastering a smile on her face, Miriam approached the table. "I hope you're hungry. I bought a good variety, hoping something would appeal to you."

"*Danki*," Aaron said with a smile. "You're very thoughtful."

"*Gern gschehne*," Miriam sat across from them and distributed the drinks. "I'm happy to help."

"I'm not hungry," Hannah muttered. "I couldn't possibly dream of eating right now."

"You must eat." Aaron placed a sandwich and bag of chips in front of his wife. "You need your strength for Lena Joy."

"He's right," Miriam said. "You said yourself that it's going to be a long night."

Hannah unwrapped the sandwich and took a small bite. "I can't stop worrying. I know that they do thousands of transplants each year, but there's always the risk of complications."

"You mustn't think that way." Miriam took Hannah's hands in hers. "Lena Joy's transplant will be routine for the team of doctors. It will be a success." She squeezed her hands.

"But there's so much that can go wrong." Hannah's voice quavered. "Just going under anesthesia is risky. I was reading in a medical book that you can have a reaction to the medication or even stop breathing. She could also contract an infection or have uncontrollable bleeding." She swallowed a sob, and Aaron took her in his arms.

Miriam took a deep breath to stop her own tears. "Oh, Hannah. You have to stop thinking this way. The whole district is praying for Lena Joy. I know in my heart it's going to be a success. You have to trust God."

Aaron rubbed Hannah's back. "Listen to your sister. She's very wise."

Hannah laughed. "*Ya*, she is." She took a deep breath. "This transplant was Lena Joy's choice. I have to keep reminding myself of that."

"That's true. Lena Joy and I were discussing it last week, and she said she hoped she'd have her transplant this year. She wants to be healthy before she starts attending social events with the rest of her friends."

Miriam nodded. "And you said it yourself, Hannah. The doctors do these transplants all the time."

Aaron glanced at Hannah and smiled at Miriam as if to thank her for her words. He then unwrapped his roast beef sub and took a bite.

"Lena Joy is going to be healthy and happy after this," Miriam continued. "Just you see."

"Right." Hannah wiped her eyes and sipped her drink. "How have things been at the bakery?"

"Busy." Miriam unwrapped her turkey sandwich and then opened her bag of barbecue chips. "But I love it."

They chatted about the bakery and then discussed news they'd heard about friends and family members. Nearly an hour passed while they ate and chatted. When they finished their meal, they moved back toward the bank of elevators.

Miriam mashed the arrow button and then stared at the wall, silently praying that Lena Joy would come out of the surgery healthy and strong. She also prayed she would be the encouragement that Hannah and Aaron would need throughout the night. Being their rock was a tall order, one that would require all of the faith and strength she had in her heart and her soul.

Hannah patted Miriam's back and looped her arm around her shoulders. "I'm so glad you're here," she whispered.

"I am too," Miriam said.

As the door to the elevator whooshed open, Miriam wished she had someone to keep her positive and strong during the surgery.

. . .

Timothy strode down the hallway toward the waiting room. During the long ride to the hospital, he replayed the conversation he'd had with Naomi over and over in his mind, wondering if he'd imagined what she'd said. She'd released him from the engagement. She'd insisted he belonged with Miriam.

She'd said it was God's will.

But how could it be God's will if Miriam loved Zach Fisher? Timothy didn't know if it was truly God's will, but he knew he had a desperate desire to be with Miriam and help her through this stressful time. No matter what lay ahead for Miriam and him, he was determined to at least be her friend. He approached the waiting room and stood in the doorway.

He spotted several small groups of people throughout the large room, while two television sets murmured above the quiet conversations. His gaze found Hannah and Aaron sitting together and holding hands in a far corner.

His heart thumped in his chest when he spotted Miriam. She stood by herself, looking out the window at the far end of the waiting room. He took a deep breath and crossed the room, thankful no one seemed to notice him, not even Hannah and Aaron, who were sharing a quiet conversation.

Timothy sidled up to Miriam, and when she didn't acknowledge him, he placed his hand on her shoulder. The contact sent electric shockwaves through his body.

She faced him. Her brown eyes widened, and her

mouth gaped. "Timothy?" she whispered. "Wh-what are you doing here?"

"I'm here to support you." He opened his arms to her and held his breath, hoping she'd accept his invitation of a hug.

She glanced down at his chest and hesitated. Then her expression softened, and she collapsed in his arms, holding on as if her life depended upon him.

Timothy blew out the breath he'd been holding in and savored the moment. Warmth coursed through him as he held her close. Resting his cheek on her head, he breathed in her sweet scent. It was just as lovely as he'd remembered—cinnamon mixed with hyacinth.

Holding her felt so right as memories rained down on him. It was as if they'd never separated, and these last four years apart from her were just a bad dream.

Miriam wrapped her arms around his waist as he rested his arms on her shoulders and rubbed her back. He closed his eyes, silently thanking God for this time with Miriam. He wished the moment would last forever.

She gasped and sobbed, and he pulled her closer.

"Miriam," he whispered. "It's okay to cry. I'm here for you. Feel free to cry all you need to. I'm sure God is going to take good care of Lena Joy. I think she's going to come through this strong."

"*Ya*," she said, still holding onto him. "I think you're right. I'm praying for her constantly, and I have faith that she'll be fine. But I still worry for her. It's a risky surgery, but she's young and strong."

"*Ya*, she is." He continued to rub her back.

She held onto him for a few more moments, and then

she stepped back and swiped the back of her hand over her cheeks. "You really surprised me. I never expected you to come here."

He folded his arms in front of his chest. "Beth Anne called me and told me you'd headed to the hospital. I thought you might like some company."

"Beth Anne called you?" She looked surprised. "When did she call you?"

"She said you'd left for the hospital, and that you were going to be here for Aaron and Hannah." Timothy glanced toward Hannah, who gave Timothy a surprised expression as she and Aaron waved at him. "Beth Anne said you might need someone to be here for you, and she suggested I come. I hope it's okay," he said, waving back at Hannah and Aaron.

She stared at him and blinked. "I must be dreaming," she muttered.

"What did you say?" he asked, stepping toward her.

She smiled and shook her head. "This can't be happening. I must've had too much caffeine today or something."

"What?" He grinned. "Are you making a joke?"

"No." She glanced past him. "Where's Naomi?"

He cut his eyes to the clock on the wall. "Home, I would imagine. She usually closes up the quilt stand around four, and it's nearly six now."

Miriam studied him. "She's not here with you?"

"No."

"Does she know you're here?"

"*Ya.*" He nodded. "She was there when Beth Anne called me to tell me the news about the surgery."

Miriam knitted her eyebrows together with

confusion, looking adorable. "I don't understand. Naomi wasn't bothered with the idea of your coming to the hospital to be with me without her?"

He frowned. "I can't say she wasn't bothered by it, but she understood."

"Oh." The confusion remained in her expression.

"Where's Zach?" he asked.

"Probably with Lilly. She has Hannah's other *kinner* at *Daed's* house."

He nodded, wondering why Zach wasn't here with Miriam. Was there significance to the comment that he was with Lilly?

"Can I get you something to eat?" he asked. "Or maybe a drink?"

"A drink would be *wunderbaar*. I want to see if Aaron or Hannah need anything." She led him across the room to her sister.

Hannah and Aaron glanced up as they approached.

"Timothy." Aaron took and shook his hand. "It's *gut* to see you. We weren't expecting you."

"I came to offer you all some support. I heard you three were here alone, and I thought you might like some extra company." In his peripheral vision, Timothy spotted surprised and animated expressions passing between the sisters.

"*Danki*," Aaron said, his eyes expressing the exhaustion he must've been experiencing. "We very much appreciate the support. It's not easy sitting here and waiting for news on your *dochder*."

"I can't even imagine." Timothy shook his head with sympathy. "Have you heard any news on the operation?"

"Just that she's gone into surgery. Nothing more." Aaron sighed. "It's going to be a long night."

"*Ya*." Hannah rubbed Aaron's arm. "We're glad you're here, Timothy. Miriam needs someone she can lean on. Did you come alone?"

Timothy nodded. "*Ya*. It's just me. I hope that's okay."

"It's perfect." Hannah smiled.

Timothy glanced at Miriam and noticed her cheeks were blushing a bright pink while she gave her sister a horrified look. He wondered what he'd missed.

"Would either of you like a drink?" Timothy offered. "Miriam and I were going to go for a walk and check out the soda machines."

"No, *danki*." Aaron glanced at Hannah. "Did you want anything?"

"No, but thank you." Hannah yawned. "I think I may try to close my eyes for a bit. It's going to be quite a while before she gets out of surgery, and I need my strength." She smiled at her husband. "I hope you like being a pillow."

Aaron lowered himself back onto the sofa. "That's my job, *ya*?"

Timothy hoped he could joke that way with Miriam sometime in the near future.

"We'll be back," Miriam said, placing her hand on Timothy's arm. "You two just relax." She led him out to the hallway. "I spotted a vending machine area down here earlier. We can see what's there. If there's nothing you like, then we can go to the cafeteria. It's not too far."

"I'm not picky. I'm sure whatever is in the vending

room is just fine." He enjoyed the sensation of her hand on his arm while they walked together down the hallway.

He wished he could sense her thoughts. He longed to tell her Naomi had broken the engagement and insisted he belonged with Miriam instead of her. He had to tell her the truth and soon. He didn't want Miriam to think he was being unfaithful to Naomi.

They stepped into the vending room, and Miriam stood in front of the Coke machine.

"Would you like a Coke?" She pulled a small change purse from the pocket inside of her apron.

He fished out his wallet from his pocket. "I have money."

"It's okay," she said, dropping quarters into the machine. "I got it." She put in the required amount and then pushed the button.

The machine rattled and then spat out a plastic bottle of Coke. When she handed it to him, her fingers brushed his, and a spark ignited the air around them. He wondered if she'd felt it too. Her eyes widened for a split second, giving him the notion that she had.

She turned back to the machine, slipped in the quarters, and then chose a Diet Coke for herself. She retrieved it from the slot at the bottom and then nodded toward a small table in the corner. "Shall we have a seat?"

He followed her to the table. "How are your legs?" he asked as they sat across from each other. "You took quite a fall at Sarah Rose's wedding."

"They're better." A little bit of a blush stained her

cheeks. "They were just a little scraped up and bruised, but they're healing pretty well. *Danki* for asking."

"How are you holding up through all this?"

She shrugged. "Okay, I guess. I'm worried sick about Lena Joy, but I'm trying not to think about it. The surgery is very risky. There could be many complications." Her eyes filled with tears, and she took a long drink of soda.

He touched her hand, which was warm and soft. "I truly believe Lena Joy will be just fine. In fact, she'll be better than fine. She'll come through this strong and healthier than ever."

Miriam squeezed his hand and smiled. "*Danki*. I appreciate your faith."

"It's the truth."

She released his hand and took another sip. "You have the most astounding faith. I always admired that quality in you."

"You did?" He raised an eyebrow in disbelief. "I thought you once said I was moodier than the weather."

She laughed, and it was sweet music to his ears, like his favorite hymn. "*Ya*, you are the moodiest person I know, but you also are the most faithful. The faith outshines the moods."

He grinned. "That's good to know." He felt a surge of confidence in her feelings for him. "What else do you admire about me?"

Her cheeks flushed again. "Oh, there are many things—your sense of humor, your laugh, your carpentry skills, your heart." Her eyes were intense and locked on his. "What about you? What do you admire about me?"

"Everything," he said.

They stared at each other in silence for a moment, much like they had when they spoke last week at the wedding. Again, he wished he could read her thoughts.

A young boy skipped into the room and stood in front of the candy machine, studying the selections before choosing a chocolate bar. When he left, the intense moment between Timothy and Miriam had evaporated. Her eyes were casual again while she sipped her drink.

"How do you think Hannah and Aaron are doing?" he asked, hoping to keep the conversation going.

Miriam shook her head and frowned. "It's difficult to say. We went down to the cafeteria earlier and ate. We talked quite a bit. When we came back up to the waiting room, they seemed to need to be alone. I walked over to the window to give them some privacy. Hannah said she wanted me here to give her strength, and I hope I'm giving her all the support she needs."

"I think just being here gives her strength. You really don't need to do or say anything in particular."

"I'll do my best, but it's not easy." Tears filled her eyes. "I can't imagine how we'd make it if something bad happened to Lena Joy. It would be a nightmare."

He squeezed her hand. "Don't think about that. God will see her through this. I just know it." It warmed his heart seeing how much she loved her niece. She would be a wonderful mother.

"*Danki.*" Her lips formed a sweet, genuine smile, and his pulse raced. "I'm glad you're here."

"Me too," he said. He took a deep breath. "There's something I need to tell you."

"Oh?" she asked, her eyes full of curiosity.

"Naomi broke up with me today."

"She what?" Miriam looked confused. "What do you mean? You're engaged."

"We were engaged. Today she saw how concerned I was about you when I found out about the transplant, and she said she had to let me go. She said it was obvious I wanted to be here with you, and it wasn't God's will for her to marry me."

Miriam studied his expression. "She did?"

"*Ya*, she did." He contemplated her eyes in return, again wishing he could read her thoughts. "What about you and Zach?"

"What about us?" Miriam gave him a confused expression.

"Aren't you courting him?"

"No, I've never courted him. We've always been good friends. He's courting my sister, but they're trying to keep it a secret."

He let out a sigh of relief. "Really? I was certain you were courting him."

"No." She waved him off. "We've never been more than friends—ever. In fact, Lilly has always been in love with him, which is why she was jealous of me and determined to break up you and me. It made her crazy that he was close friends with me and never showed any interest in her."

He ran his fingers over the cool bottle of Coke. "Lilly apologized to me about a month ago. I went to see you after she told me the story, but your *aenti* told me you were out with Zach. She said I needed to be with Naomi because you were with Zach."

"No!" Miriam cupped her hand to her mouth. "*Aenti* Edna told you that?"

He nodded. "I asked her not to tell you I'd visited you because I didn't want to interfere with you and Zach."

Frowning, Miriam shook her head. "She had it all wrong. I was never seeing Zach. In fact, the last time I had supper with him, I encouraged him to see Lilly. I told him I only wanted to be his friend."

Timothy shook his head in disbelief. How could he have had it all so very wrong? He stared into Miriam's eyes until she glanced at the clock on the wall.

"We better head back and check on them," she said, standing.

CHAPTER 28

Miriam longed to take Timothy's hand in hers while they walked back to the waiting room. Her mind whirled with questions and a storm of emotions.

Timothy and Naomi had broken up.

Naomi encouraged Timothy to come and be with Miriam.

What did it all mean? Did Timothy want to be with Miriam?

The questions echoed in her mind when they approached Hannah and Aaron. She pushed the confusing questions aside and focused on her sister and brother-in-law. She needed to concentrate on being their support and not on her jumbled feelings for Timothy.

As Hannah had predicted, she'd fallen asleep, leaning against her husband.

Miriam mouthed the words, "Do you need anything?"

Smiling, Aaron shook his head.

Timothy took Miriam's arm and nodded toward a sofa on the other side of the waiting room near a television displaying the nightly news. He led her to it, and they sat together on the small sofa.

He looped his arm around her shoulder, and she

sucked in a breath at the feeling of his body heat mixing with hers. She wondered if he enjoyed being close to
her as much as she did. She squelched the urge to lean
into his side and enjoy the feel of his muscular torso.

Instead, she kept a fraction of an inch between their
bodies and stared at the television. Although television
was forbidden by the bishop, she knew the circumstance would allow it.

Miriam stared at the screen, but the news anchor's
words didn't reach her ears. She was deep in thought,
wondering what Timothy was feeling as he watched the
newscast. Was he thinking of her or was he interested in
the latest developments in the surrounding geographical
area?

An hour wore on, and she found herself leaning
into Timothy's chest while he rubbed her arm with the
hand looped over her shoulder. Being close to him felt
so natural and so right. Did he feel the same way?

Her thoughts were interrupted by Aaron standing
in front of the television set. "I just talked to the nurse.
Lena Joy is doing well. They've removed her liver and
are beginning to transplant the new one."

"Praise God!" Miriam hopped up. "How's Hannah?"

"Doing fine." Aaron smiled. "She's on the phone
with Lilly. I'm going to call my parents after she's done.
We've got to update everyone."

Timothy stood and patted Aaron's arm. "I'm so glad it's
going well. Do you need anything? A snack or a drink?"

"I think we may make a trip down to the cafeteria
when we're done with the phone calls. *Danki.*" Aaron
crossed the waiting room to Hannah.

Miriam squeezed Timothy's arm. "I think she's going to do fine. I just feel it in my soul."

"*Ya*, me too. Do you want to go for a walk?" He pushed a lock of hair back from her face, and the warmth of his touch tingled in the pit of her belly.

She nodded. "That would be nice instead of watching television."

He took her hand, and her heart leapt in her chest. They walked around the hospital for nearly an hour, and he talked about work, telling her about the projects he'd been creating and how busy the shop had been so far this fall.

When they returned to the waiting room, they sat with Hannah and Aaron and made idle conversation about people they knew.

After a while, Hannah and Aaron headed to the cafeteria to get a snack, and Miriam and Timothy sat by the television, waiting for news on Lena Joy.

When Aaron and Hannah returned, Miriam and Timothy went down to the cafeteria and ate a snack. They returned to the waiting room and found Hannah on the cell phone.

Miriam rushed over to Aaron. "Did you get news?"

He nodded, tears filling his dark eyes. "The transplant is almost complete. They're almost finished hooking up the new liver."

Miriam cupped her hand to her mouth.

"Praise God!" Timothy said. "Everything is going well?"

Aaron wiped a tear from his eye. "It looks *gut*."

Hannah snapped the phone shut and rushed over to

Miriam, hugging her. "It's almost complete, Miriam! My baby is going to have a new liver."

"I'm so *froh*." Miriam held her sister as she cried. "God is *gut*."

"*Ya*, He is," Hannah said. "I can't wait to see her. These last couple of hours are going to be torture."

"We'll get through it." Aaron pulled Hannah into a hug. "We'll see her soon."

Miriam glanced up at Timothy and smiled. "I'm so glad you're here."

"Me too." He touched her cheek, and she thought she might melt at the tenderness of the gesture.

Why is he truly here?

Does he still love me?

Could there be a chance that we get together again— maybe forever this time?

The questions continued to tease her while they sat in front of the television for the next couple of hours. Tedious situational comedies droned on from the flat screen, but Miriam hardly noticed.

She was deep in thought, alternating between prayers for Lena Joy and thoughts of Timothy. She was determined to crack the riddle of Timothy Kauffman, who sat beside her, holding her hand and rubbing her arm. He seemed to be more than a friend, but she was perplexed by his behavior. Were they starting over as a couple or did he just want to be friends?

As the hour wore on, Miriam found herself yawning.

"You can take a nap," Timothy whispered in her ear, the tickle of his voice in her ear sending chills down her spine. "Just use me as a pillow, like Aaron said to Hannah earlier."

She tilted her head, enjoying his deep blue eyes. "You certain?"

He ran his fingertip down her cheekbone, and she closed her eyes, enjoying the touch. "I don't mind at all," he said. "Close your eyes, so you're refreshed when it's time to visit the patient with her new liver."

She smiled. "Okay." Leaning into him, she inhaled his musky scent, losing herself in sweet memories of their past. She longed to relive the taste of his kisses.

The reality of the situation roused her from her fantasies. Timothy Kauffman was no longer her boyfriend. Years had passed since the treasured days of their courtship. But she couldn't help but wonder where she stood in his heart now. Being with him felt so natural.

But did he feel it too?

She closed her eyes and soon relaxed.

. . .

Miriam awoke with a start to Timothy's voice in her ear.

"Wake up, sleepyhead," he whispered. "The surgery is over."

Miriam sat up and rubbed her eyes. "It's over? How long have I been asleep?"

"Almost three hours." He pushed her loose strands of hair back under her *kapp*. "You must've been exhausted."

She cupped her hand to her mouth to cover a yawn. "I guess so." She scanned the waiting room for Hannah. "Where's my sister?"

"She and Aaron were called back by a nurse. I guess they're going to see Lena Joy." He stretched and then grinned, causing her heart to thump due to his handsome face. "My arm's asleep. You were leaning on it."

"I'm sorry." Her cheeks heated.

"I didn't mind at all." His expression changed to a frown as he glanced across the waiting room. "There they are. They don't look *froh*."

Miriam stood and gasped when she spotted Hannah, sobbing while Aaron held her. Her blood ran cold. "Oh no," she said. "It can't be. She has to be okay."

"Don't jump to conclusions." Timothy pulled her to him. "Let's wait and see what they say. Remember, keep your faith."

"'Now faith is being sure of what we hope for and certain of what we do not see,'" she whispered.

"That's exactly right," Timothy said.

Aaron caught Miriam's eye, and he gestured for them to join them on the other side of the waiting room.

"Be strong," Timothy whispered as he put his arm around her shoulder and led her to them.

Miriam took a deep breath, but her confidence broke when Hannah met her gaze. When Miriam saw the despair in her eyes, she began to cry.

Hannah opened her arms, and Miriam fell into her hug.

"They can't wake her up," Hannah said between sobs. "My baby went to sleep, and she won't wake up."

"Oh, Hannah," Miriam held onto her and sobbed. "Oh no."

Miriam held her until Hannah pulled back and wiped her eyes.

"I can't believe it. The doctor said the surgery went well." Hannah swiped more tears, despite the continuous flow from her eyes. "The doctor said it's rare that this happens, but she had some reaction to the anesthesia. My worst fears came true. How could this happen? How?"

"She'll pull through," Aaron said, rubbing her arm. "Our *dochder* is strong. You have to believe that. You must trust God." He wiped his own tears.

Miriam bit her lip to hold back more sobs. "He's right. Remember what I said earlier about faith. God is going to see Lena Joy through this. You have to believe it. He gave her the perfect liver. He won't let it go to waste."

Hannah held onto her husband and sobbed.

Miriam covered her mouth to swallow her own tears, and Timothy pulled her to him. They stood in silence until a nurse appeared and called Hannah and Aaron back into the recovery room.

"Do you want to go for a walk?" Timothy asked after Hannah and Aaron disappeared through the doors.

Miriam shook her head. "I have to stay here in case Hannah comes back with more news. I need to know that Lena Joy is okay."

He took her hand and led her to a sofa near the doors. "Let's sit here then. There's no need to stand."

Miriam sank down beside him, and he held her in his arms. They sat in a comfortable silence, and Miriam was thankful to not have to make idle conversation while they waited for more news of her niece.

She silently prayed, begging God to bring Lena Joy back, healthy with her new liver. She believed Aaron's words that God wouldn't have given her the perfect liver and then not let her survive the surgery. It just wouldn't have made sense for her to receive the liver and then . . .

She couldn't think the word. No, she *refused* to. She silently continued repeating the verse that had haunted her thoughts all day long.

Now faith is being sure of what we hope for and certain of what we do not see.

When Aaron approached them an hour later, his eyes held hope, which she hadn't seen earlier. Miriam and Timothy stood, and Miriam held her breath, praying for good news.

"She's awake," he said. When he smiled, Miriam squealed and hugged him.

"She's okay?" Miriam asked.

"*Ya.*" Aaron held onto her. "She's fine. In fact, she was joking with us, saying that the liver felt too big."

"Oh, praise Jesus!" Miriam laughed as tears spilled down her hot cheeks. "I knew she'd pull through. I just knew it."

Miriam stepped back, and Timothy squeezed Aaron's arm.

"I'm so glad," Timothy said.

"When can we see her?" Miriam asked.

"It will be a little while. You can go get something to drink if you'd like," Aaron said. "Only Hannah and I can be back there since we're her parents. Other relatives have to wait until she's more stable." He touched

Miriam's arm. "But she's doing well. The liver is working. The doctor said it will take a while, but in a day or so, her skin will be pink. She looks great."

Miriam held Timothy's hand. "It's a miracle."

Aaron held up the cell phone. "I'm going to make some calls and spread the news, and then I'm going to go back in and see her."

"Come out in a bit and give us an update," Timothy said.

"I will." Aaron headed over to a quiet corner. "*Danki* for being here."

Miriam looked up at Timothy. "It's a miracle! A miracle!"

His stare was intense, and her heart thumped in her chest. He leaned down and when she felt his breath on her lips, she froze.

His lips brushed hers, sending her heart into hyperspeed. He pulled her close, and she wrapped her arms around his neck. His lips continued to explore hers, and she closed her eyes, delighting in the feel of his warm mouth.

He pulled back, and his smile was wide. "I love you," he said.

She reached up and touched his cheek. "I love you too," she whispered. "I always have."

His eyes brightened. "You have?"

"*Ya*, I never stopped." She smiled.

"Does that mean we still have a chance, you and me?" His eyes were full of hope.

"*Ya*, I think we do." A new confidence surged through her. "I think God is giving us a second chance, just like he's giving Lena Joy a second chance with the new liver."

He nodded. "*Ya*, I think you're right."

"When Jeremy died, I felt like I'd lost everything," she said, taking his hands in hers. "I was sure you were seeing someone else behind my back and then my family turned against me. I moved to Indiana because I thought I belonged in the *English* world. I also thought God had forgotten about me. But now that I'm back, I've found that God doesn't forget about any of us. I saw Colleen Henderson a few months ago, and she has a new baby."

Timothy's face lit up with a smile. "She does?"

"*Ya*, her baby girl, Deanna Nicole, is a little over eighteen months old now, and she's perfect in every way. The Hendersons lost Jeremy, but they have new life in their new baby." She squeezed his hands. "Just like Jesus rose from the dead to give us new life, He brings new life to us in different ways, like Lena Joy's organ transplant."

"You're right." Timothy took a deep breath. "I never stopped loving you either. I was hurt and angry when you left, but I still loved you. Always."

"Really?" Tears filled Miriam's eyes.

"*Ya*." He ran his finger down her cheek. "I dreamt of you nearly every night for a long time, and I'd think of you often. I'd see things that reminded me of you— like daisies. And whenever I had a crumbly peach pie I'd think of you because it was never as good as yours."

Miriam laughed. "You always rated my cooking too high."

He shook his hand and placed his hands on her hips. "That's not true. In fact, I never cherished you enough. I took you for granted."

"No, you didn't." She cupped her hand to his cheek. "I was young and stupid. I was so anxious to try out the *English* world that I believed lies too easily. I'm so sorry."

"No, I am." His eyes were serious again. "I was wrong to believe the lies." He leaned down and brushed his lips across hers, sending the pit of her belly into a wild swirl. When he looked down at her, his gaze intensified. "I can't lose you again. I *refuse* to let it happen."

"It won't happen," she whispered.

"I need you by my side forever," he said.

She swallowed a gasp, silently praying that his words meant what she'd hoped they meant.

"Will you start a new life with me by marrying me, Miriam Lapp?"

She squealed. "*Ya!* I would love to marry you, and I will truly marry you this time."

"*Wunderbaar.* Your words are music to my heart, my soul, and my ears." Leaning down, he kissed her again.

Closing her eyes, Miriam thanked God for second chances.

Apple Strudel

Line bottom of buttered baking dish with thick layer of apples and sprinkle with mixed cinnamon, sugar, and dots of butter.

Sift into mixing bowl:

> 1 1/4 cups sugar
> 3/4 tsp baking powder
> 1 cup flour
> 3/4 tsp salt

Break 1 egg into above mixture; mix until crumbly. Put over apples and bake at 350 degrees until crust is brown. Serve with whipped cream or ice cream.

DISCUSSION QUESTIONS

1. Miriam is devastated when she receives the call that her mother has passed away. When she arrives back in Lancaster County, she's forced to face her family after nearly four years. Do you think she made the right choice when she left Lancaster County to avoid the criticism of her family? If you were in her situation, what would you have done? Share this with the group.

2. Miriam's hurt and anger are deepened when she discovers her sister told the lies that broke up her relationship with Timothy. Were you ever betrayed by a close friend or loved one? How did you come to grips with that betrayal? Were you able to forgive that person and move on? If so, then where did you find the strength to forgive? Share this with the group.

3. Throughout the story, characters quote Luke 6:37: "Do not judge, and you will not be judged. Do not condemn, and you will not be condemned. Forgive, and you will be forgiven." What does this verse mean to you?

4. Hannah finds herself caught in the middle between Miriam and the family members who are against Miriam, including their father, Lilly, and Gerald.

Have you ever found yourself as the peacemaker due to a family, social, or work situation? If so, how did you handle the conflict? Did it turn out the way you'd hoped? Share this with the group.

5. When Miriam first comes back to Gordonville, she seeks reconciliation with her family, only to have her father, brother, and sister shut her out again. Think of a time when you felt lost and alone. Where did you find your strength? What Bible verses would help with this?

6. Timothy is determined to keep his promise to marry Naomi. Have you ever felt obligated to keep a promise even though you felt doubt in your heart? How did you handle the situation? Share this with the group.

7. Lilly truly regrets the lies she told to break up Miriam and Timothy. Do you think Miriam was wise to forgive her sister? Why or why not? Have you ever been asked to forgive someone whose actions changed your life negatively? Did you forgive this person? Why or why not? What Bible verses would help with this?

8. What are your feelings about organ donation? Have you known someone who was an organ donor or recipient? Share this with the group.

9. Which character can you identify with the most? Which character seemed to carry the most emotional stake in the story? Was it Miriam, Timothy, Hannah, Lilly, Zach, or Naomi?

10. Miriam feels that God is giving her a second chance with Timothy and that Lena Joy's transplant will

give her a second chance at life. Have you ever experienced a second chance? Share this with the group.

11. What did you know about the Amish before reading this book? What did you learn?

ACKNOWLEDGMENTS

To my best friend and mother, Lola Goebelbecker, thank you for your love, support, and encouragement. Our family would be lost without you. Thank you for enduring my constant chatter about my books. You're the best plotting partner ever! To my husband, Joe, there aren't words to tell you how much

I love and cherish you. You're my best friend and my rock. I'm looking forward to many, many more years with you by my side. I pray daily that we'll find a matching kidney for you so you can live the life you crave and deserve.

Zac and Matt, you are the most amazing boys on the planet. I love you with all my heart. Thank you for bringing sunshine into my life. And yes, Zac, I've finally named characters after you and your brother. I hope you like "Zach" and "Matthew" as much as I do.

To my mother-in-law, Sharon Clipston, thank you for sharing my books with friends and family. To my wonderful aunt and godmother, Trudy Janitz, thank you for spreading my books to your friends and customers. Love you both!

I'm more grateful than words can express to my patient friends who critique for me—Sue McKlveen, Margaret Halpin, and Lauran Rodriguez. Thank you for always volunteering to read my books and offer your opinions.

Special thanks to Jerome Menendez, nurse practitioner at the Transplant Center in Levine Children's Hospital. Your guidance was invaluable. I can't express how much I appreciate your help researching liver transplants and Crigler-Najjar Syndrome (CNS). In my opinion, you are a superhero!

I sincerely appreciate Dr. George Mazariegos, director of pediatric transplantation at Children's Hospital of Pittsburgh of University of Pittsburgh Medical Center, who took time out of his busy schedule to help with my CNS and liver transplant research. Also, thank you to Caroline Morton, with the Clinic for Special Children in Strasburg, Pennsylvania, who also patiently answered my questions. Without Dr. Mazariegos' and Ms. Morton's help, this story wouldn't be complete.

I'm very grateful to my special Amish friends who patiently answer my endless stream of questions. Your friendship means the world to me. Thank you for welcoming me into your homes. Thank you also to Katie Martin, whose personal stories of her journey with two CNS children helped shape this story. Your book, God's Golden Children, is full of information about CNS and also is an inspiration and a blessing for family members caring for loved ones with medical issues.

Thank you also to Ruth Meily and Betsy Cook for their continued help with Lancaster County research.

Thank you to my wonderful church family at Morning Star Lutheran in Matthews, North Carolina, for your encouragement, prayers, love, and friendship. You all mean so much to my family and me.

To Mary Sue Seymour—you are the most amazing agent in the world! Thank you for believing in my writing.

I'm more grateful than words can express to the Zondervan team. Thank you to my amazing editors—Sue Brower and Becky Philpott. I'm so blessed to be a part of the Zondervan family. Special thanks to Lori Vanden Bosch for editing this book and giving the story more depth, and to Emma Sleeth for your help and insights.

To my readers—thank you for choosing my books. I also appreciate the wonderful emails and your prayers for my husband. Please, if you are physically able, become an organ donor and also donate blood. By giving the gift of life, you can help someone like my husband.

Thank you most of all to God for giving me the inspiration and the words to glorify You. I'm so grateful and humbled You've chosen this path for me.

Special thanks to Cathy and Dennis Zimmermann for their hospitality and research assistance in Lancaster County, Pennsylvania.

The author and publisher gratefully acknowledge the following resources that were used to research information for this book:

Richard A. Stevick, *Growing Up Amish* (Baltimore: The Johns Hopkins University Press, 2007).

Donald B. Kraybill, *The Riddle of the Amish Culture* (Baltimore: The Johns Hopkins University Press, 1989, 2001).

Enjoy Amy Clipston's
Amish Heirloom series!

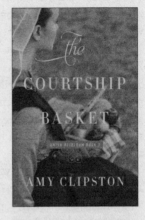
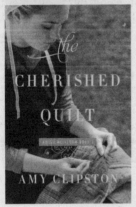
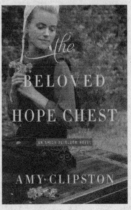

Four women working at the
Lancaster Grand Hotel find their
way through life and love.

The *Kauffman*
Amish Bakery Series